Third Man In

Book Two in The Playmakers Series
by G.K. BRADY

ISBN 978-1-7332763-8-2

Cover design by Jenny Quinlan, Historical Editorial
Edited by Jenny Quinlan, Historical Editorial
Proofread by Word Servings
Printed in the United States of America

Contents

Dedication

For hockey grinders, enforcers, and plumbers—the role players whose contributions are as vital to a team's success as the playmakers.

Chapter 1

Wrecking Ball

T J. Shanstrom skated to a stop and glanced at the jumbotron suspended above the ice like a blocky space ship. Seven-to-one. A barn burner. With his team on the wrong end of it. His eyes flicked to the red lamp pulsing like a damn beacon behind the goalie net, then lit on his opponents celebrating with a group hug. He smashed his stick against the goal, ringing it on the metal pipe.

He *hated* being schooled. Especially by his team's biggest rival—the team that had traded him years earlier.

"Kevin May," groused T.J.'s linemate, Gage Nelson, as they skated toward their bench. "That's his fourth goal tonight. He's not even that good."

Though he kept his mouth shut, T.J. fumed. That the veteran right wing from his old team was having the game of his career burned in T.J.'s stomach like a week-old chalupa. His own team's play had resembled a car driving with one flat tire: uneven, bumping along, sluggish. Off by at least one step, they'd been beaten in all the little battles that make up a game.

T.J. wanted this win tonight—badly—but his team's luck dimmed with each tick of the game clock. Since they'd traded him to the San Jose Earthquake, he'd wanted to show his old team what they'd given up. Not that he minded playing for San Jose. It had its perks—great weather and pretty women—*and* the Earthquake had a shot at winning the Stanley Cup this year. But this was a matter of pride. He wanted to rub it in their faces, but he'd barely registered a shot, much less a point. Revenge was a sweet mistress, and a chance to gloat would have put a smile on his face the rest of that night.

He clambered over the boards and plopped down, sliding along the bench to make room for his teammates. Chest heaving, he shook off a glove and grabbed a water bottle. As he streamed water into his mouth, he watched May glide toward the center line. The asshole jerked his chin at him and pointed at the jumbotron, where the goal was being replayed.

"Hey, Shanny!" May taunted. "Scoreboard!"

T.J. pictured himself wiping that damn grin off Kevin Fucking May's face.

Scoring wasn't T.J.'s main talent. Maybe it was time he rocked somebody's world and got his team pumped up. Took this game back. They still had ten minutes. It wasn't impossible.

May positioned himself for the puck drop against the Earthquake's star center, Marcus Frisk, and lost the draw. T.J. growled out a "yes."

An Earthquake player corralled the puck. A sweet pass to Frisk. He blazed toward the opponent's net. Teammates and foes closed in fast.

T.J. shot up from his seat. "Go, Frisky!"

Frisk pulled up. One of his wingers streaked toward the front of the net. "Send it!" T.J. yelled, echoed by his teammates. Frisk let fly a perfect pass that landed on his winger's blade. The winger one-timed the puck, ringing it off the post. It slid into the corner boards. A collective groan rose from the Earthquake bench.

"It's okay, boys," T.J. hollered. "We got this." His eyes swung from the corner, where several players battled for the puck, to Frisk, who was poised high in the slot.

The puck slid out, and Frisk gathered it, pivoting. May skated at him like a heat-seeking missile. Frisk didn't see him in time. May's feet left the ice, and he slammed Frisk hard. Frisk's head snapped back. He dropped to the ice.

Stunned silence swept the Earthquake bench. With a swell of rage, T.J.'s yell pierced the air. "May, you fucking douchebag!"

He barely registered an iron grip on his shoulder preventing him from flying over the boards and onto the ice to pound May into oblivion. Given the chance, T.J. would go, and his teammates knew it. It was what he was paid to do. Instead, he sat down hard as trainers ran onto the ice.

"Shanny, Frisky's not up yet," Nelson hissed beside him.

Medical staff bent over Frisk, and finally he sat upright. T.J.'s shoulders eased, lowering several inches. He hadn't realized how tight they'd been.

With help, Frisk swayed to his knees, two Earthquake players flanking him, skating him off the ice. T.J. and his teammates stood and banged their sticks against the boards in a show of support.

A whistle blew. May headed to the penalty box while the ref announced the call and signaled it by rotating his clenched fists. "Two minutes for charging."

"What the hell, Stripes?" T.J. flung an arm. "Two minutes? That's it? He injures our guy and—"

"Not now, Shanstrom," Coach Rogers growled from behind him. "We're on the power play." To the whole team, he said, "Now let's get some goals!"

Fuck that call! May is a criminal!

Not only was Frisk their best player, he was a friend, a brother, a guy T.J. had battled beside. T.J. ground down on his mouthguard, his jaw muscles bunching, his temper simmering.

The Earthquake power play mattered little because his team didn't score, registering one measly shot on goal. T.J. had been as ineffective as his teammates.

He was preparing to take the ice again when an assistant coach placed a beefy mitt on his shoulder pad and leaned in close. "Take May out."

T.J. flicked his eyes to Coach, whose focus was riveted to the ice. "Coach says it's okay?"

"Coach is down, but you didn't hear me say that."

T.J.'s insides fluttered with excitement. This would be sweet. *Take care of your own.* Though the league had gotten softer in recent years, there was still that guy who sent a message for his whole team. For the Earthquake, that guy was T.J. He'd been called a goon, dirty, unsportsmanlike. That's not how he saw it. Sure, he'd been suspended a few times, but he played the way the coaching staff expected him to, and he played his role well.

The team captain, Joe "Money" Monahan—the only other guy who'd heard the assistant's order—gave T.J.'s shoulder a shake. "Wreck that fucking hoser, Shanny. Teach him a lesson."

T.J. bobbed his head. "He won't know what train hit him."

Time for a line change, and T.J. rocketed over the boards and took the ice, his eyes on May. The arrogant bastard didn't seem to notice, skating to his bench like he didn't have a care or a conscience. *Not this shift, cocksucker, but I'll get you.*

His shifts seemed to start or end slightly off of May's as the game went on, as though some chess master was moving pieces around a board. But T.J. schooled his patience. Waited to get May in his sights. Finally, his diligence paid off when Coach threw him out against May's line. May and his boys were gassed, but they were pinned in their own zone on a penalty kill and couldn't get off the ice. T.J.'s legs were fresh, and he used them to chase May, chirping at him all the way. May shot him a smug look but wouldn't engage—which only served to bubble T.J.'s blood at a more rapid roll.

T.J.'s chance came in a breathtaking instant. As May was heading off, he slashed the back of an Earthquake player's leg. That player was Nelson, and Nelson pivoted and cross-checked May in the chest. They exchanged a few shoulder shoves, then May grabbed a fistful of Nelson's jersey, and the two men began a fighting dance. Nelson was a playmaker, not a brawler like May. And May knew it. Was about to take full advantage of it.

A coil of blinding anger, fueled by frustration, whipped loose inside T.J. He skated at May, his vision bright white, his focus lasering in on the back of May's helmet.

"May!" he yelled. May turned his head, and T.J.'s gloved fist crashed down. May's eyes rolled back in his head. He released Nelson and went down, his body thudding like a sack of grain. T.J.'s momentum carried him over, and he landed on May. T.J. rose, fist cocked and loaded. The world stopped spinning, suspended. May's half-lidded eyes were glazed. Blood leaked from his nose and mouth. The frozen second erupted when bodies piled on, and T.J. threw out an

4

elbow to shield May's head, but it didn't reach him in time. May's helmeted head, now turned sideways, was driven into the ice as more players pummeled each other on top of him.

Shouting, elbows, fists, blood, whistles.

Utter chaos.

Bodies were hauled back as refs and teammates pried players apart. Under the mass, beside T.J., lay May. Unmoving. Bloody. His slitted eyes glassy and vacant.

Heaving breaths, T.J. scrambled away when trainers swarmed May. Boos rained down on him from the crowd. Players and coaches yelled at him from the opposing bench, their words a swirl of noise punctuated by the few he made out clearly. *Goon. Cheap shot. Fucking coward.* He heard threats to separate his balls from his body and stuff them in any number of places.

"Doing my job," he yelled back. "No different from *any* of you fuckers!"

Like a bodyguard on ice, a ref skated him back to his own bench. "Third man in, Shanstrom. You're done."

T.J. should have headed to the locker room, but he leaned against the boards instead, breathing hard, his eyes fixed on May's skates. *Just doing what my coach told me. Doing my job, goddamn it.*

"Move, you fucker! Move!" he gritted out under his breath.

A trainer yelled, and a gate opened. White-shirted EMTs rolled a stretcher onto the ice and collapsed it beside May.

The ref grasped T.J.'s arm and steered him toward a corridor behind the bench. "Off, Shanstrom. Now."

Angry fans leaned over the rails, jeering, taunting. A full cup of cold, sticky liquid came crashing down on his helmet, and a wad of ice hit him full force in the face.

He ducked and hurried toward the locker room. The other team's staff made way, simultaneously glowering and gawking at him, while an inner chant looped through his brain. "May's okay. May's okay. May's okay."

It was drowned out by the fury of the crowd echoing in his ears— the crowd calling for blood. His.

Laptop and a stack of files balanced in the crook of one arm, Natalie Foster inserted the key in the lock and pushed the door open. Securing it behind her, she flipped on a table lamp, sighed, and released a long, cleansing breath.

Ah, sanctuary.

Her 1950s Denver bungalow only had two bedrooms and a bath, but it was the perfect size for her, and she loved it. It welcomed her, wrapped its arms around her, and pulled her in. If a house could embody Mom, this one did. The modest living room, with a butter-yellow couch and two Caribbean-blue armchairs, opened to a cozy but bright kitchen, where she'd perfected many a baking recipe.

Six months ago, she'd doubted her decision to upend her life and start again, but as she looked around, the sight of her quaint home warmed her. Hands down, she'd made the right choice.

The wood floor squeaked as she trod to the spare bedroom she'd converted into her office. She gratefully deposited her load atop a tidy vintage desk. A moment later, she plugged in the computer and sorted the files alphabetically, her gaze lingering on one. A frustrated sigh escaped her. She was losing this client, and already she felt the pinch in her bank account. It wasn't that she'd done a bad job. Quite the contrary. She'd done such a good job straightening their books and unearthing opportunities for them to save money that they'd gone and hired a full-timer to do what she did. They'd offered Natalie the position—a nice ego boost—but frankly, the work wasn't that challenging, and she loathed being restricted to an office, once again at the mercy of self-important bosses.

Nope, bank account balances aside, she preferred struggling and independence. Besides, she still had a tidy sum in savings—even after repaying Mom for her college tuition. She only needed to add a few more clients or sell one of her magazine articles to stave off dipping into her reserves. *Or I could accept Kevin's generosity.* She'd rather eat Ramen for a year than take money from her boyfriend—no matter that he could more than afford it, or that he'd offered her a loan.

"Enough," she admonished herself aloud. "You're fine."

Running her finger along the desk's clean edge recalled what a great flea market find she'd scored, helping her cast off her worries.

Ten feet, and she was in her bedroom, where she toed off sneaks and traded jeans and a sweatshirt covered in dog fur for a clean pair of yoga pants, a soft sweater, and socks. Though she still faced a mound of work, she gave herself permission to watch the end of the San Diego Storm game. Tonight they played their old rival, the San Jose Earthquake, and it was bound to be heated. What fireworks had she already missed?

Her father's voice often chose these moments to echo in her mind. *It's okay to take a break once in a while, Nat-Nat, as long as you remember to always do your best work. Oh, and always under-promise and over-deliver.* She smiled and silently answered. *Yes, Dad.*

Humming, she glided across the living room floor with the ballet scene from *Red Sparrow* playing in her head. Not her favorite movie— too bleak—except for the dancing. Why did ballet movies have to be so tragic?

"And now it's time for a different sort of dance," she said aloud. Really, she had to stop talking to herself. With a silent vow to do just that, she picked up the remote, and the TV screen flickered to life. She found the hockey channel and cranked up the volume.

They must have been between periods or on a TV time-out because commercials bled one into another in the background as she poured herself a measure of red wine. She glanced at her only touch of whimsy in the house, a puppy wall clock that ticked out time with its tail. Damn. Had she missed all three periods?

The ads stopped, and a name drifted from the TV, tickling her insides. *Kevin must have done something special tonight.* Dating a hockey player—any professional athlete—was different for her, and hearing his name or seeing his face on TV always rendered her a bit off-kilter, as though electrified butterflies tethered to concrete blocks were trying to fly in her stomach. Sort of fluttery while leaden at the same time.

7

She sipped her wine. Her phone buzzed, and she grabbed it off the counter. Her brother. Again.

"Drew! I am *not* bailing your ass out this time. It's *your* turn to bring the salad to Mom's. End of discussion. So put those man muscles to work and get tossing!"

"Nat. You home yet?"

Huh. No snarky comeback?

"Just got in. A dog-sitting client had me stick around to keep his furry fiend from pulling his cushions apart. I have *got* to find a new client so I can fire this one. How that feather duster of a dog can—"

"Did you catch any of the game?"

"Not yet. Just turned it on."

"Nat, sit, if you're not already." Drew's tone was clipped and grim, like the time he'd herded her into the basement when a twister had threatened Grandma's house. Prickles raced up and down her spine. Her big brother teased her mercilessly, but when it came to protecting her, he was front and center. It was one of the things she loved best about him, though she'd never admit it. Not to him.

Phone pressed to her ear, she pivoted slowly toward the TV. The sight of a stretcher being wheeled off the ice confused her. A prone figure, skates on, his helmeted head taped to a neck board. "Oh my God, Drew. Who got hurt?"

As though the TV was sentient, the camera zeroed in on the player while an announcer's grave voice said, "We've learned they're taking him straight to the hospital." She narrowed her eyes but couldn't make out the face. "We just hope Kevin May will be all right."

What the ...? Her stomach plummeted to her knees.

"Drew?" she squeaked.

Her brother exhaled. "Kevin got sucker-punched." The broadcast cut to an Earthquake player—T.J. something or other—as he stood in front of his home bench. It was hard to make out his features for the helmet, visor, and mountain-man beard. "That's T.J. Shanstrom," Drew growled, "the dickhead who put Kevin in the hospital."

As realization took hold, Natalie sank into her couch, eyes glued to the screen, heart pounding as though it would burst from her chest. She set the wineglass on the coffee table with a wobble and clapped her hand over her mouth, stifling a wail that rushed up from her gut.

Oh no! No, no, no!

Chapter 2

Do You Know the Way to San Jose?

The flight home dragged. Normally, T.J. would've plugged into music or Roman history and maybe dozed, but tonight he couldn't shut his brain off. His teammates gave him a wide berth, barely speaking to him—not the typical rally-around behavior of a team. Consequently, he sat alone. When T.J. had approached Coach Rogers, he'd gotten a terse, "Not now."

T.J. couldn't decide if everyone was leaving him to brood by himself or if they were dodging him. The vibe was distinctly the latter. Left to its own devices, his mind churned and grinded, turning over the night's events. In addition to wondering about May's condition—he had to be out of the hospital by now, right?—he tried to wrap his head around the Storm fans' vitriol. They'd waited for him outside the arena. Taunts so ugly he'd been hustled back inside the arena's underbelly until San Diego's finest could escort him to the team bus. The human barricade hadn't blocked out the verbal abuse the crowd spewed, though. Not that T.J. wasn't used to heckling. But this was heckling on steroids, and for an instant he'd questioned his safety.

"Mob mentality" was no longer a generic term to throw around. He'd glimpsed it.

And his phone? It had blown up with calls and texts from news agencies and random people leaving assorted threats that ran the gamut from slashing his tires to dismembering him. How they'd gotten his number, he had no idea.

THIRD MAN IN

On the bus ride from San Jose International to the arena, he let his fatigue settle into his weary joints and muscles, weighing him down. At least he was on friendly turf.

Or so he thought.

Along with the usual smattering of better halves and fans that typically greeted the players, they were treated to a blinding display of red-and-blue lights on squad cars positioned around the parking lot. A cop boarded the bus before the guys could shuffle off.

"T.J. Shanstrom?" he called.

Oh shit, oh shit, oh shit. I'm being arrested.

Teammates turned toward him as he stood alone in the rear, their hard gazes slicing like daggers. Stomach curdling from the emotions tossing inside him, he set his jaw and met each man's eyes with his embarrassment, anger, and growing belief they'd turned on him.

I was just doing my job! he wanted to yell. Any number of them had been guilty of injuring other players—hell, even the coaches had done it during their playing days—but all of a sudden they seemed to be suffering from shared amnesia.

Oh-so-reluctantly, T.J. raised his hand, wondering if his wrist would soon be sporting a silver bracelet. "I'm him."

The cop zeroed in on him while seeming to address them all. "We have a situation with some pissed-off people who decided they had nothing better to do in the middle of the night than get wasted and welcome our boy back home."

"Are they Earthquake fans?" T.J. asked, unable to keep disbelief from his voice. In enemy territory, he expected this. But at home?

The policeman gave him a pointed look. "Does it matter?" To T.J. it did, but he kept his mouth shut. "Just follow our instructions and no one will get hurt," the cop added.

One by one, the team exited the bus until only T.J. remained.

The cop gave him a chin jerk. "Ready for your escort?"

"That bad?"

The cop didn't answer.

T.J. sighed. "Ready as I'll ever be." He stepped off the bus behind the officer and was instantly flanked by two more uniforms. A burble in the background became a rumble, and soon loud voices brayed for "justice." A bottle shattered ten feet away, which was when T.J. noticed half a dozen policemen in riot gear advance on an agitated throng.

Jesus!

His heart had been racing NASCAR-fast but now kicked up to top-fuel dragster speed.

For fuck's sake, what dimension had he landed in?

"Keep your head down," the main cop directed. "When we get to your car, get in, lock the doors, and get the hell out."

Something akin to panic swelled in T.J.'s gut. "What if they come after me?"

"By the time they realize you're leaving, they'll be too late. And if any of them gets behind a wheel, we'll hold 'em up with sobriety checks. That should give you time. You live somewhere with security?"

"Yes." T.J. depressed his key, and his Hummer H1 chirped.

"Good luck," the cop said. "And try not to run anyone over with that tank."

He shook the officer's hand before sliding into the driver's seat. "You an Earthquake fan?"

"Fan of the team, but I can't say I'm a fan of yours."

Ouch. T.J. started the engine, closed the door, and lowered his window. "Thanks anyway."

The policeman gave him a head dip. "Just doing my job."

The next morning, T. J. stood in front of an office door, eyes flicking over gold block letters: *Dan MacNeal, General Manager.* He pulled in a slow, steady breath to keep his stomach from twisting into unruly knots. It didn't help that he still didn't know how May was doing. *Guy must be okay. He's gotta be back home by now.*

Clenching his hand in a fist so it wouldn't shake, he knocked. A voice told him to enter, and he stepped into a luxurious office he'd only seen once before. He barely registered three people, instead locking on a framed picture of MacNeal gripping the Stanley Cup, a big-ass smile on his face.

God, T.J. loved that silver tower. Never got tired of looking at it. He'd won one with the LA Kings in 2012 right before being traded to the Colorado Blizzard on his way to the Storm, and it had only made him hungrier to hoist it again. After being bounced from team to team, the quest had seemed hopeless until now. The Earthquake had a solid shot this year.

MacNeal's smooth voice snapped him back. "T.J. Shanstrom, meet our attorney, Jacob Pederson." T.J. shook hands with a sharp-nosed, gray-blond man.

The GM inclined his head toward Coach. "I've also asked Coach Rogers to sit in on this meeting." T.J. exchanged head bobs with Coach before lowering himself into a chair.

"I got word from the league," MacNeal said, tapping a piece of paper on his desk.

T.J. sat forward. "Yes, sir?"

MacNeal peered at him over the top of his wire-rimmed glasses. "You've been suspended for the rest of the season."

T.J.'s stomach launched itself into his throat. He fought to keep his voice even. "That's twenty-one games." Another thought jarred him. "Does that include playoffs?"

A solemn nod. "As it stands, yes. The *entire* season."

Fuck!

Fuck, fuck, fuck!

"That's months," T.J. choked, his mind like a runaway tilt-a-whirl. He looked from MacNeal to Coach, the latter wearing a bland expression. Or trying not to look guilty. "Am I the only one suspended?"

Coach shot him a side glare.

Pederson canted his head at MacNeal. "May I?"

The GM flicked his wrist in invitation. The lawyer pressed his hands together as though holding a moth captive. "Yours is the only suspension, and you're going to appeal. In the meantime, you will not speak to *anyone* about last night. No reporters, no fans, no strangers in

13

stores. Not your family, not your friends. Do *not* talk about it in public. Ever. I don't care how much you're goaded or how much you want to defend yourself. If people push, you tell them to contact my office. Understood?" Pederson's inflection told T.J. the lawyer credited him with all the brights of a gorilla, and while T.J. was used to the judgment, it still didn't sit well. Never had.

Pederson passed him a business card. "A word of advice. Lose the beard and get a haircut. You'll appear less intimidating with a clean-cut look, and you won't be as easy to recognize."

Nodding, T.J. accepted the card, plucked his phone from his jacket pocket, and waved it. "I have a boatload of messages from people wanting statements or interviews."

"Ignore them, but don't erase them. Let everything go to voicemail and fill up your inbox. You'll be provided a different phone and a new number. Be judicious when you give it out." Pederson gave him a pointed look.

Shit! He'd fallen asleep and woken up in a spy movie. "I've *been* judicious."

Pederson primly cleared his throat.

MacNeal raised sympathetic brows. "You can't play, but you'll practice and keep up your training. Spend the extra time on your hobbies or with your girl. She'll probably appreciate having you around."

Hobbies? Yeah, T.J. and his paints could get reacquainted, except he'd had no desire to touch them in a decade—and that wasn't about to change. As for his girl, he didn't *want* more Julia time, and certainly not at the expense of playing. Hockey was his life. All he cared about. He'd paid the price with his blood and sweat, over and over, and had no interest in taking a break for anything—or anyone.

"It's tough on everyone, what with the playoff race so tight," MacNeal continued. "Your team needs what you bring, but your fuckup takes all that away."

Pow! A pop to the gut. T.J.'s ability to speak abandoned him as three sets of accusing eyes stared at him. He clenched the armchair in gritty silence as he ran through the people responsible for his butt being parked here right now. *Coach. Coach's assistant. Monahan. May.*

"Look, at six-four, you're a big, bruising body out there," MacNeal droned on, "and sometimes that's hard to control. We get it. But to the league, you're a repeat offender, no matter your intent when you hit May. Have no doubt, there *will* be a lawsuit, which is why you need to keep your trap shut. Don't give them more ammo."

T.J. shook his head to loosen his tongue. "Is there any news about May's condition?"

On a noisy exhale, MacNeal said, "He's in a drug-induced coma. As soon as it's safe, he'll be moved to Craig Hospital in Denver. His brother's a doctor there, and his family all live nearby, including his daughter and ex-wife. He'll have lots of support."

A drug-induced coma? Bile rose in T.J.'s constricting throat, and he swallowed hard to keep it down.

MacNeal folded his arms on the desk. "Craig's one of the best."

"Good," T.J. croaked.

The GM nodded. "That's it, T.J. You can go."

That's it? T.J. bit back the words he wanted so badly to let loose at Coach—he didn't deserve to shoulder this one alone. Coach needed to step up. *This is* your *fault, fucker!*

T.J. shot him a hard look, but Coach's eyes were unmoving, unblinking, trained elsewhere.

In that moment, the full impact of what was happening hit T.J. square in his chest. He was being set up to take the entire brunt of this cluster-fuck. Sure, he'd delivered the hit, but he'd only been the messenger. And right now that messenger was shipping water and sinking like the Titanic, caught alone in a whirlpool of fury and disgust while sharks circled him.

Muttering his thanks—for what, he wasn't sure—T.J. closed the door behind him and trudged to the locker room. Several teammates were joking when he walked in but stopped as soon as they spotted him, pretending to busy themselves with their equipment. The cold shoulder from his own guys. *What the hell?* He gathered his gear and left the building.

Not ready to head home, he drove the streets of San Jose aimlessly. In a rougher part of town, he pulled into a parking lot and strode into a grungy, near-empty bar. Eleven in the morning, and only a few hard-cores. A TV hung from the ceiling, tuned to some sports channel. He took a stool and looked up when he heard his name.

"T.J. Shanstrom refuses to make any public statements. Is that how an innocent man behaves?"

Outrage swept over him in a heated wave. Shit, when had someone gotten through to him to ask for a public statement? Never!

The sportscaster was buddying with some other talking head who declared, "Well, this isn't the first time T.J. Shanstrom's been in trouble. He seems to invite it, and now's he's going to ground and showing his true colors."

"Hey!" T.J. called to a grizzled bartender. "Mind turning that down and getting me a boilermaker?"

Without a word, the bartender hit the remote, and the pundits were silenced. Shoulders hunched, T.J. glanced around the dim bar. No one recognized him. Hell, no one cared. Which was perfect. The boilermaker appeared and quickly disappeared, going down real smooth. He ordered another. And another. And another.

A text chimed. Julia's face smiled on his screen. *How did the meeting go?*

T.J.: *Not good.*

Julia: *How are you doing?*

T.J.: *Fine, after a few more boilermakers.*

Julia: *Where are you?*

The alcohol had taken hold, mercifully numbing parts of his brain he wanted to ignore. He texted her his location, then ordered a beer minus the shot. Time to take it down a notch. Before he'd finished his brew and asked for the next, Julia appeared, hands on her hips and a frown on her fair features.

"Oh boy. I'm in trouble now." He raised his empty pint glass to his new friends gathered at the bar—everyone was your friend when you bought rounds—but they weren't looking at him. They were gaping at Julia. He couldn't blame them.

Julia was one the most flawless women T.J. had ever seen, sober or otherwise. With long blond hair and blue eyes, she was slim and had a great rack. If he were honest—which was easy given all the booze in his system—her tits were by far her most appealing asset. They were what had reeled him in the first time he met her seven months ago—or was it eight?

A high-priced lawyer, Julia was gorgeous. Fun. Demanding only in bed. She made her own dough and didn't look at him as though he were her personal Swiss bank account—a plus since his suspension now meant zero dollars on his own paycheck.

Though he kept his home life apart from hers, things were comfortable. Enough sex to keep him happy, but nothing too close. Just the way he liked it. Sometimes he caught a whiff of her wanting something more serious, and that worried him. From past experience, this was the turning point that forced him to extricate himself from relationships. He wasn't going down Commitment Highway ever again. He'd only ever made that mistake once, when he'd been young and stupid.

Really stupid.

Julia snapped her fingers under his nose, and he straightened. The men around him laughed and mumbled among themselves. He caught just enough to know they'd swap places with him in a heartbeat, murmuring about willingly being pussy-whipped by *this* particular pussy-whipper.

"Had enough?" she huffed at him.

"Not yet."

The bartender shoved another full pint at him and winked.

"Look, you self-indulgent prick, either you leave with me now or stay here in this miserable dive."

Uh-oh. I am in trouble. He chugged the contents of the glass, pulled a wad of bills from his wallet, and dropped them on the bar top. "Another round for my friends," he announced. They cheered. Following Julia out the door, he waved his hand over his head.

Dazzling white seared his eyes; he quickly shaded them. "Christ, that's bright!"

"Yeah, well, it's the middle of the afternoon, when most of us have to work. Get in. We'll get your car when you're sober." Her voice was tight, as though she was fighting to keep it under control. He stumbled into the passenger side and wrestled with the seat belt.

As she drove, he winced at the stern set of her jaw. Not a good look. Maybe he could soften it. Christ, he could use a hard fuck right now—assuming his dick would cooperate—and maybe she could too. The liquor hadn't numbed him completely, and the thought of spending a few hours blanking out in her bed gained momentum. He licked his lips, eyes drifting to her breasts, where his gaze lingered. As he pictured stuffing his face between them, he inched his fingers along her arm.

"Don't," she hissed, shooting him daggers. "God, just look at yourself."

Oh, here we go. Didn't she give a rat's ass about what went down in his meeting and why he'd gotten hammered? Shoving his petulance and horniness aside, he slouched into the leather seat and closed his eyes. God, he was tired.

She grumbled something about being an idiot for dragging his sorry ass out of a bar on a workday afternoon, and he squeezed his eyes shut a little tighter. Maybe if he squeezed hard enough, the part of his brain telling him she was right would freeze and conk out for a while, leaving him in peace.

Chapter 3

But I'm Comfortable with my Head in the Sand

Days later, clean-shaven and shorn, T.J. slid into a booth at a San Jose hotel bar across from a former teammate. Beckett Miller was a beast of a defenseman who'd been a veteran when T.J. first broke into the league with the LA Kings. Miller had been T.J.'s idol and mentor, and playing together had carried over when both were with the Colorado Blizzard. That was before T.J. was traded and Miller got himself kicked off the team.

Right now T.J. needed to talk to someone who'd been in his skates. Miller had had his issues—*major* issues—but he'd gotten his life together and was having an epic resurgence in the NHL with Arizona, the team that had just arrived to play San Jose.

"Thanks for grabbing a cold one with me, Miller."

"Sure," Miller drawled. "It's good to catch up."

Their waitress, a leggy brunette in a short skirt and low-cut top, deposited two pints of beer on their wooden tabletop. She bent over their table, giving them a better look at the goods. T.J. appraised her cleavage appreciatively, but Miller barely glanced her way.

As the waitress flounced away, T.J. clinked his glass against Miller's. "So how's playing for Arizona?"

Miller took a swig and set his drink down. "Good. We've got a great team this season."

"I've seen your numbers. For a broken-down old-timer, you're having one hell of a year."

Miller grinned. "Yeah, it's been fun proving those bastards who called me 'washed up' wrong. Thirty-four and still whoopin' ass on punks like you." He jerked his chin at T.J. "So how many games did they give you?"

Could he discuss it with Miller, or did he need Pederson's permission? No, he didn't; his sentence was public knowledge. T.J. let out a noisy breath. "The rest of the season and all of playoffs."

Miller whistled softly. T.J. waited but was disappointed he hadn't added "Man, you didn't deserve it" or even "That really sucks." Confirmation from another hockey pro that May's injury was just part of the game would've counted for a lot. T.J. sure wasn't getting that from his teammates. With the way they ignored him, his moniker could've been "The Invisible Man." The silent rebuke stung.

T.J. took a long pull. "They claim they're taking it easy on me because the tape showed most of the damage was done after May hit the ice."

With a nod, Miller said, "They *are* taking it easy on you, considering it was your punch that landed the guy there in the first place." Miller's sharp words smacked T.J. square in the jaw, and he wrestled with his rising anger. Miller didn't seem to notice—or care.

The guy's attitude grated. T.J. took another drink and scanned the dark bar, marshaling his thoughts, forcing resentment back down a deep, dank hole. "I was only doing what I was told to do. What I'm *paid* to do."

Miller snorted. "Save it for the league and the commissioner. What you did is *your* shit, whether a coach told you to blindside the poor bastard or your teammates egged you on, and you decided to park your brain. Maybe May deserved to be wrecked, and you got carried away. No matter how it went down, grow a pair and own it."

Dick.

Miller paused, taking another swallow. "So what's your plan?"

In a bid to distract himself, T.J. surveyed the place again, all burgundy suffused in gold. In one corner, a group of young women looked their way and giggled. Puck bunnies. You could always find them hanging out at players' hotels, looking to get lucky. A cute blond wiggled her fingers in a tiny wave.

"Hey." Miller snapped him back to *their* table. "You invited me to this party. You still with me?"

"Yeah, I'm here."

"They aren't going anywhere." Miller tilted his head toward the girls. "Maybe you didn't hear me. What's your plan?"

"Talking to you *was* my plan." T.J. tipped the glass back and drained it. Miller raised an expectant eyebrow. The thought that Miller might be right made a brief appearance in T.J.'s stewing mind. T.J. *had* invited him, though the reason why was murky at the moment. He rummaged around his brain and found it.

"I want to know how *you* did it. You missed a whole season. How'd you keep yourself from going crazy? Didn't you worry you'd never get picked up by another team?"

"God, yeah. All. The. Time. I still pinch myself the Flyers gave me a shot. I kept my nose clean, took full advantage of the opportunity they gave me, and had a choice of teams when my time with them was up." Miller twirled his mostly full glass. "Your contract is still in force. Just keep working hard and don't fuck up. Don't give them any more reasons to ditch your ass. It sucks now, but use the time to assess."

T.J. chuffed, staring at his empty glass. Not being able to play out the season didn't just suck; it sucked canal water. The unbidden thought that May might not play out the season either poked at him. Hell, what if the guy could never play again? *Shit, where did that come from? Not my problem. Never liked the cocky son of a bitch anyway.* T.J. pushed the question aside and signaled the waitress. He needed another drink.

Miller continued. "What's done is done, Shanny. All you can do is take care of here and now, make sure your house is in order, and figure out how to do better going forward. You have money stashed away, right?"

T.J. nodded, growing more morose at the thought of a looming lawsuit. "Yeah, for now anyway."

Miller gave him a nod of approval. "Good. You're smarter than I was. Any word on May's condition?"

T.J. scrubbed a hand over his jaw. "He's back in Denver, at Craig Hospital. Other than that, I don't know much. My information comes from a buddy of a buddy, so it's a little vague. Obviously, his team's not interested in keeping me up-to-date." T.J. pointed at Miller's glass as the waitress sashayed over. "Want another one?"

"No, thanks. My limit's one when I'm playing."

T.J. placed his order, adding a double shot of Jameson. When the waitress left, he turned back to Miller. "Is the drink limit part of cleaning up your act?"

Miller gave him a half-smile. "I guess you could say that. The body can't take the punishment like it used to. I'm trying to preserve it for better things, and I see no reason to add abuse that's entirely avoidable." Though Miller hadn't said it, T.J. couldn't help believing part of that statement was directed at *him*, and heat flared in him again. He swallowed it down.

"So you plan on staying in Arizona?"

Miller shook his head. "Arizona's a stopover. Colorado's home. When my career's done, I'll settle there permanently."

The waitress delivered T.J.'s drinks, and Miller shook his head when she asked if he was ready for another.

T.J. blew out a breath. "I've been thinking about selling my place in Denver. Seems like a waste to have it sit empty, and this would be a good time to take care of loose ends." A thought struck him. "Hey, you sold your place a while back. Did you like your agent?"

Beckett let out a hearty laugh. "Yeah, I liked her. So much I married her."

"Fuck me! I didn't realize … When?"

"Last June. Name's Paige." Miller glanced at the ceiling and sprouted an uncharacteristically idiotic grin. "My gorgeous, green-eyed little redhead. I have no fucking clue why she puts up with me, but I thank Christ every day she does. You met her once—at Marty and Claudia's."

A pretty, petite woman in a bright summer dress floated through T.J.'s mind. She'd been at a barbecue hosted by the Colorado Blizzard's head coach, Marty LeBrun, and his wife. "I remember her. She with you in Arizona?"

"I wish. No, I married a businesswoman with lots of irons in the fire," he said proudly. "I don't have much time left in the NHL, so we agreed she stays there, and we get together when we can, like on this trip for instance. I'm stopping over for a night on my way back. We make it work."

And now T.J. thought he understood why Miller wasn't checking out the wildlife in the bar. "She still selling real estate? Could she maybe help me out?"

"She's throwing a party for her construction crew a few weeks from now while I'm home for a stretch. Make a trip out and meet her. You can talk to her about it then." Miller took a sip.

Suddenly, the room was abuzz. The puck bunnies' eyes flew to the bar's entrance. T.J. glanced over to see what had captured their attention. A half-dozen Arizona players spotted Miller and ambled over, turning female heads as they went. Miller introduced them, and T.J. felt their disapproving eyes on him. Though Miller invited his teammates to join them, they opted for seats at a different table. There was no mistaking the rebuff, and it cut to the core. He was being kicked off the island, summarily banned from his own brotherhood.

"Whaddya say, Shanny?" Miller's voice sounded almost sympathetic. "Stop by. We can do some more catching up then."

"Sure, why not? I'd like to get better acquainted with Superwoman."

A puck bunny broke away from her gal pals and strutted toward the Arizona players' table. When her sisters saw the warm reception the players gave her, they streamed over like penguins jumping off an ice floe.

Miller threw back his beer, stood, and grasped T.J.'s shoulder. "Time for me to take off. T.J., great to see you." He pointed at his teammates. "Boys, don't be late for morning skate."

As Miller turned away, a smoking-hot Kendall Jenner knockoff blocked his path, laying her hand on his arm.

"Beckett Miller. I've been dying to meet you. I was hoping we could get to know each other tonight," she purred.

Narrowing his eyes at her, Miller pulled back slowly, and the woman's entire body shimmied. Actually shimmied. Probably because she'd just dropped her panties. *Seriously? Jesus, how does he do that?* T.J. had always held a grudging admiration for the guy's ability to attract women, but now he was just disappointed—Miller was married after all.

Christ, is every pledge of fidelity just a two-bit promise you put away, then trot out again when it's convenient? Just like—

"Not interested," Miller said in a low voice.

T.J. found himself surprisingly buoyed.

Undaunted, the woman continued as if Miller hadn't just given her the brush-off. "I *love* the long hair on you."

Miller straightened before her outstretched fingers could reach said hair and, without missing a beat, declared, "So does my wife. She's the *only* reason I put up with the fucking pain in the ass it is." He shrugged. "But she's totally worth it, especially when she's straddling me and yanking on it. Can't get enough of that little wildcat." Miller shoved his hands in his pockets. "I have a sudden urge to call her. Well, g'night." Utterly guileless, he stepped around the woman, and his long strides carried him to the elevators.

Like the woman who now gaped after Miller, T.J. was frozen in place. Then a smile tugged the corners of his mouth, and he barked out a laugh; he couldn't help himself. Miller had just restored his faith in mankind. *Wouldn't believe it if I hadn't just seen it.* The woman turned her gaze on T.J., confusion and anger colliding on her pretty face.

He raised his hand. "Hey. I don't have long hair, but I don't have a wife either."

"Because you're an asshole," one of the players said.

Down went his beer and Jameson. He was spoiling for a fight. Just then his phone vibrated. His new phone. The caller had to be one of four people.

He signaled the slinky cocktail waitress for the check, found a discreet corner, and picked up the call. "Hey, Julia."

"Hi, babe. I'm back in town early and wondered if I could see you tonight. I miss you."

Alarm bells clanged in his head. She *missed* him? This was a new development. While he couldn't remember *every* detail of their unspoken agreement, he didn't recall missing each other being one of them.

He sifted through a handful of plausible excuses to stay away tonight. Didn't need to go rushing right over there and fuel her hope that he was warming to the idea of long-term.

"Uh, well, I'm hanging out with some buddies I haven't seen in a while. How about I call you in the morning?" He winced at his own deception.

She gave him a long-suffering sigh. "All right. I'll talk to you then."

On the way home, he picked up a few bottles of Jameson. *Just a couple of drinks to chill out.*

A couple of drinks turned into many.

Jameson after Jameson, T.J. wrestled with Miller's words, the sportscasters' accusations, the crappy way his teammates and coaches were treating him—hell, the way *other* hockey players treated him. He wasn't that guy, goddamn it! Shit, that would make him as bad as his dad. It would mean he'd broken his vow to be nothing like the vicious son of a bitch.

The liquor didn't drown T.J.'s tormented thoughts, but it did cancel some noise and serve up the raw truth with crystal clarity. And he didn't like it. Hated it. But he couldn't hide from it.

A guy who had been playing the game, *doing his job*, was lying in a hospital bed because T.J. had put him there. Was T.J. any different from the brute he'd worked his whole life not to be? He was a swatch cut from the same length of cloth. What if Kevin May was the tip of his demon-riddled iceberg? What if he could no longer contain his father's monsters living within him? The realization he might be *exactly* like his father leveled him, and no amount of Jameson would ever change the truth of it.

Chapter 4

Change is Good, Says the Person Whose Life is Static

After ten days, Kevin was finally transported to Denver. It felt like ten years. Here Natalie was, walking through Craig Hospital's doors, anxious about seeing him for the first time since the devastating hit. Her mind whirred as she looked around the large entry decorated in a subdued palette. The neutral colors were doubtless meant to soothe the frayed nerves of those who entered. No one came here for a good time.

The reception area was huge, and her eyes latched on to the main desk. She pointed herself toward it, stopping behind a young woman balancing a toddler on her hip. Natalie tried in vain to ease the coil of knotted rope in her stomach as she awaited her turn.

She found herself in no-woman's-land. Her relationship with Kevin, if you could even call it that, had just barely crossed the threshold of the early stage. Yet she'd been summoned by his brother because "Kevin needs all his loved ones around him."

Except she wasn't a *loved* one. A *liked* one was more fitting, or a *recently intimate* one, if such a term existed. And becoming intimate had been a deliberate decision on her part. Reluctant to go out with him at first, she'd been charmed by his persistence—his attention had propped up her flagging ego—and she'd grown to really like him.

THIRD MAN IN

A relationship hadn't been high on her priority list, but when she met Kevin jogging by Ferril Lake, she was ready for a fun fling. Nothing serious. Just a way to ease back into the dating thing without relying on an app. And what better way to ease back in than with a good-looking, athletic guy who, though resolute in his advances, acted every bit the gentleman? A big plus: he only lived in Denver part-time, mostly during the off-season, which gave her ample breathing space while they got to know each other at *her* pace. Though he'd made it crystal-clear he'd wanted to move that process along more quickly, he hadn't been creepy or pushy about it. No, he'd given her plenty of room to decide when the time was right—for her. And she appreciated that about him.

But just where did that leave her now?

"Next," called a man seated behind the reception desk, and Natalie positioned herself with an awkward tread and an even more awkward mindset as she asked for Kevin's room. Thank God the receptionist didn't ask her relationship to the patient. *I'm his latest conquest.*

The knots in Natalie's stomach tightened a little more when she stepped aboard the elevator. Fisting the hem of her cobalt Columbia parka, she steeled herself for whatever loomed, ready to be front and center, to be strong for him. She'd had little practice at this sort of thing. When Dad died, it happened suddenly, which had been both eviscerating and fortuitous. Though she hadn't gotten in a proper good-bye—and really, was there such a thing when you lost someone you adored?—there'd been no lingering, no drawn-out suffering. He'd just woken up one morning and by lunch was dead from massive heart failure. Years later, and the stab in her heart still throbbed.

She paused outside the door, her hand hovering. Filling her lungs with air, she pushed the door open and entered a world filled with soft lights and beeps emanating from a bank of monitors. In their midst was an enormous bed, where Kevin lay amid tubes and leads attached to his head, arms, fingers. Was this the same man she'd last seen with a devilish grin plastered on his bearded face? Right now that man's lids were closed, and he looked mortal, so helpless among the soulless machines. Where was the powerful athlete?

27

Natalie became dimly aware of other people in the room when a dark-haired woman in light scrubs turned to her.

"Can I help you?" the woman said in a hushed voice.

Natalie cleared her throat. "I'm here to see Kevin May ... I'm his girlfriend." The last bit came out as a question, and she winced inside. She drew herself up, owning her cred to be there. "I spoke with his brother, Dr. Colin May, who said I should come."

The woman frowned, then shot a look to a similarly attired man whose head came up quickly. Maskless, he wore glasses that reflected an ethereal blue, and his eyes fixed on her.

"Natalie?" he said. The woman moved aside.

"Yes. Dr. May?"

He stepped to her and grasped her hand in both of his. "Please call me Colin." His voice was soft, warm, and reassuring.

"It's lovely to meet you. I only wish the circumstances were different."

"So do I." Colin gestured toward Kevin. "He's been asking for you."

He has? "Is he ... is he awake?" *Is he okay?* She shuffled to Kevin's bedside and feathered her fingertips over his hand, surprised by its warmth. What had she expected?

"He's in and out, mostly sleeping, which is what he needs right now to heal. You'll hear the word 'contusion' a lot, which is just another way of saying his brain is bruised. They've ruled out skull fractures and internal bleeding, and he's been downgraded to a moderate TBI by his physician, which is very encouraging."

Her eyes flew to Colin's. "You're not his physician? And what's TBI?"

"Sorry. TBI stands for traumatic brain injury. And no, I'm not Kevin's physician. My area of practice is spinal cord injury. I'm just here as the brother of the injured party." He gave her a half-smile. "I can interpret the doctor-speak for the rest of the family and keep them informed."

She hinged forward and whispered, "Kevin?" No response.

"When he's conscious," Colin offered, "he's fuzzy, but he knows where he is, and he recognizes us. He's mentioned you repeatedly."

Really? A touch of self-satisfaction oozed inside. She fixed her gaze on Kevin's face. Faded, faint bruising and cuts in various stages of healing were scattered over his cheeks, nose, and chin. Her heart melted a bit, releasing an inner Florence Nightingale she didn't know she had.

"I've been reading what I can on the Internet. Maybe you can fill in the blanks?"

Colin clasped his hands at his back. "He suffers from dizziness, fatigue, blurred vision, tinnitus, and nausea—all normal, considering his injury. He also has numbness in his left arm."

She bit back her alarm and hovered fingertips over Kevin's bearded cheek, unsure what to do with them. "What's his prognosis?"

"You can touch him. It's probably good for him." Colin gave her a chin lift, and she let her fingers stroke Kevin's soft beard. "The doctors are pleased with his progress so far. He's young and in top physical shape, which helps. But head injuries are unpredictable and vary from patient to patient. Time will tell how soon he recovers—and how fully."

Wide-eyed, Natalie looked into Colin's blue eyes blinking behind his glasses. "He might not make a full recovery?"

He nodded. "But hopefully that—"

The door opened wide, and a blond woman stood in its frame, her small figure silhouetted. Colin's assistant charged toward her, but the intruder's high-heeled boots ate up the distance between bed and door before she could be intercepted.

Colin raised a hand at the attendant. "It's okay, Clara."

Meanwhile, the blond woman eyed Natalie from foot to forehead, a powerful, floral fragrance drifting off her in a rolling, invisible cloud. Natalie's nose twitched.

"Who the hell are you?" the woman hissed, her eyes narrowing as they fastened on Natalie's fingers caressing Kevin's face.

Colin cleared his throat. "Kristin, this is Natalie, a good friend of Kevin's. Natalie, this is—"

"I'm Kristin May. Kevin's wife."

Bag slung over one shoulder, T.J. sauntered through the players' parking lot toward the arena. Another gauntlet of reporters, photographers, and pissed-off people to make it past. Another practice where his teammates would either aim to crush him or outright ignore him.

Yet Kevin May was out of ICU, out of his coma, and back in Denver. Obviously, he was going to be just fine, which made these people harassing T.J. all kinds of fucked up.

At least the crowd waiting for him had been shrinking steadily; maybe they were getting tired of chasing him. Or maybe they were getting their jollies by taking to blatant speculation on the air, or in blogs and other questionable writing. Publicly, they questioned everything from T.J.'s character to his eating habits and how they affected his motives. He was evil incarnate. Next they'd accuse him of terrorizing small children and torturing animals. Which would only mean they'd confused him with his dad.

"Hey, T.J.," one of the gauntleteers called, "stolen any walkers from helpless old ladies today?"

Another guffawed. "What was for breakfast? Victims' fingernails chased with a few pints of their blood?"

He gritted his teeth, Pederson's words ricocheting in his head. *Don't talk. Don't engage. Don't defend no matter how much it eats you up inside.* The contempt wasn't just eating him up. It was devouring him.

"Shanstrom! Let me ask you a question," one guy called.

"No, let me ask *you* a question," a deep voice boomed from behind him. He whirled in time to see his linemate, Gage Nelson, address the crowd. "What is it you people do that allows you to hang around parking lots all day, and where do I get one of those jobs? If I had your kind of freedom, I'd have my butt parked in a movie theater or at a food kitchen. Those folks could really use some volunteers. You should check 'em out."

In the time it had taken Gage to lob his friendly volley, T.J. had escaped into the arena.

He turned and took in Nelson striding behind him, a grin plastered on his face. "Hey, thanks, man."

Nelson shrugged. "Yeah, no problem. Just having some fun."

"And doing me a solid at the same time."

"Hey, it's what teammates do, right?"

T.J. just stared at him, poised to deflect the sarcastic comment that never came. Nelson was sincere, guileless, and T.J. was awash in gratitude he tried to cover up with another marble-mouthed, "Thanks."

Together they entered a wide corridor that smelled like damp cement and headed for the locker room. T.J.'s first surprise came when he spotted the Earthquake GM standing beside the door. The second surprise came when MacNeal said, "T.J., let's take a walk."

"Yeah, sure." Heart hammering, palms a little sticky, T.J. stowed his bag and ambled alongside MacNeal down the corridor.

Not too many steps later, the GM stopped in front of a door, looked around, then stepped inside, motioning T.J. to follow. T.J. did, getting his third surprise. They were in the stick room.

"So …" MacNeal paused to cough. "We just came to terms with the Colorado Blizzard. You've been traded to your old team."

T.J. felt as though he was a passenger in a plane that had done a thousand-foot free fall, his stomach firmly lodging in his throat. He needed an air-sickness bag.

"Are you shitting me?" he blurted.

MacNeal glanced down at his shoes. "No, 'fraid not."

"But I'm an enforcer. Enforcers don't get traded mid-season when their teams are in the hunt."

"Except you're not playing, are you?" The man arched his considerable eyebrows. "Oh, and you won't be traveling alone. Gage Nelson's been traded too."

Stunned, T.J. raked his fingers through his hair. He might have even spluttered something. The Blizzard hadn't made the playoffs in a decade. At twenty-seven fucking years old, he was running out of time.

"Hockey's a business, T.J."

Ha! As if T.J. didn't know. He'd been on the "business" end of it far too many times.

MacNeal slid his eyes to the side. "You've worked hard for this team, but it's time for a change. This isn't personal."

Isn't personal to who? T.J. wanted to yell. His brain buzzed, bombarded by thoughts ranging from how the hell to get his Hummer to Colorado to getting his dry cleaning to missing out on his favorite sushi restaurant.

"When do they expect me?"

"First thing tomorrow morning. Plenty of time."

T.J. had less than twenty-four hours to get his affairs squared away. Good-bye, nice to know you, and, oh, by the way, good luck with your life.

Yeah, fuck you very much.

One of the equipment guys walked in, startling T.J., the GM, and himself.

"Well, all the best." The GM took off, leaving T.J. to lurch after him like a three-year-old about to take the ice for the first time. *Move your feet, kid, and try not to face-plant.*

As he stumbled to the locker room, his phone vibrated. *Julia.* He'd totally forgotten about her as he'd mentally built his to-do list.

"Hey," he breathed.

"Hey. You up for a home-cooked meal tonight?"

He looked at his phone as if he'd picked up the wrong one. Julia had never cooked for him, preferring trendy restaurants and high-end takeout. "Uh …"

"Just say yes, T.J."

"Yes, T.J."

"Good," she laughed. "I'll see you around six."

Chapter 5

Into Every Life, a Tornado Must Rage

Natalie froze in place, her mind racing to take in the tornado calling herself Kristin May. The woman was small, petite even, but pound for pound, she packed a wallop. With a mental slap, Natalie blinked and came to, hitching in a breath and putting the I-won't-be-pushed-around inflection in her voice. It had served her well in the business world once. Right now it would lend her confidence she didn't feel.

She eyed Kristin. "You are *who*?"

"Uh," Colin interrupted in a loud whisper. "Maybe we should step outside." He held his arm toward the door in invitation. Kristin's nostrils flared on an angry exhale. Had she been a dragon, fire and smoke would've accompanied the dramatic breath.

"Fine," she grumped, stepping in front of Natalie, forcing Natalie to follow in her wake.

In the corridor, Natalie pulled back her shoulders, drawing herself up to her full five-seven, and crossed her arms over her chest. Too bad she wasn't wearing her Louboutin pumps so she could add another four inches to her height. As it was, the fuzzy pink sweater she'd donned—because it was Kevin's favorite—didn't lend itself to intimidation. She looked more like a Peeps marshmallow chick than a badass.

Colin shoved his hands in his pockets and glanced at Natalie. "This is Kristin, Kevin's ex-wife." Strong emphasis on the "ex."

Natalie mindlessly extended her hand for a shake. Kristin looked at it as though it were booby-trapped. Natalie left it there until Kristin finally caved and shook.

"So *this* is Natalie?" Kristin's eyes traveled from Natalie's flats to the top of her head.

"Yes." Colin cleared his throat. "Kevin's—"

"Girlfriend," Kristin drawled. "Yeah, I know. He tells me *everything*."

What Kevin perhaps *hadn't* told Kristin was that the relationship wasn't much more than some flirt-a-thons, a few shared meals, and a one-night-stand rolled together. Pretty much squat. But it didn't keep Natalie from squaring her shoulders and saying, "Everything?"

Kristin arched a perfectly manicured brow, which neatly matched her blond bombshell look. Kevin had never said much about his ex—he'd focused instead on his three-year-old daughter—and when he *had* talked about Kristin, he'd been neutral, if not kind. *Damn.* Natalie could use some mean, Kevin-uttered words right about now because the only ones dancing in her head were *stunning*, *sexy*, and *beautiful*. All words to describe the same thing: a drop-dead gorgeous woman with a killer bod packaged in the diminutive frame men always seemed to go for. She probably wore size-two clothes and size-five shoes. *Double damn.*

Why couldn't Kristin have fat ankles and lopsided eyes? Small boobs and boring brown hair like Natalie's?

"Maybe Natalie and I should take a stroll." The blond bombshell's appraising blue gaze locked on Natalie. Natalie's return gaze held steady.

Ooookay. "Sure. Why not? Kevin's still sleeping." Natalie darted Colin a look. His eyes and mouth had gone round. "You'll stay with him for a bit?"

He bounced his gaze between them and nodded slowly.

To Kristin, she said, "Lead on."

She followed Kristin along the brightly lit hall into a deserted lounge that held clustered seating areas, fake plants, and various vending machines. *This is so—*

Kristin whirled and faced her. "Awkward, huh?" She'd snatched the thought from Natalie's mind.

"Just what I was thinking."

"Drink?" Kristin's glossy pink lips twitched in an almost-smile, throwing Natalie.

Natalie's eyes cut to the machine. "Tea, please."

When they'd settled into seats, Kristin took a quick sip and leaned in. "Look, I get that Kevin is ... fond of you. The way I see this situation, you and I," she waved a hand between them, "need to put differences aside."

Natalie opened her mouth, to say what, she wasn't exactly sure, but Kristin steamrolled ahead. "We need to form a team. Team Kevin."

To say Natalie was astonished was an understatement of epic proportion. She was still grappling with Kristin's presence in the first place, and the woman's "Team Kevin" yanked her into a surreal world that had her inwardly shaking her head to dislodge any unseen cobwebs. *Seriously? Teaming up with my sort-of boyfriend's ex? Help! I've fallen into a parallel dimension and can't get out.* She pictured herself miming pushing against an invisible box.

Kristin seemed to tune into her thoughts. "Look, I know how weird it sounds. But think about it. We care about the same man, so why shouldn't we be in the same camp?"

Even in her stunned state, Natalie recognized the logic. And really, she had nothing against Kristin. She didn't know her well enough *to* have anything against her. But the kumbaya, let's-be-BFFs sentiment might change—quickly. Could Kristin be trusted? Sharing Kevin with his ex wasn't appealing on a number of levels, including, admittedly, one that involved pride. Yet didn't Kristin have as much right to be there as Natalie? Kristin certainly had more time invested in Kevin. And it wasn't as though Kristin had proposed running Natalie off the island. Yet.

God, sometimes she hated when her inner Lily Logical stepped up and ran roughshod over her emotions. Why couldn't she embrace jealousy, indignation, outrage like everyone else? She wanted to be pissed, damn it! But pissed wasn't what she felt. More like a little buoyed at the thought of having an ally to share the load.

35

Kristin seemed to sense her warring with herself. "With two of us—"

"We'll take shifts."

"Yes! We'll avoid showing up at the same time, *and* there'll be two of us protecting him."

The woman was not living up to Natalie's expectation of a she-devil, and her internal tantrum fizzled. "Protecting him from what?"

"Crazy-ass nurses who want to poke him full of holes. Doctors who don't order the testing or therapy he needs. I watched them do it in San Jose."

This totally threw Natalie. She'd only *just* seen Kevin in Denver, but Kristin merited the VIP pass that got her to San Jose? Yeah, maybe Natalie was a few rungs down the who's-who ladder, and she just needed to get over it.

"We're still each other's emergency contacts," Kristin dropped matter-of-factly, once more reading Natalie's thoughts.

How does she do that? One for Team Kristin, a fat goose egg to Team Nat.

The sting over being reminded how small a space Natalie occupied in Kevin's life was followed by a twinge of guilt. Unlike his ex, she hadn't considered the possibility he might be mishandled in the hospital. Yeah, Natalie was an interloper all the way around. She decided to shove aside insecurities and petty pride and join Team Kevin. "Okay. I'm on board."

A genuine smile lighting her eyes, Kristin extended *her* hand this time. "Good. Let's exchange cell numbers."

Natalie took a seat beside Kevin's bed, pulling her fingers through her hair to tame it. For him, she'd left it down today, like she'd worn the sweater, though he was still sleeping and had little idea. She cupped his hand in both of hers, relishing a peaceful moment alone. Colin and Kristin had cleared out, Kristin proclaiming she'd return. With a noisy sigh, Natalie mentally stacked her attributes against the ex-Mrs. May's. On the surface, two totally different women. Physically, they stood at opposite ends of a spectrum. And their demeanors? Kristin was flash and brass balls, like a hotshot hockey goal-scorer with dazzling moves, whereas Natalie was the ho-hum forward who analyzed before dishing off a pass—the player with three times as many assists as goals.

Natalie wanted to hate her. She really did. But she suspected they were more alike than not, and she had to admit that, together, they had powerful team potential.

Though Kristin clung to the wife title, she nudged Natalie toward sympathy. She went all the way back to high school with Kevin. That merited some kind of honor badge in Natalie's life handbook, as did being a single mom. No, thanks. At twenty-nine, Natalie had entertained the idea of having a child, only to realize she preferred forming a tag team with Mr. Right first. She thought she'd come close, but her candidate had proved her wrong six months ago by transforming into Mr. So-Terribly-Wrong before her eyes.

Cody. She hadn't given him a thought in weeks. So why was she giving him a thought now? A groan from the bed saved her the trouble of exploring the question.

Blue eyes opened, locking on hers. "Nat?" Kevin's voice was a rasp, but hearing it brought stinging tears to her eyes and relief to the rest of her.

She leaned closer. "I'm here. How are you feeling?"

He untangled his hand from hers and covered his eyes. "Like shit."

"Do you remember what happened?"

Peering at her over his hand, he frowned. "Of course I do. I got knocked out, I didn't lose my mind," he bit out.

She straightened her spine, taken aback by his harsh tone. *Must be because his head hurts something fierce.* "Shall I get someone for you?"

A grunt was his response, then he closed his eyes again. Before Natalie could stand, a round, gray-haired nurse slipped into the room.

"He just woke up," Natalie offered.

The nurse nodded and fiddled with a few monitors, then patted his shoulder. "Hey, big boy, I need to get some vitals on you."

He mumbled something unintelligible, and the nurse cast her a sympathetic look. "Might be easier on him if you stepped out."

Befuddled and a bit stung, Natalie scrambled out of her seat. "Of course." Looking around, she mentally picked up, then tossed back her belongings. *Do I come back?* She must have resembled a bobblehead on steroids, her head going this way and that. Two pairs of eyes tracked her, which only made her fumble more. In the end, she snatched her purse and scurried to a water station down the hall. She grabbed a Styrofoam cup and placed it under the ice chute. Nothing. As she pulled it away, the machine spat cubes at her, missing her cup entirely. *A metaphor for my life.*

An ambling walk through circuitous corridors, a stop in the ladies' room, and a successful water dispenser encounter later, she headed back to Kevin's room, grateful to discover they were alone. She also discovered that Kevin had fallen asleep, and as she sank into the chair, she found herself grateful for that too. Obviously, she needed to get her bearings and figure out what position she filled on Team Kevin.

The afternoon passed by in a fog as T.J. packed up essentials, notified his insurance agent, and arranged to have his Hummer driven to Denver. Details in a list longer than Santa's naughty roll.

Stripped to his boxers, T.J. was heading for the shower when his phone rang. Finally, the call from his agent he'd been waiting for. He picked it up before the second ring.

"Herb."

"T.J. How's my favorite client?"

"The trade's a shock, though I can't say I'm surprised. It's no secret Coach Rogers hates my guts and blames the whole May thing on me, even though *he* ordered the hit."

"Well, you'll have a clean slate now."

38

"Not exactly, Herb. This is my second stop in Colorado. And they suck."

"You've played in Denver before, but you haven't played for *this* team. Management's changed, and they've hired a new head coach since you were there."

"Yeah. Marty LeBrun. I know the guy."

"But you've never played for him. From management down, this bunch is focused on winning. They'll do whatever it takes. Look, I'm not going to bullshit you, kid. I just found out the Earthquake was shopping Nelson before his contract was up. They wanted to get some value for him while he's still hot. But as part of that deal, whoever got him had to take you."

"Wow, now I don't just feel like shit, I feel like shit's shit."

Herb chuckled. "Well, don't. Coach LeBrun wanted *you* just as much as he wanted Nelson, so cheer up, buttercup. Someone out there likes you."

T.J. snorted. "Kevin May is a Denver son, and I doubt anyone will hand me the key to the city. I'll probably get booed the first time I take the ice."

"You're used to it."

"Not on home ice."

"So you'll grow a thicker skin. Besides, you're not taking the ice until next season. It'll all have blown over by then."

Good old no-nonsense Herb, whose favorite expression was, "Don't whine on my dime." T.J. decided to keep on whining because Herb had earned a lot of dimes off of him over the years. "If by some miracle I win my appeal, it won't matter. The Blizzard's got no shot at the playoffs this year, unlike the Earthquake."

"It's called rebuilding, T.J., and you're a key piece. Think how Nelson feels. He's going to a non-contender *and* he's gonna move from a first-line center to the third line. Plus, he's never played for another team. He's not just stupefied; he's in another galaxy because his ass got launched into outer space."

T.J.'s temper fired up an impulse to snap at Herb. Why, he wasn't sure. Par for the course. On a deep inhale, he admitted inwardly Herb was right. T.J. had seen the look on Nelson's face as they'd cleaned out their lockers. Stupefied? More like zombified. Nelson didn't make friends easily. Slick as an eel on the ice, he was a quiet sort who slipped out of bars and parties early and alone, looking as though he preferred anything to social time. Hell, the only time T.J. had seen him with a woman was when a bro, or a bro's significant other, bullied him into it.

With his family all living in the Bay Area, he seemed to spend most of his downtime with relatives. *Tight-knit family. Wonder what it feels like?* T.J. envied and pitied him all at once. There was a lot to be said for having no one but yourself to rely on.

An hour later, T.J. stood at Julia's front door, fatigue bunching and twisting his muscles like the spirals of a nautilus shell. He needed to unwind. Finger poised to jab the doorbell, he hesitated as though a magnetic field encased his hand.

What was holding him back?

So many things. Like Julia cooking him a meal. It wasn't the potential state of his digestive system worrying him; it was the intimacy of her effort. The box marked "Home Cooking" rested beside the already checked off "I-miss-you" box, and both were squarely under the heading marked "Warning Signs of a Relationship Headed into Class V Rapids."

Danger! Turn back before you're towed under.

She wanted to ramp things up; he wanted to maintain the status quo.

Would she expect to follow him to Denver? Julia was a smart woman—way smarter than him—which begged the question, why would she want to hitch herself to him? Did he *want* her to? A powerful "no" surged.

Running a hand through his hair, pulling in a deep breath, he rang the doorbell and got an immediate, "It's open," so he stepped inside.

"Right here." She was on her white couch, in her white living room, wearing a white T-shirt and jeans. One leg pulled up, chin resting on her knee, her eyes were glued to the TV. Without looking at him, she pointed toward the bar. "Heard about your trade. The Jameson's over there."

"Well, hello to you too," he mumbled.

She flapped her hand at him, shushing him.

A savory aroma wafted from the kitchen, making his mouth water as he scanned the bar. He took in two bottles of Chopin vodka—one half-empty, one full—that he'd never noticed before. Julia's poison of choice was either Don Julio or champagne.

After fixing himself a drink, T.J. ambled over to the couch and plopped down beside her, then glanced at the TV. He rolled his eyes. *Chick flick.*

He cupped her shoulder, his thumb stroking small circles. "Don't I get a hello?"

She leaned over and pecked his cheek without looking at him. "Hello." She returned to the same position on the couch, eyes still fastened on the TV.

"Something smells good," he offered, slightly annoyed.

"Just a little longer," she whispered. Her blue eyes were bright with tears. Had he ever seen her cry before? He darted his gaze back to the TV, where a man in a wheelchair was smiling at a young woman curled up in his lap.

A little alarmed, he whispered back, "What are we watching?"

She didn't answer. Just kept her brimming eyes riveted on the screen. The man was saying something that made the girl cry, and Julia shook her head.

"We're watching *Me Before You*. It's almost over." She shot him a guilty sidelong glance and scooted a little closer without touching him. "Sorry."

Sipping his drink, he watched with half his brain until he found himself getting sucked in.

"What's this guy's deal?"

Whispering again, she said, "He was in an accident that left him paralyzed, and he doesn't want to live anymore."

"Why not? The guy's rich, he's got parents who love him, a cute girlfriend—"

"Shhh." She patted him as though she were soothing a child. Then, in a dreamlike voice, she said, "He used to be this buff, active stud, and now he can't be that guy anymore. He doesn't want to live a life where his mind is the only part of him that functions. And he loves her, but it kills him not to be able to do anything about it."

Kevin May's glazed eyes popped into T.J.'s mind, shooting a bright bolt through him. He calmed his breath. *It's just a movie.*

Now the scene switched to a breezy white room. So peaceful, so tranquil.

"Now what's he doing?"

"He's in Switzerland so he can check out on his own terms. Now shush. Here comes the really sad part."

Moving Julia aside, T.J. lurched to his feet. She snapped her head up and met his eyes.

"I need more Jameson," he stammered.

Turning abruptly, he marched to the bar, clutched the Jameson bottle, and ducked into the kitchen, where he couldn't hear the crying and soft, sad speeches. His fingers tugged his hair.

It's a movie, goddamn it! Movies aren't real.

For some reason, his mind wouldn't accept what he tried to feed it, rebelling with its own line. *He can't be that buff, active stud anymore.*

T.J. couldn't remember when he began pacing, but by the time Julia appeared in the doorway, wiping moisture from her cheeks, he was in full stride.

She sniffled. "Are you upset?"

He rounded on her. "You *liked* that movie?" Add a chortle and a sneer, and he sounded just like his dad. Another parallel he'd never seen before, and it made him recoil. *Back off, asshole.*

Her mouth slackened, and a tear slid onto her lip. "Yes."

"Why?"

"Besides the fact that Sam Claflin and Stephen Peacocke are really hot? I don't know. It's a touching story. I mean, the guy had absolutely *everything* one second, and the next his world is—" Her hand shot to her mouth and covered it. "Oh shit. I should've realized ... The accident."

The "accident." Lawyer-speak for assault on ice. Like it happened on its own, and I was standing there by chance.

He gaped at her. Words leapt through his brain like a colony of elusive frogs, and he couldn't snag any of them.

"T.J., I'm sorry. I wasn't thinking ..." She paused for breath. "That guy you hit, he isn't paralyzed. He'll be fine."

Like that makes it all better.

He bent his head and folded his arms around his ears. "You don't know that! He's still in the hospital!" It was the first time he'd said it aloud. Hell, the first time he'd admitted it.

Heart jackhammering his ribcage, he leveled his gaze at hers. "One second, one turn, one move," he pinched his thumb and index finger together, "one infinitesimal deviation, and he'd be warming up on the ice right now." *Not lying in a bed thinking about how the hell he's going to walk again, much less skate or play hockey.* And if T.J. couldn't play hockey again? It was the one thing, the *only* thing, he'd ever done well. Would *ever* do well. If he couldn't play, it would be game over. Just like the dude in the movie.

Anguish rushed up from his gut, and like bile, it tasted acrid, filling his mouth with a bitterness he couldn't choke down. Alternately confusing and crushing. In that moment, he *had* to tell someone, anyone, to let out this ... this whatever the fuck it was crashing down on him like a tsunami.

He searched Julia's eyes, desperate for a lifeline, but she pulled him up short by stepping back and crossing her arms as if preparing to broadside him. "Look, I'm sorry your life's been fucked up lately. I'm even sorrier for what I'm about to say."

He shook his head and sighed. "Julia, I know I've been a jerk."

"Do you? Well, that's good because it might help you with future girlfriends."

Future girlfriends? What the fuck? "I'm sorry for what I said about the movie." He braced himself—for what, he had no idea.

She looked down at her feet before her blue eyes shot back up to his. "T.J., when we first hooked up, it was fun. Nothing serious, nothing heavy. A lot of sexy times. But it feels like ... it sort of stalled, and lately I've realized a few things."

Before he could think beyond, "Where the fuck is she going with this?" she straightened her shoulders. "I had this planned differently. I was hoping to feed you a nice meal, talk over dinner in a calm, civilized way." She drew in a sharp breath. "The real reason I asked you over tonight … Oh, hell. I'll just come out and say it. I think we should stop seeing each other."

His mouth swung open. *"What?"* He stared at her, incredulous. "Because of a goddamn movie?"

"This is not about the movie."

"The trade, then. How did you find out anyway?" *What the fuck is going on here?*

Lips pressed together, she bunched her eyebrows in a hard line that paralleled her mouth. "It's not the trade either. No, I'm talking about the fact that whenever I've even *hinted* at getting more intimate, you've reacted as if I asked you to assassinate the president."

"Wait. What did I miss? We've been *plenty* intimate. Were you in a different bed from the one I was in?"

An eye-roll. Not a good sign. "I'm not talking about physical intimacy, T.J. I'm talking about two people sharing more than a bed. Their hearts and dreams. Letting each other in. Knowing the other person better than they know themselves. Don't get me wrong. Sex with you is good. Great!" The last word sounded as if she'd thrown it in to cover a leaking wound, akin to sticking on a Band-Aid and hoping it was enough. "But other than sex, what've we got? And the sex … We don't make love. We fuck."

And what's wrong with that? he refrained from asking. Instead, he ventured, "But I take care of you in bed. I always make sure you orgasm first. Hell, multiple times." Was this about being a selfish lover? Except he wasn't. Suddenly, he felt like the dumb gigolo to her smart attorney self. Smart girls didn't waste their time with him unless they wanted a good lay. And he'd always given them that.

A thought horrified him. "Don't tell me you've been faking it." Reaching back, he gripped the counter's edge hard, steadying himself, his abused ego deflating faster than a Mylar balloon nailed by a dart.

"Oh my God!" She threw up her hands, then pointed an accusing finger. "You just don't get it, and *that's* the problem. You're incapable of real intimacy, of loving someone and letting them love you. Want the evidence? We don't talk." She began counting off on her fingers. "About our days, our careers, our futures, anything. You're going through some heavy shit, but all you do is brood and drink and put up walls. We've been together nine months, and I don't know a thing about your family. The only part of you you're willing to share is your body. And even when we're screwing, you're here, but you're not. I don't feel connected to you. You never say anything remotely romantic in bed. Shit, you don't say *anything* in bed. You don't even look at me. And cuddling? You'd think it was comparable to rolling around in poison ivy. We're missing tenderness that should be natural. That's not how intimate partners behave, T.J. Frankly, I don't think you know how to be in a relationship, and I want—no, I deserve—more than a fuck buddy." Her voice held a sad edge.

His mind reeling, he had no idea what to say.

She let out a shoulder-dropping sigh. "We're on two separate paths that are widening the farther we go, and it's time to move on."

Jumbled thoughts came at him, pelting him like he was on the wrong end of a lopsided snowball fight, but nothing stuck long enough for him to study it. Then he flashed on the Chopin bottles, and a thought hammered him.

"Wait. Is this about another guy?"

She focused on a corner of the ceiling. When she lowered her eyes to his, she raised a skeptical eyebrow. "Don't tell me you've been a one-woman man this entire time. Hot hockey player on the road, women throwing themselves at you."

Not really an answer. Aftershocks, stronger than the original jolt, rippled through him. His hand flew to his hair.

One side of her mouth curled in a smirk. "You should learn to control your tells. You give yourself away too easily."

"But I didn't—"

Her hand went up. "Not interested in if you did or didn't." She gave him a little shrug.

What. The. Actual. Fuck? "But *you* obviously did." His voice had climbed a few octaves, making him sound like someone had his nuts in a vise. Someone did—Julia.

45

Lips pursed, she nodded slowly. "It's not as if I went out looking for it. Stuff just sort of … happened, and I met someone. I want to find out if he and I have a future."

A hard slam to the gut brought up old, unwelcome shit he wanted to keep buried. Deep. With the memories came a cold rage. His iron grip on the counter was the only thing holding him in place, and he clung to it as though his life depended upon it.

"So that's it," he ground out.

Julia closed the distance, stood on tiptoe, looped her arms around his neck, and kissed him on the mouth. Her fragrance was strong and spicy, like a runaway plug-in fragrance that saturated the air, and it clashed with the acid churning in his gut.

"Thanks for everything, T.J." One hand patted his chest. He'd been dismissed.

With a cursory nod, he pulled her other arm from his neck. Countless times she'd had her hands on him and he'd liked it, but now, not so much.

She pointed at the bottle on the counter. "No one else I know likes Jameson. Let me grab a bag so you can take it with you." *Consolation prize.* She turned and padded away.

Blowing out a breath, he looked around himself as if he'd just woken up. Shreds of the Jameson label were strewn across the counter. He scooped them up and depressed the pedal of her step-on garbage can, dusting off his hands over the open container. A black label caught his eye. *Morton's.* One of his favorite restaurants. He peeked at various cartons. One was marked "Prime Porterhouse," another "Lyonnaise Potatoes." He skipped the third.

Ten minutes later, flustered and flabbergasted, his ego in pieces, he stood outside her door, nearly laughing out loud that she'd never fed him her "home-cooked" dinner before tossing him out on his ass. Nor had she told him where she'd heard about the trade.

A question kept spinning against the backdrop of his mind like an old forty-five on a goddamn turntable: How in the hell had this happened?

As he drove away, Julia's words popped up and bobbed like corks in his mind. *You just don't get it. It was physical. There's no connection. I found someone.* No, he didn't get it.

Jesus, she cheated on me!

His stomach bunched into knots, and her confession sliced into his most tender spots as though a prep chef were going to town with a well-honed blade.

Thank God he'd never fallen hard for her—not that he could've anyway. Not Julia or any girlfriend he'd had the past ten years. No, while he'd liked them all and tried his damnedest to treat them well, he hadn't deserved any of them.

His relationship with her, like all the others, was another piece of wreckage to chuck into the grab bag of things marked "did not see that coming." Maybe it was time he added "but totally should have" to that label. Maybe he should just play it safe and stop dating completely—he might be a ticking time bomb anyway. He could become Beckett-Milleresque and one-night-stand his way through life. Or maybe forego sex, at least for a while, as unbearable as that sounded.

With a headshake, he turned on the car's audio system. Time to chill out and smarten up with a little ancient Roman history. But instead of the podcast he'd been listening to, he landed on a local sports station—and froze at the sound of his name.

"Well, good riddance. Denver can have T.J. Shanstrom," some talking head spat.

Another chortled. "He can hang out with Kevin May while he waits out his suspension."

T.J. punched the knob off and slammed the heel of his hand against the steering wheel. *Damn it!* Weeks ago, his world had been perfect. Now the bird of paradise—no, a flock of them—was crapping all over him. Why?

Maybe the universe wanted him to atone. But he'd been playing a role on the ice, doing a job he was paid a lot of money to do. And Julia? He'd never promised her a damn thing.

Karma be damned. He didn't believe in that shit anyway. No, it was time to focus forward. Denver and lots of changes were coming at him, and he had twelve hours to prepare himself.

Denver. Kevin May's in Denver.

A thought niggled at him, but it was preposterous, so he dismissed it. At first. Then it basted in his brain, and a decision crystallized. It wouldn't hurt to throw some positive at the universe. Might even help him turn his luck around.

He drew in a long, shuddering breath.

Tomorrow, he would visit Craig Hospital and see with his own eyes that May was all right.

Chapter 6

The Atonement Express Runs Through Denver

Natalie gave Kevin's door a tentative knock. They'd moved him to a different part of the hospital, and she'd only just learned the new location from Kristin—who'd apparently overseen the move on her watch the evening before.

Somehow Natalie had been relegated to morning and lunchtime while Kristin had appropriated the sweet spot: afternoon into evening. It wasn't that Natalie minded visits early in the day, but often Kevin was asleep or gone for tests or therapy, which meant she saw little of him. Worse, the visits were competing with her business schedule, chewing up precious client time while she scrambled to fit everything in. Her first dog-sitting rounds started in the morning, as did calls on her bookkeeping clients. She'd been juggling appointments, missing a few assignments along the way, to her horror and chagrin. Letting a client down had never been her MO but now seemed a constant series of blips, and she teetered on the edge of losing a few bigger accounts.

And her previously healthy habits? Sleep was elusive, and her diet consisted of far too many grab-and-goes. The night before, dinner had been leftover rice and two string cheeses with an IPA chaser. Routine morning runs, once a sacred ritual, had fallen by the wayside entirely. Her go-to for calming herself, fly-fishing, seemed a vague memory.

So here she stood, knuckles poised to rap again, pondering how much time she'd spend with a conscious Kevin—or waste on a sleeping or absent one. Grace Guilt gave her a good finger wagging, and she chased the selfish thought away. But today she had little choice; her time was limited by her brother's dogs waiting in her vehicle.

Another knock, and a croaky voice called to come in. She poked her head inside, relieved to see Kevin in bed and alert, and she plastered on her best smile.

The effort was rewarded when he said, "Hey, beautiful lady," and reached out his hand. She took it and leaned in for a quick peck. Kevin frowned. "Why are you so late?"

Embarrassment heated her cheeks, and she pulled away. "I'm not that late." The crushed look on his face made her instantly regret her retort.

In a softer tone, she said, "I had to spend extra time with an important client, and that put me a little behind." A client she'd been desperate to soothe and keep from firing her ass. But she couldn't tell Kevin any of this. Colin had warned her not to put any undue stress on his brother—about anything. Besides, these were *her* business affairs, and she could handle them.

Kevin laced his fingers with hers. "I see how it is," he mocked. "Your client's more important than I am."

He'd just yanked on Grace Guilt, making Natalie rush to say, "No, it's not like that." Why did she feel the need to justify herself?

As if he hadn't heard her, he said, "I'm hungry, babe. Do you see the menu anywhere?"

She glanced around quickly. "No. Let me get one for you."

Less than five minutes later, she returned triumphantly. "Ta-da! Menu."

"I didn't ask for a menu," he growled, startling her. "I asked for a fucking cup of water. Or juice. You know, liquid?" His sarcasm had a nasty bite. "Christ, you couldn't even get *that* right."

Natalie looked around, wondering if he might be talking to someone else. Maybe he thought *she* was someone else. Otherwise, his behavior made no sense.

He hit the call button, and a moment later a nurse came in. He gave the woman a saccharin smile. "Nurse Ratched, may I please have a cup of water? My girlfriend's a little too scattered to get me one."

The nurse cut her a look that said, "Are you lame?" Natalie's face flared a little hotter, amping up her defensiveness and no doubt making her appear guilty as charged.

After the nurse delivered the water, Natalie swallowed her pride. "Do you want to look at the menu now?"

"I'm thirsty, not hungry." He reached for the cup with his left hand. While Natalie scratched her head mentally over his confusing behavior, she watched his hand tremble, splashing water from the cup. "I can't get a grip on it," he gritted out.

Natalie slid it from his feeble grasp and placed it in his right hand. "Do you want some help?"

"No." He lifted the cup to his lips and swallowed. "That worked." A tentative smile curved his mouth. "God, I hope that's not permanent."

Natalie averted her eyes, suppressing despairing tears. *So do I.* Kevin was left-handed. With a deep breath, she rallied and faced him.

He took her hand in his again, his thumb stroking her knuckles. "I'm sorry to put you through this. I'm sure my injury isn't what you signed up for."

On that seemingly lucid comment, she lowered herself into the chair beside his bed. "It's okay. So … speaking of your injury, is there any news?"

"Kris told me that T.J. Shanstrom just got traded to Colorado."

Natalie nearly shook her head. She'd expected news about results of medical tests, not hockey. And she certainly hadn't expected *this* tidbit that had her jolting to the edge of her seat. "He's coming *here*?"

"Yep. The team probably needed to move him out of California. Apparently, he's been getting crucified by the press and attacked by angry fans."

"Serves him right," she hmphed, an image of Kevin's shaky left hand flashing in her brain.

"Yeah, well, rumor has it the coaches told him to come after me."

Incredulous, she perched farther forward, anger percolating in her veins. "So he does everything he's told? It doesn't excuse him from lacking a conscience or a brain."

Kevin stared at her. "Nat, you don't understand because you've never played."

His reprimand knocked her down a few rungs, making her feel stupid and small. "I guess I don't," she groused. "I just don't like people hurting my friends."

"Hockey can be a brutal. Shit happens on the ice. Tempers flare, and guys just lose it sometimes. It's part of the game."

"I get that it's part of the game, but this was different, intentional," she protested.

Grace Guilt rushed to the fore. *Don't stress him out,* she nagged. "Ready for that menu now?"

"Yeah, sure." His voice was pure exhaustion, so different from the barky one he'd used minutes ago.

She passed it to him, and he held it in his right hand, staring. He blinked once, twice, closed it, lowered it, and dropped his head back on the pillow. "Fuck. I can't read it."

Alarm swelled inside her. Months ago, he'd bragged about his twenty-twenty vision. "I can read it to you, and then we'll order," she offered.

He covered his face with his hands, then let out a long-suffering sigh. "God, I'm so tired."

"Should I go?"

His hand shot out and locked on her arm. "No. Please stay." He blinked rapidly. Were those tears? Her heart about broke. "Maybe read from *The Hockey News* so I can kid myself that I'm still part of it all?" His eyes reminded her of a sad puppy as he peered at her. No way could she refuse.

She covered his hand with hers. "Of course I'll stay. I'm here for you."

THIRD MAN IN

Sunglasses shielding his eyes from Colorado's blazing-bright winter sun, T.J. sat beside Gage in a silver Escalade ESV. The front passenger seat was occupied by a Blizzard employee, though T.J. didn't recall her name. She'd greeted them at Denver International Airport, and now they were speeding toward the arena to meet with Coach Marty LeBrun. Tough-nosed, a ball buster when he thought it was warranted, LeBrun also had a reputation for being fair-minded. His players might not have always gotten along with him, but they respected him, and that's what mattered to T.J. And really, anyone would be better than Coach Rogers.

The girl in the front twisted her body so she faced them, rousing T.J. from his thoughts.

"So, T.J., this is your second tour with the Blizzard?"

"Yep."

"And I understand you already own a condo at Spire? That's a really nice building."

"Uh-huh."

Still stinging after yesterday's searing smackdowns, T.J. wasn't in the mood for polite chitchat, no matter how attractive she was. He wanted to wallow in the canal water that was his life, but from out of nowhere chirped Miller's annoying voice: *Grow a pair.*

T.J. let the words spin in his head, then side-eyed Nelson when the girl turned her attention on him. The poor bastard looked uncomfortable. Whether it was the girl rattling him or the shock hadn't worn off yet, T.J. couldn't tell. Nelson mumbled a few words, and they rode in silence the rest of the way.

The driver pulled into the arena's underground parking garage, and attendants took their bags when they exited the Escalade. The young woman escorted them through a series of doors and hallways. T.J. swiveled his head, reacquainting himself with the surroundings.

Familiar, yet foreign. Concrete mustiness, glaring light, a creeping chill. The last time he'd been here, he'd been on the visiting team.

But now he was entering his *home* rink. And no asshats were hassling him. Yet.

They stopped at an open door with a placard beside it declaring the space to be the coach's domain. As they stepped inside, Marty LeBrun rose from behind a desk and extended his hand. Not a huge man at six feet-ish, he was nonetheless broad and hard. He had a crushing grip and wore the battle scars of his former playing days on his face. His dark hair was flecked with silver, and intelligent brown eyes took in T.J. and Nelson.

"Come in and sit." He waved at two chairs. The girl hovered in the doorway until Coach gave her a curt nod. "Thanks, Serena. Would you please close the door on your way out?"

For the next twenty minutes, Coach focused mostly on Nelson. The office door opened, and a head poked inside. "These our new players, Coach?"

Coach jerked his chin at the newcomer. "Gentlemen, say hello to your captain, Dave Grimson, affectionately known as the 'Grim Reaper.'"

The Grim Reaper grinned, revealing a gap where three top front teeth should've been. He wagged his head at Nelson, then led him away to meet the boys—he'd be playing with them in tonight's game—and the door closed once more.

"T.J." Coach's sharp voice had T.J. sitting up a little straighter. "You've been here before, though this'll be the first chance we've had to work together."

Yep. You're the boss. Got it. T.J. gave him a head bob, and Coach continued.

"No games, obviously, but you'll practice with the team, attend meetings, all the regular stuff you'd be doing if you were on the active roster. Except travel. When we're on the road, you'll be here training—and polishing your image." He paused to take a pull on a water bottle. "Your dance card's gonna be full because you're getting extra shares of Blizzard community work. New team, new town, fresh start."

T.J. groaned inwardly. "Yes, sir." It wasn't that he didn't like community work; it was more about what it took out of him to keep up his defense shields. Lots of smiling. Lots of posing for pictures at hospitals with sick kids, pretending it was a big party. It was all about appearances. But it was no party—not for the children, and certainly not for their parents. Real parents. Parents who would do anything for their kids. Who could never imagine leaving them behind with a drunk who'd beat the shit out of them over ... and over ... and over ...

Steepling his hands, Coach jarred T.J. from his self-indulgent visit to Misery City. "You've got your same number, eighty-four, if you want it."

T.J. gave him another nod. "I'd like that. Thank you."

"So tell me what you plan to contribute to this team."

Marshaling his thoughts, he brushed his palms along his thighs and cleared his throat.

"Well, there's my usual game. Going to the dirty places on the ice and clearing guys out to make room for our top players. Beyond that, I'll be working on my shooting—on my own time. I'd like to sharpen my goal-scoring. I understand I'm no sniper, but I'd really like a chance to rack up more numbers on the scoreboard and fewer in the penalty box."

Coach's eyebrows crawled to his hairline. *Here it comes.* T.J.'s heart sank a few inches. He'd been plugged into the enforcer role for so long, told who to wreck and when, he wasn't sure he had a scoring touch anymore, but he sure as hell wanted to try. Yeah, he followed orders, and he was good at his job, but what if he could be something other than *that* guy? Play a different kind of game? Be the guy he'd started out to be all those years ago? Someone who could make room on the ice with his big body and handle the puck with enough skill to set up the goal-scorers and chip in a few himself? A right wing who could surpass his career best thirty-six points in a season and crack the fifty-point ceiling?

Coach pursed his lips. "Of course we expect the same level of toughness you've always brought. But I'm glad you want to up other parts of your game." To T.J.'s surprise, a twinkle lit his eyes, deepening the creases radiating from them. "I've seen tape of you when you first broke into the league. I also watched you before you were drafted, when you played in major juniors. You have good puck sense and vision on the ice. With your size and strength, you could be a force out there, a real power forward like the Capitals' Tom Wilson. *That's* the reason I wanted you here. And like Wilson, you'll need lots of photo ops and serious community involvement. If you do it right, you might even get nominated for the King Clancy like he was. That's my goal for you. But," Coach continued, "let's see how it goes. That all right with you?"

T.J.'s heart hoisted itself up a few rungs, and optimism sparked. Maybe Herb had been right and this trade *was* a do-over. Before he got too carried away, though, his oldest inner voice—the one planted by his father when he was just a kid—told him he was a piece of crap who wouldn't amount to anything. A waste of space and air.

Though he desperately clung to it, the spark of optimism fizzled and winked out.

It was early afternoon when T.J. pulled into Craig Hospital's parking lot and cut the engine. He reminded himself that all he needed was one quick look at Kevin May—he was sure the guy was fine—and he'd be on his way. But another minute or two to compose himself wouldn't hurt.

With a huff, he sank a little deeper into his seat and stared out the window. The sky was crowded with thick gray clouds that looked as though they were trying to decide whether to spit out their load of snow. A white-haired couple teetered toward the hospital entrance as a mother holding a child's hand speed-walked around them. What were these people doing here? Visiting loved ones? Getting help for themselves?

A blur of motion snagged his attention. He narrowed his eyes and made out a woman being dragged across the parking lot by one—no, two—dogs of different sizes. The woman yanked on the dogs' leashes and dug in her heels. T.J. half expected to see asphalt peeling up like ice cream scoops, but she stumbled instead, and a leash flew from her grasp. The dog attached to it tore for the unsuspecting oldsters heading for the entrance.

T.J. unfastened his seat belt, threw open the door, and leapt from his car in one motion. Sprinting across the parking lot, he vaulted for the furry fugitive and snatched up the leash, wrestling the animal to a stop. The couple trundled on, oblivious to their near miss while T.J. reeled the big dog in. Behind him came a gasp, and he pivoted in time to see the woman clamber to her feet, her remaining charge capering around her at the end of its lead.

"Thank you. I couldn't hold him." She was breathing hard, dusting off her jean-clad thighs, the remaining leash wrapped around her wrist.

T.J. ruffled the dog's thick-furred neck. The animal was big, its blocky head so huge T.J.'s splayed hand barely spanned its breadth. The beast gave him a sloppy slurp that striped the back of his wrist, then sat on its haunches, eyeing him with what could only be described as a shit-eating grin.

Showed her! it seemed to say with laughter in its large brown eyes.

T.J. turned toward the woman. "Yeah, no problem. You okay?" Her head was down, and when she raised it, eyes the color of an amber pendant locked on him. For a beat, he was transfixed, lost in gold and copper.

"I'm fine. I was letting them out for a walk," she said, snapping T.J. out of his daze, "when *that* one made a break for it." With a frown, she inclined her head toward the dog sitting beside him.

Even with the frown, she was beautiful. Not in a glamor-girl-perfection way like Julia, but in a natural, this-is-what-she-looks-like-all-the-time way. Healthy. Vibrant. Her clear skin had a bronze cast, as if she were bathed in sunlight. High, flushed cheekbones accented an oval face surrounded by wavy hair that cascaded over her shoulders to her elbows. Its color and sheen reminded him of glossy milk chocolate with streaks of caramel.

Her sable eyebrows eased as she reached for the leash. "Thank you so much. I don't think I could've stopped him from knocking those poor people down." She lifted her chin in the general direction of the hospital entrance.

T.J.'s mouth curled up on one side, but he held on to the lead. "Yeah, that would've been bad. Like a bowling ball on steroids, cutting a wide path through undersized pins. You sure you're ready for me to hand him over?"

"Thank you, yes. C'mon, Meathead. Back to the car." She reached for the leash again.

"Meathead?" T.J. tugged on the leash, and the dog stood, its adoring eyes pinned on him.

"He's not my dog, so I had nothing to do with the name." A little smirk played on her features. "He seems pretty enamored with you."

"Oh, so you're not his owner? Who is?" *Boyfriend?*

"No, I sometimes watch him and Annie." She inclined her head to the other dog who had heeled politely at her side. "They're my brother's dogs."

A little alarm bell rang in his head. "Is your brother in the hospital?"

"No, no. I stopped in to see someone after taking these guys to the dog park." The sun caught in her strands, gilding them in gold.

Now the other side of T.J.'s mouth curved. "I love dogs. Here. I'll help you get him back to the car."

"Um, okay. It's just there." She led him toward a red Dodge Durango with a crushed side panel.

"So, uh, the someone you were visiting … Are they okay?" He had no idea why he was asking. From sulking around Serena, he'd gone to jabbering at this unknown woman.

She caught her bottom lip between her teeth. *Oh shit. Not okay.* A moment later, she said, "I'm not sure." Then she was wrangling the leash around her arm, heaving up the hatch, and wedging in a one-by-one to hold it in place.

"Broken liftgate, huh?" He waited for the smaller dog—Annie—to hop into the back before handing Meathead over, then grasped the hatch to make sure it didn't jump the stick and come crashing down.

"Yeah. The Rolls is in the shop." She let out a warm little chuckle, obliterating her earlier hesitant expression. And that's when he noticed her mouth—full, rose-colored, soft, ripe.

As she maneuvered the dog and the gate, an enticing fragrance, a mixture of cookies and fresh flowers, wafted up his nose.

With a swift motion, she snatched out the stick, tossed it into the back, and took the liftgate from T.J.'s grip. He stepped back as she banged it shut and dusted her hands. *No rings.*

"Well, thanks again. I really appreciate it."

"No problem." He ransacked his brain for something else to say and came up short, his arsenal of jabber apparently depleted, but he kept his eyes pinned to hers. Jesus, they were the prettiest color he'd ever seen. Bronze and copper and gold, all precious metals melded together. Lost in them, he let himself forget for a moment the real reason he stood in a hospital parking lot.

"Well, I have to be going now." She ducked into her vehicle. "Thanks again."

He just stared, entranced, hoping he hadn't been drooling in front of her like Meathead.

Exiting the parking lot, Natalie glanced out her window, taking in the hulk still standing where she'd left him. He smoothed a hand over dark, short, thick curls, though it did little good. They rebelled and sprang right back up again. He'd done it several times as he'd faced her.

Thank God he'd corralled Meathead. The action had distracted her enough that she hadn't gone to pieces in the parking lot for contemplating Kevin's condition. The mood swings, his inability to do simple tasks, his waves of despair devastated her, and she was helpless to do anything. When time came to leave, she'd practically fled his room, guilt nipping at her heels the entire way—especially when his forlorn voice trailed after her, asking when she'd be back.

How many visits was it now, and she'd only caught flashes of the old Kevin? Her belly buckled with worry. Colin had reassured her it was normal—sometimes TBIs caused temporary shifts in personality, he'd said. *Okay,* she'd nodded.

She'd never been a weepy woman, subscribing instead to the stiff-upper-lip code, but her throat had been tight, and her lip had been quivering all the way to her Durango—danger signs of an imminent tearful outburst. And she'd had way too many of those lately.

Just let the dogs out to do their business then hightail it home, she'd told herself. No focus, only painful thoughts bombarding her. And that's how Meathead had broken her hold.

Just then, her phone rang, jangling her already stretched nerves, and she sucked in a breath before answering. "Drew?"

"Hey, Sis. What's up?"

"Just left Craig Hospital."

"Yeah? You don't sound so good. Everything okay?"

"No, it's not." Dear God, the tears she'd held back suddenly sprang loose. Frustrated with herself, she swiped at them with the heel of her hand as she drove.

Drew stammered, sounding alarmed. "Hey, hey. What happened?"

"Nothing. Everything. How do I describe it? Sometimes it feels like I understand Kevin's state of mind, and other times I feel like I've just landed on an alien planet and I can't get my bearings. I mean, the overriding question is will he be okay? But it's so much more complicated than that. What's in store for him, physically *and* mentally? Will he get his old life back?" The latter she wanted for him more than anything—to return, intact, to what he most loved. She sighed. "I'm sorry. You called me for a reason, and I'm dumping all over you."

"I called to tell you I was done early and can take the dogs off your hands. Wanna head to the river and see if the fish are biting? Grab a beer?"

The offer touched her, and she smiled through her tears. "No time. I'm buried in bookkeeping I have to play catch-up on. God, I am so far behind."

"Your loss," he teased.

Yeah, it was her loss. She didn't bother telling him she'd been so preoccupied she'd missed the deadline to submit her article to the

Journal of Accountancy. Never had she spaced such an important opportunity before. And now her clients were grumbling about *their* slipping deadlines; the thought spurred a panicky feeling that climbed from her stomach into her throat.

"I'll drop the dogs by your place. See you in a few." She clicked off.

She came to a sudden stop at a crosswalk when a kid on a bike flew across, completely unaware how close he'd come to getting creamed. The dogs slid in the back cargo area, and Natalie's heartbeat picked up its pace. *Just like that, everything can change.*

T.J. weaved his way through glaringly bright halls around staff and equipment as though he belonged there. A few more minutes, and he'd have eyes on Kevin May and know he was fine. He pictured the guy surrounded by giggling nurses sitting on his bed while he poured on the charm, just like T.J. had poured on the charm so he could find May in this labyrinth.

Muscles tauter than normal, nerves on the verge of fraying, T.J. barreled toward the door with May's room number before he lost his nerve. The door was ajar. Rolling his shoulders, T.J. grasped it. Opened it. Came to an abrupt halt. Sucked in a sharp breath.

Monitors glowed with bright, squiggly lines. Wires led to a lump in the bed that stirred, then croaked, "Christ, can't a guy sleep?"

T.J. took a tentative step inside the room, all of him wanting to turn and run. He forced one leaden foot in front of the other. "Hey, May. Just wanted to stop by and see how you're doing, man." His voice came out squeaky and high, sounding like it had when he was twelve.

Eyes fixed on him, squinting in confusion. "You're not the nurse," May rasped.

T.J. reached the bed. A face on a stark-white pillow took him back to a different time, a different hospital, a different face.

The guy looked like he'd been run over by a goddamn bus. Realization dawned on T.J. that May was as far from okay as Denver was from Antarctica, and a prickle ran along his neck, making his hairs rise. His palms suddenly turned clammy, and his stomach flipped upside down.

Why had he come? Better to have imagined May laughing, flirting, than seeing him like this.

For fuck's sake, say something. T.J. swallowed the bile in his throat and forced out a laugh. "Bet you wish I *was* a nurse, huh? They're a hell of a lot prettier than me."

May's eyes squinted a little harder. "Fuck. Either I'm dreaming or T.J. Shanstrom's in my fucking hospital room."

"You're not dreaming." T.J.'s calf muscles were coiled, ready to spring from the room.

May rubbed his jaw. "Jesus, you must have filled your gloves with concrete before that hit."

T.J. released a laugh—a real one—blowing some steam from his pressure cooker. "Do you remember anything?"

May started to shake his head, stopped, and winced. "Besides how badly we were beating you guys? No. One minute I was on the ice, next I woke up in a hospital. My ex showed me the hit on YouTube." May craned his head and looked at a clock. "Speaking of my ex, you better get the hell out of here before she sees you. Her mouth packs a bigger wallop than anything you can dish out."

T.J. schooled the urge to turn tail and run right then. "Yeah. Okay. I just wanted to check on you and see how you're doing."

"Not so great."

"No, I can see that." T.J. let loose a breath. "I'm really sorry, man."

"Yeah, I know."

"Be well."

When T.J. left May's room, he swayed down the hallway, dazed, his mind zigging and zagging as he tried to grasp what he'd seen. Kevin May would not be all right.

Chapter 7
Friends and Family Get in Free

Days later, Natalie was frazzled as she careened through hospital hallways to Kevin's room. Not yet ten o'clock, and her energy was nearly spent. Soon she'd be dipping into her reserves, and when those were depleted, she'd be running on fumes. Next stop: life support.

Last night, she'd tackled her growing pile of client work, which had taken far longer to shrink than she'd projected. It hadn't helped that she'd confused her clients and entered a stack of receipts into the wrong account, costing her hours to undo, redo, and recheck. When she'd last glanced at the clock, it had glowed 4:14 a.m. A bright sunrise had nudged her awake, and she'd been surprised to discover she'd fallen asleep, face plastered with papers strewn over her table. Again. No amount of showering or hot coffee could've sharpened her for the day's tasks or erased the smudges from under her eyes.

Add to her sleep-deprived state her first dog-sitting stop, where she'd been delayed by a barfing incident, throwing off her neatly planned morning like a tumbling row of dominoes. Down went the first one, and she was helpless to stop the cascade. She waited until the dog's owner called her back, reassuring Natalie the dog had gotten into some garbage that was merely "working its way" through his system. But just in case, would she please add a return visit to her already-squeezed morning schedule? Yes, of course she would.

As she was leaving that client's driveway, she'd gotten a call from a potential bookkeeping client telling her thanks but no thanks; they were hiring a different service—one with more time for them than she appeared to have.

Yeah, that one had hurt.

Glancing at her phone, she groaned inwardly. Forty-five minutes late to see Kevin. She'd tried calling his room without luck. Would he be pissed off at her today?

Out whooshed an exasperated breath that lifted the hair from her forehead. On that exhale, she told herself the best she could do now was pick up her pace.

The aroma of coffee pulled her up short, and she detoured to a nearby machine. She was already late; what would a few minutes more matter?

Delicious steam rising up her nose, she couldn't resist taking a sip of the hot brew as she rounded a corner. Where she collided with a human wall. She had no idea who yelped louder—the man drenched by her hot coffee or her, also well-doused. His cursing was definitely more voluble than hers—not to mention colorful—as he shook brown droplets from his dripping fingers.

"Jesuuus! Why the hell don't you watch where you're going?"

"I could say the same to you," she ground out. She looked up, high up, into blazing moss-green eyes set in a face contorted in irritation. Suddenly, light shifted in those eyes, and the hard line of his mouth softened, turning up at the corners. He looked familiar, and she reeled in her anger, spluttering instead, "Are you hurt?"

By now, all attention was focused on them, and she felt like a bug pinned to a board for all to see.

He looked her over and gave himself a cursory scan. "Looks like you got as good as you gave."

She narrowed her eyes. "Do I know you?"

Brushing at his arms and chest, he nodded. "From the parking lot a week ago. You seem to lose things easily."

She shot him a bemused look.

He returned it by arching a dark eyebrow. "Meathead?"

Recognition brightened her brain. "Right. You caught him for me."

"Yep." He bent to pick up her now-empty cup and handed it to her.

Contrition settled in. "Oh crap, I can't believe I got coffee all over you. Can I buy you another cup?"

A frown drew his brows together, yet his mouth curved into a generous smile. Like rain coming down while the sun shone. He pointed at the cup in her hand. "I believe that was *your* coffee, not mine, though it appears you were trying to share it with me. Very charitable of you, by the way." His smile widened. She was pretty sure he was snickering behind that smile.

She pressed her hand to her forehead. "Oh God. I'm sorry. I'm usually not such a ... It's been ... Today's been ... challenging."

"Ms. Foster?" a feminine voice called behind her, and she whirled to one of Kevin's nurses. "He's anxious to see you, hon."

"I'll be right there." Natalie wheeled back to the tall stranger and jabbed her thumb over her shoulder. "I have to go. Again, I'm so sorry. At least let me pay to clean your clothes."

He held up a hand and shook his head. "Don't worry about it. I'm fine. My clothes are fine. It's just jeans and a shirt." His gaze darted to the ceiling. "Well, socks and underwear too." Amused hazel eyes landed back on her. "But who's counting?"

Magnanimous of him. She let a little sigh of relief escape. "Okay. Well then ..."

He tilted his head. "Well then."

She turned and hurried away without a backward glance, steeling her shoulders, chin, and resolve to face whichever Kevin awaited her today. *Dear God, let it be the pleasant one.*

After a stop home to change his coffee-stained clothes, T.J. stood on Miller's doorstep and rang the bell. With a smile and a shake of his head, he recalled literally running into the lovely Ms. Foster an hour earlier. What were the chances? Obviously, she was visiting someone on the same floor as Kevin May. Twice now he'd bumped into her around the same time. If he planned it right, maybe he'd see her again, get a chance to find out who she was and who she was visiting. He found himself hoping it wasn't a romantic anyone, just as he hoped for another encounter—minus the scalding coffee, that is. God, he'd been pissed. But when he'd looked into those enormous, horror-filled amber eyes and realized who they belonged to, his anger had fizzled faster than a dud firework.

The heavy wooden door groaned open, bringing him back to Miller's front porch. Dwarfed by the massive arched oak was a petite, auburn-haired woman with light green eyes. Just as he remembered her.

Paige's face lit up with a dimpled smile. "T.J., come in."

He handed her two bottles of wine. "Thanks for having me."

She held the door wide for him, motioning him in as she glanced at the labels. "Oh, my favorite Zinfandels! Thank you so much. Beckett's in the kit—"

"Right here, pixie." Behind her loomed a familiar form. "Hey, my man Shanny. Glad you made it, bro." Miller pulled him into a hug, pounded his back, and dragged him into the foyer while Paige closed the door. Then Miller slipped an arm around her shoulders, drawing her close, and kissed the top of her head.

Pixie? Yeah, I get that. The size difference was almost comical. What was that old cartoon strip—Mutt and Jeff?

With a proud, beaming smile, Mutt Miller said, "Let me introduce you again. T.J., my wife, Paige Miller. I call her Andie."

T.J. squelched his amusement. Was this grinning idiot really his old teammate, the mentor he'd once idolized for being a badass and a chick magnet who could wheel the ladies like none other?

"Congratulations, although it looks to me like you got the short end of the stick, Paige." T.J. winced. *Christ! Did I just make a short joke?* "Uh, Andie?"

Freeing herself from Miller's grip, an easy laugh escaping her, Paige tilted her head at her husband. "Hulk here gave me that pet name back in college. These days I answer to either, so feel free to call me whichever one strikes you." Her eyes bounced between him and Miller. "I'd forgotten how close you two are in size."

66

T.J. jerked his chin at Miller. "I think I have several inches and a few pounds on you."

Miller clamped a hand on T.J.'s nape. "Not a chance. Doesn't matter anyway. I can still whoop your ass."

"Boys." Paige rolled her eyes and motioned toward a hallway where a burble of voices blended with muted music. "Everyone's back here."

T.J. traipsed after Big Miller and Tiny Miller, passing an enormous wood-and-iron spiral staircase that swept past floor-to-ceiling windows at least twenty feet high. Miller stopped short.

"Pixie, I'm gonna show T.J. my man cave first."

"Okay," she sang over her shoulder.

Miller motioned for T.J. to follow him down a side hall. "So Andie surprised me when we moved into this house," he began. He came to a wide, solid door, opened it, and stepped through, T.J. on his heels. "I had no idea she'd designed this and had it built until it was finished. She's sneaky that way."

"Hoooooly shit!" T.J. looked around at an enormous open space with gleaming gray granite floors. High above was a tray ceiling lined with spotlights that shone down on vehicles stacked on car lifts two-high in the most luxurious garage T.J. had ever laid eyes on. In the very center, as if it occupied sacred space on a showroom floor, sat a vintage Corvette convertible in cobalt and silver.

T.J. had never been a car buff, but *this* beauty could make a convert out of him.

Miller laughed. "I know, right? C'mon. Let's grab you a beer."

Head on a swivel, T.J. stumbled after Miller into a lounge area—it looked like an in-home theater had had a baby with an upscale car dealership waiting room—where Miller pulled a few beers from a stainless fridge. He handed one to T.J.

T.J. popped the cap and took a long gulp, bathing his parched throat in cool liquid while he reined in his incredulity. "She *gave* you a garage filled with a classic car collection?"

"No, just the 1960 Corvette over there, to replace one I had to sell a while back. I've been having fun filling the rest of the racks." He pointed at the Corvette with his beer bottle. "I had no clue about any of it until she blindfolded me and walked me in here last Thanksgiving.

The house was still under construction, but she had the garage finished before she did her big reveal. We spent the whole damn night here. Christ, that was hella fun. Best Thanksgiving *ever*."

T.J. regarded his old friend for a few beats. "Fuck, Miller, you've always been my role model."

Miller quirked an eyebrow.

"Not the drugs, man, but the rest of it. The game, the women." T.J. chuckled. "But all this domestic—" He stopped himself before blurting "bullshit" and shook his head. "You've gone in a whole other direction." *That I don't see myself following. Ever.* He tipped his beer bottle to his mouth and took another generous swallow.

Miller's expression shifted, and his eyes landed on some remote spot, as though he were watching something on a different plane. "Don't knock it till you've tried it. I used to think settling down was for suckers until Andie waltzed back into my life. Christ, I had no idea what I'd been missing." He turned his gaze to T.J. "It's nice having someone you give a damn about who gives a damn about you. Know what's even better?"

"Being in bed with *all* the Dallas Cowboys Cheerleaders at the same time?"

"Forget it. You're an asshole."

T.J. belted out a laugh. "I didn't mean to ruin our moment. Tell me. Please."

Miller scowled at him. "Since you asked nicely." He grew serious. "It's knowing she's got my back, that she's always in my corner. The world can go to shit, and she's there. No matter what."

T.J. nodded as if he understood, except he didn't. And he never would because that meant a lot of touchy-feely crap, and that wasn't him.

Miller cleared his throat. "Well, good talk." Then he launched into ticking off the Corvette's list of intricacies. T.J. pretended to listen while his mind meandered to the NHL draft when he'd been eighteen, back when he'd given a damn about someone he'd believed had given a damn about him. He'd been young and crazy in love—and utterly blind. The LA Kings had picked him in the second round, and no words had existed to describe his pure joy. He'd been on top of the world, the love of his life beside him. It couldn't have been sweeter. The best fucking night of his life. Hours later, it had transformed into the worst night of his life.

Miller's voice pulled him from his walk along Gloomy Lane. "How's Denver treating you so far?"

"No complaints. Haven't been ambushed by any haters yet, and I'm liking the team's mindset. Tomorrow they turn me loose in the community to see if my rep can be salvaged."

"Any updates on May?"

"Funny thing about that. I wasn't hearing a damn thing, so I snuck into his hospital room to see for myself." T.J. shuddered at the memory of May that first time, the one that flooded him with guilt. Guilt he'd been trying to squelch ever since.

Miller's eyebrows shot to his hairline. "Are you fucking kidding me?"

"Nope. In fact, I just saw him again today. He was looking a little better." More like a full-size sedan had hit him instead of a truck.

"Shit, that takes some cojones." Miller seemed to assess him over a long, thoughtful swallow.

"That first time, definitely. But today he almost seemed happy to see me. Asked me to come back." T.J.'s chest tightened as he recalled the slur in May's speech. Shit. Was that permanent? Whatever it was, T.J. couldn't say no.

"Jesus, you must have really dislocated his brain. Can't imagine why else he'd want to see you, of all people."

T.J. shrugged to mask his unease. "I think he wants to talk hockey. His teammates are all in San Diego, so he's with family who don't understand. And that family includes an ex and a girlfriend. Talk about a juggling act." He paused to chuckle. "Girlfriend was running late this morning, and he was twitchy as hell." The later she was, the more anxious May had become, his mood darkening, leaving T.J. to wonder if the head injury was to blame. Finally, he'd told T.J. to leave, half-assing a joke that if T.J. saw how gorgeous she was, he'd try to steal her away—like T.J. would ever pull a stunt like that. Especially on someone he'd wrecked in a completely different way. Especially since it had happened to him.

69

May had probably been worried about the girlfriend sticking around for the long haul, and justifiably so. Women could mess with your head that way. And if this one was in it for the money, she was probably halfway out the door already.

"Your lawyer know you're talking to May?"

"No."

Miller set down his beer on a side table and pulled out his phone. "I'm texting you *my* lawyer's contact information. Tom Carlisle. He's helped me through a few scrapes, and he's damn good." Miller pocketed his phone and looked back at T.J. "Call him. You need someone looking out for *your* best interests, not a lawyer working for your old team. Neither one of them gives a shit about you." A beat later, he said, "Ready to join the party?"

T.J. warmed to the idea of switching gears, especially if it meant forgetting the shitfest that was now his life. "Let's do it."

They made their way to a great room, where about a dozen people were lounging, talking, laughing. Expectant faces turned toward him, and T.J. held his breath. *Please don't recognize me.*

"Everyone, this is T.J., an old buddy," Miller announced. The faces broke out in smiles and hellos.

Paige appeared at his side, took him by the arm, and led him around the room, introducing him to her construction crew. Some guy named Norm complimented him on his style of play, and T.J.'s lungs relaxed.

They came to a dark-haired young woman with brown eyes behind big, round red glasses. She was attractive in a girl-next-door kind of way, though she wasn't T.J.'s type. Blond-haired, blue-eyed, sex-on-legs were the combination that usually snagged his attention, though lately a certain amber-eyed brunette was making frequent appearances in his imagination.

Paige bobbed her head. "This is Katie, my assistant." Katie, reclining in a corner of an oversized leather couch, lazily scratching an ear attached to a big, black fuzzball of a dog, gave him a smile. The dog watched T.J. from hooded eyes, its huge purple-black tongue lolling out one side of its grinning mouth.

"And that's Hugo, Katie's BFF," Paige said.

Dropping on his haunches, T.J. scratched the pooch's chin. "What kind of dog is he?"

"Part-Chow, part-Lab, and God only knows what else. I rescued him five years ago, and they didn't know much about him."

Hugo panted hot breath on T.J.'s hand. The dog seemed docile, content to have his chin and ear stroked simultaneously. T.J.'s knees creaked and complained, so he stood. Hugo whined.

"Hugo really likes you, which is rare. He's pretty particular." Katie's smile broadened. "You must be a dog person."

"Used to be."

Her smile shifted into skepticism. "What does that mean?"

"Nothing." A familiar pain lanced him. "Just haven't had one since I was a kid."

Thankfully, Paige's expectant gaze fell on him, saving him from further Katie prodding. "Beck said you wanted to talk to me about maybe selling your condo?" She cocked her head toward the kitchen. "Why don't you follow me so we can talk?"

"Sure." He fell in line and shot Katie a backward glance. She was still eyeing him with a question mark etched on her face.

With a devilish grin, Paige handed him two huge-ass bowls and an even huger-ass bag of chips in the kitchen. "You have to help while we talk. Refill these for me?" She bent and scraped a mishmash of scraps off plates into the trash while he washed his hands. "So you're thinking of selling?"

A few chips found their way into his mouth before he finished his task, folded his arms over his chest, and leaned against the counter. "I'm not sure. I own a place in the Bay Area, and before I got traded, I thought I'd sell the condo here. Since everything's changed, I'm considering selling them both and buying something bigger in Denver."

She began rinsing and stacking plates. "Do you plan to live there alone?"

The question caught him off guard. Wasn't that kinda personal? She continued, her back to him. "I only ask because a sweetheart, kids, parents, anyone that might live with you all come into play when you're evaluating a potential home. For instance, if seniors were to

71

move in with you, you'd want to look at something on one level. A girlfriend with kids, on the other hand, would mean searching in certain school districts."

He chuffed—loudly. "Neither of those scenarios applies. Nor will they ever."

She pivoted partway, eyes wide. "Never? Are your folks gone?"

"Good as gone." He could hear the bitterness in his own voice. Something flashed across her face before she turned back to her dishes, spurring him to move on before she could utter the question no doubt playing in her mind. With a cough, he said, "And as far as girlfriends, with or without kids, that's not happening either."

A knowing nod. "Ah. You don't *do* relationships. Nothing permanent anyway."

Excuse me? Unsure exactly why, her remark both unsettled and irritated him. A second later, he understood why she'd made it. "I take it when you met Becks, he didn't *do* relationships either."

She chuckled. "He changed girlfriends as often as he changed socks."

Genuine curiosity seized him. He moved closer, resting his hip against the counter beside her. "So how did it all happen? I mean, I thought he'd wear the King of Bachelors crown the rest of his life. No offense."

"None taken. For the record, I never set out to take away his crown." Her gaze slid to the side and grew dreamy. "We just … We happened to both be wrangling with difficult situations and sort of fell into a friendship. Nothing physical. I guess we became each other's comfort zone when everything got out of control, without any expectations. The rest fell into place."

Huh. Not what he'd expected to hear. At all. "Friends first?"

She swung her gaze to him, giving him a smile that lit her green eyes. "Uh-huh. We got to know each other and grew close. We were intimate without being intimate, if that makes sense." A happy little shrug. "And here we are."

Intimate. There was that word again, the version of it that didn't include sex, and it persisted in puzzling him. As he opened his mouth to ask her what, he wasn't sure, Miller appeared from nowhere, and

T.J. took a few paces back. Miller curled an arm around his wife's waist, pinning her from behind.

She craned her neck, giving Miller a smoky look, pecked his lips, and stroked his arm while whispering something that sounded distinctly like, "I love you, tiger."

They'd obviously traveled into their own zone, apart from everyone else.

Awkward. T.J. ducked out of the kitchen with the chips and blended into the group, losing himself in banter that had nothing to do with hockey, blanking out the last few weeks—without having to be halfway through a bottle of Jameson. A nice change of pace, sparing him the guilt that usually accompanied the drinking.

Hours later, a little lighter in spirits than when he'd first arrived, T.J. climbed into his Hummer. "Never thought I'd see the day Beckett Fucking Miller was stupid-in-love." T.J. shook his head. By settling down, Miller had broken some kind of bro code—well, bachelor code anyway—and T.J. felt like he was all alone in a lifeboat, drifting aimlessly in a vast ocean. But he'd never seen Miller happier, and he couldn't shake the thought he was missing something. Something vital.

T.J.'s own objections to letting himself fall again reared up like an oversized, creepy jack-in-the-box, shocking him from even contemplating going down the same path as Miller's. The visual was bone-jarring. No, that life was *not* for him.

Chapter 8

You Before Me

Days later, T.J. was driving to the arena when his phone buzzed. He swiped the screen.

"Hey, Millsy."

"What's up, Shanny?"

"Just heading in for a Blizzard PR appearance. Where you at?"

"Boston. So how're things with the new team?"

"They're a good bunch of guys." And unlike his old teammates, these guys actually talked to him, worked with him. They hadn't exactly fallen over themselves to welcome him, but that was normal. It was up to T.J. to fit himself into *their* routines and rituals. He'd already learned not to skate up the middle after a three-on-one drill. That area belonged to one of his linemates; he'd discovered that the hard way. Besides earning T.J. a spate of curses, the guy had sulked for hours, grousing that T.J. had messed with his mojo.

"Yep, and LeBrun's one of the league's best. San Jose might've done you a big favor. So you still planning on selling your place?"

"Maybe. Paige, er, Andie's been sending me some houses that make it damn tempting. But I haven't decided, so she's taking a low-key approach, which I appreciate."

"My girl's all kinda smart like that." T.J. didn't miss the note of pride in Miller's voice.

"Yeah, except she married you, which brings some of those smarts into question."

"Asshole. Look, ah, she's one of the reasons I called."

A little siren clanged in T.J.'s head. "Everything all right?"

"Yeah, everything's great—more than great. But I'm on the road for a few weeks and won't get a chance to see her. So do me a solid and check in on her from time to time? She, ah ..." He paused and cleared his throat. "She's pregnant." His voice cracked on the last word.

"Shit, that's great news!" *Or is it?* "I mean, it *is* great news, right?"

Miller barked out a laugh. "Fuck yeah! I'm over the moon. But she's only a few weeks along, so we're not telling anyone yet. Besides being smart, though, she's all kinds of stubborn, so don't let her know I asked."

"You got it, dude. Tomorrow's pretty open. Why don't I stop by in the afternoon?"

"Perfect! But make up some excuse that doesn't sound too pathetic. Then shoot me a text and let me know how she's doing."

"Happy to."

"Thanks, man," Miller said. "I owe you big-time. We're family now, and I'll do the same for you someday. But first you gotta get a girl."

"Ha! Maybe you can send me one of your castoffs?"

"What, you're so lame you can't find your own action? I'm sending you jack, dickwad. Not only do I *not* remember their names, but I deleted all their numbers when Andie and I got together." He paused a beat. "I remember you used to date that one ..." Miller's fingers snapped in the background. "The blond with legs that went on for miles. A stripper, right?"

T.J. laughed. "No, she danced for the Mammoth Wild Bunch. You're thinking of Gillian."

"Why not look her up? Unless she's married with five kids now."

Gillian. Maybe he should. After all, it had been a while since Julia. Memories of steamy sex with the cheerleader streamed through his consciousness. She'd been a fun fuck. Different recollections suddenly slammed into him, jarring him. Gillian was nuts. The same crazy that made her fun in bed also made her downright psycho. They'd dated for a few months, had a good time, and then she'd become obsessed—marriage, kids, the whole package—and had gone batshit when he'd reminded her it was a casual thing. Yeah, that hadn't worked out well for him. She'd gone from batshit to ballistic, and he'd backed way the hell off. More like he'd run for his life.

"No way. She was my own version of *Fatal Attraction*. That woman was out of her mind."

"Most of 'em are. So work on finding yourself a good one."

T.J. let out another laugh. "Andie got any sisters?"

"Sorry, man. She's one of a kind."

The tender inflection in Miller's voice caught T.J. off guard, and a fresh doubt jabbed at him like a dentist's pointy tool. Was T.J. missing out?

"Think I'll get a dog instead," he replied. "I hear they're loyal."

The arena parking lot was nearly empty when T.J. pulled in. Nelson drove in a moment later, and T.J. gave him a chin lift and waited.

"Gentlemen," a cheerful female voice called. They both looked over at the same time to see Serena waving at them. "Ready for your meet and greet today?"

"Yep." T.J. tried to match her exuberance but fell way short.

Nelson chimed in with something polite in his typical soft-spoken manner.

They followed her through the labyrinth of hallways into a small meeting room with tables and chairs set up like a classroom. A box of black Sharpies stood between two stacks of jerseys—his and Nelson's. She pointed to a different cluster. "Here's a box of pucks and some silver pens. I know it's a lot, but we need to build a supply since you're new. Plus, with the silent auction and benefit you'll be attending—"

T.J. interrupted. "What's that?"

She blinked at him as if processing information that wasn't included in her programming. Blink, blink. "It's a black-tie charity event."

"Are the players expected to attend?" He already knew the answer. Of course they were.

"I'm sorry, T.J., I thought I included a schedule in the packet I handed you that first day. It would've been on that." She darted her eyes to Nelson.

"I saw it," he offered with a somewhat smug look.

T.J. couldn't even remember where he'd put the damn packet—which he'd never opened. "Thanks, asshole," T.J. threw at him.

Nelson shrugged. "Anytime."

"It's a few months away." Serena coughed. "Well, um, I'll be back in a flash, and we'll be on our way." She had an inflection that made everything sound like a question. If she weren't smiling so brightly and didn't have such a nice ass, T.J. would've found the habit annoying.

He and Nelson settled in and began signing—more like scrawling. By the time Serena returned with more boxes and bags, he and Nelson had built an impressive stack.

"Really?" He narrowed his eyes at the load she carried.

"Don't worry," she laughed. "These are just team hats, T-shirts—stuff like that—for you to pass out. They always put smiles on faces."

T.J. knew the drill. They'd visit the kids in the hospital healthy enough to have visitors and hand out gifts while the entire thing was captured on video. Then their good deeds would end up on the Blizzard's website and PR clips—maybe even a local news feature—and the community could gush about what good guys they were. Even a goon like him.

They rode in the silver Escalade and, a half hour later, pulled up to a low, square building. A pair of camera operators were waiting for them in front of a sign that read "Spalding Rehab Hospital."

What the hell was *this* place? "We're not going to see kids?" T.J. asked.

His question seemed to fluster Serena. Apparently, while Nelson was the kid who had all the right answers, T.J. was the one who missed the assignments. She gave an exasperated little sigh, then plastered on a saccharin smile. *Yeah, I'm the dumbass of the class.* "No, the team did that last month. Today, you're visiting some patients recovering from brain trauma, and the hospital wants us to follow a few rules ..."

She recited those rules as he and Gage shrugged on their jerseys and tugged Blizzard ball caps on their heads.

They were shuttled into a reception area, where a hospital spokeswoman greeted them, thanking them for coming. "We're not as popular as Children's Hospital when it comes to attracting our city's star athletes, so we're especially pleased you chose to come here today."

T.J. felt a little sheepish. He hadn't chosen anything—he'd just come along because he was told to. *Just doing my job.* Shit, that was getting old. In that moment, he felt like a sheep following along blindly, pushed here and there by a sheepdog.

The lady's voice brought him back to the present. "... and you'll be visiting a group of adults whose abilities to interact vary ..."

Brain injury. Shit! His breathing sped up, and he concentrated on slowing it down while cold beads of sweat broke out on his forehead. *May'll be okay. He'll be okay. Youcandothisyoucandothisyoucandothis.*

And like the sheep he was, he followed the procession down the hall to the first room. Swallowing a lungful of air, he braced himself and mustered his best smile.

Natalie was circling Craig Hospital's parking lot, hunting for a parking space, when her phone whistled. The *Kill Bill* whistle, to be exact. Her heart sank. She couldn't keep putting her brother off. With a swipe, she pressed the phone between her shoulder and ear and continued searching out that elusive spot.

"Drew, I just got to the hospital, and I'm running late." *Again.*

"Well, hello to you too, Sis."

She realized how harsh she'd sounded. "Look, I—"

"Just drop the 'tude, okay? I don't give a fuck if you bark at me, but don't pull that shit on Mom. That's jacked up, Nat."

Heat fired up Natalie's cheeks, followed quickly by angry tears stinging her eyes. In that moment, she could've imploded. Might've even welcomed it. "I didn't bark at Mom," she fired back instead, a little choke in her throat. From anger or guilt, she wasn't sure.

"I *heard* you when she called you this morning. I was standing right there."

Natalie pulled into a spot on the edge of the parking lot, slipped into park, and closed her eyes. She *had* gotten testy in their very brief phone call, but it wasn't Mom—it was the question she'd asked so sweetly, so Mom-like. *Do you need financial help, Natbug?* No, damn it! Never mind that Natalie had just made a sizeable withdrawal from her previously untouched savings account to cover her mortgage payment. She wasn't about to admit any of it to her family.

"Nat?"

"I'm here," she sighed. "I didn't mean to come across that way. I'll call her and apologize when I'm done here."

His voice softened. "She's not looking for an apology. She's just really worried about you. Hell, *I'm* worried about you. Not only have you been MIA from Sunday dinner three weeks in a row, but you aren't calling either."

Yeah, go ahead and heap on some more guilt. "I'm treading water, trying to keep from drowning here, Drew. The hours I spend with Kevin are hours I used to spend dog-sitting, bookkeeping, marketing myself. I have to carve time out somewhere because I am *not* going to abandon him."

"Who says you're abandoning him? Maybe you don't see him *every* day."

"Not happening."

"Fuck, you've got more time invested in him *since* his injury than you had beforehand."

Her cheeks flamed once more, and her protective shields surged. "You don't know what the hell you're talking about, Drew."

"Listen to you getting all defensive. That's not who you are, Nat. Where's my thoughtful, logical little sister?"

"Are we done here? Because I really have to go. I'm already late," she bit out.

The more unreasonable she became, the more reasonable he sounded. "Nat. Deep breaths. Come to the river with me this afternoon. Cast some line. You need your Zen. Or if you'd rather blow something up, let's go shoot some sporting clays. I'll even let you beat me."

This pulled a chuckle from deep in her chest. "Ha. I wouldn't be offering to put a gun in my hands right now if I were you, Bro. I might mistake you for a target. Look, I'm fine. Really." She gathered up her belongings, climbed out of her Durango, and locked it.

An exasperated sound came from the other end.

"Okay. Gotta go now." She hung up as soon as he uttered a resigned, "Bye, Nat." God, she felt like a douche. Could women be douches? Whatever the female equivalent was, she was it.

As she scurried across the lot, irony struck her. She was running toward a situation that was slowly sucking the life from her. When Kevin's well-being had commandeered her energy a lifetime ago, she'd imagined a temporary upheaval. But weeks were stretching into unexpected months with no end in sight. And if Kevin's condition was permanent? What had started—and not gone past—a fun fling had become mired in messy muck she'd not been prepared for. If he'd been her brother, her mother, a husband, she'd have a well of resiliency she so desperately needed right now.

But that wasn't fair. Time together shouldn't matter. No, no. Kevin needed her. She could *not* let him down; she had to *be there* for him. Like a rock. Yep, she could do this. She and Kristin. Team Kevin. Except she'd become the lifeless team member while Kristin seemed to race a little faster each day. And Natalie admired her for it. The girl had spirit, spunk. Her determination never flagged, or at least she never showed it like Natalie, who resembled a worn dish towel.

On the elevator, it occurred to Natalie that Drew was right. Her reserves were dry, and she needed a refill—so she could stay strong for Kevin. Who better to fill it than those who nurtured her? Her mom, her brother—the ones she'd been treating like shit. How had everything become so twisted?

With a tired sigh, she heaved herself off the elevator and headed for her version of the Room of Requirement—a magic room that housed the coffee dispenser. As she prepared her cup, a couple of female voices drifted from the other side of a partition. Their gossipy tone captured her attention, and she found herself sucked into a different world.

"Well, it's not even like they were *dating* that long. Why insinuate yourself unless you have ulterior motives?"

"You don't know that," the second voice scoffed.

"No, I don't, but look at the evidence. She's a nobody; he's a superstar. His ex-wife is here all the time, but so is *she*. Like she's scratching for territory so she can sink her claws into his fortune."

"How do you know he *has* a fortune?"

"He's a pro athlete. Of *course* he has money! Look how much he gets paid every year!"

Natalie's blood, along with her hand, froze.

"Well, she doesn't seem like the type to me. A dog-sitter has to be kind; therefore she can't be a gold digger."

A chortle. "That's some far-fetched logic. Money does funny things to people, and gold diggers come in all shapes and sizes. And then there's the fact ..." The conversation moved away, and though Natalie heard no more, she'd heard plenty.

Heart crushed, she rested her forehead against the dispenser, pulling deep breaths into her lungs. *You can do this, Nat.* Straightening on another inhale, shoulders back, she plodded to Kevin's room. As she walked, she couldn't help but wonder if it was all worth it. Grace Guilt admonished her noisily; her self-doubt and self-pity had to take a hike. Poised to open his door, she dug deep and dragged up what remained of her reserves.

T.J.'s "assignment" had been four individuals, but he ended up spending time with nine. It hadn't been as bad as he'd imagined, and in some ways it was far better than seeing the kids. In some ways. The patients spanned from nineteen to seventy-four, and their injuries were just as varied as their ages, ranging from car accidents to plain old bad luck. Some were working on their motor skills while others were trying to remaster short-term memory. Simple things, like how to remember they'd just lit a stove so they didn't walk away and start a fire. Basic stuff T.J. never thought about—stuff these people had never thought about either until they'd been injured.

On his way back to the reception area, he took a wrong turn and passed an auditorium. A blond guy in a wheelchair was talking to a cluster of men also in wheelchairs. A few rolled their chairs back and forth as they listened, like a hockey player might shuffle his skates on the ice during the singing of the national anthem. One guy popped a wheelie.

The blond man's eyes found T.J.'s, and he smiled. The guy was young—T.J. pegged him for his mid-twenties—but the smile made him look downright boyish. Before T.J. could duck away, the guy called to him, "Come in. Join us. I'm just going over the rules before I turn the team loose."

Twelve or more pairs of eyes stared at T.J. He felt as though a bright spotlight had just been illuminated, pinning him in front of a black curtain.

"He can't play," one guy yelled good-naturedly.

Another piped up. "Yeah, he's got legs that work. He'll just slow us down." A low rumble of chuckles passed through the group. That's when T.J. noticed they all wore black T-shirts stamped with the words "No Excuses!" in neon yellow.

The blond man said, "It's okay. Maybe he's just here to pick up a few pointers, or he's my line judge. With the way *you* guys cheat, I need all the help I can get." He jerked his head at T.J. "Come in. Don't be shy. We don't bite."

"Unless you've got the ball," another called out. Another group chuckle.

It was then that T.J. realized the only thing moving on the blond guy was his head, which rested against a brace behind him. A wide webbed strap looked to be holding him up. The wheelchair itself was equipped with all kinds of unidentifiable gear, including an arm that held something by the guy's mouth.

With a faltering gait, T.J. walked inside the room and stood off to one side. "Hey, how's it going?" he said with a small wave. His hand dove into his hair, and he shifted his weight, unsure what to do next.

His discomfort must have been obvious because one guy chuckled. "Relax, dude. You're not playing, so you won't get the hell embarrassed out of you by us schooling you with our sick moves."

T.J. let out a laugh, which released some of the tension in his shoulders.

"Hey, you're T.J. Shanstrom, aren't you?" someone from the back said. All eyes fastened on him again.

Ah, shit. He raised his hand and pointed toward the door. "Guilty. I'll just leave now."

Blond guy looked him over. "You don't have to leave on our account. Some of these guys used to play hockey."

A ginger lifted his chin at Blond Guy. "Yeah, like Troy before he crashed headfirst into the boards." T.J. looked at Troy.

"True story. Got tangled up and went into the boards. Unfortunately, they won that battle."

"How old were you when it happened?"

"I'd just turned seventeen. That was six years ago."

Jesus. T.J. schooled his features to squelch his horror—and pity. The guy had likely seen plenty of both and didn't need his added to it.

"Don't feel sorry for him," the guy who'd popped the wheelie said. "He did it on purpose. Ladies dig guys in wheelchairs, and he couldn't get one any other way."

"Desperate times call for desperate measures," Troy joked.

"And, man, were you desperate," Wheelie Man retorted. This made all of them crack up. "Hey, I'm Mark, by the way." Wheelie Mark stuck out his hand, which T.J. shook, then called out each man's name in turn.

"T.J.?" a feminine voice said. All eyes, including his, turned toward the sound of his name. The hospital spokeswoman stood in the doorway. "There you are! I thought we'd lost you. I see you've met the basketball team."

"We were just getting acquainted," he replied.

"Well, I think your ride's leaving soon, so I'll escort you back."

T.J. scanned the guys' grinning faces before turning back to Troy. "Hey, pleasure meeting you." He stuck his hand out, realizing too late what an idiot move it was, and snatched it back again. "Jesus, I'm sorry." Flustered, he stood there like he was stuck to the floor.

Troy seemed to sense it. "No worries, man. It's nice to know you *wanted* to shake my hand." He gave T.J. a knowing, genuine smile. "I actually do secret handshakes. They're so secret you can't seem 'em."

T.J. laughed. "Hey, it's been a real pleasure. Thanks for letting me crash your party."

"Anytime. Come back and watch us play."

"I'd like that." T.J. nodded at the group and followed the spokeswoman into the hallway.

"How often do they play ball?" he asked her.

"Once or twice a week. Troy's a great coach."

"Wait. He coaches them? Even though he's ..." His voice echoed along the hallway.

"A quadriplegic? Oh yes. He runs the whole thing. He organizes the teams, coordinates practices, and schedules games. They even hold an annual tournament."

"No way."

She laughed. "Troy and those men you just met acknowledge they're disabled, but they don't let it keep them from living. They're adventuresome, willing to believe in the impossible. Most of them live independently, are in long-term relationships, and contribute to the community. In many ways, they're more *alive* than many whole people I meet. They possess the same kind of strength and determination you have." She stopped at a pair of closed doors.

"Uh, that *I* have?"

"Of course. How else would you have made it into the NHL?" She smiled up at him, a warm, genuine smile. "And graced us with your presence today?" She stepped through one of the doors and held it open for him.

Jesus, this woman was giving him way more props than he deserved, and he shrank a bit inside.

"Thank you again, so much, for coming today. It means the world to everyone here."

"I meant what I said. I'd like to come watch the guys play sometime."

"You're welcome anytime, Mr. Shanstrom."

God, that was nice to hear.

Natalie squeezed through the door and treaded softly to Kevin's bedside. He seemed to be sleeping. She exhaled a shoulder-dropping breath. *Thank God he doesn't know I'm late.* She shed her coat, piled it on a chair atop her purse, and sat beside him. This was her new normal—her Kevin Conundrum, as she'd dubbed it, though she kept that bit to herself. Is this how love affairs were supposed to go? Spiky feelings and stomach roiling of the I-need-a-Tums variety, not the I'm-so-freaking-excited-my-blood-is-on-fire variety?

When she was around Kevin, she felt as though she tiptoed along the edge of a crumbling precipice, one step away from sliding uncontrollably down a scree slope. He had his good days where it appeared he was conquering his TBI, but then he'd have a bad day, and it seemed his progress unraveled. One step forward, three steps back. If that wasn't bad enough, their fledgling relationship included not only Kristin but his daughter, Emma. Natalie had only met her a few times, and though the girl had been shy, her questioning glances had Natalie feeling as though she were a heartless homewrecker. *A gold digger.* The moniker stung.

Had Natalie not committed to coming every day, she might have just drifted away like so much smoke. For now, she was trapped in a strange twilight between obligation and possibility with a man she barely knew.

Chapter 9

I Can't Talk Because My Foot's in My Mouth

T.J. made his way to Kevin May's room. The door was ajar, and he knocked softly before stepping inside.

May's eyes flew to his, and he looked … panicky?

Christ, doesn't he recognize me? "How you doing?" T.J. came off sounding like a guy who'd just had ice shoveled in his breezers. High and squeaky. He cleared his throat and plowed on. "I brought you the latest *Sports Illustrated*. It has an article about the league, and oh, just happens to be the swimsuit edition."

"Shanstrom, this isn't—"

A squeal came from the door, and a whirlwind tore in, fine blond curls bobbing like an angel's soft halo.

"Daddy!" A child ran to the bed, stopping short at a woman's sharp cry.

"Emma May!"

T.J. turned and took in a Pamela Anderson lookalike whose eyes traveled from the child to his face. As shock overtook her features, tension grew palpable—heavy and sticky like a Midwest summer.

"What the hell are you doing here?" she hissed.

Oh shit.

May raised a hand and laid it on the little girl's head. "Kris, this is—"

Her eyebrows crashed together. "I *know* who this is," she yelped. "T.J. Shanstrom, the asshole who cheap-shotted you. Did you come to check your handiwork?"

T.J. raised his hands in surrender. "Maybe I came at a bad ti—"

Kris planted her fist on her hip. "You bet your ass you came at a bad time."

"Language, Kris," May said. "Emma—"

"I wanted to check on him," T.J. said lamely, panic swelling inside him.

Kris flung out her arm. "You checked. Now leave!"

"Maybe I'll come back another time." Eager to flee, T.J. inched toward the door.

She stabbed a finger in his direction. "Oh no, you won't."

"Kris." Kevin's tone was laden with weariness. Emma's big eyes bounced between the adults as she perched on the bed.

T.J. called out a soft, "Later, Kevin," and squeezed through the door. He was latching it behind him, but a powerful yank ripped it from his grip. He rocked backward as Kris exploded toward him.

Though she stood at least a head shorter than he, she got in his grill, fearless as a rabid bulldog. She stood so close he could smell her cloying perfume. "You ever set foot in here again, you bastard, and I'll call security," she snarled. "Capisce?"

He gave her a quick head bob and retreated. "Got it."

Down the hall he went, willing himself not to break into a run. He shot a glance over his shoulder. Kris was still standing guard outside May's door, her face twisted in bright pink fury.

He ducked around a corner, then streaked onto an elevator. On the ground floor, he stepped to a window, and though he looked through it, he registered nothing beyond its broad pane. Kris's tirade had thrown his emotions into overdrive. He needed to throttle them down. Bracing his hands on his knees, he dropped his head, catching his breath, trying to lock out the feelings fighting for space in his psyche. Guilt, anger, and a few others he couldn't—and didn't want to—identify. *Deep breath in, deep breath out.* Bringing himself upright again, he ran a hand through his hair.

He scanned the space, expecting to be confronted once more by the blond firebrand. Instead, his eyes landed on a vision across the cavernous foyer. Sure he was dreaming, he shook his head, but the vision remained. An angel with dark hair cascading down her back.

The sight of the beautiful Ms. Foster lifted him. Was it mere coincidence she kept appearing, or something altogether otherworldly? He didn't care.

She headed down a corridor marked "Cafeteria." More like swayed. Floated. Her lithe body moved effortlessly, like a dancer's. He was spellbound. He inched away from the window, debating. *Stay put? Follow?* His body overrode the argument in his head, and his feet began shuffling after her. What would he say when he reached her? *Hey! I'm stalking you because I'd like to know if … If what? You're gorgeous, and I'm wondering if you'd like to rock my world.* Yeah, *that* approach wouldn't put her off. No, she'd just run away screaming for security.

Despite his qualms, he kept trailing her. Why? Because just *looking* at her was rocking his world. Big-time.

He found himself at the wide entrance to a mostly empty, fluorescent-hued, white-and-stainless space. To one side, pushing along a plastic tray, was Ms. Foster, slender and supple, and he locked on to his target. She lifted her tray and carried it to a booth. He caught a glimpse of her caramel-colored eyes as she slid along the bench, and his breath hitched. Beauty and grace. The combination knocked the air from his lungs like a bone-rattling check.

A purpose crystallized in his mind. He wasn't hungry, but he grabbed a tray and loaded it with a few plates of eats, paid the cashier, and took long strides toward Ms. Foster's booth. As he approached, he slowed to a casual stroll. Her head was down, her dark hair like a curtain hiding her face; he couldn't tell what she was looking at.

"Mind if I sit here?" He lowered his tray and cocked his head to look at her.

Her head snapped up, her eyes wide and … wet. *Oh shit! Is she crying?* His stomach, which had been dancing only a second before, now lurched and sank to his knees.

"Um ..." She swiped at her cheeks. The food on her tray was untouched.

Why is she crying? "I, ah, I saw you sitting here, and I wanted to find out if you'd had any more canine or coffee ... capers," he stuttered. *Capers?* He mentally smacked his forehead. "I'll leave." He grasped the tray, feeling as lame as he sounded.

She studied him, her forehead furrowing in delicate lines that mimicked soft waves. Amber eyes brightened. "The coffee! Did you get your clothes clean?"

He nodded slowly, hovering his ass by the booth, hopeful. She sniffled and, waving her hand across the table, offered him a half-smile. "Sit, please."

Unsure if she was just being polite, he stayed rooted beside the seat opposite hers. And stared. God, those eyes. The color of warm whiskey. He hadn't painted in years, but those eyes had his mind flying through paint tubes. *Gold Ocher, Raw Sienna, a little Venetian Red.* And that mouth—sultry strawberry lips screaming to be tasted and nibbled and sucked.

His cock stirred, overriding all thoughts of paints, straining to say hello. He told himself his reaction was wholly inappropriate—she'd been crying after all—and to knock it off. No doubt he was intently zeroing in on her because sex was too far distant a memory. Really, he needed to do something about his drought. Except no one else who'd registered so much as a blip on his radar lately had affected him like she was affecting him right now.

He fidgeted with the tray and cleared his throat. "You sure? I don't want to interrupt anything." *What is wrong with you? Just shut up and sit the fuck down.*

"Yes, I'm sure. I was just having a pity party, and it's time I got over myself." One sweet breath escaped her lush lips. He chased out the dirty thoughts lurking in his mind, instead focusing on her shimmering eyes and her words. Flaming desire winked out like it had been doused with a bucket of ice shavings, replaced by tugging heartstrings. He didn't know this girl, but all of him needed to fix whatever the hell was wrong in her world.

And he had absolutely no idea why.

"So. Visiting someone here at the hospital?" He stuffed a bite of roll in his mouth that tasted suspiciously like a roofing shingle.

A sigh heaved from her body, and her shoulders folded in around her. "Yeah. You?"

He nodded. "A buddy. How about you?"

"Um, a friend. With a territorial ex-wife."

The thought of her being with someone made his stomach clutch and ripple, threatening to eject the roll. "Uh, so your boyfriend?"

She nodded, and her hair shifted like a silken drape around her shoulders. "Sort of."

His stomach eased. "What's a 'sort-of boyfriend'?" He kept his tone casual, dreading what came next. Did he really want to know about a boyfriend, even a sort-of one?

Her eyes traveled to an upper corner of the room. "A guy I hadn't been dating very long when he wound up here. I'm trying to be as supportive as I can."

"That's gotta be … daunting?"

"Not to mention super awkward." She swept a thick tress behind her ear but didn't manage to get it all, leaving strands sticking out that he was sorely tempted to catch in his fingers. "Sorry. You asked a simple question, and here I am, going all TMI on you. How about we change the subject?"

T.J. swallowed the cardboard crumbs, chasing them with chocolate milk. "Sure. Tell me about you. Are you from Denver?"

A little chuckle. Good. They were going in the right direction. "No, I grew up in a little town southwest of here called Salida. Ever heard of it?"

He shook his head.

Her eyes lit up. "It's at the foot of the Sangre de Cristo Mountains on the Arkansas River. The most beautiful spot in the world, hands-down. How about you?"

"Northern Minnesota."

"Is your family there?"

Cruising back into choppy waters now. "No siblings, and my parents are gone," he lied. Sort of. No siblings he cared to talk about, and while his parents weren't dead, they were definitely gone.

"I'm so sorry." She looked genuinely distraught. He didn't tell her it was a waste of time. "I'm Natalie, by the way." She extended her hand across the table.

Natalie Foster. What a pretty name. It suited her.

T.J. accepted her hand, a thrill shooting up his arm, and he held it, just held it. It was soft and small in his, and he caught himself before brushing his thumb across her knuckles. She tilted her head to the side, and he gave her hand a quick shake. "I'm—"

A dog barked. Natalie held up a finger and pulled her phone from the seat beside her. *Her ringtone.* "Sorry, I need to take this. But stay put. Hello? Natalie speaking."

He pretended to look around, poked at his food, trying to give her some modicum of privacy. That effort lasted several seconds—up until the first, "But I thought ..." rushed out of her. Followed by a silent second. Brows furrowed, she stared down at some unknown spot on her tray with glazed eyes. "But we agreed on three months, and I set aside ..." Elbow propped on the table, she dropped her forehead into her hand. "Are you able to share the reason why?"

Oh shit. Doesn't sound good. He squelched an urge to squirm.

"I understand." She closed her eyes and shook her head. "Thank you. Yes, I appreciate that." She swiped her phone, set it down, and let out a long-suffering sigh. She straightened, seeming to remember he was there.

"You okay?" he asked softly.

An absent look, not directed at him, as she ran her hands over her arms like she was chilled. "Yeah, I'm fine."

Her phone chimed, and she looked at it as if it might explode before plucking it off the table and staring at it. Thumbs tapped a message, then she dropped the phone in her purse and swung sad eyes to him.

"You don't *look* fine."

"Well, thanks for that." She gave him a weak smile.

He shook his head. "Not what I meant. I meant you look like you just got bad news."

"Depends on your perspective, I guess. I just got fired by a new dog-sitting client. On the bright side, it frees up my schedule. And the text was from Kevin's ex, telling me I'm off duty. I guess I've been double-dismissed." She threw up her hands and plastered on a ridiculously fake grin. "All kinds of spare time now."

"Who's Kevin?" As the question left his mouth, puzzle pieces began clicking into place, forming a picture that was all wrong. His hand flew to the back of his neck as a jolt shot through his bloodstream.

"Kevin's my boyfriend," she explained. Another massive sigh. "He's a hockey player who took a dirty hit about a month ago that landed him here."

The bottom fell out of T.J.'s stomach. *Oh shit, oh shit, oh shit! Just kill me now.* He picked up a spoon and shoveled it under wobbly neon-yellow Jell-O, which he promptly lifted to his mouth and sucked in. Hard. At least the goo was wet and slippery in his suddenly parched throat. Appraising eyes scanned him. *Does she recognize me?* Panic, in the form of adrenaline, flooded his system, and he tensed, ready to vault from the table, the cafeteria, her.

But she hadn't realized who he was—yet—as evidenced by her next words. "Don't get me started on the scumbag who sucker-punched him."

Scumbag sitting right here. T.J.'s roiling stomach sank lower, nearly dropping to his knees. "I heard something about that. Didn't he get a long suspension?" He surprised himself with the nonchalance he faked, given his heart was hammering like a runaway nail gun and an urge to heave was swelling inside him. He eyed the remaining Jell-O. *Not helping.*

A head bob. "The rest of the season. Kevin thinks the league was too tough on him, but he's being too forgiving, in my opinion."

He wiped his palms along his thighs. "So you agree with the suspension?"

Fiery amber eyes locked on his. "No. I think the goon that went after him—T.J. Whatever—should miss as many games as Kevin does. He punched him! For no reason! You can't tell me that's 'just part of the game.' The guy crossed a line." She let out a little hmph, then fired up again. "And irony of ironies, he got traded to Denver! I hope I never run into him—unless it's with my car."

Something with sharp edges twisted inside him. He'd been doing his job. Even Kevin May, broken as he was, understood that—but Natalie Foster didn't, and God, she must hate him! With any luck, she wouldn't recognize him—not in his presence anyway. His old Earthquake mug shot, the one that had continually aired on the sports channels, showed him with long, unruly hair and a full beard. Thank God he'd been in lazy manscaping mode then.

"Just kidding about that last part." Her voice had gentled. "I wouldn't actually *run over* him. Maybe nudge him a little with my bumper." Her lips curved into a smile as she nibbled at a forkful of something orange.

Definitely does not recognize me.

Her smile softened his—what? Anger? Outrage? Shame? Fear? Guilt? Irritation?—and helped him slide whatever it was past the wedge in his throat.

They spent the next few minutes talking about a guy who'd stolen a bulldozer and run it into a city building a week prior. Inconsequential stuff—at least to him.

"I'm sorry, but I never caught your name," she said sweetly during a pause.

Fuck me and the horse I rode in on. A royal battle began raging inside him, one where his conscience yelled at him to end this. Pronto. Yank the damn Band-Aid off in one clean go. But curiosity—and something a hell of a lot like powerful attraction—won out.

"Tyler," he mumbled, his tongue twisting around his half-truth.

"Well, Tyler, it was kind of you to sit here patiently, listening to a stranger rant about her troubles." And there were those eyes again, the ones he could look at the whole damn day.

"That was a rant?" he chuffed, amused.

She shrugged as they stood. "I try to stay positive. Some days are easier than others."

With a nod, he took her tray, sliding it onto his. "I'll walk you out," he said before he could second-guess himself.

As they ambled out of the cafeteria, he asked if dog-sitting was her full-time job.

"No, but it pays the bills. Well, some of them. I have a few career paths I'm exploring at the moment." Her eyes twinkled, and he breathed an inner sigh of relief. Because happiness had just flitted across her face.

He sped up to open a door for her. "Yeah? Like what?"

"Oh, like bookkeeping, financial auditing, and writing for magazines."

"Seriously? What kinds of magazines? You must be really talented." He slowed his stride, partly so she could keep up and partly because he wanted to linger. She fell in, matching his gait.

"Ha! Maybe you could tell the editors I'm talented? I don't think they've caught on yet. I write for accounting trade magazines." They strolled through the concourse and headed toward the main doors.

He must have looked confused because she raised her hand as if being called upon. "Recovering CPA here. Hated the work—and the work environment—but I love the theoretical practice and studying tax law." She let out a little laugh and crinkled her nose, which happened to be sprinkled with pale freckles. "I know. Weird, huh? I guess that makes me a tax nerd."

Glass doors whooshed open, and they stepped into the brisk air.

"Not at all. More like smart." *Way smarter than me, that's for damn sure.* Why was he always attracted to smart girls?

"If I could live on what the publications pay, maybe teach a little on the side, I'd do it full-time."

"Huh. I never knew there was such a thing. Does it pay much? The writing, I mean. Authors make lots of money, right?"

Her eyebrows inched up her forehead. "No way, unless you're Dan Brown or Malcolm Gladwell. But I love it. Bookkeeping and dog-sitting are steadier, and up until recently they supported my writing jones."

His hands slid into his pockets. "Have you lost more than the one dog-sitting client?"

"Unfortunately, yes, along with some important bookkeeping clients."

"Because?"

"Well," she cleared her throat, "since Kevin got hurt, I've been spending more time on him and less on my clients. He counts on me being there for him, and I don't want to disappoint him. I hate letting my clients down, but his recovery has to come first."

Bands of guilt cinched T.J.'s chest.

They were approaching the battered red Durango, the sight of which only fueled his remorse. The fault for her struggles fell squarely on *his* shoulders. The thought leveled him.

Just like I leveled May.

When he'd hit May, he hadn't had a thought in his head, especially about unintended consequences. Consequences beyond the injury itself. Consequences like the one walking beside him.

"And speaking of clients, I should hurry. I need to take a *paws* and check on a sick one." She smiled broadly, that smile transforming her features into something positively breathtaking. "Get it? It's a little joke. You know, pause and paws?"

Nodding numbly, he ignored the clenching in his stomach that had annihilated the warm fuzzies floating there only moments before.

He scrambled mentally. Could he figure out a way to make things easier for her? Bookkeeping, dog-sitting, and magazine writing weren't services he needed. As for anything financial, he'd hired a damn good planner years ago who was worth her weight in gold. And while he possibly had no right to come to Natalie's aid—she hadn't asked for it—an urge to help her pitched inside him.

A scheme flared in his brain, and he shut down the accompanying murmurs telling him it was a really *bad* idea. As long as Natalie Amber Eyes didn't find out who he was, he could help. *Yeah, right. This has to top the list of the worst ideas I've ever had.* The thought, however, didn't prevent him opening his mouth. "Are you looking for new dog-sitting clients?"

Stopping beside the car, she folded her arms, seeming to appraise him. "Always."

He ran a hand through his hair. "I only ask because I have this friend who has a dog, and, uh, he left it with me ... because ..." Another brainwave struck, and he rushed on. "He's the one I've been visiting in the hospital. I've been trying to figure out what to do when

I'm, you know, at work. Would you be able to take on one more?"
*What the actual fuck, dumbass? Thinking on your feet is not working
for you. At all.*

She turned her head, a glint in her gorgeous gaze. "What kind of
dog?"

An air dog because it's pure fabrication. "Uh, just a mutt." He
shrugged, drawing a blank. *Shit.*

"Big mutt? Little mutt? Red dog? Blue dog?"

"Ha! *Go, Dog. Go!*"

One of Natalie's delicate eyebrows dipped, and a tiny vertical
crease formed along its front edge.

Right. Moving on. "Nothing as big as Meathead. A Lab mix."
Everyone loves Labs, right? "He's a great dog. I helped train him," he
blurted, piling it on the rest of the crap he was vomiting. "Why don't
you give me your contact info?" he quickly added.

T.J. had abided by the motto "Keep your yap shut, and people won't
know how big an idiot you are" for most of his twenty-seven years.
Hell, it had been how he'd survived his childhood. For some reason,
his mouth had revolted today, gone rogue, and completely abandoned
that time-tested maxim.

Chewing the inside of her cheek, she studied him. He was pretty
damn sure she could see every single gear grinding behind his
façade—not to mention the façade itself—which made him squirm
inside.

"Where do you live?"

This threw him. "Why?"

She rolled her eyes, and he was pretty sure she was thinking he was
a dumb fuck. "So I can figure out if he'd fit into my route."

"Route?" A hopelessly dumb fuck.

"I make stops several times a day at each dog's home, and if yours
is close en—"

"Oh shit! I mean, I get it. I didn't realize you come to *their* houses."
Well, fuck me. First visit she'll figure out who I am.

His mouth plowed on. "That's not always doable. What if I did like
your brother and dropped the dog off? I'm willing to pay for twenty-

four-seven service a few months in advance, even if I don't need it every day."

She resumed chewing her cheek.

In for a dime, in for a dollar. "Hey, I don't bite. Neither does the dog." He kept his voice as even as he could, considering he'd never done anything like this in his whole fucking life, and he was on ground shakier than the Calaveras Fault running under Hollister. "I can always introduce you to the furry rascal. Do you interview your dogs?"

Her face lit up with a laugh. There it was again. God, she was beautiful. Kevin May was one lucky bastard. *Except he's lying in a hospital bed.*

"I meet them, yes. I have to be sure we'll get along. As for bringing the dog over, he'd have to pass the Annie-Meathead test."

He let relief twitch his mouth into a grin. "That works. So how do I get a hold of you?"

She opened the driver's door, leaned in, and began rummaging around in her vehicle. Which gave him the perfect opportunity to take in her long, graceful legs and round, shapely ass. His cock jumped to attention as he pictured his hands on said ass. Reason kicked in. *Do. Not. Go. There.*

A voice inside his head told him to run. Fast. Besides the glaring fact that this girl belonged to someone else—Kevin May, no less—she wasn't a candidate for casual. No way. She would be somebody's long game—exclusivity, commitment, the girl you brought home to meet family, the one you showered with I-love-you's, anniversary gifts, and a white picket fence. The girl you had babies with. *Not* the girl for him.

But another voice shouted the first one down. *I* have *to do this. For her. To set everything right.*

"What's the dog's name?" she called over her shoulder.

He coughed. "Uh, Fido."

She ducked out of the car and skewered him with her exquisite eyes. *Oh shit. Did she see me checking her out?* "Fido? Seriously?"

He shifted his weight from left to right. And back again. "I know. Lame, huh? Actually, that's his middle name. His first name's, ah ..." A car rumbled past. "Ford." He mentally smacked the heel of his hand against his temple. *Jesuuus!*

"Ford Fido?" She let out a little snort, as if she were swallowing a full-blown belly laugh. Not that he could blame her. She handed him a business card, and he glanced down at it but had no idea what was written there because he was still busy whacking himself upside the head for his epic fail in naming his nonexistent dog. "And his last name?"

Now his hand was back in his hair, tugging. "I'm Tyler Johnson, so …"

"So he's Ford Fido Johnson?" She narrowed her eyes at him. "Wait. I thought he wasn't your dog?" On her pretty face was an expression he could only describe as part-bemusement, part-smirk.

She knows I'm a total dumbass. Smart girl.

"It's actually sort of a joint custody situation."

A look he couldn't make out flitted over her features. *She's probably debating whether to call the Looney Tunes police to haul my ass away.*

"A joint custody situation as in a breakup that resulted in sharing the dog with your ex, uh, partner?" she offered.

If he'd just swallowed a drink, he would've sprayed it all over her. *She thinks I'm gay. Because I told her a guy owned the dog. Well, shit.*

He bounced on the balls of his feet. "No, nothing like that. I've taken care of my buddy's dog for so long it feels like he's mine." God, he sucked at lying. "I like women," he added for good measure. "A lot." That was most definitely *not* a lie, but Christ, why couldn't he keep his damn mouth shut?

She dipped her head—he could've sworn she was trying not to laugh—and raised it again. "Look, I haven't decided if I'm ready to take on a new client."

Not one who's nuts anyway. "I totally get that."

"I won't make any promises," honey-eyed Natalie said. "But you've got my card, so feel free to give me a try."

His dick gave a rousing cheer. *Hell yeah, I'll give you a try.* With some effort, he reminded himself—again—he wasn't going there. "Yeah, sure."

He stood tongue-tied as she hopped into her car and buckled up. "Well, it's been nice chatting with you, Tyler."

"Yeah, sure," he repeated, as though his entire vocabulary had been reduced to those two words. He tapped the side of her car twice and stepped away.

She was rolling out of the parking lot when he finally read the card. Her name, website, email address, and phone number. What more did he need?

Oh right. A dog. And to remind himself—over and over—that he was only doing this to help Natalie Foster. Because he'd been the one who'd put her dead center in this mess. And that was the *only* reason.

She's Kevin May's, and she's absolutely off-limits.

He'd need to tell himself a few thousand times more.

Chapter 10

This'll Work, I Just Know It Will

Natalie took one quick peek in her rearview—just enough to glimpse Tyler's tall, broad form as he tried in vain to tame his rebellious curls.

Was she considering taking on his "shared custody" dog? God, yes! She'd tried not to come off as desperate, but she was, in fact, desperate. Payment in advance for twenty-four-seven dog-sitting would be like hitting a jackpot in Central City. And the guy seemed … Well, nice. Not to mention polite. His stolid expression hadn't reflected even a ghost of a wince when she'd cracked her awful paws joke. *So lame, Nat.*

Driving out of the parking lot, she mused that talking to him in the cafeteria had suspended her wallowing, if only for a short time. It'd felt good to work out her rusty smiling muscles and unwind some of the tight coils in her shoulders. Laughter therapy.

The few times he'd smiled at her, it had lit his dark golden-green eyes like a shaft of sunlight in a forest's depths. *Bet he breaks a lot of hearts with that look.* Oh well. Not her problem. He was a potential client, and she didn't mess in her clients' personal lives, though she already knew this one liked women. *A lot.* He'd certainly made that clear. A chuckle bubbled up inside her. Ford Fido. She shook her head.

"God, that has to be the *stupidest* name I've ever heard," she snorted as she drove. "I hope the dog has a sense of humor."

Her own sense of humor grew more fleeting the closer she got to her sick-dog client's house and, like wisps of smoke, disappeared entirely when her Durango conked out and stubbornly refused to be coaxed back to life. She dropped her head against the steering wheel, banging it repeatedly in a feeble attempt to break loose *some* plan of attack. *Get it together, Nat. Can't afford to lose what's left of your sanity.*

A white cruiser pulled up behind her, and a policewoman stepped from the vehicle. "You okay, miss?"

Damn it, she barely knew anymore.

An hour after leaving Craig Hospital, T.J. stood outside Miller's house, ready to fulfill his pledge, buoyed because he'd found a way to help Natalie. Never mind that it was a *really* bad idea.

Paige opened the door and stepped aside. "T.J., how nice to see you. Come in." She wore a look that was part-bewilderment, part-fluster. He'd only texted her fifteen minutes ago to find out if he could stop by. "Beck's out of town." She shut the door behind her.

"I'm here to see you, not him." T.J. was pleased he could tell Becks his wife looked perfectly healthy.

"Oh! Is this about your condo?"

He nodded.

"Great. Let's have a seat in my office."

A few strides, and she motioned for him to sit before settling behind a large desk stacked with paint decks, a kitchen faucet, and a precarious pile of carpet samples. He could have been looking at a miniature home improvement store.

"Sorry about the mess. Can I get you coffee? Water?"

"No, thanks."

She folded her arms on the desk and leaned forward, a smile playing on her lips. "How can I help you?"

"So those houses you've been sending me … There was one I really liked, and I wondered if we could take a look at it?" T.J. patted himself for coming up with *this* ruse.

Paige began tapping away on her computer. "Which one?"

He scratched his neck. "Uh, it was a brown one in Highland, I think. Or maybe the Tennyson District."

Eyes on her screen, she smirked. "That narrows it down." Before he could counter her sarcasm, she said, "Doesn't matter. All the ones on the west side of I-25 are under contract."

He mustered disappointment. "Oh."

She raised an eyebrow. "Gotta move fast in this market."

"No kidding," he laughed. "I guess I'll hop on it quicker next time. Which leads me to the reason I wanted to move to something bigger." He cleared his throat. "I need a dog."

Just then, Katie appeared in the doorway and stopped in her tracks. Both women looked at him expectantly. "*Need* a dog?" they chanted together.

He held up his hands in surrender. "Long story."

Paige pointed at Katie. "Katie's your go-to dog expert."

Katie plopped behind a desk. "I'm a dog lover from a long line of dog lovers." Her eyes bounced between T.J. and Paige as a proud smile spread across her face.

Just as T.J. was contemplating for the millionth time what a bad idea this was, something wet nudged his hand and flipped it on top of a furry head, startling him. When T.J. looked down, Hugo stood beside him, acting for all the world as if he wanted in on this conversation. The dog seemed to smile before bumping his hand again.

T.J. obliged him with a head scratch. He'd always liked dogs. Had always *wanted* a dog, even after his dad had killed the first and only one T.J. had ever had. A steely stab, sharp and deep, assailed his chest, sucking air from his lungs. With one clearing breath, he recovered and locked the painful memory back in the dungeon where he'd buried it so long ago.

"Hugo comes to work with you?" he said, his voice a little croaky.

Katie nodded. "Yep. A perk of working for Anderson Homes."

"I don't suppose you lend him out?"

She shot him a quizzical look. "Lend him out?"

"Never mind."

Her puzzled expression quickly morphed into skeptical. "So what kind of dog do you *need,* and why?"

"I need a Lab mix. Male. For a friend."

Paige lifted her head and joined Katie in peering at him, questions etched on their faces.

"Can you help me?" he asked.

Katie seemed to appraise him, then surrendered a sigh. "Virtual shelter time."

He must've looked as flummoxed as he felt because she followed this up with, "Shelters have pictures and descriptions of their animals online. Let's see who's got what so you can figure out where to go. Although, if you're as big a softie as you seem, you'll only make it to one shelter."

The comment completely threw him. "Softie? Me?"

Hand on her mouse, eyes focused on her computer screen, Katie nodded. "Um, yeah. Right, Paige?"

"Yeah," Paige echoed. "You might be a big, tough hockey player, but we," she waved her index finger between Katie and herself, "have superpowers that cut through that crusty outer layer and expose your gooey marshmallow center."

Despite his efforts to hold it in, T.J. let out a laugh that morphed into a snort. "And judging from the guy who *used* to be Beckett Miller, you also possess the power to turn that marshmallow center inside out, am I right?" *And that guy is definitely* not *me. So why the hell am I getting a dog again?* He pushed the pesky question aside.

Katie, whose glasses mirrored an eerie computer-blue glow, craned toward her screen. "Only Paige has the power to turn the mighty Miller into goo. Speaking of goo, look at this cute guy!"

T.J. rose quickly, ducked around Katie's desk, and stood beside her, staring at the screen. She was pointing at a goofy-looking black-and-white dog with one ear up and the other at half-mast.

"That's a Lab?" T.J. frowned at the furry face. "No way." His attention slid to the right and landed on an all-black face with crossed copper-colored eyes. He pointed. "What about that one?"

Katie read aloud, "Buddy Boo. Labrador Retriever mix, male, sixty-three pounds, two years old. High-energy guy who needs a walking buddy." She twisted her head and looked T.J. up and down. "Do you walk?"

"Seriously?" he chuffed. "Can this dog do wind sprints? Heavy rope training? Weight lifting?"

Seemingly ignoring him, Katie turned her gaze to Paige. "Permission to abandon ship this afternoon for a dog rescue mission at the Dumb Friends League, boss."

Paige cupped an ear. "Don't I hear ledgers screaming for attention?"

Katie shot T.J. a dejected look. "We're drowning in bookkeeping. I suck at it, and boss lady is even worse. We've been looking for someone who knows what the actual hell they're doing, but no luck so far. Which means I need to stay put."

An idea winked on like a five thousand-lumens flashlight in T.J.'s brain. "I know a bookkeeper. I'll text you her contact info." Two sets of eyes locked on him. "She's a CPA, and bookkeeping's what she does. Well, one of the things she does. She also dog-sits." He could barely contain a fist pump; he'd found another way to help Natalie.

"Why don't you enlist *her* help to get a dog, then bring her by here?" Paige posed logically. "That way she and I can chat and find out if there's a fit."

T.J. began backpedaling. "I'm not sure she's the right one to help with the dog."

"Why not?" Katie asked. "Surely a dog-sitter would be on board for this very important animalatarian undertaking. Unless ..."

"Unless what?"

Katie pulled her glasses down her nose and scrutinized him. "Unless you're just getting this dog as a ploy to meet women at the dog park."

T.J. swallowed a chuckle. *Don't need a dog, or a park, to meet women. But to help Natalie out? Definitely.* "Dog park? Is that a thing?"

"Have you ever had a dog before?"

An unbidden memory of a dog's whimpered cries rushed at him, and he pulled in another deep breath to counteract the twisting in his gut. "We weren't allowed pets growing up."

Paige chimed in. "Why get one now?"

"Being suspended means I'll be around. Seems like the right time." He glanced between their suspicious gazes. "I really do like dogs."

Katie took over the tag-teaming. "What happens when you're back on the road?"

The third degree. Jesus, he didn't like being on the defensive. "Other hockey players have dogs," he tossed out. "Besides, I've got that covered."

Paige arched an eyebrow. "The bookkeeping dog-sitter?"

"Her name's Natalie Foster." He glanced at the ceiling, marshaling his thoughts. "She's ... I owe her. You can't let her know I'm behind this. In fact," he paused a beat, "I need a promise from both of you."

The women waited expectantly.

"She knows me as Tyler Johnson, and I'd like to keep it that way."

They narrowed their eyes.

"T.J. stands for Tyler Johnson," he offered.

Paige said, "Which still doesn't explain—"

T.J. threw up his hands in surrender. "Do you know who Kevin May is?"

They nodded together like a pair of bobbleheads. "The guy you injured," Paige added helpfully.

Yeah, thanks for that reminder. "Natalie's his girlfriend."

Paige and Katie stared at him as if a pair of elk antlers had sprouted from his head. "Oh, this is better than TV," Katie chuckled.

T.J. blew out an exasperated breath. "I ran into her in the cafeteria at Craig and didn't know who she was until after we'd been talking a while. She's trying to balance being there for him with work." He smoothed his hair. "I thought she'd freak out if she knew who I was, so I introduced myself as Tyler Johnson, which, as I said, is my actual name, minus the Shanstrom. I just want ... Christ, I want to help, but if she knows who I am—"

Paige held up her hand like a traffic cop. "Wait. Does she actually *do* bookkeeping, or is she some puck bunny who needs a calculator to figure out what two plus two equals?"

"She's a CPA, and she knows her shit." Heat began rising in his chest as the urge to defend Natalie took hold. Not a good kind of heat.

Paige crossed her arms. "Huh. You do realize this can blow up in your face, right?"

So much. He nodded.

"You're a masochistic do-gooder who enjoys playing with fire. A weird, but interesting combination." Paige closed, then opened her mouth, only to be cut off by the *Thor* soundtrack.

"Ah. The God of Thunder is calling," Katie said blandly.

Paige picked up her phone, breathing, "Hey, handsome."

Katie turned to T.J. and mouthed, "Beckett," as Paige scurried from the office.

"Thor?" he mouthed back.

"Oh yeah. I think his ringtone for her is 'Hot Stuff' or something just as ludicrous. Those two are disgusting." Katie shook her head. "You'd better escape before you see me barf."

"So do I pass the Katie smell test? Can I have a dog, Mom? Please?" A grin tugged his lips.

"You can have a dog." Then, in a conspiratorial whisper, she added, "Natalie will never learn your true identity from me." She mimed a key-locking motion in front of her red-lipsticked mouth.

Somehow, her promise did little to curb the feeling he was wading deeper and deeper into Shit Swamp with neither canoe, paddle, nor life preserver.

Natalie fought the urge to face-plant on her couch after she dragged herself and her crap out of Drew's car into her house. The reason she resisted was on her heels, and she didn't want him to glimpse what lurked just beneath what she believed was her stoic mask.

Drew sauntered to her fridge and opened it, stared for a moment, then wheeled toward her, looking disappointed. "So you good without wheels until Mom's off work and we can do the car swap-a-roo? If I didn't have hockey tonight, I'd loan you mine."

His offer warmed and crushed her at the same time. She *hated* needing his or Mom's help. They'd been exceedingly supportive since the fallout seven months ago, and she hadn't even scratched the surface of paybacks.

"I'm good. Thanks for chauffeuring me around to my dogs and covering the tow to your place."

"Yeah, no problem. You caught me between consulting gigs, so the timing was perfect. I'll head home now and take a look at the Durango." He gave her a sympathetic smile on his way out. "Hang in, Sis. It'll get better."

She flopped into an armchair. Its normally soothing color didn't cheer her; it only made her realize she was as deeply blue as its upholstery. Mid-afternoon snow clouds glowering outside her window didn't help either.

The Kevin Conundrum, work—or lack thereof—a broken car, and her debits column outstripping her credits were coalescing into a massive bait ball that dragged her into inky depths. Her only consolation was that since her client list had been shrinking, so had her workload, freeing up time to do as she wanted. And she wanted to do … nothing—except climb into bed and pull the covers over her head, but she couldn't motivate herself enough to get out of the chair, much less change into PJs.

Her phone vibrated on the coffee table, startling her. *Who's this?* Maybe it was Opportunity. She always took *those* calls. With a swipe of her screen, she forced a song into her voice. "This is Natalie."

"Hey, this is Tyler Johnson," a male voice rumbled. Trying to place him, all she could get out were a series of stammering "ah's."

"From Craig Hospital? The cafeteria?" he added helpfully. "Meathead?"

The big guy who needs a dog-sitter! Natalie shook her head, hoping it would dislodge her tongue. It worked. "Yes, of course. You ate Jell-O, and I had mac and cheese."

He let out a throaty chuckle. "Is *that* what that was?"

"I know, right?" she barked a little too loudly. *Cool it, Nat.* "I think they're in the same-color food group." Her mouth suddenly dried up like the Eastern Plains in July, underscoring her desperation to reel in a

107

new client. "I assume this is about Ford Fido?" The name almost made her snicker, counterbalancing her hip-hopping nerves.

"Well, yes and no. My, uh, buddy's made other arrangements, so I don't have the dog anymore."

Disappointment rocketed all the way to her toes. She tried to keep it from her voice. "Oh. That's too bad."

"Yeah, *but* I have this idea." He sounded downright cheery, obviously none too broken up. "I'd like to get a new dog, one that's all mine, and I could really use your help."

Her spidey-senses revved up to standby mode. What was he up to? "My help to ..."

"I found one online, at a shelter, that looks *just like* Ford, and I'm anxious to get him, but I need a professional dog-whisperer to go with me so I can be sure we're ... uh, compatible."

"A professional dog-whisperer?" Skepticism surfaced. "As in someone who can evaluate the dog's personality for a match?"

"Yeah. That."

"I'd like to help, but I'm not qualified. My mad skills only go as far as looking after them."

"Seems like somebody's selling herself short. Look, I just need guidance from an expert, and you handle dogs way more than I do, so you have all the credentials I'm looking for." He ran on. "I'd be happy to pay you for your time. Then, of course, I'd hire you to watch him like we talked about."

Oh, so tempting—if he's not a serial killer. "When were you thinking of doing this?" Her brain began flying through her schedule.

"Right now."

Brain thrown totally off balance. "Um ..."

"You doing anything this second?"

"Yeah, talking to you." Ah. There was a sliver of the snark she'd been missing. Good to know she hadn't lost it completely.

He muttered something that sounded suspiciously like "smartass," making her lips quirk in an almost-grin. "I'll swing by and get you," he insisted. The guy was persistent. Shouldn't her intuition have roared from standby into high alert? But not even a flicker.

She cast frantic glances around her kitchen and living room. How long would it take to tidy up? And to tidy herself? Couldn't be covered in dog slobber, hair, or other unsavories when meeting with a potential client after all. "How long will it take you to get here?"

Warmth in another dark, husky laugh tickled her insides. "That all depends on where you live."

Trapping the phone between her shoulder and ear, she began corralling a few dirty dishes. "I guess that would help, huh?" She gave him her address in South Park Hill, and twenty minutes later, in a fresh hoodie and jeans, her hair brushed back in a neat ponytail, she hovered by the front window. A big-ass black SWAT-looking vehicle rolled slowly along the street. *Oh shit! Drug raid?* She narrowed her eyes and concluded her block was *not* under attack. It was just one of those badass, gas-guzzling Hummers. As vehicles went, it was overkill—the Arnold Schwarzenegger of SUVs. Who drove something so impractical anyway? And why?

The shiny black behemoth nosed along the curb across the street and stopped, so large it blocked the view of her neighbor Yvonne's house. The driver's door opened, and a man whose face was shadowed by the bill of a ball cap hopped out and trotted to the Hummer's back doors. Natalie couldn't see his face, but she did take note of the broad shoulders filling out his form-fitting navy waffle-weave, his trim waist, and his very fine ass displayed in faded denim. *Yowser! Yvonne's upping her game.* Yvonne liked men, and she liked them young. While Natalie had no idea how old the woman was, she was pretty sure the flaming redhead could be a poster girl for "cougar."

"More power to her," Natalie muttered aloud. "When I'm her age, I hope I get the kind of atten—"

The man's face came into view.

Oh shit! Not only had Natalie derided her potential client's ride, but she'd been ogling him shamelessly.

As she pulled on her jacket and gathered her purse, she scolded herself not to do *that* again—no matter how much it improved her mood.

Chapter 11

Dog Daze

T
J. opened and closed the back door that had rattled all the way over, then took in the quiet street bordered by grassy medians. Trees with trunks as big around as tractor wheels stretched skyward. The vibe was working class, comfortable—like where he'd grown up, minus the comfortable part. Glancing across the street, he checked house numbers and surveyed his target, a tidy light gray bungalow with dark gray shutters and a purple door. He ran through a color palette in his head. *Plum or eggplant or ... What else is dark purple? Bruises. Nah, they'd never name a paint that color.* Whatever it was, the color combination worked. He told himself this to forget his heart was jackhammering his ribs, which it had been doing since he'd heard Natalie's voice on the phone. Trotting across the street, he braced himself for the inevitability she'd recognize him.

Apparently, the inevitability wasn't happening today because she greeted him with a gorgeous smile when she opened the door.

"Hey." He took her in, all bundled up, her cheeks pink. "You look ready."

"I am. Let's go rescue a dog."

Right. Rescue. T.J. hadn't thought about it in those terms until now. *Look at you, going all humane society on yourself.* He led the way to the passenger door, opened it for her, and offered his hand to help her maneuver the high step. She didn't take it, grasping the door frame to hoist herself up instead. Her jacket hit her at the waist, and as she climbed into the cab, it rode up at the same time her jeans rode down, giving him a tantalizing glimpse of two perfectly placed dimples above a sliver of something lacy—and red. His heart shifted into top speed while a few things south of his belt began rearranging themselves. Suppressing a groan, he shut her door.

Rescue. Right.

Turns out the Dumb Friends League shelter at 20th and Quebec was only a short drive. On their way, Natalie continually scanned the interior of his H1 as though she were looking for an escape route.

"Something wrong?" he asked.

That seemed to startle her. "Not at all. Just checking out your, uh, big wheels."

He wasn't quite sure what to do with that, so he chuckled.

"Do you take it off-roading in Afghanistan?" she quipped.

He wasn't sure what to do with *that* either, so he let it go. Was she giving him shit about his Hummer? In San Jose, it had fit right in, but Denver had a lower flash factor, and he considered that the H1 was maybe, just maybe, a hair over the top.

"The exterior *looks* rugged," she continued, "but this interior might be a little plush for transporting a dog."

Panic set in. This was really happening. "You mean I'll be taking him home with me *today*? Isn't there a waiting period or something?"

"Nope. Assuming you and the dog get along during the visit, it's cash and carry."

Oh shit. Should've thought this through a little better. Should've thought it through period.

A reddish building with dark green trim came into view, and he turned into the parking lot, slid into a space, and killed the engine.

Before he could reach her door, Natalie hopped out, her eyes bright. "Let's do this!"

The process was a blur of sterile meeting room, dog, shelter staff, and paralyzing paperwork that T.J. dodged until he could steer Natalie to the pet store, giving her carte blanche to pick out whatever she deemed the dog needed. As soon as she was out of sight, he filled out forms, scrawling his real name and flashing his California ID, along with a copy of his electric bill to prove he was a Colorado resident. Finally, he caught up to Natalie surveying dog food.

She glanced over her shoulder at him. "All done?"

Dragging a hand through his hair, he puffed out a breath. "Yep. I'll get him when we're done here." His eyes scanned the food bags and zeroed in on the highest-priced one.

"Dr. Chewy's," he read aloud. "Fresh herbs. Organic fruits and vegetables. Regional blueberries and carrots. Organic meat, free-range chickens, and fish caught in the wild. Huh. It even has kelp, marigolds, and juniper berries." The fancy ingredients no doubt justified the outrageous price tag. He reached for it.

Beside him, Natalie's rosy lips quirked into a smile, looking as though they were holding back a laugh. "Dogs in the wild don't eat blueberries and carrots. Or kelp. Or marigolds. Not as a general rule anyway."

He retracted his hand and exaggerated a crestfallen look. "No?"

She plowed on. "Proteins are good, and the more they resemble what he'd eat in the wild, the better. You don't have to pay through the nose for healthy dog food."

Pretty and *practical.* "And you wondered why I wanted to bring you along." He caught a whiff of her hair as she turned, appreciating other good reasons to have her there.

At checkout, he caught himself as he was going for his credit card—his *real* name was on it—switching gears to cash. Though he rarely spent much, he usually carried a lot. The clerk told him the amount, and T.J. opened his wallet and pulled out a wad of bills. Out came a condom that hit the counter with an unnaturally loud *thwack*, as if announcing itself to the whole goddamn world.

The clerk's eyes bounced between him and the foil packet. At least she kept her comments to herself. He didn't dare look at Natalie because he was pretty damn sure his face was on fire. The harder he tried to pick up the damn thing, the more it eluded him, making the effort agonizingly slow and humiliating. *Damn it!* Natalie's graceful hand deftly grasped it and dropped it into his open palm; she didn't utter a sound.

"Thank you," he mumbled.

They made their exit, heads down, and he picked up on choking noises coming from her—or were they snorts? He wasn't sure, but whatever they were, he felt like a total moron. Of course, he didn't need to hear her laugh to feel that way—he was good at reminding himself what a dumb fuck he was.

Looking up at him, she flashed him a brilliant smile. "You must've been a boy scout."

"Because?"

"Because they're always prepared."

Smartass. Shaking his head, he sprouted his own smile to hide his epic embarrassment. "I wish I could say that was the case." *Sadly, it's been in there so long I forgot about it.*

She quickly cast her eyes away before he could read her expression. Did she believe him? The more compelling question was why did he care?

He unlocked the Hummer's doors. "Let's stow this stuff and get my dog."

While he arranged the goodies in the cargo space, she handed him bags. "Have you decided on a name yet?"

Hell, she already knew how stupid he was. Might as well leave no doubt. "Yep. Ford Fido Johnson."

Amused eyes snapped to his. "Seriously?"

"Seriously."

To her credit, she didn't laugh her ass off.

Fifteen minutes later, T.J. was driving her home, being serenaded with alternating whines, barks, and cries as the dog paced—or tried to—back and forth on the pristine leather seats, clambering and stumbling over the back console. T.J. darted his eyes to the rearview mirror repeatedly, catching flashes of fur and panicky cross-eyed dog face, wincing at the thought of sharp claws puncturing the perfect leather.

T.J. flinched after one particularly sharp whine. "He's really vocal, isn't he?"

Natalie looked over her shoulder and extended her hand to the dog, who added heavy panting to his routine. "He's just scared. Aren't you, buddy?" she cooed. "From what the shelter told us, he was abused and abandoned. It'll take time for him to fully trust you."

Yeah, I can relate. It suddenly dawned on T.J. that the role he'd just signed up for was a reversal from his childhood. The enormity hit him square in the chest. He'd just taken on the care of another living thing. Jesus! Was he capable of doing better than had been done to him?

Natalie continued placating the dog. "It'll be okay, Ford. Even though Tyler gave you a really lame name, he'll take good care of you." The animal let out a high-pitched moan that sounded distinctly like a dog scoff—the equivalent of calling bullshit. Undeterred, Natalie broke into incomprehensible baby-talk babbling.

T.J. swiped his hand through his hair. "Christ. Do *I* have to talk to him like that?"

"No," she continued in a singsong voice, "but it soothes him."

"That's soothing? I thought there were two of you howling instead of one." He sent her a wink before he could stop himself. She didn't appear amused.

At a red light, he turned to look at Ford. The mutt chose that moment to yip and cry like a coyote—no, a pack of coyotes—hunting their next meal. Then he yakked all over the seats. It dribbled onto the floor mat.

"Fuck me, Ford! Did you really have to do that?"

Ford followed up with stepping in the mess and spreading it all over the backseat, the floor mats, the console.

"He can't help it," Natalie admonished. "If you were a better driver—"

T.J. gawked at her. "*Better driver?* You think his puke pile is *my* fault?"

She flicked her index finger at the windshield. "Light's green." He could've sworn she sported a smirk. Yeah, she definitely knew what a dumbass he was.

Agitation popping and fizzing in his veins, he gripped the steering wheel and put eyes on the road.

Ford made choking noises, then resumed the high-pitched whining until T.J. parked in front of Natalie's house. Keeping his voice even, T.J. side-eyed her. "I should clean this up."

A little nod. "I'll get you some paper towels. And a piece of advice? Don't do a perfect job because he's just gonna throw up again on your way home." She grinned at him as she opened the door.

Fan-fucking-tastic!

"Oh, and by the way, they make doggie seat belts. Maybe invest in one?" She slid out of the seat and stood on the sidewalk.

Incredulous, he followed suit and stared at her for a beat before coaxing Ford out. "And you couldn't tell me this while we were *in* the store?"

"Didn't even think about it." She shrugged.

He wanted to be annoyed, but she looked so damn cute in her short, poufy jacket—which unhelpfully brought to mind the red lace concealed under her jeans—that all he could do was chuff and watch her disappear into the house. He steeled himself and looked into the backseat. The view hadn't gotten any better; neither had the smell. The dog whimpered at him.

"Yeah, you *should* be sorry, you little fucker." He scratched Ford's soft ears, and the dog trained crossed eyes on him, pink tongue flapping in time with his panting.

Natalie returned, took Ford's leash, and paced him around while T.J., muttering colorful curses under his breath, cleaned up and tried not to retch.

Finished, T.J. leaned against the car to watch Natalie work the dog.

"Sit," she said, and Ford obeyed. Just like that. "What a good boy you are!" Ford wagged his seriously long tail.

"He seems to listen to you."

"Because he's had some training." She handed T.J. the leash. "He'll listen to you too."

He took the leash and reeled Ford in. "Have you told *him* that?" The dog cast a longing glance at Natalie. T.J. couldn't blame him. "Hey, I still need to pay you for today and the next three months."

She tilted her head. "Much as I'd love to take your money, let's hold off on the three months until Ford's met Annie and Meathead."

"What about *your* dog?"

"I don't have a dog."

T.J.'s jaw dropped. "How do you not have a dog?"

She slid her gaze to the side, her hands twisting her ponytail. "Well, I *sort of* had a dog, but you might say I lost her in a joint custody kind of thing." Her whiskey-colored eyes rose to his.

The statement nearly rocked him backward. "You were married?"

"It didn't get quite that far. And she wasn't mine to start with, but I still miss her. The way I see it, though, splitting up with Cody and losing out on his dog spurred me to be a dog-sitter, so good came from it."

A picture of a stud cowboy rodeo star poked at T.J., and jealousy surged, unsettling him. He shook it off. It was none of his damn business anyway.

She slipped her hands in her back pockets. "Now I get to love on other people's dogs without actually having a dog, *and* I get paid to do it. It's like this other business I've toyed with starting—a little fantasy of mine."

She'd had his attention before, but now his focus sharpened to a pinpoint. "What kind of fantasy?"

"I call it Bucket of Puppies. You work with a shelter and borrow their puppies to rent out for a half hour on special occasions—birthdays, anniversaries, proposals. Instead of flowers, picture someone offering their sweetheart a basket of squiggly puppies—maybe there's a ring tied to a bow around one puppy's neck. Irresistible. How could anyone say no to that?" As she spoke, her eyes flashed and sparked as though tiny diamonds were catching the light and firing it back. "You'd help the shelters by exposing the pups to potential owners, and folks would get a puppy fix without the work. Win-win." She sighed. "Tricky logistics, though. Like I said, a fantasy."

"Sounds like a great idea to me."

She shrugged, a little blush pinking her cheeks. "Take Ford home, let him get adjusted, and in a few days when the other dogs are here, bring him back for a playdate, and we'll go from there."

"And in the meantime, I can call you whenever I have no clue what I'm doing, right? You'll be my dog-whisperer on retainer?"

A smile tugged one corner of her pretty mouth. "You won't need my help. You'll do just fine."

He pulled his billfold from his back pocket. "Still not convinced." As he flipped it open, the condom mishap seized his brain, and he was suddenly awkward, no longer cocksure. Gingerly, he slid out a hundred and offered it to her.

Surprise flicked over her features. "What's this?"

"For today."

"I don't think I have change."

"I wasn't expecting change."

Eyes widened. "A hundred bucks for a few hours? That's a little extravagant."

Her words hauled his mind to a different kind of service, and he tried not to chuckle at the double entendre. Yeah, of course his mind went there. "You were totally worth it."

She gave him a blank stare. He shook the bill at her, canted his head, and grinned. "For today *and* your retainer. I figure this buys me one call." His mind now leapt to her on the other end of a sexy phone call. He rubbed his hand over his jaw, enjoying the flirting—even if it was one-sided.

A dark eyebrow arched. "And if you need more than one?"

Now it was *his* turn to stare, tongue-tied, as what she said and the way she said it traveled straight to his crotch. Was she flirting back? Hope soared.

Her brows furrowed in confusion, and he realized he was reading *way* too much into the conversation. His attempt at silver-tongue had just nose-dived and settled him on the scale somewhere between "lame" and "awkward." Smart girls did that to him, and this one was smart and so out of his league. *Yeah, dumbass, and don't forget there's at least one boyfriend in the picture.* A letdown any way you sliced it.

She wrapped her arms around herself. Was she cold? As if in answer, a snowflake landed on one of her long lashes. He cleared his throat as he cleared away his dirty thoughts. "Uh, if I have to call you more than once in the next twenty-four hours, then you get to pick the payment. Cold, hard cash or ... service." *What the hell does* that *mean, Shanny?*

"What does that mean?" she echoed.

Hell if I know. "Say you need," he glanced over her shoulder, "a leaky toilet fixed or a lock changed or some other household repair. A service for a service."

Was she fighting a smirk? Yeah, no doubt. "So you're saying you're good with your hands?"

He nearly choked. "I guess I am. Saying that."

"I'll keep that in mind ... if I need anything fixed."

Please. Do. He loaded Ford into the backseat, and she waved at the dog. "Bye, Ford. Try not to give your dad too much trouble tonight."

Dad? Yeah, no.

T.J. flapped his hand at her. "Pfft. I got this." His voice broadcast a bravado that was definitely missing.

"Okay. Then I won't expect to hear from you." With an impish smile, she spun and hurried inside her house.

He slid behind the wheel and glanced over his shoulder. Ford sat on his haunches on the less-pristine leather. The mutt cocked his head, chuffed, and bleated as if to say, "What the hell, dude? Why'd you let her leave? She's the only one who speaks canine."

Such a bad idea on so many levels.

As T.J. was pulling away, the dog vaulted over the seat and crashed onto the front floorboards with a *whomp* and a whimper. T.J. came to a gear-grinding stop and threw the shifter into park mode. "What the fuck, Ford? You okay?"

Ford climbed into the front seat, clawing into the leather for leverage. Sixty-three pounds of slobbering, whining black dog sat up in the passenger seat like he owned it.

With a resigned sigh, T.J. resumed driving. Bracing an arm against Ford's chest at every turn and stop, he stuttered his way to the condo. By the time he parked in his building's garage, dusk had settled in and snow was steadily sifting from the clouds. He wrestled the dog, a fluffy dog bed, and countless bags out of the car and watched in horror as the dog lifted his hind leg and peed on the back tire of a Mercedes beside T.J.'s H1. A cry came from a few spaces away. T.J. locked eyes with an older woman who tsked and berated him about his "filthy animal."

He speed-walked to the elevators, chased by the woman's indignant threats—to do what, he wasn't sure, and he didn't stick around to find out. When they were safely on the elevator heading to the thirty-fifth floor, Ford looked up at him innocently. "What? I had to piss," he seemed to say.

In that moment, it struck T.J. he'd have to take the dog outside every time he needed to relieve himself. How often did dogs go? Where the hell did he take him? *Not to the garage, that's for damn sure.* And for the hundredth time this past hour alone, he mentally smacked himself. *All for a girl ... who's not yours.*

Inside his apartment, T.J. bounded around the eight hundred-square-foot space, closing its few doors. The dog watched him blandly, as if thinking, "So I can't get into the coat closet, the bathroom, or your clothes closet. Big fucking deal." For the first time since he'd bought the place, T.J. wasn't digging its open floorplan.

As he emptied shopping bags and washed out two dog bowls, he kept a wary eye on Ford. He filled one bowl with water and placed it on the floor beside the kitchen island. The dog stuck his paw in it, tipping it and spilling the contents. Then he gave T.J. a cross-eyed stare.

"Seriously?" T.J. grabbed towels from the bathroom and mopped up the mess. "Okay, so you're not thirsty."

Ford on his heels, he set the dog bed in front of the living room's floor-to-ceiling windows, then grabbed his smartphone and plopped down on the couch. "Where's the closest park?"

Ford sat on his haunches, his body between the couch and the coffee table, staring.

"Now what?" T.J. said. "Take your dog bed for a spin. It's got a prime view, and Natalie said that bed," he stabbed his finger toward said bed, "is every dog's favorite. Smells like magical dog food or something. Or even better, girl dog."

Ford continued staring at him. "What, did your tail run out of wag? You used it all up on Natalie and there's none left for me? Fine. Be that way."

Trying to ignore the eyes boring into him, T.J. entered "dog parks near me." To his surprise, the first one to pop up was on the third level of his building. "I guess I *do* take you to the garage. Sweet! Who knew?"

Ford blinked, then launched himself onto the couch, knocking the phone from T.J.'s grip.

"Shit!" T.J. scooted him off and retrieved it. "This is people furniture, not dog furniture. You have your own bed." He pointed to Ford's sleeping spot again, but the dog merely placed his paws back on the couch. T.J. gave him a sharp "no," and Ford turned a few circles, wrapping his leash around his legs. The leash T.J. had forgotten to unclip.

"Oh, for Christ's—" The dog tripped and landed hard against T.J.'s knees. "You okay? I thought dogs landed on all fours."

When T.J. had Ford's legs unencumbered, the dog, still on its side, bicycled all fours and upended the coffee table, scattering everything it held, including a bowl of Goldfish crackers. He quickly pounced on the crunchy orange bites, stamping some into the carpet.

T.J. sprang to his feet. "Looks like a goddamn bomb went off!"

Except where the Goldfish had been. That area was spotless.

He picked up his smartphone and slid his thumb over the screen, hovering over Natalie's name. "Don't do it. You'll just give her more reason to laugh at your stupid ass. Save your one call for a *real* emergency."

With a frustrated huff, he sat back down and pulled up YouTube videos of people training their dogs to do basic dog stuff. Sit. Heel. Come. *If these yokels can do it, so can I.* It all looked so simple, so straightforward. Snacks figured heavily into the training. One more reason to appreciate Natalie—she'd made him buy treats, a good thing since he was pretty sure those were the last of the Goldfish crackers.

Empowered, he decided it was time to try a few lessons, but when he looked around, Ford was nowhere in sight. *Oh shit.*

"Ford?" No response. "Dog doesn't know his name," he muttered. He ventured a "Buddy Boo" as he searched his bedroom with no success. He opened the closet door, sure the dog couldn't be in there, and cursed a blue streak when he discovered the dog was, in fact, in the closet, immensely enjoying the taste of T.J.'s shoes, including his favorite—and most expensive—pair of Nikes. But worse was the carnage the dog had inflicted on T.J.'s pee wee stick, the one he'd scored the tournament winning goal with. The dirty white tape that had held the knob in place was mangled beyond recognition, as were the knob and the blade tip.

"Shit, shit, shit!"

Beyond the slobber-coated shreds of shoes and the remnants of stick stood the gaping bathroom door, and he slapped his forehead. He'd left it open when he'd grabbed the towels to mop up the water.

As realization of what Ford had just ingested struck him, T.J. panicked, and he lugged the dog out of the closet, snatched his phone, and hit Natalie's number, hissing, "C'mon, c'mon, c'mon." Nothing but ringtone. Chest heaving, he kept one eye glued on the dog, expecting it to keel over momentarily.

She picked up.

"Ford just ate my shoes. And my ... A memento. Where do I take him to get his stomach pumped?"

"Calm down. How much did he actually swallow?" She was using that soothing voice on *him* now. Oddly, it worked.

"I don't know. Looks like he shredded a couple pairs of shoes and chased it with ... other stuff."

"Hang up and text me a picture of the damage."

T.J. did, and she called him back, declaring the dog to be okay. "Did I see the remnants of a hockey stick?"

"Uh, yeah."

"Just keep a close eye on him. And be sure to take him out frequently to go potty. Has he had dinner yet?"

T.J. glanced at his watch. 6:38 p.m. "Shit, I totally forgot."

This garnered another laugh. "He's probably hungry. Give him some real dog food, then take him outside. Take two aspirin and call me in the morning."

"What? I give him aspirin?"

"No! Never give a dog aspirin. I was referring to you, and that was a joke."

He slumped in relief. "I think I'll take two shots of Jameson instead."

"*After* you feed Ford and take him outside to do his business. Then I suggest pulling out some of those chew toys you bought today. "Night."

"Wait! Does this count as two calls or one?"

"Well, let's see. You called me, and I called you back. Pretty sure it counts as one call."

The call over, he cracked his neck, easing his shoulders. Until he remembered the mess. *God, my stick!*

T.J. picked up the biggest pieces and laid them reverently on the top shelf of his closet as though preparing a body for burial. It had been his good luck charm. Now he was out of work and out his lucky stick. How the hell was he ever going to get back to where he'd been?

From out of nowhere, it occurred to him that Kevin May was likely asking himself a similar question.

Chapter 12

Who (the Hell) Let the Dogs Out?

After cleaning up the mess and giving Ford his *real* dinner—which the dog promptly scarfed—T.J. took him to the third-story dog park. The term "park" was, at best, the product of an overzealous imagination. Flanking one side of the parking garage, the open space consisted of artificial grass and colorful plastic shapes that reminded T.J. of play structures.

As he inspected the all-important dog-waste-baggie dispenser, he didn't see the little foofy dog until Ford broke his hold and pounced on it, eliciting a sharp, yippy bark. Ford sprawled on his belly, nudging the white ball of fur with his nose.

The snippy lady from the garage began wailing, "Oh, Coco!"

T.J. hadn't noticed before, but the woman was a dead ringer for Marge Dursley from *Harry Potter* before she blew up and floated away. When she spied T.J., she pointed a crooked finger at him. "Get your miserable mutt off my Maltese!"

"Ford!" T.J. ordered in his sternest I-am-the-supreme-commander-of-your-ass voice. Ford didn't care that T.J. was supreme commander and ignored him. T.J. grabbed the leash and tugged. The dog didn't move, so riveted was he on the sharp-barking mop. The woman howled, so T.J. gave another quick jerk. Ford rolled over and lay docilely, letting the miniscule dog sniff his junk. *Dude, seriously? Man up!*

While Marge screeched, her dog pranced around a prone Ford. T.J. reached out and rubbed its little head—why, he hadn't a clue—and it wagged its curly tail. He scooped the dog up and handed it to the woman. "Your dog's fine."

She slid T.J. a scathing scowl. He gave Ford's leash a yank and was surprised when his dog not only got up but sat on his haunches at T.J.'s side like a master. T.J.'s chest might have puffed.

Unwilling to tempt fate and get stuck in an elevator with Marge, T.J. lingered in the freezing park. Hands in his pockets, watching Ford poke around, he began pondering what the hell he was supposed to do with the dog when he went to the arena for training tomorrow.

Hadn't thought that through either.

What a dumb fuck! He never should've walked out of the shelter with the damn dog in the first place. But how could he not with Natalie Amber Eyes enthusing over what a great guy he was for rescuing the mutt? Yep, not the first time logic had deserted him because of a pretty face. Beyond that, though, there had been something that twanged his heartstrings when he first saw pathetic Buddy Boo—a name even more ridiculous than Ford Fido, if that was even possible.

The animal had looked at him with his head tilted and those crossed copper eyes, and he must have read "Sucker" on T.J.'s forehead because he'd intensified the look and held T.J. spellbound, telepathically pleading to be saved. Little did T.J. know what a great actor this dog was. Or maybe he'd simply seen his own past reflected in the dog and decided that, this time, he'd make things right.

Having solved the mystery of the dispenser, T.J. picked up Ford's mess, along with a Coco-sized deposit—*nice going, Marge*. Back in the condo, T.J. poured himself a double Jameson, hoisted his feet on the now-upright coffee table, and clicked on the TV, settling in to watch his new team's away game. Ford leaned against his legs like he belonged there, and T.J. patted his head. The dog let out a whine. The crying grew more persistent, so T.J. leashed him up, threw on a hoodie, and returned to the chilly park. Only to watch Ford sniff around and do absolutely nothing akin to relieving himself while T.J. froze his balls off.

This little game repeated itself several more times over the course of the evening until Natalie texted him to ask how Ford was.

He's a pain the ass. Visited the dog park 4 x the past hr alone.

Dog park? No yard?

I'm in a condo. It's temporary.

Especially temporary now. A backyard had just moved to top spot on his priority list.

You know he's working you, right? she texted helpfully.

Figuring that out. How's ur SUV?

Fixed. Also, A & M are here day after tmw so bring Ford over.

Ok. Hey, does this count as a call?

More helpfulness from Natalie, reminding him what an asshat he was. *No, it's a text.*

So I can text u all night and it won't count?

Night, Tyler.

Wait. Forgot to tell u I gave ur name to a friend, Paige Miller. She needs a bookkeeper.

That's so sweet!

Her words inspired another chest-puffing. Yeah, he was a dog rescuer *and* sweet. At least in Natalie's amber eyes, and for as long as it lasted, that was plenty. He ended with *My pleasure.*

Glancing at the TV, he realized he'd missed the entire game for all the rides up and down the elevator. *Damn it.*

Before he climbed into bed a while later, he cleaned up more spilled water and discovered how hard kibble is on bare soles. He coaxed Ford into the very plush, very expensive dog bed—in vain. The dog would have none of it, whimpering at T.J.'s bedside instead. Short of sleeping in his closet or the bathroom, T.J. couldn't escape the beast. Giving in to fatigue, he let the thing climb into bed with him to shut him up.

"Do *not* get used to this," he told Ford firmly between yawns. "Tomorrow, you're in your own bed."

He tried not to contemplate how pathetic it was that the first warm body he'd slept with in over a month was furry.

Natalie tossed her head side to side, trying to mold her pillow into something comfortable enough to help her block the numbers marching across the ledger sheets in her mind—the ones continually jumping into the negative column. If only she could suspend them, she could float off to sleep. God, she needed sleep! The open laptop on her bed flickered with the end credits to *Kate and Leopold,* a movie that never failed to fill her with happy bubbles she could drift away on. Except tonight. And this was the third romcom tonight.

"Hugh Jackman, you're yummy, but you're no Keanu," she told the TV. Squeezing her eyes tight, she tried conjuring Keanu Reeves's John Wick into a nineteenth-century duke waltzing her around an elegant ballroom. She almost had the image. Just as he tightened his grip on her dainty waist—it was *her* fantasy after all—her phone chimed with a text, popping her eyes wide, kick-starting her heart. It was either Drew, Mom, or Tyler. The first two were panic-worthy, and she prayed it was neither of them. The third? He'd be flummoxed, reporting the latest Ford antic, which she'd find entertaining, a distraction that *could* get her back to her bubbly place. Plus, she'd amuse herself compiling a list of "services" she could extract—it would be a long one.

She snatched the phone from her nightstand and sagged with option four—she hadn't considered Kristin. *Sorry it's so late.*

Natalie drew in a sharp breath and exhaled all thought of Keanu. *Everything okay?* She cringed, hoping Kevin was all right.

Yes. Just wanted to shift tomorrow's sked. Can you come earlier?

Natalie's first reaction was all snark, but Grace Guilt demanded she take the high road.

No problem.

Thx. Have a good night.

"Yeah, what's left of it," Natalie hmphed.

She mentally rearranged her morning, her heart growing more leaden as she pondered tomorrow … and the next day … and the next.

The doctors said Kevin was getting better, but what did "better" mean? Would he one day be the Kevin she'd started falling for or someone entirely different? And when did his healing end? Two months? Two years?

She'd fallen into Alice's rabbit hole and was becoming more distraught trying to make sense of a world that made no sense. As she tried to do the right thing, be the rock Kevin needed, she was losing herself in a quagmire. How could she be there for him when she was unsure where *she* stood?

Scrolling through her phone, her thumb landed on an earlier text exchange. She laughed aloud at a late message from Tyler: a heavy-lidded selfie with Ford sound asleep on his shoulder. *Ur bearing witness to the last time this happens. Ever. Ur welcome.* She'd have to educate him on the finer points of crating the dog.

Staring at the sweet image, her heart grew a smidge lighter, airier, as if she'd been dosed with helium. The picture depicted Tyler from mid-chest up, his head on a pillow, the dog cradled in his left arm. He wore a black tank that revealed parts of a detailed tattoo along a muscular bicep, shoulder, and chest. The colors were vivid: reds, yellows, blues, greens. Tattoos weren't her thing, but this one piqued her curiosity because it looked like a gorgeous piece of art. What did the whole thing look like?

Her mind began to unwind as it found another focus, wandering back to this afternoon. She'd felt normal for the first time in a long while, lost—even happy—in the part she'd played in Buddy Boo-Ford's adoption. Laughter had come easier today, sparked by Tyler's brawny persona brought to his knees by the adorable, cross-eyed dog. No lie, she'd witnessed moments between the two that had warmed her heart. Tyler's selfie summed up the man-dog relationship succinctly and went along with her perception of him as a cream puff.

If the interaction with the dog hadn't been enough to out him, he'd outed himself by giving her name to a potential bookkeeping client—a solid one, based on Natalie's research. Paige Miller, owner of Anderson Homes and a finalist for Denver's Woman Entrepreneur of the Year, held an impressive resume. How did Tyler know her?

Tyler. When he'd started his tank, Roman history had blared—not X Ambassadors or OneRepublic—and he'd shut it off with an embarrassed smile. Though she'd hidden it, she'd been impressed. Intrigued. The guy was sharp-witted, and she'd enjoyed their easy back-and-forth. She'd sensed a flirtatious undercurrent, and though she refused to examine it too closely, it had been fun trading banter. And if he *had* intended the double meanings? Fun *and* flattering, but it wouldn't go any further. She couldn't do that to Kevin.

As for Ford, if Tyler hadn't adopted him, she'd been tempted. With personality-plus and a zeal to please in those crossed eyes, the animal had captivated her heart.

All in all, the afternoon had turned into a bright island in a morass—a refuge of sorts—and she found herself looking forward to Ford's visit.

Done with his workout in the Blizzard training room, T.J. stopped by Serena's office to collect Ford. "Hey, thanks again for watching him."

"No problem." She smiled sweetly. "I just couldn't stand to think of him locked up in your car for hours."

T.J. *had* planned to check on him frequently, but Serena had seen him with Ford during his first check-in and offered to watch him.

"I *love* dogs," she'd exclaimed. T.J. had been grateful. It saved him interrupting his training and kept him from worrying about Ford. A win-win.

As he clipped on Ford's leash, he glanced at Serena. "I owe you."

Her smile slid from sweet to sinful. "Maybe we can figure out a way for you to repay me?"

Shit. This girl wants to play. Messing with the staff was *not* a good idea, especially for a guy on the team's tightrope.

"Uh, sure," he threw out as he hurried from her office. If he hadn't had a good reason for Natalie to watch Ford before, he certainly did now.

He settled the dog in the back, climbed into the driver's seat, and before he could scroll through emails on his smartphone, Ford stationed himself in the front passenger seat. As T.J. was shaking his head, a text caught his eye. He tapped the number.

"Yo, T.J. Brother, what's up?"

Brother, my ass. "Hey, Money. Haven't talked to you since San Jose." *When you blew me off.*

"Been busy. You know how it is. How you doing?"

"Oh, you know. Living the high life of a benched NHL player. It's just one fucking funfest. So you're coming to Denver?"

"Yep. We play your Snowflakes in a few weeks. Let me buy you a beer. You can repay me by introducing me to the local wildlife."

T.J. mentally scratched his head. He and Money had never hung out before, though he couldn't say why. Why was the dude all friendly now? "Sure, though I gotta warn you, I'm not all that familiar with the *wildlife* around here."

"Ha. Yeah, right. So have you been following the standings?"

T.J. let out a mirthless laugh. "Of course I have. What else am I gonna do with myself?"

"Well, I can think of a few things that involve being buried in lots of tits and ass. Can't think of a better way to help a man forget his troubles." He paused to laugh. "Your new team's not doing so hot, my man."

"Thanks for that newsflash, asshole. I really needed you calling me to tell me that. So besides your worthless offer of a beer, why the hell *are* you calling me?"

Money chortled. "Because I was worried about you, of course."

"Yeah, well your timing's impeccable."

"How so?"

"I just got word from my new coach that the arbiter is siding with the league. My suspension stands."

A low whistle from the other end. "Fuck, that's gotta hurt."

T.J. heaved a huge sigh. "No surprise." *But it still hurts like a mother.* "Doesn't matter anyway since the Blizzard has zero chance of making the playoffs."

"Well, you really screwed the pooch when you put the hit on May. Guy wasn't even worth it."

Was that scorn? Sarcasm? Whatever it was, it sent a jolt through T.J. *He's laying all the blame for this cluster-fuck at* my *doorstep?*

Schooling his rising temper, T.J. casually said, "Hey, Money, about that. Let me ask you something."

"What's that?"

"Coach Rogers told the assistant to tell me to mess May up, right?"

A long pause, followed by a throat clearing. "How would I know?"

"Because you were sitting *right there.* You heard him. *You* told me to 'wreck the hoser.'" T.J. kept the sound of his gritting teeth from his voice—a feat at which he was accomplished.

An awkward laugh. "Fuck, Shanny. No one has to *tell* you to wreck anyone. It's what you do. Like a switch flips on, and you're on autopilot. Everybody knows that. You might wanna keep your hallucinations to yourself." A female voice tee-heed in the background. "Hey, good talk, Shanny, but I gotta go. See ya next month, man."

"Right," T.J. grumbled.

Seething thoughts racing back and forth, he punched the gas, Ford fighting for purchase in the passenger seat. T.J. backed off his road raging and began pondering. Had he imagined being told to destroy May? Coach Rogers had denied it from the beginning—vehemently. But T.J. remembered it like it was unfolding right there in the driver's seat. His memory, like the arena lights, was bright and clear. In his mind's eye, he saw which players were on the ice, where the refs were positioned, and Money giving his shoulder a shake. Who'd been next to him on the bench? Nelson.

Funny. They'd never discussed it. Not after the game, not when they traveled to Denver. But then, Nelson had been in trade shock. Maybe T.J. should have a chat with him.

T.J.'s focus sharpened on his surroundings, and he realized he was ten minutes from Spalding Rehab. An idea struck, and soon he was pulling into the parking lot. He looked over at Ford. "What do you think of visiting some folks who need cheering up? And there's a basketball team I'd like you to meet, if they're here today. Think you can pull off behaving like you belong?" *That applies to both of us.*

Chapter 13

Taking Care of Business

When morning came, Ford's bed still hadn't been slept in, while T.J.'s was covered in dog hair. Paige and Katie's words danced in his head, and he tried not to think about what a wuss he was as he towed the dog along on a distance run in the crisp air. Ford's stamina, his eagerness to match T.J.'s running rhythm, and his mostly civilized behavior at Spalding the day before helped T.J. overlook the sleeping situation. For now.

T.J. had been surprised their impromptu drop-in had been welcome at the rehab center. Patients and staff alike loved Ford, and he'd returned their attention with his overly zealous tongue. Of the No Excuses! team, Wheelie Mark had been around—turns out the guy volunteered there—and they'd spent the afternoon shooting the shit with convalescents about sports and food—T.J.'s favorite subjects. He'd lost track of the day, and when he'd finally left, night had fallen.

Now his mind wandered to seeing Natalie, hopeful Ford could pass the "test." He couldn't see the dog staying alone at the condo. Bringing him to work had, at best, been a one-time desperation move. Leaving Ford in the Hummer for hours or with Serena and her expectations wasn't going to fly. No, Natalie Amber Eyes was his best bet.

He laughed at himself. What had begun as a way to help *her* might've been morphing into something T.J. needed too.

And he was finding he was okay with that.

A while later, T.J. pulled up to Natalie's house. "It's showtime, Ford Fido Johnson. You ready?"

Apparently, Ford was. T.J. had installed a barrier and put Ford in the cargo area. When he opened the back door, before he could clip on his leash, Ford pressed his advantage, sailing out, spinning T.J. like a cheap amusement park target. The dog took off, loping down the sidewalk, head on a swivel, tongue flapping, tail pointed up and swiping from side to side like a wiper without a windshield.

"Ford!" The dog kept going. "Ford!" *Christ! So much for training.*

Natalie's front door opened, and there she stood. Her fingers flew to her lips, and out came a shrieking whistle. Ford froze, glanced over his shoulder, and did a one-eighty when she began clapping and trilling, "Come on, Ford!" He ran at her, ramming his head through her outstretched hands and square into her crotch, staggering her backward. She recovered and laughed, the sound plowing into T.J.'s chest as forcefully as his dog had plowed into her legs.

T.J.'s strides chewed up the walkway. "Jeez, I'm sorry. Ford! Bad boy." The dog ignored him outright. And who could blame him? He was having a licking lovefest with an angel who cooed and caressed. He buried his nose in her sweet spot again. *Ha! Bad dog, but fucking smart. That's my boy.*

She yanked Ford's chin up. "He's not a bad dog—he just needs to mind his manners." To the dog, she said, "Who's handsome and sweet? You are, aren't you, boy?" She had an iron grip on the dog's chin as his tongue windmilled, trying to land a slurp. "Can you sit, Ford?"

Damn if the mutt didn't park his butt in front of her! How the hell did she do that? T.J. had only gotten him to do it a few times, and he suspected it had been pure chance. Ford glanced at T.J. with a broad dog-smile, and he could've sworn the damn thing winked at him before turning all his adoring attention back to Natalie. *Yeah, I'm on to you, you fuzzy fucker.*

She shaded her eyes with her hand. "Do you have a release command?"

"Release command?"

"Yes. It's what you say to release him from his sit." Her eyes caught the afternoon sun and reflected it back in gold and copper. Liquid fire.

His brain froze. "Uh …" Not that he had a release command to begin with, but he couldn't even form a thought, let alone find a word to throw out there.

She leaned down to Ford. "Okay?" The dog stood. "Right. That's a common one."

"Yeah. Okay." *What just happened?*

She grabbed Ford's collar and beckoned T.J. to follow them inside. Unable to stop himself, he stood back, eyes flicking over her gorgeous, well-defined ass. T.J. felt himself tighten. *No, not going there.* He followed said ass, dimly aware she led him through a living room, then a kitchen, into a glassed-in patio. The sunporch opened to a winter-yellowed lawn where large, leafless trees ringed the perimeter. Two dogs ran from one corner of the yard and pressed wet noses against a glass door separating them from the patio. Their oscillating tails brought to mind the back end of a Chinese dragon dancing in a parade.

"Okay, Ford. Ready?" She opened the door, nudging the dogs out of the way, and released Ford's collar. He surged into them, and the three dogs began a spirited smell-fest.

Sliding the door closed, she paused a moment and grinned at the fur ball swarm. "I have a feeling they'll do just fine, but we'll keep an eye out to be sure."

He pulled in her light, clean fragrance—vanilla? Flowers?—trying to keep his wits as he stood beside her, watching the dogs. They remained that way for some time. When the dogs flopped on the ground, panting, she turned to him. "They seem to be getting along. We can watch from the kitchen. I've got fresh coffee cake and coffee. Interested?"

"Absolutely."

Though her kitchen was tight, it was tidy. White cabinets and dark polished stone counters in a U-shape opened onto an area just big enough for a wood table and two chairs. Cinnamon and something else that made his mouth water hung in the air. She motioned him to the table, stretched to a shelf, and plucked down a cup, which she filled from a half-full coffee pot. "Do you take anything in your brew?"

He lowered himself into a straight-backed wooden chair with a puffy red seat cushion. Not frilly, but definitely feminine. "Just black, thanks. You make coffee the old-fashioned way."

Her eyebrows knotted together in a question mark.

"You don't do those single serves. Not that I'm complaining."

She handed him the cup and smiled, and warmth pooled in his gut. "Regular brewing is budget-friendly. Besides, I pound coffee like water, though I've reached my quota for today. If I have more, I'll start twitching." She stuck out her tongue, crossed her eyes, and executed a goofy, jerky dance-in-place move, pulling a laugh from him before she snapped back into normal person mode.

"What was that?" he snorted.

"My twitchy self. Big slice?" she asked, knife poised over a whole coffee cake that looked homemade.

"Is there any other size? Please."

"Good. Leaves less for me to eat." She slid a plateful under his nose and handed him a fork, then cut herself a small slice.

He pointed at his plate. "Did you *make* this?"

"Yep. I love to bake."

Before he could censor himself, he blurted, "I love to eat."

She grinned. "Well, good. I like baking for an appreciative audience."

"Wait. You made this specially for …"

"For you? I guess I did." She was standing, looking out the window, nibbling away, looking nonchalant as hell. Except … Was that color rising on her cheekbones? The notion she'd done this for him, and was self-conscious about it, cracked something open deep inside him. Was that good or bad? *Not sure.*

He shoveled in a forkful, stifling a groan. Best damn cinnamon-blueberry coffee cake he'd ever eaten in his life. "This tastes incredible. Do you make other stuff too?"

"Mm-hmm. How about you? Do you cook?"

"Nope. I just eat."

Wow. Just, wow. She's hot, smart, and cooks. The perfect trifecta for turning a guy into her tool. Good thing he wasn't in the running. Nope. Nor would he be.

"Looks like the dogs are doing great together."

Intent on the food, he'd completely forgotten them. Some dog parent *he* was. "So does this mean Ford's in?"

"It's looking good. If you need to run errands or get back to work, you can leave him here for a while."

He took in his surroundings. Table, chairs, pale yellow walls, a half-empty mug of coffee before him, some crumbs scattered on a white plate. A crazy-ass dog clock with a swinging tail. Simple, uncomplicated, homey. It occurred to him he didn't *want* to leave. "I can hang out a little longer, unless I'm in your way."

She shot him a look he couldn't read. Not that he was good at reading her—or any woman—though he found himself wanting to sign up for *her* course.

"You're not. Since you're staying, more coffee cake?"

"Thought you'd never ask." He rose, handing her his plate as he put eyes on the dogs, each indifferently sniffing in a separate part of the yard.

She cut him another piece and placed it on the table, and he retook his seat, following it as surely as one of the dogs would trail a rabbit's scent.

"Thanks again for referring me to Paige Miller. I'm meeting her in two days," she said.

Delight took him by surprise. "That's fantastic. You'll love her. Smart lady, and she's super chill."

Natalie leaned against the counter. "How do you know her?"

"Paige?" He swallowed a bite, mumbling around it. "She's married to a buddy of mine."

Eyebrows furrowed in astonishment. "Wait. Isn't she married to Beckett Miller?"

T.J. stopped chewing. *Oh shit.* "Uh, yeah. You've heard of him?"

Now her eyebrows shot to her hairline. "Are you kidding? Wait'll I tell my brother! He's Drew's favorite defenseman in the entire NHL. Drew's a D-man himself in a rec league, and he studies the guy's moves. Of course, he's in a totally different class."

T.J. registered little of what she said. He was too busy freaking out over the brother whose dogs were presently in her backyard—the brother who'd show up sooner or later and probably recognize him. "Are Annie and Meathead here on a set schedule?" More bewilderment on her features. Yeah, he'd shifted gears pretty quickly on her. "I only ask because Ford really seems to be enjoying himself, and it would be nice for him to play with them regularly." *Smooth, Shanny.*

"It's random, although lately they've been here a lot. Drew's an IT consultant, and he's been spending more time at client sites. He hates leaving his pups alone."

"So Drew follows hockey?" T.J. was proud of how casual he sounded over his jackhammering heart.

"Oh God, yes. He knows each player on every single team and can recite their stats. He's a tad obsessive." She used air quotes on the last word and added an eye-roll.

Shit, shit, shit!

"He must be thrilled you're dating a hockey player."

"I guess so." Her expression grew wistful, as though she'd traveled someplace distant. A story lurked behind that look, and he winced, imagining that story had to do with the fact that said hockey player was lying in a hospital.

"How's he doing, by the way?"

She seemed to wake up. "Hmm? Kevin? He's coming along." *Not promising.* Her sad half-smile yanked at heartstrings that had only recently been put into play. They'd either been rusty or nonexistent until he'd met her, and now they hurt for the workout they were getting. He swallowed another bite, though it now tasted like sawdust.

She glanced out the window. "Looks like Ford's passed the test."

Joy, mixed with relief, swelled inside him, making him forget the brother. "So I can sign him up?"

"Let's do it." She plucked a form from a folder on the counter and handed him a pen. "Just fill this out. And don't forget to include your work number so I can reach you in case of an emergency."

He scanned the form, then flicked his eyes to hers. "My cell *is* my work number."

"Oh. What do you do?"

His brain froze. Unease rushed up from his gut, stomping on the pleasant feels, and wedged in his throat. Though he'd practiced this, his mouth was temporarily stuck. He mentally swiped imaginary sweat from his forehead.

"I'm in the entertainment industry." Her questioning expression pulled more practiced parlance from him. "I, ah, sell sports." He plowed on before she could fire another question. "Which reminds me. I'm on the road a lot. Do you do sleepovers?" His hand shot to his nape, and he shook his head over his blunder. "For dogs, I mean."

Her eyes lit with mischief, and her full lips quivered as though she held back a laugh. He couldn't help but dip his gaze to them.

"Yes, I do dog sleepovers." Her brows converged in an appraising look. "Are you gone for long stretches or just overnights now and again?"

Shit. This slope gets more and more slippery. If he didn't navigate carefully, his twisting truths would augur him into the ground.

"A little of both, though I don't expect to be traveling for a while." *Not for another few months anyway.*

"How about we cross that bridge when we come to it, then?"

He pulled in a relieved breath and got to work on her form. "That works."

Natalie suppressed the happy dance her feet were itching to break into. A new client! Who was paying in advance! And his dog was sweet and fit right in. For now, she was okay with not knowing *exactly* what he did for a living because ... he was paying in advance!

Tyler jarred her from her daydreams. "All done." He slid the form over the tabletop. "Can he start tomorrow?"

She shoved her hands in her front pockets to keep them from fidgeting. "Of course. What time?"

"Is seven too early?" He seemed to cringe. "I can pick him up by three."

"Not at all, if you don't mind me taking him along on my rounds. He'll stay in the Durango while I do my thing."

"What about your hospital visits?"

"I'll work something out until Ford's comfortable staying on his own, if you're okay with that." Hopefully she could finagle shortening her visits without upsetting Kevin—and Grace Guilt would keep her judgments to herself.

Tyler rose and seemed to consider. "I wouldn't want to take you away from time with your boyfriend."

A distinct possibility, though she'd never tell Tyler. "They've increased his therapy, so he's more occupied as it is." Not a lie, but not the entire truth. They *had* stepped up Kevin's therapy, though it generally didn't conflict with her visits.

Grace Guilt shook her head in disdain; Natalie could practically *hear* her.

"Works for me, then. But do you trust Ford in your vehicle?"

"Puh-leeze," she chuffed, drowning Grace out. "There's nothing he can damage."

Tyler beamed at her. "Okay, CPA. Calculate what I owe you. What's your daily rate?"

"For two in-home visits a day for one dog, I usually charge twenty-five. Keeping a dog here would be a little less."

"That doesn't make sense if he's with you the whole time. What do you charge other clients?"

"I don't typically board dogs, besides Drew's, and we barter."

Tyler's golden-green eyes darted to the ceiling. "And kennels charge ..."

"Around here? The average is thirty a day."

138

"So let's say fifty since he's getting personal care, and sometimes I might run late."

Did he just wink at her? *Pretty sure that was a wink.* Now he was scrutinizing her, grin pasted on his face, and her cheeks began heating. She opened her mouth to protest, but he held up his hand. "So what does ninety days work out to?" He snapped his fingers. "C'mon. Let's see those mad math skills."

Unable to keep it in, she let a laugh burst from her. He was being ridiculous. In a very nice way, but still ridiculous. She faked counting on her fingers. "Forty-five hundred." The full impact of the sum hit her. "Oh my God! That's too much." But he was already going for his back pocket. His wallet? Surely he wasn't going to pay cash ...

He pulled out a rubber-banded wad of hundreds and offered them to her. "There should be forty-five hundreds, but double-check."

Her mouth moved, but nothing came out. She was too busy staring at the bills in her hand. "Wait. Did you ... You already had this worked out, didn't you?"

"I did a little research." He shrugged broad shoulders. "So are you going to count it? I wouldn't trust me, if I were you." When she didn't move, he took the bills and counted them out on her table. "All there," he declared. "And for the record, I'm not taking it back. It's hard to sit straight with a lump that size in my pocket. Doesn't balance the wallet on the other side."

"All there," she repeated, a bit dazed, her mind going at warp speed as it blazed through his possible occupations.

He leaned in and waved his hand in front of her face. "Hello?"

When she nodded, he straightened and headed for the backyard, stirring up a heady man scent that drifted off him, a combination of a woodsy, musky fragrance—like Creed Aventus, one of her favorites. Something altogether distinct and masculine. It smelled wonderful, and she fought the urge to sniff, zeroing instead on what she needed to do. *Write a receipt! No, write it on the form. Cash received, forty-five Benjamins. Holy house payments, Batman!*

Five house payments, to be exact.

The numbers—and her vibrating phone—snapped her back, interrupting her mind's meandering along the putt-putt course of life. She picked up. "What's up, Drewbert?"

"Hey, Nat. Headed your way to pick up the dogs. You home?"

"Yep. How soon will you be here?" She walked to the expansive living room window and peered out at the enormous black Hummer. *What the hell does the guy do for a living? Please don't let it be illegal.*

"About ten minutes."

The back door opened, and heavy footsteps creaked on the kitchen floor then stopped.

"See you soon, Bro." She hung up and pivoted to find Tyler eyeing her warily. "Drew'll be here in a few minutes."

Tyler turned and stalked back to the kitchen door in a nanosecond. "I should go."

Ooookay. "You don't have to leave because he's coming over."

"No, uh, I just remembered someplace I gotta be." He practically hurled himself through the doorway. Gone were the grin and the playful persona. He was all business.

"Um, okay." Confused and somewhat sheepish, she followed him outside into the backyard, where he stood, eyes on his dog.

"Ford!" The dog ignored him. He tried to corral Ford, which proved highly entertaining, though Natalie felt a stab of guilt for enjoying it. The animal seemed to disregard him completely. Tyler growled something undecipherable as he lunged, nearly face-planting on the grass. The whole scene reminded Natalie of a greased pig contest, and she had to fight back her amusement. She lost the battle, and a snort escaped. To disguise it, she bent over and drummed her thighs. "C'mere, Ford. Come on, baby boy. Let's go, sweet thing."

Ford loped over to her. She fought the urge to smirk.

Between breaths, Tyler jerked his chin at her, and a slow, lazy smile began spreading over his face. "Maybe you can teach me that thing you do."

"Thing?"

"Getting him to come *without* having to go all girlie." He grasped Ford's collar.

"Right," she scoffed. "Because it would be so easy to peg you for girlie."

He gave her a headshake. "Welp, I'm out. See you tomorrow bright and early."

"See you then." She walked him inside and gawked as he sprinted through her house to his Schwarzenegger Special, afterburners practically shooting from his heels.

No sooner had he pulled away than Drew's Subaru rolled alongside her curb. As Drew unfolded himself, she contemplated whether she'd done or said something wrong. Maybe she'd pissed off Tyler with her smartass attitude, the one that seemed to pop up effortlessly whenever he was around. No, he'd teased her too.

Before she could ponder it for long, Drew walked over, watching the big black behemoth roll down the street. "Whose Hummer?"

"My new dog client, Tyler," she replied absently, eyes still glued to the vehicle. *California plates.*

"What does the guy do?"

"No idea, but he paid me in cash. Forty-five hundred bucks."

Drew's brows shot to his hairline. "Seriously?"

"I know, huh?"

"You didn't ask what he does?"

"I did. He said something about entertainment. He wasn't specific."

Drew let out a low whistle as the Hummer disappeared from sight. "Be careful, Sis."

T.J. glanced in the rearview at Ford, who stared cross-eyed from the cargo space. "Christ, that was a close call!" Ford cocked an ear. "One run-in with hockey bro, and you and I would be out, my friend. O-U-T." He exhaled noisily. "You look as tired as I feel."

Eyes strafing Natalie's street right before he turned, he caught on her tidy little house. He pictured her pretty eyes widening as he counted out the cash. God, that had been fun!

His thoughts had raced along an emotional spectrum—and not just in one pass, but several—as he'd sat in Natalie's kitchen. He'd seesawed between lust, protectiveness, a yearning to soak in her serene vibe, and something unidentifiable but way too touchy-feely. Altogether *girlie*. Maybe he needed a *Game of Thrones* marathon or to cue up a couple of *John Wicks* for some serious ass kicking. Maybe what he *really* needed was a little horizontal R&R. When no candidates came to mind—other than the beauty he'd just left, and she was *not* a candidate—he pushed the thought aside.

"We're in, buddy. Did you have a good time?" he said aloud. Ford tilted his head, making his eyes appear even more crossed. "I mean, how could you not with Annie licking you all over? Too bad you don't have all your parts anymore."

The dog seemed unaware of what he was missing because he looked as though he were grinning, his big pink tongue hanging over pointy white teeth.

T.J. snorted. "Just go with that. You're God's gift to the bitches. A total badass stud muffin."

Ford disappeared from view. "Yeah, go ahead and lie down while I'm trying to prop you up. Man's best friend, my ass. What the hell am I doing talking to a goddamn dog anyway?" *Not to mention paying someone a lot of cash to watch said dog.* For not the first time, T.J. shook his head at the convoluted house of cards he was building.

When—not if—would it come crashing down?

Chapter 14

A Fine Mess

The next morning started well, and it showed in Natalie's step. Her bank account wasn't on life support, Tyler had dropped Ford off promptly, and she'd been able to text him that his dog had been great company on her morning rounds—without lying. Now she was right on time to see Kevin, and a bright winter sun illuminated an azure backdrop so vivid it nearly hurt to look at. Life was blissful perfection.

Natalie slid out from behind the steering wheel and shut the door. Ford whined. The windows were cracked open, and she wiggled her fingers through a gap. "I know you don't want to be left alone, but it won't be long, I promise. So no honking the horn or joy riding, okay?"

With a few furtive backward glances, she hurried toward the hospital's entrance, her last view of Ford promising. He sat in the driver's seat, ears up, and was looking around with great interest.

Approaching Kevin's room, uproarious laughter surprised her. She stepped inside to find the TV on, and the laughter was coming from him. "Whatcha watching?" she ventured.

Seated in an armchair, he didn't spare her a glance. "Some stupid game show."

She pecked him on the cheek. "Funny, huh?"

"Just look at the idiot in a dog suit, for Christ's sake!" he wheezed between chuckles.

Natalie darted her eyes to the screen, baffled by what he found so amusing. At least he was seeing clearly today.

They cut to commercials, and he finally swiveled his head toward her. And frowned. "You're all bright and cheery. What's going on?"

Should she *not* be cheerful?

"I have a new dog-sitting client, and he referred me to a possible new bookkeeping client. I'm meeting with her tomorrow." Giddiness over the meeting began percolating in her bloodstream. "And funny coincidence, she's married to Beckett Miller, who plays defense for Arizona."

"I know who Beckett Miller is," Kevin snapped, startling her. His attention returned to the TV. "What's the asshole's name?"

Bewildered, she asked, "What asshole?"

"Your new client."

"His name is Tyler Johnson, and he's not an asshole," she bit out.

Kevin's eyes remained fixed on the TV, and another overblown laugh came from him. When she looked, a gray-haired man with a laser-white smile was urging viewers to call an eight-hundred number for life insurance. This was funny?

"Guy's probably a phony setting you up," Kevin grumbled.

Right. Moving on. "Depending on how long the interview lasts tomorrow, there's a chance I won't make it in, unless Kris won't be here in the evening and I can swing by then?"

"Kris hasn't missed a visit, and she hasn't been late. Not once."

Ouch! Yeah, and Kris doesn't have to work because you support her! Not that Natalie expected him to support *her*. Nor did she want that. But the stinging rebuke was patently unfair because the comparison was skewed. Part of Natalie wanted to lash out, to tell him how pretzel-twisted-complicated her schedule had become while she juggled him and her other obligations. Did he even give a shit?

The other part of her was plain tired, emotionally exhausted. The happy bubbles she'd brought with her this morning had all popped, and it wasn't like she got that many these days to begin with. Even so, she held her tongue. *No pity parties. This is about Kevin healing. Team Kevin is on the job.*

Seeking benign ground, she asked, "What show is this?"

Kevin clicked off the TV and looked at her, now with a charming smile. "What're you doing way over there?" He patted his thighs.

Natalie was in Whiplash Central, her head spinning at blurring speed as she tried to keep up with Kevin's strange shifts. "Give me a minute. I need to check on the dog in my car." Without waiting for his response, she hurried from the room and straight into Colin.

"Hey there," he said cheerfully. "Where're you hurrying to?"

"I need to check on a dog."

"May I walk with you?" Dressed in street clothes, Colin looked like a rumpled college professor, complete with a kind, patient smile. He pushed his glasses up the bridge of his nose.

"Of course."

He fell in beside her, and they walked in silence until they were beyond the hospital doors.

"Natalie, there's something I've been wanting to say to you."

The smile was still on his face, but warning bells went off in her head.

"You've been ... so good to my brother, in spite of his erratic behavior, and I can't thank you enough. I understand how difficult this must be for you. You'd just started dating when he wound up here, and you're probably wondering what you got yourself into, yet I've never heard a single complaint from you."

A mirthless laugh. "If you listen to the gossip, I'm only in it because I'm a gold digger."

Beside her, Colin nodded. "The people who matter know that if you were in fact a gold digger, you'd have ditched him and moved on to someone with a more promising future."

An alarming statement. "So his future isn't promising?"

He gave her a cautious look. "Unclear. TBIs are unpredictable. But any way you slice it, Kevin's got a long road ahead of him. And at his age ..."

Colin didn't need to finish the sentence. At thirty-three, Kevin was already old by NHL standards. And by the time he got through rehabbing and training to get back to the level he'd been at when he was injured? The odds weren't in his favor. Her heart broke for him.

She had eyes on Ford now, still sitting up straight behind the wheel, and he had eyes on her—his wiggling and whimpering gave him away. The sight gave her a miniscule lift as she and Colin stopped beside the Durango.

Colin cradled her hand in both of his, eyes filled with sympathy. "Natalie, I know you're here because you're loyal and you have a big heart. Even Kris agrees, and she's a tough one to impress." He paused a beat. "I suspect you also have a stubborn streak, which means you won't give up, and frankly, that worries me. You need to consider what's best for *you*. No one would fault you for getting on with your life."

"But it hasn't been that long!" she spluttered. "What kind of person would I be—"

"*There's* that stubborn streak." He patted her hand. "It's been months, Natalie, and his future is, at best, murky." Releasing her, he pivoted away, then glanced at her over his shoulder. "Think about it."

She *had* thought about it, she shamefully admitted to herself. When she'd signed up for Team Kevin, she hadn't fully comprehended what was in store; there had been no job description, nothing to prepare her for putting her life on hold indefinitely.

Grace Guilt sparked to life. *Kevin didn't expect* his *life to be on indefinite hold either. Get over yourself.*

Confusing emotions boiled inside her and, like heavy, wet steam on a mirror, clouded her ability to reason. Tears pricked her eyes. Were they for Kevin? For herself? For this shitty situation? *All of the above,* she decided as she opened the car door and laid her head on top of Ford's. His fur was soft, and she buried her nose in it. He seemed to understand, this dog, and settled his chin on her shoulder while she hugged him close and let the tears come.

Hours later, at three sharp, the Hummer pulled up. Tyler practically ran up her walkway. "How'd he do?"

"Awesome! And when you drove up just now, he started whining and wagging. He recognized you."

Tyler stepped inside and dropped to a knee as Ford hurtled straight at him. Tyler caught him, but the dog practically bowled him over in a jumble of dog and man legs. The pooch licked and squirmed, and Tyler tossed him on his back and scratched his belly. "Well, it's because we're sleeping together now. Right, buddy?"

She nearly choked but composed herself and refrained from asking if girlfriends also whined and wagged when they saw him. *Probably.* "I thought that was only the first night."

"Nah, I'm too easy. I let him talk me into two nights. But last night was absolutely the last time."

Giggles rose up and transformed into uncontrollable, tear-wrenching belly laughs. God, it felt good to release the tension! So much better than bawling. Though he sported a bemused look, Tyler laughed right along with her. When she regained most of her composure and gasped for air, he said, "I have no idea what's so funny, but you should laugh more often. It looks good on you."

In that moment, she realized she hadn't laughed, really laughed, in a long while—not even with Drew—and the epiphany saddened her.

T.J. regretted the words as soon as they left his mouth. Natalie's smile, blindingly brilliant a moment before, slid from her face, and she straightened. He climbed to his feet, inadvertently encroaching on her personal bubble. Standing so close to her made it hard to breathe. He took a backward step. "So … anything fun planned for later? Like a trip to the river?"

A ghost of a smile returned to her pretty face. "Not today, but Drew and I were talking about going this weekend, which reminds me. I'd be happy to bring Ford along and see how he does. Drew's bringing his dogs."

T.J side-eyed Ford. "What do you think? Ready to try fishing?" The dog gave a barky cry. T.J.'s gaze traveled back to Natalie. "He says yes."

"Good."

"Oh, and since you're meeting with Paige tomorrow, I won't bring him over."

She pursed her lips and frowned. It was a cute look on her. He was beginning to think pretty much any look was cute on her. Or gorgeous. Or sexy as hell. "What'll you do with him?"

"I've got time off, so we might head up to Boulder and hike Chautauqua or Mount Sanitas."

"Ooh, that sounds like fun."

An awkward silence followed, and he rushed to fill it. "I should probably let you get on with …"

"I have a few doggie visits to finish."

His mouth apparently had its own agenda. "Do you need a ride?"

One dark eyebrow quirked. "To my doggie visits?"

"Right. Your Durango's fixed," he stammered. "Never mind."

A knowing smile curved her lips. "But my sliding door could use some love. Do you have a minute to take a look at it for me?"

His heart kicked up a notch. "Happy to."

He followed her out into the enclosed porch and tested the door. "It's off its track. This is an easy fix." He pointed up at the frame. "See?" She leaned in and peered upward, standing so close he smelled shampoo and a clean, fresh fragrance that was all her. His brain locked up.

"For *you*, maybe it's easy," she snorted.

In a bid to distract himself, he nudged her out of the way, grasped the door, and wrenched it—hard—popping it off the track completely. *Yeah, I meant to do that.* He squared it up and hefted it back in place, grateful when his synapses began firing again.

"Um, isn't that kinda heavy?" she said.

Dusting off his hands, he turned to her, feigning a sheepish modesty over his unplanned Hercules move. "I lift weights," he offered.

"What kind of weights? Do you toss horses?"

"Nah. I've only worked up to ponies." He suppressed a wink. "If you have silicone, I can touch up the track so it slides easier for you."

"Silicone? Sorry, I'm home-improvement impaired."

"A candle instead? One of the skinny ones you see on fancy tables."

She disappeared, and he tested the door again, this time noticing the lock was wonky. When she returned, she gave him a candle and a perplexed look.

Dropping to a knee, he ran the candle over the lower track. "The wax will help it slide. Did you know your lock's broken?"

"It's been like that since I bought the place."

"That's not safe." He shot her a look over his shoulder. "I can fix it."

She let out a laugh. "Are we bartering? How many dog calls do you expect in exchange?"

He rose and shrugged. "None. I like doing this kind of stuff, and I don't get a chance in a condo." Technically, he wasn't lying. He *didn't* get a chance because the condo didn't need much, and he couldn't have cared less. But fixing things for *her*? He liked that. A lot. One more way to help her.

"Wow. Ford *and* a handyman? How can a girl turn down an offer like that?" A smile shone in her eyes, adding another foot to his six-four frame, and his chest might've expanded another ten inches.

Yep, he was Mr. Helpful.

"A twofer." He grinned. "I'll take some pictures and get measurements, then make a Home Depot run and pick up what I need."

"What, you mean today?"

Her astonishment had him backpedaling. "We don't have to, but I don't like the idea of this broken lock."

"I always bolt the door between the porch and kitchen."

"Good." He teased his phone from his pocket and took close-ups of the lock. Before she knew what he was up to, he snapped her photo. Twice. *What the hell is the matter with me? I'm acting like a moronic six-year-old who's crushing on his teacher.*

David Lee Roth sang out in T.J.'s head about being hot for *his* teacher. *Shit.*

"What are you doing?" She seemed borderline amused.

149

Great question. What am *I doing?* As soon as he realized she wasn't freaking out over his stalkerish behavior, he allowed a self-congratulation for his genius move. Genius moves were rare for him. "So I don't forget whose lock I'm fixing. For the record, I usually don't do this kind of stuff."

"You don't fix locks?"

"No, I meant I don't, uh …" *Act like an asshat.* "Goof off."

Natalie's graceful fingers covered her mouth, but they didn't hide her curving lips. Or hold back a giggle. "No goofing off. Duly noted."

T.J. looked into entrancing amber eyes, and his heart bumped against his ribs a little harder. For a beat, he swam in those eyes, lost, while he recorded every golden copper hue and chocolate fleck.

Her eyebrows crinkled in a silent question, and he cut his gaze back to the slider, his hand shooting to the back of his head, smoothing his hair. New thoughts raced through his brain, like why the hell being around her made him nervous. It wasn't just the ever-present threat she'd discover his identity—the threat that hung over his head like an executioner's ax. No, it was something deep in his chest, the pit of his stomach, that rumbled and rippled and rolled and made him short of breath and brain power.

Women he was attracted to usually inspired one body part, and it for damn sure wasn't in his chest. But with her, *every* body part seemed to engage, as if his entire being was drawn to her. And it scared the living shit out of him.

Normally women pursued *him*, and if they hit that certain chord, he'd more or less roll into a relationship, whether it lasted a week or a year—although since Melissa, he hadn't gone a full year. Those girlfriends got tired of not getting what they needed, what he was incapable of giving, and the wheels invariably came off the relationship bus. But the next one would appear and take her place. If the breakups bothered him at all, it was a surface scratch, nothing more. Like Julia. Sure, he missed the sex, but he'd been over her when his plane had touched down in Denver.

Was something seriously wrong with him? Were crucial pieces of his heart missing? Did he need to replace them? *Intimacy.* The word streaked through his brain like a dying comet.

If he were honest, the disappointments from broken relationships only grazed his outer layer because that's as far as he let those relationships get.

But the woman in front of him, with her penetrating whiskey gaze that set off all kinds of zips and zaps inside him, affected him differently. Since meeting her, he was inspired to do better, to be better, to look beyond himself. Maybe it was because he'd injured her boyfriend, but he suspected it ran deeper. He didn't get it and didn't want to examine it. But deep down, he quietly acknowledged if he ever let her in, she could bring him to his knees.

None of it mattered because nothing was going to happen. She was devoted to Kevin May and showed no hint of being attracted to T.J. And he sure as hell wasn't going after her, no matter how much he wanted to.

Kevin May was a potent deterrent. Not as a rival, but because T.J. had stripped the most important part of May's life from him when he put him in the hospital. For all T.J.'s reputation as a heartless thug, he refused to steal another precious piece from the guy.

Chapter 15

Just Jameson and Me

The next morning, T.J. ran errands, Natalie never far from his mind. God, he hoped Paige hired her. He'd left Ford alone in the H1 and was now cruising Home Depot's aisles, searching out what he needed—including a can of silicone.

It had been a long time since he'd been in a hardware store. The smells and neatly stacked merchandise brought back better memories, memories of being shipped off to work at his uncle's. The guy was cut from the same gruff stuff as T.J.'s dad, but while he'd lashed T.J. verbally, he'd never hit.

Plus, he'd seen something in T.J.'s game and had pushed him to play smarter, to play all out. And he'd paid for it all, out of his own pocket—the leagues, the equipment, the travel. Hockey hadn't been T.J.'s first love, but his uncle had given him a way out of his hellhole. T.J. could lose himself in playing the game and working with his hands, fixing things, building something with only wood and nails. His uncle was a master carpenter who had taught him how to puzzle out solutions to problems, who had taught him to use his brain *with* his brawn. Too bad the guy hadn't lived to see T.J. make it to The Show.

All these thoughts were streaming through his head as he scanned his purchases in the self-checkout, so he didn't pay attention to people around him. Until a guy at the register beside his said, "Are you T.J. Shanstrom?"

T.J. glanced over. A burly guy in a Storm jersey was eyeing him, and it wasn't a friendly look. *Shit.* Before he could answer, the guy turned to other customers and called out, "It *is* T.J. Shanstrom," then swung his eyes back to T.J. "Why the fuck aren't you behind bars, asshole?"

This charged T.J.'s bloodstream with pissed-offness, and he told himself to calm the fuck down. Tangling with some random jerkoff, physically *or* verbally, wouldn't end well for either of them. Zeroing in on getting the hell out of the store, he quickly inserted his credit card as a wide-eyed clerk in an orange apron took a step toward the angry fan. "Sir, if you could just—"

Burly Guy shot her a warning glare. "Don't even think about telling me to keep quiet, lady. This guy's a criminal. He shouldn't even be—"

T.J. couldn't hold it in. "Look, dude, why don't you give the lady a break?" He grabbed his receipt and bags.

Burly Guy snorted. "Or what? You gonna sucker-punch me like you did May? Fucking cheap shot."

A small crowd gathered. T.J. squared himself up and faced the guy. This dickhead would be easy to drop. *Don't engage, don't engage, don't engage.* He pivoted to leave.

"Ha! Big man's nothing more than a little pussy. Look at the chickenshit run away as soon as someone gets in his grill. Guess you only take on defenseless guys, huh?"

Confining the flaring anger inside him, T.J. pulled in a huge breath. *Buddy, you do not want to go there with me.* He wheeled. Months ago, he'd have clocked the guy. Instead, with every ounce of control at his disposal, he took a page from Gage Nelson's handbook and gritted out, "Hey, I admire your loyalty. Hockey needs more fans like you."

On a spin, T.J. caught the guy's confused expression. He gave the terrified-looking clerk a nod and strode from the store. Behind him, the guy must have found his tongue because he started hurling more insults that T.J. took a pass on acknowledging.

Reaching the Hummer, relieved to find it and Ford intact, T.J. practically vaulted inside. No one was coming after him when he checked his rearview. "At least my dog likes me," he muttered. Ford yipped as if backing up his statement.

As T.J. nosed it onto the street, a number he didn't recognize rang. Maybe it was Troy or Mark from No Excuses!, telling him they'd finally scored some court time for their next game. He was excited to attend.

"Hey."

"Mr. Shanstrom?" a clipped male voice said.

"Speaking."

"Jacob Pederson here."

The name jangled a bell … and a nerve.

"I'm the attorney for the Earthquake, Mr. Shanstrom. We met the day after," a dramatic pause, "the unfortunate incident."

Gray-blond hair and a ferret face floated into view. T.J. leashed his distaste. "What can I do for you, Mr. Pederson?"

"I'm calling to let you know ownership has been served with an intent to sue for a laundry list of groundless offenses. As you were a team member at the time, your name is listed. I wanted to personally alert you that you'll be receiving a copy."

Dumbfounded, T.J. stared out the windshield, vaguely aware of cars moving all around him like spawning salmon. "But they still don't know if he'll recover. Can they do that?"

"They can do whatever the hell they want."

Christ, the guy was a total asshole. "What are the ramifications?"

"Nothing for now. But I reiterate it's best for all concerned, especially yourself, if you continue to respect the gag order. I also caution you against moving assets. Courts don't look fondly on people trying to hide their money." On *that* cheery note, Pederson hung up.

Fuck. Fuck. Fuck.

The inevitability had just arrived, coming up on T.J. like a pissed-off semi in the rearview mirror. Blaring, bearing down, all grill. This shit was unsettling, and it was just getting started.

He rolled to a stop at a red light and roved his eyes over a trio of ragged homeless people sitting on flattened cardboard. No way to tell if they were men or women. *Wonder if that'll be me after May's taken everything I've got?* Oddly, the thought of losing the money didn't bother him as much as it should have. He'd been raised without it and had consequently conditioned himself not to count on it. NHL careers were short. After blowing through paychecks early on, he'd throttled back and turned his earnings over to his financial advisor. Yeah, he owned an expensive Hummer, but it was his only vehicle, unlike a lot of guys he knew. The house in San Jose and the condo in Denver were upscale but not stupid extravagant—neither had its own bowling alley, racquetball court, or gold toilets.

The light was still red, so he scrolled through his phone and swiped a name he'd put off calling for too long. When the receptionist picked up, he said, "Hi. I'm T.J. Shanstrom, and I was referred by Beckett Miller. I'd like to speak to Tom Carlisle, please."

Natalie parked along a tree-lined curb. She'd always loved the homes in the 7th Avenue Historic District. The one outside her window was newer—probably built after knocking down a few old brick ones—but not garish. An understated, cream-colored stucco and stone affair set back from the street, it reminded her of Rocky Mountain Mediterranean, if there was such a thing. Definitely someplace a successful businesswoman and her pro-athlete husband would live.

Natalie rang the doorbell, taking in a peaked entry with a leaded window that topped an enormous set of oak double doors. One of the doors opened, revealing a small, auburn-haired woman.

"You must be Natalie. I'm Paige." Hand outstretched, Paige stepped toward her, her smile wide. Natalie had only seen a few pictures of Paige Miller online—professional headshots—but she was still surprised by the diminutive woman sporting navy flats, faded jeans, and a denim-collared shirt under a burgundy sweater. Paige Miller was all girl-next-door, of the Colorado variety, and Natalie felt an instant kinship with her.

She accepted the woman's warm, firm grasp. "I am. It's so nice to meet you." Paige led her into a marble-floored foyer and closed the door with a solid thud. Natalie's eyes darted to an elegant, wood-paneled office with two paper-littered desks. Opposite was a pristine sitting room with a fireplace and a baby grand piano. Two completely different worlds.

"The mess there is my office," Paige motioned to the desks, "and that's Beckett's refuge when he needs to bang out a classical tune or ten."

"He plays piano?" Natalie couldn't mask the incredulity in her voice.

"I know, right?" Paige trilled. "Imagine my surprise when I discovered there's more to hockey players than fists." She headed toward a desk. "Katie, my assistant, is out in the field. The files we need are on her computer, so let's take a look at the rat's nest we lovingly call accounting." She pulled in a breath. "I'm hoping we're a fit."

Me too. You have no idea how much.

Ten minutes later, peering over Paige's shoulder at Katie's computer screen, Natalie had a solid idea of what they needed. She held her rising excitement in check because what they needed, she offered. Working for Anderson Homes would be substantial *and* interesting.

Paige shot her a backward glance. "What do you think? Is there hope?"

"There's always hope," Natalie laughed. "It'll take some time putting things in order, but it's totally doable. Once that's done, it's a simple matter of keeping everything on the rails."

Paige motioned for her to take the seat opposite and leaned back in the chair. "I understand you're a licensed CPA."

Natalie laced her fingers in her lap and squeezed them. Hard. "I was with Hennings and Barton until recently."

Paige's eyes widened. "Oh wow. They're *big*-time. How long were you there?"

"I interned my sophomore year of college, so nine years in all." Natalie braced herself for what was coming next.

"How far did you get up the food chain?"

"I was up for junior partner when I left."

Paige seemed to appraise her. "And you left to start a bookkeeping service?"

There it is. Yeah, I'd be skeptical too. "I was burned out on corporate and wanted to make a move before putting myself and the firm through the junior partner dance." The answer came out smoothly—no doubt because she'd practiced it many times.

"And how are you liking the change so far?"

Natalie eased a bit. "I enjoy being the boss of me. I like picking and choosing clients and setting my own schedule. So far it's been really positive." *And no grabby bosses.*

Paige leaned forward, forearms on her desk. "You obviously know what you're doing. The job's yours if you want it. How soon can you start?"

Elation soared. "How soon do you want me?"

Paige beamed at her. "Last month! Seriously, how about Monday?"

Natalie nodded vigorously, trying to hold back the yippee ki-yay threatening to burst from her lungs. "Perfect. I can't wait to get started." She meant every word.

Dripping with sweat after a workout in his building's fitness center, T.J. rode the elevator to his floor, smiling about the busty blond bombshell who manned the front desk. Jazzlyn something or other. She'd checked him out as she'd checked him in, flirting shamelessly. Not that he was complaining. He needed the practice, and his ego sure could stand the lift—among other parts of him. His dry spell was running long, making him twitchier by the day.

Funny thing was whenever he frequented a target-rich environment, none of the "targets" appealed. His indifference wasn't from lack of choices. Women who signaled that "hey, let's play" look seemed to be everywhere: bars, the gym, the arena. And dog parks! Jesus, Ford was the best chick magnet T.J. had ever seen. Though it didn't matter because T.J. always fell short of sealing the deal. Which left him wondering if his libido had developed an allergy to sex … Except said

157

libido enthused in the presence of a certain dark-haired dog-sitter with eyes the color of tawny port.

Distracted by thoughts of what the hell was the matter with him— *Jesus, where to begin?*—he opened his front door and was about bowled over when Ford flew out, all dog licks and leaps.

"Jesus, Joseph and Mary!" T. J. closed the door while Ford capered around him, tongue darting out like a cheek-seeking missile.

"I like that you're excited to see me, but give a guy a little room, huh?" This was answered with a whine, and T.J. obligingly patted Ford's head.

He paced to the kitchen and tossed his key card on the granite counter, Ford so close on his heels he nearly tripped.

"Insecure much?" T.J. chuffed.

He picked up his phone. And smiled at Natalie's text.

Got the job!

He whooped out a "yes!" and pumped his arm. *Of course u did. Had no doubt.*

A reply chimed moments later: *You were right. I really, really like Paige.*

She's a sweetie. He paused a moment, took a breath, then let his thumbs fly over the keypad. *U ready for me to fix that door now? Afterward I'll treat u to a celebratory drink.*

He hit send before he could reconsider. *What the hell, Shanny?*

Thx, but not today. Maybe you can fix the door when you bring Ford over this weekend?

Damn. "As it should be, dumbass," he muttered aloud. Ford cocked his head, and T.J. went on. "Why am I a dumbass, you ask? Because my attorney says so. Because I have no business inviting her out. Because even if I hadn't been the one to wreck her boyfriend, what does a smart, beautiful woman like her want with a dumb fuck who's got a lawsuit hanging over his head? She could do way better. She *is* doing way better. Injured or not, May's the better bet."

He let out a dejected sigh and sent her a reply. *Ok. C U then.*

Tom Carlisle's voice ricocheted in his head, telling him his contact with Natalie was a surefire catastrophe in the making. Of Yellowstoneblowing-up proportions. And Tom had blown up himself when T.J. had told him about hiring her.

"Are you a fucking idiot?" he'd ranted. T.J. had winced but hadn't been surprised by the reaction. What had gotten his hackles up, though, was the next bit. "You're tapping *his girl*," Tom had said, "to find out about his condition."

"I'm not *tapping her*," T.J. had shot back. "Fuck, you make her sound like a piece of ass. Which she's not."

"Okay, okay. So you're not tapping her, but any way you slice it, you're at least smart enough to see how bad this looks, right?"

T.J. had conceded the point. "So, Counselor, what do I do?"

"Get as far away from her as you can."

"Got another answer?"

"How's this? I promised my good friend Beck I'd take your case, but if I were a smart man—and usually I'm a *very* smart man—I'd send you to my worst enemy for representation."

T.J. had ignored him. "When will they file the actual case?"

Tom had scrubbed a hand over his face and blown out a huge breath. "It could take years. Until they have a solid grasp on what May's future holds, they can't put a number to it. But you can bet your balls it'll be a big number."

"I fucked May up, Tom. If I had it to do over, I'd skate away, but what's done is done, and I need to make it right. Helping her helps make it right."

"Jesus, please tell me you haven't told *her* that."

"She doesn't know who I am."

Tom had cackled—an incredulous, you-are-so-screwed cackle. "Fuck me, this just gets better and better." He'd given T.J. a pointed look. "I'll take your case if for no other reason than I want a front-row seat to this fucking disaster. I'll sell tickets and make a fortune. I'd tell you to stop seeing her, but I'm pretty damn sure you won't listen, so if you insist on being stupid, at least don't talk about May, the lawsuit, or hockey. Make sure *she* doesn't talk to you about May. Make sure you're not being recorded. And let your financial advisor keep managing your money because she's been doing a damn fine job sheltering it for you. Hiring her was the smartest decision you've made. In fact, *I* might hire her."

T.J. had left the attorney's office with a mixture of relief and abject fear.

This shit was real.

May might never play again, and the fault lay squarely on T.J.'s shoulders. It had thumped him in the heart, where he didn't like being thumped.

That he'd let his temper rule him with disastrous consequences had been making its way into his consciousness like a splinter working its way out of a finger pad. Slow, festering, painful. And God, while he hated like hell to admit it, the power to stop it had been in *his* hands. If he'd done the *right thing* instead of his *job*, he'd have taken heat, but May would still be playing right now—and enjoying life with Natalie.

His phone buzzed with a text, giving his heart a lift. *She changed her mind.*

But this message wasn't from Natalie. It was from Serena. *Uh-oh.* Worse than Serena possibly stalking him was Serena telling him Duffy Shanstrom was trying to reach him.

Fuck.

Fuck.

Fuck.

Long minutes passed while he stood in place, his mind reeling. *What does he want? I'm not giving him a damn thing.* His finger hovered over the screen. *What if something's wrong? No, he'll just try to manipulate the hell out of me. Maybe he's heard from Mom.*

Shit.

Sucking in a deep breath, he hit the number Serena forwarded.

Muscles instinctively clenched at the sound of a familiar, gruff voice barking out a "yeah" on the other end.

"Duffy." T.J. was gratified his voice held up, even and deadpan, instead of the telltale breaking squeak that would've broadcast his weakness. It had been years since he'd spoken to his father, but he was instantly back in quivering kid mode, arrows of fear slicing through him. He swiped his fingers across his suddenly sweaty forehead, reminding himself his old man couldn't touch him. Not anymore.

Duffy cackled. "Well, hell. The bigshot hockey player *finally* graces his old man with a fucking minute of his precious time."

T.J.'s hatred for the son of a bitch surged, liquefying his fright and turning it to spine-fusing steel. "Yeah, it's great to talk to you too. What do you want?"

"Nothin'. Saw you got traded after the beauty punch you landed on that candy-ass. A chip off the old block." This he said with a prideful tone T.J. had never heard growing up.

T.J.'s stomach curdled, then bottomed out with the thought he carried the same DNA and couldn't do a damn thing to change it. "So everyone's okay?"

"How the fuck would I know? No one talks to me. Your sister doesn't give a shit about me. *You* don't give a shit about me. Your mom betrayed us all. I thought my kids at least would show a little appreciation, but no. Ingrates." He spat the last word.

T.J. pinched the bridge of his nose. "Why were you trying to reach me?"

"Well, my disability's check's just not enough, and I figure you owe me. It was thanks to me you got into hock—"

Stomach muscles buckling tight, T.J. pinched harder. "We both know you did squat, Duffy. Unless you count the times you messed me up so bad I nearly got dropped because I could hardly fucking play."

"I was toughening you up, boy," Duffy growled. "And look where it got you. Maybe you'd rather be Princess Pansy-Ass playing with your sparkly paints."

As a kid, T.J. had loved to paint as much as he'd loved hockey, but he'd had to hide his small stash or suffer the wrath of Duffy.

"I don't have time for this, Duffy." *You worthless piece of shit.*

"And this is my thanks for giving you my best?" He cursed a string bluer than a Colorado sky, most of which T.J. didn't hear.

"Duffy, do us both a favor. Don't call me again." T.J. hung up.

He inhaled and released several long, steadying breaths, waiting for his hands to stop shaking so he could block the number. Normally, he'd take his spiky energy to the ice and channel it into bone-rattling hits. Like his dad, but controlled. Sanctioned. But there was no practice today, no outlet.

His eye caught on a bottle of Jameson, light bouncing off the glass, beckoning him. Just like booze beckoned his dad. *Chip off the old block. Shit.*

"What do you say we get hammered, boy?" he asked Ford, who sat attentively on his haunches. "Yeah, I know it's only 3:47, but it's cocktail time somewhere."

He poured a three-finger shot and tossed it back, letting it burn away the sour taste on its way to his belly. And poured another. "Definitely getting hammered." Ford, who'd been seated by his side the entire time, gave a little yip. "I know. It's not the answer, yada, yada." Muscles and nerves began uncoiling.

T.J. ruffled the pup's ears, which surprisingly soothed him. "Look at you, being all obedient dog." Ford gazed at him with those crossed, adoring eyes he'd favored Natalie with. "Yeah, you *are* a good dog. Natalie's right, but don't tell her I said so. Women like to lord it over you. Just sayin'. That's my tip for the day. You're welcome."

Ford's floppy ears straightened, seemingly upon hearing her name.

"Ha! You recognize her name? Can't blame you. If we're sharing secrets here, thinking about her makes parts of me stand up and pay attention too."

He sank into the couch and pulled up the pictures he'd taken on his phone. Settling on one, he studied it, and different elements came to life. The light had illuminated her eyes in such a way that they appeared to have gold dust sprinkled in them. *Beautiful.* Warmth pooled in his stomach as he pictured Natalie hugging Ford's neck, and he drifted for a moment, his shitty day compartmentalized in a virtual penalty box.

An errant thought struck him. Thinking of her made him hungry, and not for food.

Christ! How fucked up was that? *I nearly kill May, then move in on his girl.* No, he hadn't moved in on her. But Jesus, he wanted to. Bad.

Refusing to give it any more thought, he fed and walked Ford, then poured another hefty drink. He lowered himself into an overstuffed recliner, staring through the floor-to-ceiling glass at the mountains beyond. He raised his drink to the window and the world on the other side of it, then threw back a mouthful. Ford submarined his nose under

162

T.J.'s forearm, and T.J. stroked his head reflexively. As he ran his hand over Ford's fur, a different texture snagged on his fingers, and he pulled a dark brown strand from the dog's neck. It seemed to go on and on. Turning his hand over, he inspected it closely.

"Huh," he muttered. "Now she's leaving her hair on you, you lucky mutt." An image of Natalie hovering above him floated into his mind, a dreamy smile on her face. Her soft hair cascaded over her shoulder onto his, looking like chocolate draping a cake. She was naked, her bare skin kissing his. His fingers sifted through her tresses, and her eyes fluttered closed, her ripe lips parting. He clutched a handful of hair and pulled her to him.

Ford's yelp yanked him from his fantasy. The imagined hair T.J. had been relishing was the dog's coat, so he released him with an apology and groaned at the manifestation of his daydream.

"I'll deal with you later," he mumbled to his stiff cock. To himself, he said, "Gotta get her out of your head, dude."

He refilled his glass.

Sometime in the night, he awoke facedown on his bed, his head pounding as though an army of monkeys had been let loose on bongo drums. Gingerly, he lifted it and looked around. One bedside lamp glowed, revealing that he was fully clothed in the same sweaty gym clothes. But for the outline his body had pressed into the comforter and the drool where his mouth had been, his bed hadn't been disturbed. Ford lay beside him, head on a pillow, squeaking softly, his paws quivering in a frantic imitation of full-out running.

Shit! Did I let him out one last time before passing out? Jesus, maybe having another living thing depend on him was a really bad idea.

T.J. rolled over cautiously and pulled himself up, wincing at the steady tattoo in his skull. He wobbled into the bathroom, flipped on a light, and peered at himself in the mirror. A strange reflection stared back at him, and he blinked. Blinked again. It didn't help. Venturing another peek, he cringed at his reflected image.

What the actual hell?

Streaks of gold, canary yellow, red, rust, pink, and brown streaked his hair, his shirt, his shorts. His fingers were covered in color. He looked as though he'd been bombarded by a flock of loose-boweled fowl. Stumbling to his living room, he stiff-armed the wall to keep himself upright. Where the birds had blitzed *him*, something else entirely had blown up his condo. Paper was scattered among tubes of paint—acrylic *and* watercolor—pencils, brushes, pallets, and jars filled with cloudy gray water. An art store had been attacked and detonated in his living room. And dining room. And kitchen. When his eyes landed on the empty Jameson bottle, fuzzy puzzle pieces began fitting themselves together.

Yes, he had taken Ford out one last time—*Thank Christ!*—which also meant the brown stains were *not* from the dog. Yes, he had hauled out every artist's accessory he owned—and hadn't touched in a decade—and attempted to paint … What?

Sinking to his knees, he began sifting through scads of paper. Evidence of his inner Claude Monet, sadly, was absent. A mess of dabs, blobs, and lines of color convinced him he'd been going for a Picasso-crossed-with-Andy-Warhol theme in an imitation of a disjointed Campbell's soup can. Or Van Gogh with a dash of Salvador Dali. Definitely *not* Monet. This artist extravaganza was a mixture of Jameson and Shanstrom all the way.

The farther into piles of paper he dug, the more recognizable the images became. Eyes? He'd been trying to paint eyes? Or brown peacock feathers? He shook his head and immediately regretted it.

Aliens transported me to a science lab and investigated the paint while I was being experimented on. Or the condo was *the science lab.*

"And what the hell was man's best friend doing to protect me while all this was going on?" he mumbled aloud.

T.J. unearthed a piece of paper about six inches by sixteen and stopped short. A pair of amber eyes layered with copper and bronze shone from beneath long, lush sable lashes. The sweep of a forehead above dark, arched eyebrows showed a sliver of gleaming chestnut hair—just enough to hint at its silkiness and touchability. The aspect was slanted, as if the woman was side-eyeing him. Guile, amusement, and something unidentifiable but altogether alluring danced together in a sensual, tantalizing combination that held a promise of pure delight. It was as if he'd taken the photo and added an essence—Natalie's essence—that transcended the picture itself.

Damn, it was the most beautiful piece he'd ever painted.

He'd never been good—a rank amateur who found a sort of grounding pleasure in applying strokes that blossomed into a world of shapes and color—but this was a vision worthy of staring at all day long. Apparently, he did his finest work in the company of Jameson. Or was it the subject?

After clearing a spot on the kitchen island, he carried the painting over as though he were handling a delicate tower of spun sugar. He placed it carefully and softly blew specks from its surface.

Curiosity sent him searching for his phone to compare the photo against the painting. And that's when he saw texts he didn't remember sending. Scrolling through the screen, his eyes widened and his stomach lurched.

Oh shit, oh shit, oh shit! When the hell did I send these? He checked the time on the first message. Apparently he'd started at 10:33 p.m. Well into the Jameson. His jaw clenched as he began reading.

T.J.: *What ur doing?*

Natalie: *Did you mean to text me? This is Natalie.*

T.J.: *Absolutely. Ur the one I want. Ur amazing.*

Natalie: *Just figuring this out?*

T.J.: *Suspected it since I met u.*

Fuck! His other self had text-flirted while he'd been checked out.

Natalie: *See you in a couple days.*

T.J.: *My dog seriously loves u, Natalie Amber Eyes. Gonna paint em right now.*

He nearly slapped his forehead, remembering at the last minute that it would hurt like a mother if he followed through. He groaned instead.

Natalie: *Um, not sure I understand?*

T.J.: *Making pickle of u.*

According to the time stamps, some period passed before her answer. Smart girl.

Natalie: *Are you ok?*

T.J.: *No but ill make a pickle n everything will b gd cuz ill cu.*

Another groan escaped him. *Jesus H. Christ on a damn fucking cracker! She must think I'm nuts! Or brainless. Or both.* He gulped a lungful of air and read on, dreading it to his very core but unable to look away from the car wreck that was the text conversation.

T.J.: *U there?*

Natalie: *I'm here but signing off now. See you later.*

T.J.: *Yes u will my dog loves u more than he loves me.*

Natalie: *I'm sure that's not true. Good night. Heading to bed now.*

T.J.: *Wanna come with u. Sooooo bad. U have no idea. I thnk about it. All. The. Time. In the shower in bed on the couch all the fucking time. Promise ill let u come first trust me im good that way.*

He stared at the last text, and his baked brain went in all different directions. Who could he blame this on? *A monkey broke into my condo and stole my phone! Autocorrect on crack! I swear!* How soon could he catch one of those space station shuttles and get dropped on another planet? Should he just tell her who he was and blame it on the Shanstrom gene?

An undecipherable orange word flashed at him beside the text. He scrunched his eyes and peered closer. "Draft," it said.

His heart surged and pumped relief into every limb. "I didn't send it!" he exclaimed aloud, then broke into a maniacal laugh. "It's in my fucking drafts!"

He pulled in three cleansing breaths and prepared himself as though he were one of those bomb guys on TV about to cut the red wire that would either annihilate the entire fucking world or save it from destruction.

"You can do this," he told himself. His hand shook.

Back arrow, back arrow, back arrow. And again. And again. Then he shut off his phone and dropped it on his counter like it was on fire, palmed his face, and sat perfectly still for what felt like hours. At last, he found the wherewithal to put himself to bed. But before he did, he stole one last glance at the painting.

Enough alcohol remained in his system that his internal battle stations were compromised. His cloaking device or the cloak of invisibility or whatever the hell it was that hid him from himself was temporarily on hiatus. In his weakened condition, he acknowledged an inner, undeniable truth—a confession of his closely guarded heart. Natalie Amber Eyes had not only taken up residence in his head, but she'd brought all her belongings and was making herself comfortable in his heart.

He had to evict her.

Chapter 16

Karma's a Bitch

Natalie awoke like an Energizer Bunny whose batteries had just been replaced. It was going to be a great day, damn it! She raced through her chores in record time and arrived at the hospital ahead of schedule—conceding that, yeah, having fewer dog clients might have speeded things up a bit, but hey, she wasn't going to dwell on it.

When she reached Kevin's room, a nurse said he was in therapy, so Natalie settled into one of the chairs and waited. And waited. And waited.

An hour later, she was pacing the room, beating herself up for not having brought work with her. She had so much to do!

The door swung open, and Natalie spun, gluing a smile on her face. Only to have it land on Kristin.

"I'm glad I caught you, chica," Kris said.

"Pretty even chance since I'm always here this time of day." Natalie regretted the snark as soon as it escaped her.

Kristin dismissed Natalie's remark completely, instead bouncing in place and silently clapping. "They're talking about moving Kevin to a rehab home. It might happen as early as tomorrow."

"That's great news!"

Kristin seemed to grow misty-eyed. To Natalie's horror, she choked out a, "Yeah, but he won't need me as much."

Not up on the latest etiquette for comforting one's semi-boyfriend's ex, Natalie approached like a one-legged goose and gave her a tissue and an awkward shoulder pat.

Pooling blue eyes looked into hers. "Natalie, you have to have asked yourself, 'Why is this crazy bitch here all the time?' I know *I* would have."

Huh? "I assumed because you still care."

Kristin let out a mirthless laugh. "That's one way of putting it."

"Kris, I'm not sure I—"

Dabbing at her watery eyes, Kristin sat. "Sit for a minute?"

Natalie lowered herself into the chair beside her.

"Did Kevin ever tell you why we broke up?"

Natalie shook her head, bracing herself for what, she wasn't sure.

"I cheated on him," Kris whispered.

Whatever else Natalie might've expected, it wasn't this confession, and her head jerked before she could stop herself. "You *what*?"

"I know." Kristin drew in a breath. "Looking back, it was beyond stupid, but hindsight and all that crap." She swiped her eyes. "I felt fat and ugly after Emma was born. Kevin was on the road a lot, and I felt like I wasn't getting enough attention when he *was* home." A faraway look came into her eyes. "So I looked for attention elsewhere. And got it."

Fascinated, horrified, Natalie sucked in a breath.

Kristin huffed out a sigh. "End of story, end of marriage." Her eyes filled again. "But I've never stopped loving him, you know? And now I just want to give him whatever he needs. Maybe I'm still trying to make up for my sins."

"And maybe you still love him. Do you ever think about getting back together?" Natalie cringed inside, unsure which answer she wished for.

Nodding, Kristin dropped her gaze to her lap and the now-shredded tissue. "I wish we were a family again. Not just for Emma, but for me too."

The words didn't surprise Natalie—they confirmed what she'd suspected—but they whiplashed her nonetheless. Wasn't this a betrayal?

Kristin's doleful eyes searched hers. For forgiveness? Permission to take her husband back? Whatever it was, the look touched Natalie's soul. She *knew* how it felt to lose someone you loved, and her heart ached for this woman, this family.

What was best for Team Kevin?

A moment of exquisite clarity settled over Natalie.

Among T.J.'s cringe-worthy attempts at sexting Natalie, he'd found another text. This one lifted his spirits.

Finally got court time. Be at Twentieth Street Rec tomorrow. Price of admission is beer and women. No excuses!

It *was* tomorrow, and T.J. had run through a solid workout with the Blizzard trainers. Shooting practice with a few guys from a Denver rec league—one of them a damn good goalie—had followed. They'd chatted afterward, the guys telling him how much they appreciated the opportunity.

"It's hard to get ice time," one guy said.

"Yeah, with the explosion of youth hockey, even the 2:00 a.m. slots are filled. About our only option is driving four hours to fucking Steamboat when they're *not* having a tournament," another guy grumbled.

"Used to be you could party all night, then take the ice and work it out of your system," the goalie chortled.

After showering, T.J. drove to the No Excuses! game, his mind working over a common problem for the adult rec leagues: lack of places to play consistently. Scrambling for access to decent facilities, competing for scarce resources would suck big-time, especially for a group like No Excuses! And they were worthier than just about anyone he could think of.

An idea sparked. Could he help them? At a stop sign, he scrolled through his contacts and placed a call.

"Millsy? Got a minute?"

Natalie sat flipping through a foodie magazine while she waited for Kevin in his room. Her mind had been spinning like a runaway water meter since her conversation with Kristin, and the magazine was doing squat to distract her—it only reminded her how hungry she was.

The door swung open, and Kevin rolled in attempting a wheelie, an exasperated attendant behind him. His eyes caught on Natalie.

"Hey, pretty lady," he said. "I thought Kris might be here too."

Was that disappointment in his voice?

"She had to pick up Emma from preschool, but they'll be back. How are the headaches?" Natalie kept her butt firmly planted in the seat and waited. An odd thing happened. Kevin went straight to a nearby chair and hoisted himself into it, bypassing his usual kiss and hug. She felt like the other half of an old married couple that didn't bother with affection anymore.

The attendant left the room with the wheelchair, and Kevin exhaled, his relief palpable. "My head feels like just one snare drum's pounding and not a whole drum kit today."

Natalie studied him. Was he giving off a different vibe, or was she just hypersensitive? "I hear you might be upgrading to new quarters."

"That's what they tell me. So I can learn how to turn off lights and shower by myself." His tone was sarcastic, but then he abruptly switched to playful and waggled his eyebrows at her. "I'm pretty sure I can't handle the shower alone."

Astonishment twisted her tongue, and she couldn't form, much less utter, a word.

"You're ignoring me." He grinned—no, leered—at her. "How about a sponge bath instead?" Yep, he'd totally meant what he'd said. A shiver of something—disgust, guilt?—raced along her spine while *awkward* sang out in her brain.

This was not normal Kevin behavior. Then again, what *was* normal Kevin behavior? She was adrift with no way to gauge, but a definite creep factor was settling in. One she didn't like.

"Um, I think it's best to leave that up to the nurses."

He rolled his eyes to the ceiling and left them there. "Yuck. The only nurses I get are the dudes and the old fatties." His eyes returned to hers, then slid up and down her body. "I'd like one that looks like you or Kris. Maybe you can put on one of those sexy nurse outfits—"

Okay. Now he was pissing her off. "Ask Kris," she snapped. But what exactly was making her mad? That he included Kris in his little fantasy, or something else? A large dose of inexplicable defensiveness surged.

A soft chuckle. "Damn. I was hoping I could talk you both into it."

She narrowed her eyes at him. "Apparently you *are* feeling better."

"Maybe," he sighed. "Christ, Nat, I don't have a fucking clue. All I know is I want the hell out of this place. Not just this room, but the whole damn situation. It just feels like time's at a standstill."

Shit. Now she felt like a total jerk. She softened her tone. "It must be frustrating. Have you thought about what going home looks like when they finally release you for good?"

He turned his head and looked at her. "What do you mean?"

"I mean, do you hire someone to help around the house? And what about PT visits?"

He blinked. "I have no idea."

She inhaled quickly, saying aloud what she'd been practicing for the last half hour. "Have you thought about staying with Kris and Emma, at least until you're back to where you were?"

He turned his head away. "Kris and I have talked about it," he said softly.

A virtual gut check had Natalie's blood rising again. But it was a weird dynamic: part-hurt and part-relief. Relief over what, exactly? She told herself it was because someone who loved him would take care of him twenty-four-seven, but underneath lurked a different sort of relief, a wholly selfish one. Grace Guilt rose up and wagged an accusing finger at her. Natalie ignored her, her mind tracking in another direction.

She laced her hands together. "Do you ever think about getting back together with Kris?"

Guilt-ridden eyes jumped back to hers. "Sometimes," he croaked.

Something tugged in her chest, and she felt like a wriggling fish that had been unhooked and placed back in the water. She could breathe again. It told her volumes she wasn't prepared to examine yet, such as: How much of her magnanimous gesture was driven by her waning stick-to-itiveness? By her desire to escape her Kevin Conundrum?

She patted Kevin's arm. "Kris really cares about you. If there's an iota of a chance …"

"What about you?"

"This isn't about me. It's about you getting better, and … maybe getting your family back at the same time. I think you should give it serious thought."

There it was. Her blessing freely given. More like borderline foisted, if she were honest.

He gave her a half-smile. "Yeah. Maybe I should."

T.J. watched from aluminum bleachers, humbled. In addition to inspiration, he got a fair dose of shame. His perfectly working limbs were an embarrassment of riches around the No Excuses! team, yet they were the well-adjusted ones. Go figure.

The wheelchair team blew him away. Not because of their athletic skills, which were impressive, but because of their attitude, their loyalty to one another, their fierceness to not only live, but *own* a world that had shit on them.

He sat among wives and girlfriends cheering from the sidelines, women who obviously loved and cared about these men. Who were in their corners. And he found himself envying the disabled guys. They reminded him of all he'd never had, all he hadn't deserved.

The game ended, and Mark rolled over and tugged a pretty woman into his wheelchair. She landed on his lap with a squeal, and he laid an embarrassingly long kiss on her lips.

He scanned her face and, looking at her with a beaming smile, said, "T.J., this is my wife, Carla."

Firmly wrapped up in Mark's beefy arms, Carla gave T.J. a shy hello. Guy had no legs—they were blown off by an IED in Afghanistan—yet he'd met and married Carla *after* he'd gone through what would have crushed most men's spirits. He'd told T.J. he'd had plenty of down days but finally decided nothing was going to change, so he might as well live as though each hour was his last. No excuses.

T.J. thought he knew what that meant, but he'd been wrong.

Mark gave him a chin jerk. "Bring your girl next time."

T.J. raked his fingers through his hair. "Haven't got one to bring."

Carla's brows climbed her forehead. So did Mark's. "Right. You're just afraid to bring her because you *know* once she gets a load of us studs, she'll drop your ass in a hot second." Mark's eyes darted to his wife, still in his lap. "Right, babe?"

Carla gave him an eye-roll, then to T.J. she said, "I've got a cousin—"

T.J. held up his hand. "Thanks, but I'm not in the market." *Because the only woman I'm remotely interested in is so out of bounds I'd need a special permit approved by five different government agencies to be with her.* He shot Carla an apologetic look. "No offense, Carla."

Her smile told him she hadn't taken any.

He stared at the couple for a beat, then his uncensored mouth went rogue. "It's nice you two got together." Where the fuck had *that* come from, and why the hell was he going all soft and mushy lately? He had no clue, but his man card was on the verge of being revoked. Permanently.

Funny thing was it hadn't been a hollow platitude. He *was* glad Mark had someone like Carla, just like he was glad Miller had Paige.

His mind jumped to May and Natalie, and his ridiculous, squishy feels evaporated, especially when he realized how alone *he* was—and how that wasn't about to change anytime soon.

Shoving his pity party down deep, he focused instead on these guys and the idea that had sprouted in his head and grown legs after he'd talked to Miller. If he couldn't help himself, he might as well help *them*.

Chapter 17

Of Porn Stars and Drug Dealers

The next morning, before T.J. could corral him, Ford bounded from the car and hauled his dog ass to Natalie's front door, where he sat and barked. She opened up, a grin splitting her face. Her demeanor told him his texts hadn't put her off. *Thank God.* He wasn't about to remind her by apologizing. Instead, he considered it a bullet dodged and let the whole awkward episode go.

"Is my handsome boy happy to see me?" she sang to the dog. Ford jolted upright and began cavorting around her legs. She was dressed in bright, stretchy pants that hugged her lean, shapely legs.

T.J. released an inner sigh, picturing himself the object of her affectionate cooing. His mind nimbly segued to those legs wrapped around his waist. Following her inside, he conceded that if not for Kevin May, he'd be in deep, deep shit with this woman who both enchanted *and* terrified him.

He pulled his hand through his hair. "Uh, sorry about the texts." His eyes caught on a boxy green nylon bag, a cowboy hat, and a pair of gray waders. "What time will you be back?"

She glanced at a sportsman-style watch strapped to her wrist. "Drew has a hot date, so four-ish. Does that work?"

"Perfect. I've got plenty to do today." *And I'll come back late enough to avoid the brother.* Practice, extra training, and team meetings awaited. All things Kevin May *couldn't* do. Shit, he hated when those stealth thoughts blindsided him, which they did *way* too much.

T.J. hadn't seen May since his ex had thrown him out, and his updates had mostly come from Natalie. Tom Carlisle's warning to stop intel-gathering replayed in his head, but he couldn't resist one last chance.

"So how's your boyfriend doing?"

Natalie flinched, and his stomach clenched. "Better. Looks like he's moving into a brain retraining facility soon." Her words left him breathing easier—guy was on the mend—but why did she sound so unhappy? Girl should've been over the moon.

"Is everything okay between you guys? Not that it's any of my business." He held his breath.

She stared at him, her eyebrows riding up and down her forehead like the elevators in his building. Christ, he wished he could read her.

"Um ... for now."

He held his gaze steady, trying not to infer too much from her cryptic comment. Her amber eyes dimmed a bit, then quickly livened again when Ford launched himself into T.J.

"Jesus, dog! How many times I gotta tell you not to knock me over?" Ford's response was to smear himself against T.J.'s legs.

Natalie laughed. "Maybe he doesn't want you to go."

He ruffled Ford's head. "I'll be back this afternoon. Maybe your pretty dog-sitter will have more coffee cake for us."

A flush crept up her cheeks. It was a good look on her, turning her smooth skin a beautiful shade of light bronze. He could've sworn a spark flashed in her coppery-gold eyes. His tongue tied itself in knots, and he was pretty sure he gaped. *God, just look at her.*

She stole his breath away.

Puck after puck, shot after shot, T.J. aimed top shelf, short side, five-hole, blocker side, stick side. He practiced wraparounds, bank shots, and sliding the puck under the goalie's pads. Extra ice time where he and Nelson worked on their give-and-goes, on setting each other up.

Several teammates watched from the sidelines. Some cheered; others taunted. Hopeful signs they were beginning to accept him. Practice had been a little rough, but T.J. locked it out.

Sweat pouring off him in rivulets, he began gathering up pucks on one side of the net while Nelson corralled those on the other side.

Dave Grimson, the "Grim Reaper," skated over. "So, Shanny, you practicing to be the next Gretzky? Thought you were more of a brawler."

Wiping his face with the bottom of his practice jersey, T.J. side-eyed his captain. "Never hurts to work on my shot." *Here it comes: You're no goal-scorer. You're an enforcer. A grinder.*

"I'll work with you if you want." Grims shrugged. "In fact, I bet most of the guys here would." He swept his hand toward the onlookers.

Taken aback, T.J. blinked. "Yeah, Grims. That'd be great."

"All right. Get these pucks picked up and stop batting your eyelashes at me, or the guys'll think you're trying to kiss me." With a wink, the captain skated away. Mid-ice, he stopped, seeming to remember something. "Some of us are grabbing dinner at the Chophouse tonight with our SOs," he hollered. "Eight o'clock." He pointed at Nelson. "Admiral, you're invited too."

Relief—and something a little warm and fuzzy—surged inside T.J., and he forgot about the cuts and bruises he'd earned in practice. Right now he was only focused on dinner with the guys. Yeah, that was something he would *not* miss.

"We should bring Mom next time." Natalie stowed her gear in the cargo box atop Drew's Outback and climbed into the front passenger seat, satisfaction oozing through her. What a perfect day. Enough clouds to make hungry, cagey fish rise in the shadows and take the flies she'd cast on the water's swirling surface.

Ford had snoozed with Annie and Meathead in the SUV, ending the day with a woofing, splashing romp in silty pools along the muddy bank. Caged behind the vehicle's net barrier for the drive home, the dogs smiled and panted. And, man, did they stink! She'd have to clean Ford before Tyler came for him.

"I asked her, but she was too busy." He used air quotes for "busy" as he slid behind the wheel. "I swear we never should have started her on Netflix."

Natalie chortled. "Maybe it's not TV. What if Mom has a boyfriend?"

"*What?* Oh hell no. Nuh-uh."

"Why not? Mary Foster's a vibrant woman. She's a catch." Natalie grinned at her own joke.

"She's our mom. Moms don't … Shit. I can't believe you just put that thought in my head. Now I've gotta bleach it out. You are the suckiest sister on the planet, you know that?"

"I try. Seriously, Drewbert, Mom might find someone before *we* do."

He eyed her warily. "*We?* When did you join me in singledom?"

"Not sure I have. My hold on coupledom's a little shaky, though." Saying it out loud didn't bother her as much as she'd expected.

"Why? What's going on with Kevin?"

"The right question would be what's going on with him and his ex?"

Drew's eyebrows traveled to his hairline. "Seriously?"

Natalie nodded. "They still have feelings for each other. And I'm okay with that. I'd rather see a reconciliation, especially where Emma's involved. Besides, Tyler said I was pretty this morning." Yep, she'd scarfed up the "pretty dog-sitter" compliment like a pie-eating contestant hell-bent on winning.

Drew shook his head.

"What?" she retorted.

He stopped at a red light and shot her a warning look. "Don't fall for his lines, Nat."

Her deflector shields locked into place. "He just threw it out there, Drew. He's a *guy*, so it probably didn't mean anything. But it's still nice to hear once in a while."

The light turned green, and they rode in silence for a few minutes.

"Did I tell you Tyler knows Beckett Miller, and he set up a meeting with Beckett's wife? She's my newest bookkeeping client."

Drew's eyes widened, and his mouth swung open. "*The* Beckett Miller?"

Natalie smirked. "Mm-hmm. So be nice. I *might* introduce you someday."

"Wait. How does Hummer Man know Miller?"

"He says they met a long time ago."

Drew rubbed a finger over his chin. "Any more clues about what he does for a living?"

"Nope." The question—one she'd been asking herself over and over—bothered her more than she wanted to admit.

Drew let out a derisive snort. "Guy drives an expensive vehicle, doesn't do a nine-to-five, and is in quote *entertainment* unquote."

She shrugged. "He says he sells sports, which fits because he's really ripped and has this gorgeous tattoo that goes from here to here." She traced a fingertip from her upper arm to her shoulder. "Maybe he's one of those Beach Body workout guys."

"How do *you* know he's really ripped? And how did you get a look at his tattoo?"

"You can't miss his rippedness," she stammered. "As for the tat, he texted me a picture of him lying in bed—"

Her brother dropped his chin, looking as though he might charge her.

"Shit. This isn't coming out right. Let me rephrase. He sent me a picture of Ford curled up in bed with him. He *happened* to be wearing a tank, which is how I saw the tat. Just his arm and part of his shoulder. That's it. That's all I saw."

The more she spewed, the guiltier she sounded, though she'd done nothing wrong. She'd merely noticed some exceptional muscle definition ... and his butt. But she was only appreciating the male form.

Drew's skeptical look fastened on her. Hopefully, he couldn't read her runaway thoughts.

She pointed her index and middle fingers at her eyes then at the windshield. "Eyes on the road, Bro."

He faced forward. "Nice try." A beat later, he added, "The guy's either a porn star or a drug dealer. Maybe he was Miller's dealer. They went on those wild cruises together—you know what I'm talking about. The kind your clients used to charter. Where each guy picks two or three chicks for a long weekend. Wealthy guy stuff."

A laugh bubbled up inside her despite her best efforts to squelch it. "Where the hell do you get this crap? I swear you watch waaaay too much TV."

A sliver of a doubt crept in, like a determined weed growing through a crack in the sidewalk. Was her new client one of *those* guys? Damn. She thought the career change had deloused her of men like that.

Drew tapped a finger on the steering wheel. "Annnd, his screen name is 'Big Hummer.' I guess that could be his dealer handle too."

She rolled her eyes. "So he either wags the 'Little Hummer' in porn flicks or he sells drugs?"

He grinned. "Yeah, that about sums it up."

"Well, you'll just have to meet him for yourself. I doubt he looks anything like those porn stars you're talking about."

"How would I know? I'm not into porn, but if I were, I sure as hell would *not* be zeroing in on a dude."

She looked out the window to hide her flaming face. Surely it was as red as a chili pepper.

When the temperature in her cheeks cooled a degree or two, she cleared her throat. "There's no way someone with a dog as sweet as Ford could be either of those things."

"Keep telling yourself that, Nat."

God, how she wanted to wipe that smug look from his face—as much as she wanted to wipe Tyler's finer attributes from her mind. *Pretty dog-sitter* and *I like women* stubbornly danced in her brain. No doubt women liked him too—a lot. But jeez, she couldn't go there.

Nope, it was a moot point.

Ford was clean, dry, and fluffy by the time Tyler arrived. Natalie was also clean and dry, wearing a fluffy sweater and still riding the day's high.

"Sorry I'm late," he huffed at her door.

"No worries. C'mon in. Can I get you anything?"

"Water would be great. Then I'll get to work on your door." He dropped a tool tote and a Home Depot bag by her couch.

"Nothing stronger than water?" It was nearly six after all. She shot him a smile over her shoulder.

Ford bounded in, and Tyler reached for him. "Hey, buddy. How's it going? Wow! Look at you. Did Natalie Amb—did you get a bath? You even smell like dog bubble bath."

Natalie Amb? What the hell is that? Tyler's text popped into the jetsam bobbing around in her brain. *Natalie Amber Eyes.* An unexpected thrill zipped through her. *Stop it!* "He really needed it after playing in the river."

Tyler jutted his jaw so Ford could lick his chin, then rose with panther grace. He looked taller than she remembered. Six-four? Six-five? He was sporting a bruise along his jawline and a cut above his right eyebrow. *What the hell?*

She gave his face a good once-over. How had she not noticed how handsome he was before? He possessed a certain rugged appeal and intensity that slung a few chills through her.

Gold starbursts surrounded his pupils, bleeding into deep green. His lashes were long and thick, making the combination quite striking, especially when layered on chiseled cheekbones and a strong jaw. A little scar decorated the top lip of his full mouth, somehow enhancing his good looks. And if it had detracted, his hard body would have more than made up for it.

Wonder what it's like to kiss a guy with a scarred lip?

He crossed his arms over his chest, making it look broader. "So do you have your own fishing vest too?" He seemed to suppress a snicker, which yanked her from her wayward thoughts.

Chauvinist. "Yep, and a rod, a reel, and boxes of flies I tied with my dad. I prefer fly-fishing, but I've been known to land a sailfish or two, eighty-pound tunas, dorado, and roosterfish. I even handle live bait without squealing like a girl." She faked a gasp, then perched a fist on her hip. "Oh, and I shoot guns too, better than most men I know."

His eyes went saucer-round, and he raised his hands in surrender. "Whoa there, sassiness. I didn't realize I was dealing with a seriously badass outdoorswoman. Don't shoot me, please." His hands dove into his front pockets, and his lips quirked, making his scar twitch.

He was pretty damn cute, and she suppressed a laugh in spite of herself. "Sassiness? Sorry about the 'tude. It's just that when people act astounded that I fish—"

"I'm not astounded," he protested. "I'm jealous. I mean, you've landed a sailfish. How cool is that? I've tried, but I've never reeled one in. And I've known women who'll hang out on boats, but fish? Nah."

Oh shit! Were they women on a hedonism cruise? She bit back the urge to ask.

Tyler flashed her a wicked grin. "I think it's great you fish. So ease up and quit busting my chops, smartass."

She clamped her mouth shut to keep a laugh from bursting out.

"So fishing. Shooting," he said. "You like guy stuff, huh?"

She gave him an eye-roll. "Yeah, well, no point in letting guys have *all* the fun."

He flashed her that devastating smile again. "So now you know I've got all the manners of a misogynistic dumbass," he continued. "Please be gentle when you whoop my ass at fishing."

Momentarily stunned by his comment, Natalie put her mouth back to work. "So *do* you fish? I wouldn't want to school a beginner and leave him floundering."

"Did you just say that?" he snorted. "And mean to?"

She inched her nose up a bit. "I certainly did."

"Where do you get your jokes? The back of a cereal box?"

"My dad taught me everything I know, and believe me, I've got a million of 'em."

"Good to know. I am now on high 'bad joke' alert." He winked at her. Actually winked. Goosebumps erupted on her arms, making her hairs stand on end as though charged with electricity.

"You're deflecting," she laughed. "Do you fish or not?"

He puffed and assumed an insulted look. "Of course I fish. I'm from Minnesota."

"Which means diddly." *Oh, stellar comeback, Nat!*

He dropped his hands at his sides and leaned against a wall, all casual-like. As if he belonged there. "Well, Christ. If you're going to abuse me, I *will* take something stronger to drink. But be forewarned, I cannot guarantee the quality of my work."

"Beer? Sangria? Crown Royal?"

With his palm flat against his chest, he tapped out a rhythm. *Thump, thump, thump.* "Interesting assortment. Beer's fine."

"IPA? Pilsner? Stout?"

"Seriously?" he laughed. "I'll go with the IPA."

She headed for the fridge, sensing him right behind her. "Well, good thing that was your choice because IPA is all I have." She plucked out a cold bottle, popped the top, and handed it to him.

One side of his mouth hitched up in a smile. "Is it safe to assume you don't have the Crown Royal, or the ... what was the other one?"

"Sangria."

"Right. I knew it was random." He tipped the bottle to his lips.

"Sangria is not random, but you'd be right. I don't have any."

He gave her a scrunched-forehead look like he thought she was utterly banana balls.

Picking up his stuff, he headed for the enclosed patio and the troublesome sliding door. She followed and watched him get to work. He bent over the lock, his broad back stretching a long-sleeved shirt molded to his upper body like Spiderman's suit.

A little cough escaped her.

"Bless you," he called over his shoulder.

"Um, thanks, but that wasn't a sneeze."

He stood, reached for his beer, and took another swig, his eyes boring into hers over the bottle.

She searched for a bit of conversation to anchor herself. Unfortunately, her mind U-turned to women on boats, and curiosity prevailed. *As long as he already thinks I'm nuts ...* "Ever gone on one of those every-guy-gets-two-women hedonism cruises?" she blurted.

He sputtered and sprayed beer, dribbling it onto his chin. His hand shot to his face, covering his mouth. "Excuse me?" he said from behind his fingers. He seemed to be laughing.

She handed him a paper towel and grinned. "Sorry. Sometimes the random thing takes over, and I can't stop."

"Duly noted." He set down his beer and dragged the towel across his mouth. "Or you enjoy pushing people's buttons."

"A little of that too."

He chuckled and went back to work, removing the lock. "I'm not sure where you find a hedonism cruise, but it sounds interesting. I'll research it thoroughly and get back to you. It may take me a few weeks, though, so you'll watch Ford for me?" He looked up at her, hazel eyes twinkling. Obviously, he was getting a kick out of this. So was she, and she responded with a belly laugh that busted all kinds of anxiousness loose. God, it felt good to let go!

He rotated a shoulder as he lined up the new lock, and the shirt crept up, exposing a swath of skin, giving her an enticing view of hard-ridged muscle. No fat here. No tattoo either. She tried not to picture it under his shirt, curling around his beefy bicep.

"So what's up with the California plates?"

He didn't flinch. "I keep putting off going to the DMV." His voice was smooth and deep, and it rumbled like a low growl of thunder.

"How long have you been in Colorado?"

"Not quite a year."

Not really an answer.

Though he wasn't looking at her, she made a circle with her forefinger and aimed it at him. "How did you get the scar on your lip?"

Seemingly without thought, he touched the scar with his fingertips. "Took a stick to the mouth."

She frowned. "What kind of stick?"

Wide eyes flew to hers, like he was a deer caught in a hunter's crosshairs, before landing back on the locking mechanism. He flicked a lever and pulled. The door held. "Hockey stick. I played hockey as a kid. We all did. Pond hockey."

She nodded slowly. "Ah. Minnesota in winter."

With an easy grace that broadcast his comfort in his own skin, he turned his back to her and tested the door a few more times. He had a very nice back. It matched the rest of him. *Yeah, he could totally be a porn star. Not that I would know what a porn star looks like in his clothes. Or out of them. He'd have to be pretty buff, though, right? No fatties with floppy bellies.*

Tyler took another pull from his beer bottle. A long, throat-pulsing pull.

Natalie turned for the kitchen. "Think I'll have a beer too."

She didn't realize he'd been on her heels until he said, "So did you have any luck today?" Startled, she spun with her bottle, and he held out his hand. When she gave him a quizzical look, he nodded at the beer. "I'll open that for you."

Passing it to him, she told him, in minute detail, about the *enormous* rainbow she'd caught, her mouth galloping away from her. Tingles were zipping through her bloodstream, but they weren't because of the fish.

Within minutes, she and Tyler were seated at her kitchen table, exchanging more barbs and laughing in a comfortable cadence. It was the best time she'd had in a very long, long while, which was remarkable, considering she was pretty sure her sort-of boyfriend was about to dump her.

A minute became an hour, and she found herself not wanting him to leave. Being with him made her forget her worries, and she wanted to hang on to the feeling. When was the last time she'd spent Saturday night like this? So long ago.

"Are you hungry?" She got up and stuck her head in the fridge. "I can whip something up if you are. And I have more beer. Or Crown Royal. I like Crown myself. And it's Ford's suppertime, isn't it? I'll feed him." *Jeez, blither much?*

Tyler laughed as though he were trying to slide out of an awkward situation—like the girl he didn't like just asked him to a Sadie Hawkins dance while the hot girl he *wanted* to ask him hadn't gotten to it yet and he was looking for a way to stall. Or like his dog-sitter was getting too friendly. Yeah, that.

He surprised her when he said, "I've been holding out for the coffee cake, but I'm not seeing any encouraging signs."

"I'm on it." Her back to him, she began pulling ingredients and measuring spoons from cupboards. Behind her, Tyler had grown very quiet. Maybe he'd been kidding. She pivoted on her heel and caught him staring at her, an unreadable look on his face. They locked eyes for a long, heated beat, and her tummy teeter-tottered.

"Um, so ... coffee cake. I owe you ... I mean, the door and all," she babbled.

Why was the air suddenly thick and ripe as though charged for a lightning strike?

He stood abruptly and headed toward the back door to let Ford in. "I should probably go. I've got this thing ..."

In Natalie's life dictionary, *thing* translated to *date*. "Right. Sorry. Didn't mean to hold you up."

He shot her a hazel-eyed glance. Lord, he had long lashes. "Although, I gotta say, coffee cake ... Got any Jameson?"

"No, but there's a liquor store down the street."

"You probably have stuff to do."

"I do. Like make you coffee cake. And you're going to help."

Dark, thick brows crawled up his forehead, and a lazy smile curved his lips.

"First things first," she rushed on. "My baking's much better with a shot of Crown."

"I guess this is the part where I hustle out to get my Jameson?"

"This would be that part. But hurry, or I'm taking the good apron."

He barked out a laugh. "The *good* apron?"

She nodded, and he stepped lively to the front door. "Shit. On my way. Wouldn't want to get stuck with the *bad* apron, whatever the hell that is."

Minutes later, she was still laughing to herself, clattering measuring cups, when the door opened. "Back already?"

"Back? From where?"

Natalie whirled. "Mom! I wasn't expecting you."

Her mom sashayed over like a Southern belle, not the Colorado cowgirl she was. Natalie loved that about her. Her mom leaned in and kissed Natalie's cheeks, wrapping her mom smell around her. Natalie loved *that* about her too.

"I was headed this way and thought I'd drop off some ham. Ooh, what are you making?"

"Coffee cake." Natalie peeked beneath a tall foil tent covering a platter her mom held. "This is Easter dinner for eight, Mom. It won't fit—"

"You've been looking a little scrawny lately, Natbug." Mom, the Queen of Tetris, began rearranging the contents of Natalie's fridge to create space for the platter. "Men prefer women who have a little something to grab."

Natalie was biting back a laughing protest when someone knocked at the front door. It opened, and Tyler filled the entire frame. He held a big box. "Brought back a little extra—" His eyes darted to Mom, and his mouth swung open. "Oh, sorry, I ..."

Waving him in, Mom took in his entire form in one thorough sweep. "Don't mind me. I was just dropping off some goodies for Natalie. I'm Mary, her mom. And you are?" She said it so sweetly no one could have taken it for the mama bear question it truly was.

Tyler ducked his head. "Tyler. Johnson. Natalie's, uh, dog client. Nice to meet you, Mrs. ..." Mom cocked an eyebrow, and Tyler changed course. "Uh, Mary." He stood stock-still.

"Come in, Tyler. Please. I was just leaving," she assured him.

He shuffled inside, looking utterly unnerved. Natalie reached for the box, but he stepped around her and deposited it on the kitchen table. His eyes bounced between her and her mom.

Natalie peered inside the box. "Did you buy out the whole liquor store?"

"I just thought I'd replace the beer and ... looks like you're low on red wine and ..."

"Aw, you didn't have to, but thank you." Suppressing a snicker, Natalie pointed to a ruffly magenta apron draped over the back of a kitchen chair. "That's yours."

He hesitated, then surprised her when he slid off his jacket, picked up the apron, and pulled it over his head. Natalie burst out with the laugh she'd been holding back, and Mom joined in. Grinning, Tyler held up his arms. "What do you think?" He pivoted. "It's my color, right?"

"It's perfect!" Natalie chortled. "Except the ties aren't long enough."

He looked down at himself and shrugged. Mom side-eyed Natalie with a look that said, "I like this one." Natalie answered with an eye-roll.

Tyler offered Mom a drink as he poured Natalie one, but she declined and left—after telling him that "dinner was in the fridge."

He poured himself a hefty helping of Jameson. "Does your mom always do that?"

"What? Bring over dinner for a football team? Rarely. Not sure what possessed her, but it's a good thing you're here to help me eat it." *Look at you, Nat, sliding that right in as smooth as silk, you sneaky bitch.*

He let out a noisy sigh. "I think I love your mom."

"Careful. She might adopt you." She smirked at his getup. "You don't have to wear the apron, Tyler."

"What? No way. I'm in this to win this. So get busy and boss me around."

"You know you look ridiculous, right?" *And not like a porn star at all.*

"Be nice. I'm getting my girlie side on."

She let out a *pfft* and shoved a measuring cup at him. "Sugar. One cup."

"Yes, your sassiness. Wait. Did you just call me 'Sugar'?"

She pressed her lips together. *Don't laugh. Don't encourage him.* Even though that was exactly what she wanted to do. Instead, she said, "So what about your *thing*?"

He beamed her a devilish smile. "Canceled it."

189

Chapter 18

Merging Traffic Ahead

Such a bad idea. On so many levels.

T.J. had blown off his teammates—the first dinner they'd invited him to—so he could stand beside Natalie in her kitchen, wearing a ridiculous pink apron, getting covered in flour under the pretext of helping her bake *him* a cake. Yeah, he hadn't told Grims what he was *really* doing, though the guy had guessed. Sort of.

The text exchange had gone something like:

Sorry, Grims. Can't make it. Something came up.

Something like your dick?

LOL. Next time?

Next time.

T.J. just hoped there *would* be a next time.

Despite Tom Carlisle's voice yapping in his head, he hadn't been able to resist the chance to spend Saturday night with Natalie. Especially after she'd given him a look like he was fucking Superman when he'd fixed her lock. If he'd been smart, he'd have run like hell, but he wasn't smart—unlike that mouth of hers. The mouth he was dying to sample.

Yeah, being here was a bad, bad idea.

He side-eyed her. "More Crown?"

"A short pour. Please." Her focus was lasered on a bowl that held cinnamon-sugary goodness. Sticking out her little pink tongue, she sprinkled the stuff over a creamy batter—batter he kept dipping his finger in just to get a rise from her. So easy, so fun.

Don't get carried away, Shanny, or she'll hook you like the damn trout she caught this morning. Then she'll know the reason you got a dog was to wag your way into her life.

So why was he here, exactly? Because she was all sass and flashing brown eyes and questions firing at him. She kept him dancing on his tiptoes as though he were Mikhail Fucking Baryshnikov. The woman was fearless, fascinating, and terrifying all at the same time. And he was eating it up.

He swallowed a smirk, thinking about how she'd blindsided him. Several times. A hedonism cruise? He'd heard about that stuff, but other than an occasional quick and dirty fantasy, he'd never given it much thought.

Had she been serious? He couldn't tell with her. Maybe one day he'd get to know her well enough to understand what in the name of two-for-one tacos had spurred her to pursue that particular line of questioning.

In your dreams, Shanny.

He tugged a hand through his mop. *Shit, that's my "tell," isn't it?*

Besides being off-limits, what would a woman like her want with a guy like him? She was filet mignon, and he was stew meat. And once Natalie found out who he was? Ground chuck. His stomach lurched at the thought.

"Hey." Her eyes darted to the back of his head, glimmering with mischief. "You just rubbed flour in your hair."

"Yeah? Well, you've got flour on your nose." He tapped the end of her nose, putting flour where it hadn't been. She crossed her eyes to look down at the spot, pulling a grin from him. "And now you look like Ford," he said.

With a little headshake, she opened the oven and pulled out a pan covered in foil, replacing it with the cake, then set a timer.

"What's that?" He pointed at the foil tent.

"The ham dinner my mom brought. Baking's my thing, but overcooking is *her* thing."

"Do you bake pies too?"

"Oh yeah. I make a mean peach pie, but I also do banana chocolate cream, Dutch apple ..." She began pulling off her apron, and all he could do was stand there salivating. God, he loved pie. And ham. And the sight of her. And every smell in the kitchen at that moment—especially hers.

She held her hands out for his apron. "Ready to eat?"

He bit back the X-rated answer vibrating in his throat, smoothing the apron over his chest instead. "You mean I don't get to keep this for being such a great help?"

A little laugh escaped her. "If you insist."

"Maybe it clashes with the seat cushions." He pulled it over his head, getting tangled in the ruffles. Up on tiptoe, she helped free him, then stood back, looking him up and down, wadding the apron in her hands. "You're a good sport for playing along. And here I thought you were on bad joke alert."

His hand shot to the back of his head—again—and he let out a nervous laugh. "Not when I'm the bad joke."

She arched an eyebrow, after which she poured wine, lit candles, heaped their plates, and placed a salad and hot rolls on the table.

He pointed at the side dishes. "I've been standing here the whole time. When did you make those?"

A little shrug. "While you were standing here the whole time."

He pulled out a chair for her. "You're a kitchen ninja." The seat wobbled as she slid into it. "Your chair needs tightening. I can take care of that." He took his own seat, a mismatch but sturdier than hers. "And I'll go over this one too."

Could he get used to this? Yeah, he could.

She dropped her napkin in her lap and gave him a smile that lit her eyes. "Wow. I must be doing something right to deserve my very own handyman."

You are. You're breathing. They toasted to her repaired lock, and he dug in. He didn't stop until he heard groaning and realized it was coming from him. "So good," he mumbled.

Natalie watched him over the rim of her wineglass. "Your girlfriends must not feed you."

He stopped mid-chew, then shook his head. "Not 'girlfriends' plural. I'm a one-woman kinda guy." Clueless as to why, he added, "Although at the moment, I'm a no-woman kinda guy. I just recently broke up with someone. Well, technically, *she* broke up with *me*." What the fuck was wrong with him? He never divulged this much information, but somehow he couldn't stop spewing nuggets he normally kept secreted in his vault. If he didn't watch himself, he'd hand Natalie the keys to said vault and let her have at it.

Regret stamped itself in her pretty features. "I'm sorry."

"Don't be. We weren't … It was casual." *Always is.*

"So," his mouth trumpeted uncensored, "how about you and your ex-boyfriend? Cody?" Mentally, he patted himself on the back for not spitting out his food along with the guy's name. He shoveled in another bite and watched her.

Her eyes widened.

"Sorry. None of my business. Didn't mean to bring up bad memories." His own bad memories came roaring at him, and he twitched one side of his mouth in an attempt to lighten the mood, though he suddenly felt heavier than a grounded blimp. Traveling back in his past always did that to him.

She darted her eyes to the tabletop. "No, it's okay. I … You caught me off guard." Candlelight reflected in honey-colored eyes that were shadowed by a melancholy touching every feature on her pretty face.

A bolt fired straight to T.J.'s chest, and he couldn't decide if it was the thought of her being hurt by someone that disturbed him or if it was that someone had gotten close enough to hurt her.

Her eyes delved deep inside him. Did she see everything he'd locked away with no intention of ever hauling up again? He squirmed inside, but he didn't look away.

"Were you together long? High school sweethearts?" Now he was careening into familiar territory—achingly familiar—and his innards felt as though someone had stuck a fist in them and twisted. Anger bubbled up.

Do. Not. Say. Your "priorities changed."

His inner words scratched out harsh tones in his head, and he struggled to rein himself in. *Jesus, get your temper under control.* He eased the glare he was pretty sure he was giving her, though she couldn't have noticed because she'd shifted her eyes to the ceiling as if the words she searched for were inked there.

Her gaze landed back on him, scanning, as if reading some coded information. Did she trust him with her answer? "I need more Crown. Jameson?"

He declined. "Sticking with water." Though he damn sure could've used the Jameson.

She rose gracefully and poured herself a measure.

His heart fell off a high dive. Her look, coupled with her words, doused the flames that had ignited in him.

Ford, who'd been contentedly curled up in her living room, padded in and laid his head on her lap when she retook her seat. Yeah, T.J. had been about to Hulk out, but somehow this damn cross-eyed dog had sensed some disturbance in the Force and had acted more human than T.J.

Twitchy as hell, muddled emotions tap-dancing in his stomach, he rested his fingers on the edge of her table and began drumming. Which did *not* help with the whole appearance of nonchalance he was going for.

She cradled the Crown. "In a nutshell, my boss wanted me to sleep with him, and my fiancé of four years accused me of turning a molehill into a mountain. I filed a harassment claim, and Cody walked the same day. My world fell to pieces."

What. The. Actual. Fuck?

"Excuse me? He didn't go after the guy?" T.J.'s hands curled into fists on his thighs. *Fuck me, if some douche told my girl to spread her legs, I'd fucking tear him apart. They'd never find all the pieces.* "And then he *broke up* with you?"

She shrugged. "I think he was embarrassed. He worked for a sister firm."

"That's no excuse." T.J. kept the growl in his belly from his tone.

A sad smile curved her lips. "He moved on pretty quickly, though. A month later, he was living with someone."

Ferocity speared T.J. The intensity took him by surprise. He hadn't felt a primal surge that powerful since NHL draft night. Where the hell had it come from?

He choked out a "Seriously?"

"Yeah. Not gonna lie, that hurt." A mirthless laugh, then her features softened. "But it worked out in the end. I stood up to very influential people. Lawsuits suck, by the way. So do lawyers. Mom and Drew had my back, and my dad was cheering from heaven." She paused a moment to swipe at her cheek. "Knowing my family was there for me gave me courage. It helped me come to terms, and I embraced a completely different lifestyle. One I like."

Aw, man. Don't cry. Please don't cry. T.J.'s seat suddenly felt too tiny, and he perched a little higher and shifted his weight. "What's happening with the lawsuit?"

"It's over. We settled. I didn't do it for the money. If that had been my reason, I'd have hung in for a bigger payday." She sniffed and dabbed at her nose. "The culture was screwed up, and it wasn't just bosses. It was rich clients who pawed and grabbed, and no one stopped them. Female employees were encouraged to 'play along.' I didn't want the same crap happening to someone who might not fight back, so I filed."

He wanted to do something, hurt someone, but he couldn't. So he just sat there, stewing in frustration.

She cocked her head. "But there's a huge silver lining. I'm stronger. I know what I want. I discovered I didn't miss my job—I was part of the slimy set, like the other snakes in that god-awful pit. Sure, I rocked Louboutins, drove a swanky Mercedes, dined at the best restaurants, and drank two hundred-dollar bottles of wine like they were Two Buck Chuck. But I didn't like myself."

Mesmerized, he watched her as she gazed somewhere far off, trying *not* to picture her long, bare legs in stilettos that screamed, "Fuck me!" Her next words blew that image right out of his head.

"I've become a dog-sitter extraordinaire in my grubby jeans, covered in dog hair and dog slobber."

"But your ..." He inhaled the words *financial trouble.* "Do you ever think about restarting that career?"

"Nope." She sipped her Crown. "My life's simpler now. I have more independence than I've ever had. Money's tight, but in time that'll change." She beamed. "I'm like the mosaic table on my patio."

"The what?"

"It's a collection of glass splinters that've been put together, and it works somehow. It's beautiful that way."

So are you.

Rising even as he tried to ground himself, he cleared the table to give himself something to do to settle his roiling emotions. Anger and frustration tempered by amazement and sadness. Being with her made him think too much, poked at his sore spots. Part-pain, part-pleasure. Confusing as hell.

Standing close beside him, she dried dishes he washed in comfortable silence, her light floral scent tempting him to pull in a deeper inhale. He leashed the urge to lean in. Instead, he imagined her warmth reaching out, tendril-like, floating on a soft, fragrant breeze and wrapping itself around him.

After covering the coffee cake—another ninja move since he'd never seen her pull it out of the oven—she excused herself. He wiped the counters and hung up her kitchen towels. Jesus, he'd fallen into a Norman Rockwell painting without knowing how it happened.

Ford whined beside him as if to say he *liked* being in a Norman Rockwell painting.

"What? You're a mind reader now?" T.J. tapped his forehead. "Quick. What number am I thinking of?" He put his hand on Ford's head, and the dog rubbed against it. "*Bzzt.* Epic fail, bud. But you're right about the other thing. I'm gonna have to tell her."

The thought made him want to hurl his dinner.

Chapter 19

All in the Family

The week whizzed by, T.J. never seeming to find the perfect time to confess. It was as elusive as that perfect scoring shot. Between his and Natalie's hectic schedules, he only saw her during the morning and afternoon Ford exchanges. Occasionally, he struck upon brilliant excuses to stick around when he picked up Ford—*Hey, how do I get him to fetch me a beer?*

What the week did bring were numerous chances to watch the No Excuses! On Friday afternoon, they let him play in their scrimmage. In a wheelchair. As the game went on, he realized their nefarious purpose. He was their entertainment, for all the occasions he wound up on the floor and they had a grand old time laughing their asses off.

He was a decent baller upright on his two feet—hell, he was a good all-around athlete—but he'd sucked in *this* game. Big-time. Each side had foisted him off on the other because he was that bad. A handicap who unfairly tipped the scales, they'd protested. Yeah, that hurt. But to be fair, he'd spent more time figuring out the damn contraption than actually playing.

But being there had been less about the games and more about hanging with the guys, hearing their stories, and learning what drove them. Every minute he spent with them opened his eyes a little wider, and his respect and awe grew exponentially. With all his parts intact and in working order, T.J. should've felt like the fortunate one, but he didn't. And it had nothing to do with his poor play.

"We *might* tolerate you as long as you bring the beer and women," Mark had chortled.

"Beer, I'll bring, but no way am I sharing my women with you," he'd fired back.

"Ha! Yep, I'd keep them away from us too 'cause we're that awesome, and you're just ... not."

"In your dreams."

One of the other guys had piped up. "Your women *are* in my dreams."

The joke would've been on them if they knew what was really going on—that he was lusting after a woman who was off-limits, and if she ever became fair game, it didn't matter. She was about to find out who he was and drop him like a hot rock. It was totally FUBAR. Which left him charting a Friday night with a mess of Santiago's breakfast burritos and a half-dozen episodes of *Forged in Fire* while the wheelchair-bound badass ballers were making plans with their girls for a *real* night of fun.

Wow. Lighting the social scene on fire, Shanny. Look out, Denver.

Saturday would be no more scintillating because Natalie was fishing with her mom and brother and would dine with them at the end of the day. Another cozy Rockwell scene, only he wasn't part of it this time. The thought gave him a twinge of ... sadness? Nah. Never mind that he'd enjoyed his night with Natalie *way* more than he dared admit and had been angling for a repeat. It was probably good it never came since he seemed unable to coast in neutral.

As he drove home from the game, he envisioned Natalie Amber Eyes in waders, clomping in squishy boots along a riverbank while catching her rod tip in low-hanging tree branches.

I handle worms and don't squeal like a girl. I wouldn't be laughing my chauvinist man ass off if I were you.

His cock perked up, just as it had when she'd rebuked him a week ago. Hell, it had been hard pretty much that entire evening.

Disgusted, he glanced down at himself. "She calls us out and you salute her? Dude. We need to talk." Nonetheless, a chuckle escaped him. He'd laughed, really laughed, during their exchanges, and it had felt so good, like a spring had uncoiled deep inside him and let off enough tension that it didn't feel as though it would snap. He loved that she didn't take his shit personally and that she lobbed it right back at him. He wanted nothing more than to spar with her because it pumped him up. He craved it, bad jokes and all.

Burritos and TV alone weren't going to cut it as Saturday night distractions went. At a red light, he scrolled through his contacts, stopping on the one he was searching for. Staring at the screen for a beat, he debated, his thumb hovering. He hit the green phone icon. Two rings, and his call was answered.

Hours later, a six-pack down and half of a second one gone, T.J. and Nelson were watching two talking heads dissect the LA Kings' play against the Winnipeg Jets during the game's second intermission. They'd been watching sporadically—just enough to pick apart this and that player's game, sparing no one.

"Listen to these two go on and on about how great Ferguson is." T.J.'s voice rose in a falsetto on the last four words. "Christ, they should start their own fan club and get it over with."

Nelson snorted as he deposited a platter of steaming wings glazed in fiery orange-red sauce on the coffee table. He dropped onto the opposite end of the couch, and T.J. slid a few wings onto his plate, then plucked celery sticks dipped in ranch dressing from a cup. This was the third batch Nelson had made. They were the best wings T.J. had ever tasted. Ford, curled up close by, raised his head, looking for all the world as if he'd sniff the scent right out of an invisible trail wafting from the oven.

"Nelson, if I'd known you cook the hell out of wings, I'd have invited you over a long time ago."

Nelson licked his thumb. "My mom's from Buffalo, and she taught me how to make wings the 'right way.' Her words."

"Did she teach you to make anything else?" T.J. tore a strip of meat from the bone and chased it with a swig of beer.

On a nod, Nelson took his own bite and chewed. "A few things. Perfect Italian meatballs, barbecue sauce, and New York-style cheesecake. I make killer brisket, but that I taught myself."

T.J. guffawed. "Shit, will you marry me?"

Nelson shook his head. "Your plumbing's all wrong. I'm saving myself for someone a little softer and sweeter, who smells a hell of a lot better than you do."

"That wouldn't take much." T.J. crunched down on a celery stick. On the TV, the two teams were facing off for the beginning of the third period. "Hey, there's something I've been meaning to ask you."

Nelson wiped his chin, then jerked it at him. "What's up?"

"The night I put the hit on May ..."

Nelson seemed to become hyperfocused.

T.J. pointed a wing at him. "First of all, I don't think I ever thanked you for being the only teammate who didn't ignore me after that went down."

Nelson gave him a shoulder shrug. "Shit happens on the ice."

A recollection of his searing, white-hot anger blasted into T.J.'s brain. Maybe he hadn't been in his right mind. More food for thought some other day.

"Do you remember Monahan talking to me after the hit on Frisky?"

"I remember that he leaned down and said something, but I didn't catch it."

Well, shit.

Nelson took a long pull on his beer. "What I *did* catch was what Coach Rogers said to Joe right before that."

Oh, this had all of T.J.'s attention. "Yeah? What did he say?"

"I don't recall the exact words, but his meaning was clear. He told Monahan to sic you on May. Even promised a bounty to whichever player took May out of the game, and he'd up it if the guy wound up in the hospital."

T.J.'s eyebrows flew to his hairline. "He actually used the word *bounty*? You heard him say that?"

A grave nod. "Yeah. Did Coach Rogers ever pay you?"

"Hell no! I had no idea!" T.J. flung out a hand. His stomach knotted, and suddenly he wasn't hungry anymore. Outraged, shocked, offended were more apt descriptions for his current state of mind as the full force of Nelson's reveal hit T.J. like a slapshot. "I considered it part of my job to lay the guy out, but I never dreamed I was supposed to play Dog the Bounty Hunter. Fuck me! That's not how I play the game."

Did this explain why his teammates had shunned him? They thought he'd wrecked a guy for bonus money?

Nelson raised a skeptical eyebrow. "So no one said anything about a reward for laying May out?"

T.J. shook his head numbly. "Not only that, but Monahan and the coaching staff claim I heard everything wrong. That no one ever gave me an order." Dumbfounded, T.J. stared at the edge of the coffee table without really seeing it.

Nelson licked his fingers. "Hey, you still seeing that pretty blond in San Jose? Isn't she an attorney or something?"

The question caught T.J. off guard. "Julia?"

"Yeah. Julia."

T.J. frowned. "No, she dumped my ass the same night you and I learned about the trade."

The sportscasters were talking about an out-of-his-mind save by a goalie, and Nelson glanced up. "God, I love Kathryn Tappen," he said wistfully.

T.J. followed Nelson's gaze to the beautiful blond MC directing the discussion between the hockey pundits. "You and millions of other guys."

Nelson grunted. "She's the perfect woman. Gorgeous, smart, and she knows her hockey."

Not sure what to make of Nelson's remark—until tonight, T.J. hadn't even been sure which side of the fence the guy swung on—he just stared at the screen, and a long silence stretched between them.

Nelson cleared his throat, eyes still fastened on the screen. "I'm pretty sure Monahan's seeing Julia."

T.J. jerked his head around, mouth swinging open. Nothing came out but a choking, barking noise. Ford raised his head and cocked his ears.

Nelson side-eyed him. "Sorry, Shanny. I thought I saw them together at dinner one night, but I wasn't positive, so I kept it to myself. Then I ran into them at a Warriors game. Figured it wasn't any of my business."

Stunned, mad as fuck, T.J. snapped his mouth closed and blinked. A familiar heartbreak echoed from his past, but it wasn't jealousy that was throttling him.

Julia knew about the trade. Did Money set me up because of Julia? What the hell happened?

"I'm supposed to meet him for drinks next week when the Earthquake's in town." The thought of meeting Monahan made T.J. sick. He picked up his phone, ready to text a cancelation.

"That'll be interesting," Nelson deadpanned.

T.J. did a mental one-eighty and pulled in a long breath. "Looks as though he and I have a few things to discuss."

Making her way to Kevin's new room, Natalie was late because she'd parked on the wrong side of the building. She hadn't seen him in several days, staying away to give him time to think, nor had they revisited the conversation about him getting back with Kristin. Consequently, Natalie felt as though she was swimming upstream in murk, unable to see what lay before her, and her mind spun on a wobbly axis for all the unknowns.

She hated unknowns. She'd have made a lousy emergency room doctor. *I won't treat you if you can't time your injury between the hours of ...* No, she was a precision planner, and she liked that about herself. X plus Y equals Z. No surprises, thank you very much.

Questions corkscrewed in her head. The same ones over and over and over. Would Kevin *ever* recover fully? Where was their relationship headed? Could she take the mood swings, the endless rehab, and God knew what else? With everything he was going through, could she, in good conscience, broach the subject of ending their quasi-relationship? Because that was exactly what she was contemplating. Ending things, regaining her freedom, her equilibrium. And that made her a bad person, a disloyal person. A person who pulled out when things got too tough, just like the gold digger the nurses had described.

Another question bobbed in her limbo soup: Did Kevin *want* her to be part of his new normal?

She'd find out.

Today.

His door was ajar, and she knocked and stuck her head through the gap. Kevin pivoted from the window, eyes wide.

"Sorry I'm late," she huffed, pushing through the door.

"Hey, no problem," he said softly. He seemed to swallow hard. When she leaned in for a kiss, he lightly brushed his lips against hers. "Thanks for coming."

"Of course." She studied him for a beat. "Did you get bad news?" Panic began swelling inside her.

"No, nothing like that." His eyes shifted from side to side, never resting on her.

"What's going on, Kevin?"

An enormous sigh rolled from him. "I have something I need to tell you. Maybe you should sit?"

Natalie's heart sped up, and she crossed her arms, manning her defenses. "Why? Is what you have to say going to knock me on my ass?"

"Natalie, Kris and I, uh … Natalie, I'm so sorry."

Oh shit. Is this it? "About what?"

He dragged his hand over his chin. "You've been there for me every step of the way, and I'm so grateful. God, Natalie, you're beautiful, you're smart, you're sweet, you're fun. You're every guy's fantasy."

Her heart kicked into a higher gear. "I hear a *but* coming."

He dropped his head.

Spit it out. She wasn't inclined to go easy on him, though she didn't know why.

When he leveled his gaze back to hers, his face reflected anguish, and she felt small and mean. Hell, hadn't she just been thinking of breaking up with him? Yeah, her feelings were hurt, but it was her pride that was bruised—her heart, not so much.

"Natalie, only God knows if Humpty Dumpty will ever be put back together again. That's a life sentence, and you deserve someone … someone who's not broken," he said.

She pulled in a deep breath, and her voice got a little quaky. Damn. "I know how hard this has been for you." *And the road ahead won't be any easier.*

"You know I care about you, right? A lot. If it wasn't for Emma … I don't know." He gave her a rueful look. "Natalie, the guy who gets you will have won Powerball. I mean that with all my heart."

She certainly didn't feel like a prize in that moment. "But that guy's not you."

He shook his head. "That guy's not me. I'm so sorry." He spread his arms tentatively.

Oh God. He was giving her the puppy eyes, tugging at her brittle heartstrings. Now she was going to cry. Damn it! She walked into his embrace before he could see her unshed tears.

He enfolded her and laid his cheek on her head. "Take good care of yourself, sweetheart."

"You too," she managed.

A quick, chaste kiss, and she turned and left.

When she settled herself in her car, her phone pinged. A text from Kris.

Please don't hate me.

Natalie let out a shuddering sigh. *I couldn't even if I tried. Good luck to you both.*

The tears that stung her eyes were part-grief, part-hurt, and a boatload of relief.

Suited up, waiting on Nelson, T.J. pulled his phone from his locker and leaned against a wall. He hadn't seen—or talked to—Natalie for a few days. Self-preservation.

T.J.: *Catch anything Saturday?*

A response chimed almost instantly, and his spirits rose.

Natalie: *Skunked. Mom caught the only one.*

T.J.: *If ur not busy this aft, I can stop by and fix ur chairs.*

Natalie: *Today's not good.*

T.J.: *Everything ok?*

Natalie: *Yes. Just some suckiness happening.*

He didn't like the sound of that. Should he push? Did he want to know? He settled on low-key. Sort of. *Do I need to kick someone's ass?*

Natalie: *LOL. No. I can kick my own ass.*

T.J.: *Wow. That's a move I'd like to see.*

Natalie: *You know what I mean.*

T.J.: *Maybe. Hey Ford and I could come cheer u up.*

Natalie: *Promised Paige I'd finish her books by tmw. Up to my eyeballs in QB.*

Spirits tanking, he tapped out a reply. *Queen beeship? Quantum biometrics? Questionable banter?*

Natalie: *LOL. QuickBooks. You?*

T.J.: *Holding up a wall waiting on a friend.*

Natalie: *Where's Ford?*

T.J.: *Home alone. He hasn't called me even though I got him a phone.*

Natalie: *Fat dewclaws.*

T.J.: *???*

Natalie: *Canine version of fat thumbs. He's prolly fine haha.*

"She must be hot."

T.J.'s head snapped up.

Nelson, grinning, gave him a few chin jerks. "Judging by the stupid look on your face."

T.J. flipped Nelson off, then shoved his phone back in his locker. "Screw you."

205

Nelson barked out a laugh. "That lame comeback says it all, dude. She's *definitely* hot. You asking her to the big charity event?"

"Shit. I need a date?"

"You don't *have* to take a date. I never do."

"What's up with that anyway?"

"Holding out for Kathryn Tappen. She'll notice me one of these days. Seriously, though, why not ask *her*?" Nelson pointed at T.J.'s locker.

"Can't."

Nelson's eyebrows crawled up his forehead. "Married?"

"Not exactly. It's complicated."

"With women, it's always complicated. Especially one you've fallen for."

T.J.'s first reaction was to deny and protest. Just as quickly, he realized he'd only play into Nelson's hands and make him look like he'd guessed right. And Nelson was wrong.

Right?

T.J. pushed himself off the wall. "What makes you think I've fallen for her?"

"Your face."

"C'mon, Dr. Phil," T.J. growled. "Quit yammering and let's get in some shooting practice so I can hit you with a few pucks."

Staring at her computer, Natalie let out an enormous sigh. She could usually lose herself in numbers—especially when she was playing forensic detective like she was with Paige's screwed-up books—but she was still processing the breakup, untangling emotions twisted like skeins of yarn that had been attacked by pouncing kittens.

On one hand, she felt a sense of loss even as she smarted from the rejection. But on the other hand, there was relief so profound that Grace Guilt made an appearance with a stern warning: *No displays of happiness allowed.*

But Natalie couldn't deny the gladness. No more fetters from her constant, corkscrewing inner conflict. Though he'd never know, Kevin had liberated her from a jail cell of her conscience's making by calling it off. And whatever his future held, he had a happy ending that touched her heart and made it easier to let the thought of him go: he was back with his family.

She scrolled through her texts from Tyler, unable to stifle a smile. Another touch to her heart. Him asking if she needed cheering up. If he needed to beat someone's ass. For her. His rush to defend had sent warm tingles from her middle to her digits. Yeah, she could take care of herself, but knowing someone besides Drew wanted to have her back ... It turned her insides a little gooey.

Her phone buzzed with a new text, and her heart surged with the thought it was Tyler.

Hey, Natbug. Just wanted you to know I'm thinking about you.

Mom, how do you do that?

Do what?

Know when I'm blue.

What's wrong, sweetie?

Natalie called and told her about Kevin.

"I'm so sorry, honey." And by the inflection in her voice, she totally was, but then her tone changed. "There's a bright spot you may be overlooking, Natbug. Now you're free to pursue that delicious Tyler."

Natalie belted out a laugh. "Mom! First of all, he's a client. Second of all, I think I'm gonna need a little time to get over Kevin dropping my ass."

"Natalie Rose, ladies do not swear."

"Mom. Seriously. How long have you known me? And you're still trying to convince yourself I'm a lady? That ship sailed when I was five."

"A mother's most powerful survival tool is her eternal optimism."

"And you are the eternal optimist, Mom," Natalie said with affection—and hope that she'd inherited that particular gene. "So what are you up to this evening?"

"Drinking wine and watching TV."

"Sex and the City?"

"No, that series is so last month. I'm watching *Outlander*. The wedding episode."

"Ew, Mom. Just ew." Yeah, Drew had had a good point about the brain bleaching.

"The stork did not deliver you, Natalie, no matter how much you want to believe," Mom hmphed. "But Santa Claus does in fact exist."

Laughter rumbled and rose from Natalie's belly. God, the release felt good! When she caught her breath, she swiped at her moist cheeks.

"What's so funny?" her mom asked in her patient "Mom" voice.

"My mom's got a more interesting virtual sex life than I do."

They hung up, and Natalie felt lighter. So light that she tackled her work, finished it, and came up for air just in time to catch part of the wedding episode herself. She fixed herself a wee dram and settled in, envying a fictional woman named Claire for the lengths her equally fictional husband, one lovestruck Jamie Fraser, would go to for her. Talk about your knight in shining armor, er, kilt.

I need one of those. Kilt and shining armor optional.

Chapter 20

Man Plans, and God Laughs

T. J. was about halfway through his four-block walk when his phone vibrated. His team captain, Dave Grimson.

"Yo, Reaper."

"What's up, T.J.?"

"Just on my way to meet my old captain at the Euclid."

"Ah. Excellent choice. Love the poutine. Listen, I was just wondering if you've found a date for the banquet."

Sidestepping a car in the crosswalk, T.J. rummaged around in his brain, unearthing the black-tie charity affair. *Shit.* "No, still working on it." Serena had pressed to be his plus-one, but he'd dodged her so far.

"Maybe I can help you out," Grimson said. "My girlfriend's sister will be in town, and Nicky would like her to attend. Sis doesn't want to be the fifth wheel, so I thought I'd hit up you new guys. You're not seeing anyone, right?"

"Uh, no. Did you ask Nelson?"

Grimson guffawed. "I started with him. I figured Kendra would prefer a good-looking date. Sounds like he might have someone already."

He's going stag.

Grimson continued. "Don't tell Nicky I said so, but Kendra's ... Wow! Smokin' hot. Blond, blue-eyed. Not as hot as Nicky, of course."

"Of course," T.J. said dryly. His mind bounced to whom he truly wanted on his arm at the to-do. A picture of Natalie's long legs in high heels floated through his mind before he shut it down.

"You want me to text you a picture?"

T.J. quickly weighed his options. Go with Serena and fight her off all night. Go stag and fight Serena off all night. Take the sister, which would shield him from Serena *and* make up for blowing off the Chophouse invite. He sighed. "No need. Sure, I'll be her escort."

"Sweet! Thanks. I'll text you her info."

It only hit him he had a date after he'd hung up. Huh. He couldn't say he was excited, but he wasn't exactly dreading it either. Maybe it would be good to get out, have a distraction, keep him out of his own head for a while.

Money's voice cut through his thoughts, and T.J. looked up to see him standing in front of Euclid, a wide grin on his face. T.J. wished he could muster the same sort of enthusiasm for seeing his old teammate.

The place was cranking, and they grabbed a quiet corner table by the bar. T.J. ordered his usual Jameson and beer, and Money ordered a vodka martini—Chopin vodka.

T.J. took a sip of his water while they waited for their drinks. "Didn't know you were a martini drinker."

"Me and Bond, man."

T.J. stifled a snort.

A cute waitress deposited their drinks and hurried off. Money's eyes followed her until she rounded out of sight. "Oh, man. I'd like to tap that."

"Yeah? Thought you were seeing someone." T.J. sipped his whiskey while Money's eyes widened and quickly narrowed again.

"Who told you that?"

T.J. shrugged, belying his rising annoyance. How had this asshole become captain? "Heard a rumor. Is it true?" Jealousy was not in play, but rather an uncharacteristic protectiveness. He owed Julia *something* for putting up with his dickheadedness for nine months.

Monahan lifted the martini glass to his mouth. The drink looked out of place, as though he were a gorilla going pinkie-up with a demitasse of fine china—nothing like the impeccable King of Class that embodied Bond.

"It's casual, and what she doesn't know won't hurt her." He winked, pursed his lips, and slurped from the edge of the glass. "I'm taking a page from Shanstrom's Handbook on Women. Get just close enough to enjoy the benefits."

T.J.'s stomach rolled over. While he hadn't cheated on Julia, the cavalier way he'd treated her was uncomfortably close to what he saw in Monahan. And he didn't like it. He'd never given a fuck before, so why the hell did he give a fuck now? This girlie "getting in touch with yourself" shit had to stop.

Conversation moved into benign terrain—players, the standings, the approaching playoffs—until it migrated toward T.J.'s new team.

"So how's it working out so far, Shanny?"

T.J. fiddled with his phone. "No complaints. Lots of practice, lots of training, and lots of community service. Also working on my goal-scoring."

Money quirked an eyebrow. "Why?"

"Coach thinks I can contribute on the scoreboard."

Money erupted in a laugh. "If I were you, I'd spend more time sharpening my boxing skills. That way next time you hit someone, you can land it in the right spot and not KO the bastard."

A rush of heat flared in T.J.'s gut like the flame from a striking match head. Money's face was split in a leer—which T.J. ached to knock off his mug.

"About that hit, Money. I don't think you came clean."

The grin slid from Monahan's face. "What're you talking about?"

"Your amnesia—the part where you don't remember telling me to hit May right after Coach's assistant said Coach was down with it."

Money's head jerked, and his eyebrows crashed together in a scowl. "Careful, Shanny."

T.J. rose partway and planted his fists wide on the table. Monahan seemed to shrink back. "No, *you* be careful, asshole." T.J. leaned in, but he kept his fury in check and his voice to a low snarl. "I've got witnesses who heard exactly what I heard on that bench, and my attorney's got their names—including yours. If I'm going down, you, Coach Rogers, and the rest of the organization are coming with me."

He never knew until that moment that Monahan had blue eyes. Right now they were swimming in a sea of pink, the contrast bright. T.J. leaned in a little closer, picking up the medicinal smell of the vodka. Julia's words about meeting someone special, about wanting to give it a serious try, raced through his mind. For such a smart woman, she chose her men poorly.

"Julia deserves better than a fucking weasel like you, but she's a big girl and calls her own shots. But I swear to God, you mistreat her, and you're dealing with me." T.J. jabbed a thumb at his own chest. "You got that, dickwad?"

Monahan began regaining his composure. "She *dumped* your ass," he hissed. "You think she's going to appreciate you making threats?"

"Let me be clear. That's no threat. It's a promise."

Licking his lips, Monahan ran his palms over his chest in a nervous gesture. "Look, Shanny, let's leave Julia out of this for now. There's bigger shit at stake here." He leaned in conspiratorially. "About May … I only did what Coach told me to do. I was doing my job."

T.J. laughed mirthlessly. "You're stealing my best lines, Joe, and I have a feeling that whole 'it's my job' shit's gonna turn out just as well for you as it did for me. Especially when everyone hears about the *bounty* Coach put on May's head. The bounty you both conveniently forgot to mention."

Now Monahan looked panicky. "Coach'll make good on the reward, Shanny. He told me to tell you that. He'd just like you to keep it on the QT."

Still leaning toward Monahan, T.J. waved a hand between them. "So he knows about this little reunion?"

"He's the one that suggested it."

This revelation rocked T.J. backward, bringing him fully upright. "You can tell him for me to take his fucking money and shove it where the sun don't shine."

The surrounding tables had stopped buzzing, and all eyes were riveted on them.

T.J. didn't care. He shook his phone. "Thanks for the interview, *Captain.*"

Money's eyes bugged. "Shanstrom, wait. You *recorded* us?"

"Damn straight." While Monahan gawped, T.J. liberated a few bills from his wallet and slapped them on the table. "For my drink."

T.J.'s recording might not have been legal, but he didn't give a flying fuck. *Let the attorneys fight it out.* He was done with this shit-show. Yeah, he'd delivered the punch, but these guys went beyond the pale. Pivoting on his heel, he strode through the restaurant, ignoring the curious patrons. The moment he hit the pavement, he crossed the street and didn't look back.

Despite the weight of Kevin May's injuries, despite the lawsuit pressing down on him, despite the looming admission to Natalie, T.J. felt a lightness in his step as he walked.

He was staking a claim on his life.

One more hurdle to jump.

He pulled in a breath and tapped Natalie's number. "Hey, I need to see you."

Natalie's spidey-senses had been on high alert since Tyler's call. He needed to see her about what? Not about fixing her chairs, surely. Maybe he was canceling his dog-sitting contract. Her stomach bottomed out at the thought. Not only would she be returning a chunk of money, but she wouldn't get to see Ford anymore. Until that moment, she hadn't realized how attached she'd grown to the cross-eyed pup.

Not seeing Ford also meant not seeing Tyler. Her heart wobbled. Apparently, she'd grown attached to Ford's owner too.

When the Schwarzenegger Special pulled up outside, and its well-cut owner and his dog hopped out, she braced herself. Tyler headed up her walkway, his expression broadcasting he wanted to kick someone's ass. Why?

"Guess you're about to find out, Nat," she murmured to herself.

But a funny thing happened when she opened the door. His features softened into a smile that said he was happy to see her. It slid into sadness, which really perplexed her.

"Hey." She stood aside to let them in.

"Hey. Thanks for letting me bust in on you at the last minute."

Ford went straight to the back door, and Tyler followed, opened it, and let him into the sunporch. Such natural, casual actions, yet the air felt charged, electrified, like a storm was about to unleash its fury. Did he feel it too?

Hand still resting on the doorknob, Tyler turned to face her. Even in the muted light, she made out the flash in his hazel eyes as he fixed them on her. The look was blazing, intense. Her skin tingled as though it might catch fire.

Self-conscious, she sidled to the refrigerator. "Can I get you anything?"

"No, I'm good. Thanks."

Arms folding across her chest, she leaned against the fridge. "You said you needed to talk to me?"

"Maybe I *will* have something."

Okaaay. That bad, huh?

She pulled out two beer cans, popped their tops, and handed him one. He studied the label way more intently than it merited. "Echo Brewing? What's Echo?"

She waved her hand vaguely over her head. "A craft brewery about twenty-five miles north."

He took a long sip, the maelstrom still stirring behind his eyes. "So how's your boyfriend?"

Not what she expected, and it threw her. "I'm not sure."

He arched an eyebrow at her.

"I haven't seen him for a few days," she explained. "Nor am I likely to."

Hyperaware of his every move, she gauged how long it took him to register what she'd said. Slowly, deliberately, he set his beer down. The intensity seemed to drop a few notches. "What happened, Natalie?"

She mirrored him, setting down her own untouched drink with a sigh. "Kevin and Kristin patched things up, which means I'm out."

Natalie's words hit T.J. like a bucket of crushed ice—shocking, freezing, melting on contact as the chips slid to the ground. Had he heard her right?

"He broke up with you? After what you sacrificed for him?" Stunned, he stared at her for long beats. A moment ago, he'd been thinking, *This is it, moment of truth,* and he'd been dreading it more than he'd dreaded his dad's beatings.

But now he was blown off course, pissed as hell at Kevin May.

"It's okay. *I'm* okay," she said soothingly. He believed her. "It's the best outcome. For everyone, especially his daughter."

A tremor of hope rippled through him even as reality wrapped its steely arms around it and choked it off.

Do. Not. Go. There.

"I'm happy for them. Truly," she added.

The outer crust of his heart may have cracked a fraction, though he couldn't name all the reasons why. Sympathy. Relief. Sadness. Being knocked on his ass by her incredible kindness.

Was she being stoic, merely hiding the hurt that surely was there? He knew only too well what that did to a person's soul. "What about *you*?" he said.

She gave him a wistful smile. "I'll survive." In that moment, he made up his mind. He wouldn't pile on more shit by telling her who he was. Not yet. *Confession temporarily derailed.* Give her a day to recover. Three. Then he'd tell her. For sure.

Appraising him as if reading his every thought, she crossed her arms over her chest. "So you needed to talk to me about something?"

Shit. What lie to come up with now?

"It's about Ford, isn't it?" she prodded.

Wow. She'd just made it easy. He pulled both hands through his hair and laughed nervously. "You must be psychic. I actually have a favor to ask. There's this … thing I have to go to in a few weeks that could go late, and it might be easier if he stays with you overnight. I'll double your rate."

Natalie wasn't sure why, but Tyler's request—which should have made her breathe a sigh of relief because he *wasn't* firing her—gave her a hard, fast jab instead. "What thing?"

"A black-tie charity event."

The jab dissolved into inexplicable disappointment. She pictured him all dolled up in Armani with a gorgeous woman hanging on his arm. "Um, sure. Just let me know what day, and I'll put it in the schedule."

"Awesome. That helps a lot."

She sagged a little. A porn star. *Going to a charity event. With his voluptuous co-star. A benefit to raise money to restore old X-rated films.*

His voice pulled her from her idiotic thoughts. "Hey, got any of that ham left?" Gone was the hard edge, replaced by his usual playfulness.

"You're hungry?"

"Always." He gave her a mischievous smile that sent her heartbeat into a gallop.

What is wrong with me?

All casual-like, he took another pull of his beer and stepped closer, so close she felt his heat caress her arm and got a whiff of his heady, masculine scent.

"In exchange," his deep timbre resonated dangerously, "I'll overhaul your chairs. Show me one of your favorite fishing spots tomorrow, and I'll fix your leaky bathroom sink *and* your running toilet. Bet you'll see a drop in your water bill."

Her mouth opened, but nothing came out, so she snapped it shut. She'd forgotten about her bathroom—and every other repair the house needed—but *he'd* noticed. And now he wanted to go fishing with her? "Did you just say 'a drop in your water bill'?"

He flashed her a grin. "You caught that."

"Your jokes are as lame as mine."

"Not even close. Do we have a deal or not?"

"Who's bringing the food?"

"You are. Unless you want food poisoning. I'm capable of eating twenty-four-seven, but anything beyond microwaving pizza rolls taxes my culinary acumen." His grin broadened. "So you taking me fishing or what?"

"Be here at five sharp."

With all the fizzing in her blood, she wasn't sure she'd get any sleep tonight.

Chapter 21

Dangerous Curves Ahead

What the hell is wrong with me?

The same question had been on a loop in T.J.'s head since he'd wormed his way into the fishing trip. His logic—if he could call it that—had gone something like, "If she gets to know me, likes me a little, maybe she won't throw shit at me when I tell her the truth."

So here he was, riding in Natalie's Durango as she maneuvered a curvy mountain road. In the back lay Ford, rods, and bags of gear, one of which held waders and boots belonging to her brother that she'd finagled for T.J. He was pretty sure that not having his own fishing gear was an offense worthy of stripping him of his man card. Worse, *she* was behind the wheel—not that she wasn't a good driver, but Jesus, she was putt-putting around a curve as though she drove a go-cart with no go.

He side-eyed her. "Aren't you going kind of slow?"

Not looking at him, she said, "You've got to respect the curve."

His brain short-circuited for an instant and unfortunately came back on line at half-capacity. "I respect the hell out of your curves," he blurted. *Every. Single. One.*

Now she did look at him … as though he were insane.

Dragging his hand across his jaw, mentally backpedaling, he pointed straight ahead. "Keep an eye on the curves ahead."

And I'll keep an eye on yours.

Soon she pulled onto a narrow dirt track, coaxing her POS vehicle over ruts and mud until she reached a sandy crescent, where she parked. Ford had been emitting high-pitched, barky noises from the back, and when T.J. put eyes on him, the dog's whole body wagged. Apparently, Ford was excited they'd arrived.

"We're here!"

Natalie threw open her door and was outside before T.J. could spit out, "Where?"

He followed her out of the car and took in his surroundings. Trees and bare bushes crowded together, looking like a tangle of giant birds' nests. Through their screen, a narrow trail descended a twenty-foot embankment, below which a stream of clear water rippled in somber tones.

Behind him, Natalie pulled gear from the car, cooing to a whimpering Ford. "No, sweet boy, you can't come out for this part. But we'll let you out later and you can splash around all you want, okay?"

Down went a tarp. Next she set up two camp chairs, dropping a bag beside one, and pointed T.J. in its general direction. "C'mon. The fish aren't gonna just hop into our nets," she said.

"So we're keeping them?"

A grin split her face. "Just long enough for pictures, then we'll release 'em."

She wriggled out of her jeans and plopped into a chair. *Hello, standing right here.* But she was all business, oblivious to his ogling. Instead of the racy red panties he itched to get a closer look at, she was wearing the pink thigh-hugging leggings from before.

Glancing over at him, she ran her eyes from his feet to his … crotch? Could she see what was happening behind his zipper?

"You going to put on your waders?" she asked.

Unlike her, he only wore knit boxers under *his* jeans, and at the moment, they were doing little to contain the growing problem brought on by the sight of her in the skintight pants. "Uh …"

She gave him an eye-roll. "Take off your pants and pull the waders on. If you're not wearing long underwear, then leave your jeans on and try not to get them wet."

Bossy. He liked it.

Once dressed, she led him down the path to the water's edge and pointed out a few places fish would be hanging out. He couldn't see it. While he messed with his line, trying for all the world to look like he knew what the hell he was doing, she waded surefooted into the swift current, stepping her way over large rocks.

"Eyes on me," she called. He had absolutely no problem with that. Mesmerized, he watched as she smoothly cast a line that lay perfectly flat on the water, just like he'd seen on the outdoor channels. She was a natural ... and pretty damn sexy, concentrating hard as she worked the line fluidly. Turning, she flashed him a brilliant smile that made his heart stutter. "Did you see how I rolled my wrist when I cast the line?"

Uh, no. He'd been too focused on other parts.

Since when had a girl in waders turned him on? Never. Until right now. More puzzling, that hot fisherwoman stood on a pedestal *he'd* apparently put her on, and he couldn't knock her off. Worse, he'd convinced himself—wink, wink, nudge, nudge—that he was safe from falling for her as long as Kevin May was in the picture. But that safety net was gone, stripped away. Nothing left to keep him on the straight and narrow.

Damn.

A few sloshes brought her to him. "Ready?"

His competitive nature warred with practicality. With a huge puff of air, he said, "I have a confession."

Her eyebrows went up.

"I don't fish." That hurt to admit.

"Your dad never took you fishing as a kid?"

"Nope." Another stab, though of a different sort.

She seemed to appraise him. "No worries. I'll teach you."

And she did. That is, she tried, but the instant he figured out teaching meant a whole lot of hands-on—*her* hands on his hips, his arms, his back—he slowed his learning roll. Admitting to his lack of fishing ability was turning out pretty damn well as she attempted to maneuver his stance.

Competitive juices began flowing, and he got serious, letting her move off as he lost himself. Beauty and serenity enveloped him.

Though he hadn't landed anything more than a stick, he reveled in the hypnotic burble of water, the rhythmic casting, and the liquid gold reflected in the stream as the sun climbed. Understanding settled over him. No wonder this was Natalie's church.

So enthralled was he that he didn't realize how far upstream he'd gone until Natalie's shout skipped across the gurgling river.

"Watch out! It drops off there."

Twisting to locate her, his boot slid off the slimy rock he'd been standing on, and he lost his balance, toppling into the icy water with a splash and a bracing gasp.

She reached his side quickly, setting aside his rod, tugging on his wader straps to help him sit up. Water swirled and lapped around his chest.

"You okay?" she asked.

"It's f-f-fucking freezing!"

She whooped. "That's what happens when you don't pay attention!"

"Smartass," he hissed.

Still laughing, she extended her hand. "Need help?"

He gave her a fake glower. "Oh, *now* she wants to help." Grasping her hand, he gave it a quick yank, and she plopped into the water beside him with a gratifying yelp. "That's what happens when you stop paying attention," he mimicked in a falsetto.

"No fair!" she cried right before she burst into laughter and splashed him.

He splashed back with a guffaw. "We're doing this?"

Laughing, yelling, they exchanged icy splashes and chased off any fish within miles. Cold, soggy, panting, they struggled out of the water and flopped on the tarp.

As she caught her breath, she gave him one of her dazzling smiles. "I sure hope you brought that change of clothes I told you to bring."

"I did. See? I listen." He winked at her.

"Sometimes," she chuffed.

Hoisting himself to his knees, he stripped off the boots, waders, his shirt and undershirt, leaving him to make his way to the car and his bag in nothing but squishy jeans.

With a backward glance, he asked if she needed anything from the car, but she'd gone quiet and stock-still. He rushed back and crouched beside her. "Hey. What's up?"

"N-nothing. Just cold."

"Well then, let's warm you up."

Holy hotness, Batman!

Natalie's ability to speak went missing the moment Tyler bared his torso, exposing defined muscles running the length of his forearms, his biceps, across his powerful shoulders and solid chest. Sweeping up his arm and spilling over his shoulder onto his pec, his tattoo was on full display in stunning, vibrant glory. Rolling her tongue back in her mouth as she fought the urge to gawk, she registered a wing, a clock, a rose, and a heart inked over his own heart, with a scroll beneath it. Flowing script adorned the scroll, though she couldn't make it out without gluing her eyeballs to him more than she already had.

When he dropped beside her, her breath quickened; she marveled she hadn't gone into cardiac arrest. The only thought that came to mind was a Jack London quote: "Show me a man with a tattoo and I'll show you a man with an interesting past."

Middle school English Lit was hastily shoved aside as the man beside her morphed into someone far more interesting than the man he'd been a few minutes ago. She was seeing him in a new light. Mysterious, borderline dangerous, and sinfully hot.

As far as the whole package went, Tyler was a testament to testosterone. A walking advertisement for all that was breathtakingly, beautifully masculine—all that power, all that hardness, all those angles. She was ready to clamber up on a stage and shout out its praises.

Tyler rose, bringing her up with him, giving her a full frontal view. "Sure you're okay?"

She blinked, then nodded. *Omigod.* Did her ovaries just flutter? Maybe they cheered. She wasn't sure because her brainpower was suspended. Yep, Hailey Hormones was driving the bus at the moment.

As he leaned into the car, Tyler's smooth back flexed and rippled before he emerged with his bag and faced her. Unable to stop herself, she flicked her gaze over his sculpted chest to his six-pack, cataloging every muscle along the way. His wet jeans dragged low on his hips, where a tantalizing V-shape carved from a wall of male muscle descended to parts unseen. Parts she could only wonder at. Natalie had pegged him for a guy serious about fitness, but this? Nope. And unlike his ridiculous vehicle, Tyler's physique wasn't Arnold-Mr.-Olympia freakishly bulky. She stifled an image of her hands and mouth skimming the planes of his perfect, chiseled body.

He smirked, the cocky bastard. No doubt he was used to blatant goggling.

Realizing she was licking her lips, she cast her eyes to the side, pretending to be totally engrossed in the river. *Yeah, like that could melt my kneecaps.*

Tyler's deep voice, throaty as a muscle car, rolled over her like hot, sweet fudge. "Yo, Natalie. Shouldn't you get out of those wet clothes?" She swiveled her head to him, thankful *and* disappointed a shirt now covered all that magnificence.

"Um, yeah." *Just let me strip right down. You can hold me to keep me warm.*

As if he knew *exactly* what naughty thoughts were streaking through her mind and lighting her body on fire, his mouth curled up in another smug half-smile, the scar slashing his upper lip like a white stitch. He shook water from his curls.

Wonder what it would feel like hearing him purr in my ear while I sink my fingers in that thick mop?

"I'll take Ford to the river and give you some privacy?" Hazel eyes bounced between her and the dog, whose nose pressed against the back window.

She felt a flush creeping up her neck as she wove her way toward him. *Right. Focus, Nat.* She mustered a wimpy "okay," her brain

223

otherwise stuck on Tyler's body. Under Tyler's body. Over Tyler's body.

"Hey." He lightly tugged on a wet strand of her hair. "How about we grab a cup of coffee to warm you up on the way home?"

Concern replaced amusement in his rugged features. *He thinks I'm in shock.* Truth be told, she was, but it had nothing to do with the river's chill.

T.J. was relieved when Natalie seemed to return to herself. He wasn't sure where she'd gone. At first he thought she was raking him with her eyes—and liking what she saw—but then she'd gone blank, and he'd worried she'd gone hypothermic.

They stopped for coffees to go, and as she sipped her cappuccino, she said, "I'm curious about your tattoo."

"And?"

She seemed to pull in a breath. "Whoever designed it is amazing. It's a beautiful work of art."

"Thanks." He shot her a sheepish look. "That would be me."

Wide brown eyes met his. "*You* designed it?"

"Don't sound so surprised. I have a few hidden talents." *A few I'd like to show you.* Things south of his belt began stirring, and he groaned inwardly.

Don't go there. Picture her covered in dog fur. Nope, not helping.

Add up numbers on license plates. Five, seven, and two equal fifteen. Shit. Fourteen.

Her cheeks pinked, and she appeared flustered. Maybe she'd read his dirty thoughts. "So you're an artist?"

"No. I mean, I like to dabble, but it's only a hobby."

"So what does the tattoo mean?"

He looked through the windshield at the vibrant blue overhead. Not even a hint of a cloud. Had he ever seen a prettier color than a clear Rocky Mountain sky? He turned, studying her profile as she drove.

"It's about perseverance and second chances." Yeah, he'd leave it at that.

She cocked her head. "A second chance at ...?"

"Everything." He sipped his coffee. They were careening toward the edge of Calamity Cliff, and he braced himself for her next question. Oddly, his gut wasn't seizing like it normally did when someone probed.

"What does the scroll say?"

"No excuses." His most recent addition.

"Meaning?"

"Meaning there aren't any do-overs in life. If you're gonna do something, then do it. *Trying* doesn't cut it."

In an awful imitation of Yoda, she growled, "There is no try. Only do." Then she giggled.

His heart might have melted a bit.

They coasted to a stop at a red light. "Good words to live by," she added, popping the lid to her drink, dipping her finger in her cup to capture a dollop of foam, and sliding it oh-so-slowly in her mouth, her tongue licking it off.

All the blood in his system rushed to his pants, and it took a moment for her words to sink in. And when they did, the possibility occurred to him that he'd been making excuses his entire life. Just like he'd been lying to Natalie since he'd met her.

He shoved the thought aside in favor of studying her gorgeous face. The shift wasn't a hard one to make, but it brought a pang of sadness. A woman like her—confident, intelligent, capable, kind, funny, beautiful—wouldn't want a guy like him for more than a roll in the hay. Why should she? And that was *without* knowing his real identity.

After Tyler and Ford left, Natalie fixed herself a cup of cocoa, blanketed the top in a double layer of mini marshmallows, and added a healthy froth of whipped cream for good measure. A little treat after a perfect day on the river. She slid into her now-solid kitchen chair with a sigh.

An image of shirtless Tyler popped into her brain—again—and she told herself to knock it off. Again. No lusting after clients, especially good-paying ones. These speeches might have been all she needed if Lily Logical was in charge. Unfortunately, Lily had gone on hiatus and relinquished control to Hailey Hormones. Hailey was lighting tiki torches and assembly-lining Jell-O shots in preparation for one hell of a party.

Drew's conclusions about Tyler's occupation had seemed ridiculous at first, but the notion had worn a gap of doubt in her mind—to the point she'd added male stripper and escort to the virtual list. Not the type of guy she was into.

On the table beside her were a pad and pen, and she began doodling absentmindedly until she drew a vertical line down the middle, scribbling *Pros* on one side and *Cons* on the other. Under cons, she listed Tyler's negatives: *mysterious; broods; possible porn star, gigolo, stripper, or drug dealer.* She jotted down *MMA fighter*— explaining the scrapes on his face—before finishing the list with *Lives in California?* Tapping the pen against her cheek, she searched for more negative attributes but failed. *I'll come back to that.*

Hailey clamored to list his positives, so Natalie relented and began writing. *Loves dogs; super smart; wicked sense of humor; fun to talk to; gorgeous eyes; gentleman; swoon-worthy body; generous; tall; really hot; handyman.* This list was flowing much easier than the other had. She stopped before she could write another variation of *great body* or *really hot.*

Another sip, and Natalie perused her lopsided lists. Reviewing the cons, she realized she actually found brooding men attractive, so she transferred it to the pros column.

Hailey clapped and let out a *Woot woot!* Natalie was sure that girl was fist pumping.

"This isn't working," she muttered aloud.

The pros column had to be counterbalanced—there was an order, a symmetry to the universe after all—so Natalie got back to work. The hot chocolate had become a sweet white sludge; she savored a few

more sips, revisiting her interactions with Tyler today. This shook a
few more ideas loose, and under cons she added: *guarded; evasive.*

On the bottom of the page, she wrote: *Man harboring a secret.*

She hadn't a clue what that secret might be.

Chapter 22

You Might've Missed a Spot

Over the next few weeks, winter seemed to melt into spring. Between Ford, practices, and the No Excuses! team, T.J. had settled into a deceptively comfortable routine. Deceptive because he hadn't told Natalie. He was buying time to make every repair her house needed. Once she tossed him on his ass, there'd be no more handymanning his way into her life, and he didn't want her left with projects—or so he told himself. Sadly, her list was dwindling. However, she'd mentioned needing a bookcase. He could build that. And from there …

Occasionally, she fed him. They even jogged together once or twice. Always, they talked. Laughed. Bantered. He loved every minute of it.

Mary stopped by once, kissing him on the cheek like he was part of the family, amping up that whole scary-as-shit Rockwellian vibe. Strangely, he didn't mind. As long as "family" didn't involve meeting Brother Drew, T.J. could kid himself he belonged. With Natalie. Trouble was he still walked a knife's edge because she continued firing questions about his *occupation*. And looming fast was the damn charity dinner. If he'd been unenthusiastic about taking Kendra before, his interest had positively shriveled.

A constant tug-of-war seesawed inside him, and while he *knew* being around Natalie was a spectacularly bad idea, he seemed unable to control himself. Not unlike the lack of restraint he'd once displayed with his spiky temper. For the moment, the anger was peacefully slumbering in a quiet, foggy place in his psyche. So there was that.

But he couldn't keep deceiving her. It tore him up inside. The more he was with her, the more tenaciously he clung to the fragile, hopeful thread tying him to her. Each day, he grew more anxious about what life looked like once that string was snipped. Friends weren't exactly in his corner.

"So, thoughts?" Paige asked as he surveyed the interior of the last house on their showing list.

"I like that it's new, but the outside looks like a collection of boxes, and I'd need a microscope to find the yard."

"So I take it this one's out. Do you have a number one?"

"Yeah, the one *you* remodeled. I like the exposed brick, it's next to a park, and the yard's perfect for Ford. Maybe I should have Natalie take a look."

Paige's eyebrows inched up her forehead. "So you two are …"

He grinned at her. "What? She doesn't talk about me at work?" He reminded himself of a thirteen-year-old girl.

Paige crossed her arms on top of her barely there baby bulge and frowned. *Uh-oh.* "When are you going to tell her?"

His hand shot to the back of his neck. Shit, he had to stop doing that. "Haven't found the right time."

"Seriously? How is that even possible? You see her, what, every day?"

He deflected. "So she *does* talk about me at work?"

Paige gave him a disgusted little snort.

"The thing is," he said, "as soon as I tell her, she'll kick my ass to the curb."

"As she should. And the longer you wait, the harder that kick'll be. If you want a shot at staying in her life, you need to tell her. Pronto."

"Wow. Do you ever hold back?" *But she's right.*

"My bluntness has nothing to do with your approaching disaster. Buster, you are skating on ice so thin you can see fish swimming below the surface. I know it's none of my business—"

A cheerless smirk. "But you're making it your business?"

This garnered an exasperated eye-roll. "Look, you're Beck's good friend, *my* friend and client, and *she* works for me. Things could get real messy real fast. I don't want to dance on eggshells around you, and I don't want either of you getting hurt." Her expression shifted to concern, tugging at his chest.

"You're sweet to worry, but it'll be fine." If only he believed it. He felt as though he'd swallowed a brick, and it was lining the bottom of his stomach.

Hours later, he was leaning against Natalie's counter, one ankle crossed over the other, watching her chop vegetables while he told her about Paige's house. He loved watching Natalie. He imagined her in *his* new kitchen as she was now, her shimmering chestnut hair skimming her shoulders, floating around her as though made of silk. Intelligent, golden-brown eyes caught the light, reflecting it like the sun on the river. Her body—supple, graceful, fluid—moved with mesmerizing ease. He could watch her all day, all night, and never grow tired of it—or get enough of it.

Running his eyes over her—for the hundredth time that hour—he pictured exploring the smooth terrain of her body, the dips, the valleys, the curves beckoning from under her tight jeans and her clingy white blouse. She was fully clothed, but she was that much sexier somehow. He felt himself tighten.

Stop it.

He dropped his head and rubbed his neck, trying to think of unpleasant things—the stink of a locker room, bloody teeth on the ice, the pain of a stitched lip—so his cock would calm the hell down and he could move. Didn't help.

Then he thought of telling her.

That did it.

Game over.

Pulling in a breath, he let it back out in a quiet sigh. God, he didn't want to lose this. Lose her. Even if he didn't really have her, he had a piece of her. That piece had stealthily transformed into something more precious than anything he'd ever known, and he hadn't seen it coming.

Focused on how to tell her, where to start, he watched her lips move, barely registering what she was saying. He nodded vaguely, and she kept talking about the stew she was making to take to her mom's.

How would she react when he told her? Different scenarios playing through his mind, he cringed. None of them had him coming out intact in any way, shape, or form.

Abruptly, she stopped what she was doing and studied him, though he couldn't tell what thoughts played through her mind. He wanted desperately to understand her, to know her well enough that he could recognize a look, a twitch of her soft mouth, a graceful quirk of her brow, the way her eyes lit up or dimmed. Regret filled him—he'd never get that chance.

"You okay over there?"

He startled back to the present and plastered on a grin. "Me? Yeah. Absolutely."

She took a step toward him, enveloping him in a dizzying cloud of wildflowers, baking cookies, and fresh sheets—the best of everything he loved. Intoxicating. As his thoughts began melting into mush, he shoved his resolve to a far corner of his mind and let full-throttle desire rise up in its place.

With a soft hip check, she nudged him out of her way. "Someone needs his Jameson, I think." Pulling a bottle from the cabinet beside him, she placed it on the counter with a pirate smile that about caved his knees. "You know where the glasses are."

God, he wanted to kiss her. Just once. Just a taste before he told her everything and she never spoke to him again.

Ford, who'd been curled up on Natalie's doormat, suddenly popped up on all fours and loped over, rubbing against Natalie's legs. She dropped to a knee and grasped his head in her hands. "Such a handsome baby."

This. A slice of heaven T.J. suddenly craved.

Ford's tail wagged so hard his back end swung from side to side. It was a wonder he didn't fall over. The dog gave him a cross-eyed, eat-your-heart-out look that said, "This is better than a juicy T-bone any day," and T.J. couldn't disagree. *About how I'd react if she called me a handsome baby.*

He released a laugh, diffusing his tension while the mutual adoration volleyed between Ford and Natalie. Yep. He was going to miss this, and an ache formed in his heart. "I should just give you the damn dog. He likes you more anyway."

She rose, hovering at the edge of his bubble, causing his nerves to fire. "No, he doesn't."

Why did standing next to her make him feel like a fucking fourteen-year-old? Another nervous laugh escaped him. His brain was disconnecting—probably because all his blood was redirecting elsewhere—and he begged it to stay in play and help him out.

He slid his eyes to a corner of the ceiling and distractedly took note of a dot. Spider? Errant paint dab? When he lowered his gaze, her lidded eyes were focused on his mouth. His cock had been stirring with great interest and now stiffened to full mast, as if to say, "Ready to party here."

When women came on to him, he let them take the lead, acting his part capably enough to get them into the bedroom, where they both wanted to go. An easy role to play, and it saved him having to be the aggressor, which saved him from an ego-spearing shutdown.

Natalie was sending the signals, but he was in over his head here, drowning in desire.

He wanted her more than he'd ever wanted anyone.

A whisper away, her body hadn't moved. "What's going on in your curly-haired head?"

Lust and honor jousted inside him, leaving him tongue-tied. Bound up in knots. All he could do was answer honestly, his voice a rasp. "I have absolutely no idea."

"None?" Her lips formed a very kissable pout.

Just a kiss. Just one. No, you can't. One taste, and you'll crave more, and taking more would make you an even bigger douchebag. She'll hate you ten times over.

She leaned in, her face so close, a hint of warm breath tickled his chin. He could pick out the sweet freckles banded over the bridge of her nose. Her fragrance made him woozy, and her nearness hijacked the air from his lungs. Between their bodies, the atmosphere crackled, charged as though lightning sizzled in the narrowing gap.

Long, thick lashes swept her cheeks when she fluttered them closed. What did she look like when she slept? Or when she—

"Tyler?"

Reason fled. As if acting on their own, his hands rushed to her face, cradling it. Surprise flitted through her eyes. Angling her head, he drew her mouth to his. Her eyelids lowered in surrender, and his lips landed on hers.

He took it slow, pressing gently. She tasted so much sweeter than he'd imagined, and he savored the perfect softness of her lips. Of her skin beneath his thumbs. He cupped her head, sliding his hand in her hair, tangling, tugging. With the other hand, he stroked her neck, her back. She glided her hands under his open flannel shirt, fisting them in his T-shirt. A musical mewl rose from her throat. Her touch traced a sizzling trail that drove off what was left of his mind, and he crushed her to him. As her warm curves molded to his fever-fueled body, so did her mouth mold to his, lips parting with a nudge of his tongue. The kiss deepened, soft and wet, as they explored each other's mouths.

Lushness and heat.

Sucking, nibbling, tongues rolling and caressing like they belonged together. He couldn't tell where his lips ended and hers began. All hot mouth and tongue, they fused together. Urgency ramped up.

Sensations burst and began raging through him, igniting him. Fierce, primal. A visceral force possessed him. He spun them, pressing her against the counter. His hands ran over her back, her waist, her hips, squeezing, recording every curve, marveling at how well she fit him. In turn, her hands roamed all over him, her touch like ghosting handprints that pulsed shivers through his body. Layers separated them, and his mind zeroed in on removing them, of her skin sliding against his, hot and smooth. His cock strained his zipper, aching to let loose its load.

No one, ever, had rocked him like this.

He was lost.

Their lips uncoupled, and he kissed his way over her jaw, his tongue flicking, tasting her as he went. Her mouth was on his neck, moist, warm, thrilling, and when she reached his ear, she whispered, "Tyler." So much promise in that one word.

Tyler.

The sound of his name—*that* name—thumped him rudely, bringing him out of a lust-filled fog. He could never have this. He couldn't have *her*. Didn't deserve to.

Breathless, he pulled back, staring at her as her lids lifted lazily. He stepped back, putting space between them to keep himself from plunging back into the succulent depths of her mouth. Cold rushed in, puckering his skin where their bodies had been cinched together.

"I shouldn't've done that," he stammered.

Breathing unevenly, her expression zoomed from languid lust to embarrassment. "No." She rushed to smooth her hair and blouse. "Momentary lapse of judgment."

Those words hit him like an ice bucket challenge.

She peered at him, her lips rounding into an O. "I meant *my* lapse of judgment, not yours. I shouldn't be kissing clients. I *don't* kiss clients."

"My fault." He was shaking his head like the idiot he was. If he shook hard enough, maybe it would fly off his neck and save him from explaining.

"I really like you." He mentally slapped himself. When was the last time he'd told a girl he *liked* her? Eighth grade? And the last time he'd told a woman he loved her was ten years ago, the same night she'd ripped his heart out and crushed it under her cowboy boot.

Natalie cocked her head. "Um, I like you too?" An awkward pause followed, and he couldn't think what to say next. She saved him by speaking first. "Are we talking *I like you* in a let's-be-BFFs kind of way? Your-playlists-are-so-cool kind of way? Or an I'm-into-you-and-want-to-kiss-you-again kind of way?"

Stuffing his hands in his pockets to prevent them wandering—and to rearrange himself south of his belt—he locked eyes with her and rocked on the balls of his feet. "That last one. Yeah." Pausing a beat, he took stock of his heart slamming against his ribcage. Then hauled in a steadying breath. "And that's a problem."

Her brows scrunched together. Frowny McFrownface. "Because?"

Fuck. Because I'm T.J. Shanstrom.

Her glossy hair reflected the light in shimmering gold. He longed to reach out and tangle his hand in it again, feel its silky texture sift through his fingers.

Checking the urge, he sagged with regret. "Because I'm all kinds of fucked up, Natalie." *And being around you is making me in-fucking-sane.* He raked his fingers through his hair. "I should go."

She blinked rapidly, then seemed to retreat, hooding her eyes. A too-casual smile curved her lips, masking her blush of embarrassment. "Was it that bad?"

It was his turn to blink. "Was *what* that bad?"

"The kiss. I *am* a little rusty."

Stunned, he reared back as if she'd slapped him. "Jesus, no! How can you think that?"

On a chuckle, she waved her hand between them. "You're standing there, I'm over here, and now you're leaving."

Fan-fucking-tastic. Best kiss of my life, and she thinks ... Nice job, asshole. "The truth ..." he stammered.

Dark eyebrows arched expectantly.

A groan rose inside him; he stuffed it back down with a sharp inhale. "Truth is kissing you was un-fucking-believable. But if I do it again, I won't be able to stop myself. And you don't want that." Astonishment shone in her eyes. "You deserve a *good* guy, Natalie, not someone like me, who will only disappoint you."

She stared at him a beat. "Not sure how you could disappoint me, but let's just, um, hit the reset button. Pretend it didn't happen and go back to what we were doing."

Which was me ogling you, fantasizing *about kissing you. Nope, pretty sure pretending isn't going to wipe that kiss from my mind.*

She shot him an impish grin. "C'mon. Don't let me feel awkward all alone here."

His shoulders dropped a few inches in relief, and his lips twitched in a smile. He hadn't realized how tightly wound he'd been.

"Ah. Good. There's one of those elusive smiles," she teased.

"Hey, I'm always smiling," he said feebly.

"Says the guy who broods half the time." She pointed at him and looked sideways as if she were speaking to someone. "Yo! We've got a brooder here!"

He snorted, grateful for the lighter vibe. "You're such a smartass. Who says I brood?"

Her index finger tapped her chin. "Oh, you brood."

"Watch it," he mocked. "I've been getting in touch with my feminine side, and I might burst into tears at any moment."

A loud scoff as she picked up the knife and went back to work. "Is that all men think women do? Cry?"

He shrugged. "No. We're just envious because we don't have a superpower as awesome as yours. Not to shine your apples or anything, but one tear—just one—can bring a man to his knees. It's like kryptonite, and it's damn terrifying."

Eyes on the cutting board, she shook her head and chuckled.

Covertly, he stared at her for a beat while the memory of kissing her flickered through his head. He ached to kiss her again. Over and over.

She sent him a conspiratorial look, as though she knew about his very alert dick still straining his fly. Hell, she *did* know because he'd been grinding it against her only minutes ago.

This goes no further.

Sadness, staggering loneliness swept through him, catching him off guard. He'd been closed off for so long, and this ... this *whatever* flaring between them ... tore him open, laying him bare.

He craved the closeness—he craved *her*—like his lungs craved air, yet self-preservation overpowered him, urging him to sprint for his life.

Women you love leave. All the time. Never forget that.

Preparing to go, he tried to swallow around the puck lodged in his throat.

An hour later, stretched out on his bed, hands clasped behind his head, T.J. stared at Natalie's framed eyes hanging on his bedroom wall. He'd once more skated away from the inevitable, and while it didn't make him proud, he was thankful to catch his breath. Live another day in a world where Natalie Amber Eyes didn't hate him.

Those amber eyes. He hadn't been inspired to create anything since the night he'd painted them. Maybe he'd used up every ounce of talent he had, and he'd never paint again. Had the Jameson inspired him? Nope. He'd had plenty of Jameson before without being roused to that level. Had to be those eyes and the girl they belonged to.

I am so fucked.

Ford hopped up beside him and circled once before settling in, head on T.J.'s shoulder. This time the dog laid a paw on his stomach, as though offering comfort.

T.J. stroked his head and ears while the dog nudged his palm. "Yeah, you get it. She'll never want to see us again when I tell her the truth." *How did I get myself into this mess? An overdose of stupidity and a stroke of lunacy.* "At least I got you out of the deal, and I can't believe I'm saying this, but I wouldn't change that for the world, buddy. Nope, I wouldn't."

The dog's adoring, cross-eyed stare fastened on him. "What if I were just some random guy? I'd call right now and ask her to dinner, hold my breath, and pray she'd say yes. Then I'd take her someplace fancy with white linen tablecloths and candles and listen to her bad jokes." *Just to hear her voice.*

He waggled his eyebrows. "After that, I'd take her home and take my time kissing her, undressing her—"

Ford whined.

"No, dude, you wouldn't be there."

T.J. looked into wise copper eyes that seemed to telegraph sympathy. He rubbed the dog's silky ear. "Yeah, you're right. Our days are numbered. Why torture myself?"

A rush of something bitter and unbidden crammed his throat, and he couldn't clear it. Just like he couldn't pry the feel of Natalie's lips and body against his from his mind. How could something that felt so damn right be so damn wrong?

Chapter 23

Of Course He's a Great Kisser; He's a Porn Star

Glass of Crown Royal in hand, Natalie stared at her dog clock. Back and forth its tail went, wagging in time with its ticking and tocking, doing nothing to regulate her own rhythm. It was after midnight, and she was a little confused and a whole lot of hot-and-bothered as she mentally hit the replay button on Tyler's heart-stopping kiss.

Whoa, mama! It had done things to her insides, lighting up places she'd forgotten—or didn't know—she had. *Especially* when he'd cranked up the burners.

Definitely adding kissing to the pros column.

He'd caught her by surprise when he first kissed her, though admittedly she'd been hoping for it all along. What he'd initiated began slowly, softly. But then he'd taken charge and transformed it into raw need and hunger, possessing her mouth, his hands on her as though he was pitching a stake in her marked "mine." As though a dam of pent-up desire had just busted loose inside him.

God help her, she'd loved it. She longed to get swept away in the flood.

He'd stirred deep, primal urges inside her. And there was no mistaking how it affected *him*. His arousal, thick and hard, had nestled between them when he'd pinned her against the counter.

She hadn't guessed at the tornado of passion spinning inside him. He was good at concealing it. But beneath that restrained demeanor and all those glorious muscles, Tyler Johnson harbored a scorching, slow-burning blaze fueled by carefully leashed power she wanted *unleashed*. On her.

Before the kiss, his eyes had been brimming with heat, roaming over her like he wanted to devour her. And when he kissed her, he *had* practically devoured her—in the very best of ways. But then it came to a screeching stop, slamming into … the Great Wall of Tyler.

Had she misread the signals?

Yeah, no, because he'd been right there with her, riding a tidal wave of lust. But something had reeled him back, shut him down.

Beneath his hunkiness and kissing skills, Tyler Johnson had secrets he kept well-guarded alongside his heart.

Demons and danger lurked in his penetrating golden-green eyes. He was the black-leather biker, cigarette dangling from his full lips, that every mom warned her daughter about—the guy with an edge. Lethal. Natalie had never contemplated falling for *dangerous* or *fucked up*. Until now.

Throw caution to the wind, Hailey Hormones begged. Girl had a point because, good Lord, Natalie's knees had yet to stop quivering. She could have locked lips with Tyler for days, foregoing food and water, and died in his arms. Her family would've found her emaciated body entwined with his, lips forged together.

Another sip of Crown slid down smoothly. She propped bare feet on her kitchen table, smiling at his unexpected admission. *I like you.*

Yeah, the guy carried baggage so weighty he couldn't talk about it, but it lent him a boyish vulnerability that tugged at her. Like a rescue dog. The whole package was growing unnervingly irresistible. Intrigue compelled her to chip away at his thick crust, searching out his chinks. Therein lay a paradox. Natalie wasn't about to "fix" a man, thank you very much, even if he was hotness personified. After all, who *was* Tyler Johnson?

Porn star.

Being a dynamite kisser was probably a requirement for *that* job. Wait. Did they bother kissing in porn flicks? *Never mind.*

She'd googled "Tyler Johnson" and come up with an NBA player, an actor, and a pro hockey player only an inch taller than she was. None of them looked a thing like her Tyler Johnson.

Her?

Spidey-senses tingled, urging her to steer clear, while Drew sounded off in her head. But something about Tyler made her brighten like a warehouse full of ignited Roman candles when he was around, turning her into a mass of giggles and shivers. No one had ever affected her the way he did, and it was addicting. Just like that kiss.

So when he texted her at midnight, inviting her to lunch day after next, she didn't hesitate.

Yes.

Anticipation made her tummy hop as though a net of ping-pong balls had just been released inside. No sleep for her tonight.

Casey's Bistro & Pub in Stapleton was a casual, comfortable restaurant humming with diners enmeshed in conversation. Bringing Natalie here was a massive gamble, but T.J. had never been here, no one knew him, and he banked on her suppressing her reaction in public. Yeah, probably another seriously bad idea that he'd add to the mountain of other bad ideas.

They sat in a quiet booth. She was opposite him, talking animatedly about her growing role at Paige's. He was happy for her, glad he'd had a hand in it.

Chin cupped in his palm, he studied everything about her as she enthused. Blood pounding in his ears, his stomach rolling like a log on a river, he stopped registering what she said. His attention was riveted on her beautiful, expressive face. He drank her in, memorizing everything about her. God, he would miss looking at her.

As she talked, she tilted her head from side to side, and her gleaming hair swung like a curtain ruffling in the breeze. Her bright eyes were deep gold today, the flecks of copper and brown so easy to pick out. He spied a shade he hadn't noticed before—was that russet?—committing the color to memory.

The light pink nubby sweater she wore under a matching pink jacket set off the bronze tone of her flawlessly smooth skin. And though he couldn't see them at the moment, blue skinny jeans—highlighting her very fine assets—tucked into brown ankle boots. She'd about knocked the breath from his lungs when she'd bounded out of the house and into his H1.

Insides wound tighter than a garage door torsion spring, a familiar thought sparked. Maybe he could put this off for another day, another week, after the season was over.

Man the hell up!

They'd placed drink orders, and a server approached with a tray holding two pints of beer. *Thank God.* He had cotton mouth, and he felt as though something clawed his dry throat. The tray slid onto the table, and a woman set their glasses in front of them. In his periphery, she went still.

"T.J.?"

He snapped his eyes up, the hair along his nape standing on end.

His blood froze as he stared into Gillian's blue eyes. She looked as shocked as he felt.

Oh shit, oh shit, oh shit!

A white-toothed smile split her face. "It *is* you!" she squealed, making him flinch. "I tried calling you as soon as I heard the Earthquake traded you to Colorado, but you changed your number. Oh my God, and here you are at my table!"

Before he could shift his gaze to Natalie, Gillian blocked his view by leaning over, wrapping her arms around him, and pecking him on the lips. A familiar, cloying scent assaulted his senses.

"I've missed you," she breathed against his ear, then pulled back—just enough to grin at him. "How've you been, you sexy man?"

He darted his head, glimpsing Natalie's confused expression. As he was opening his mouth to beg her to stay, a meaty hand pressed down on his shoulder, and he nearly launched from his seat.

"T.J. Shanstrom, right?" *Fuck!* A man with his hand held out crowded Natalie, pinning her in the booth. "Jesus, man, it's great to meet you. Diehard Earthquake fan since I was a kid, and a T.J. Shanstrom fan since you entered the NHL. And now you're a Blizzard!"

T.J. lurched upward and automatically shook the man's hand, the motion echoing his frenetic pulse. He tried to press himself out of the booth, tried to glimpse Natalie's face, catching only a flash of pink.

The man continued pumping T.J.'s hand, obstructing his exit. "Sorry about your suspension, man. I really miss seeing you play." Now a rumbling crowd began gathering around their booth.

"Uh, thanks." T.J. reclaimed his hand, then darted his gaze to Natalie.

She was still seated, and a series of expressions flitted across her face like flash cards in odd combinations. Shaking head. Gaping mouth. Crashing brows. Sparking eyes. Cheeks drained of color. Hurt pinching the corners of her mouth. It reminded him of old movies where the human morphed into a monster in stuttering stages.

People pressed inward, trapping him and Natalie in the booth. He barely registered they were fans *happy* to meet him because, right now, it didn't matter. Only *she* did.

The guy was patting his shoulder now, announcing his presence to the diners, while Gillian yakked at him and took pictures with her phone.

Natalie gathered coat and purse in a flurry and rolled sideways, somehow escaping the booth. T.J. used every bit of his size to power his way through the group. "Hey, man. Sorry. Gotta go." He plucked his wallet from his back pocket, fished out a few bills, and threw them on the table, thanking everyone for their support as he turned and loped after Natalie.

In the background, Gillian shouted, "Call me!"

Outside the pub, hand in his hair and a string of curse words on his tongue, he scanned the sidewalk until he locked on Natalie's slender frame scurrying away at warp factor nine.

"Natalie!"

Without slowing, she flew him the bird over her shoulder. He took a few strides, stopped, and strode again. His hesitant steps mirrored his

242

faltering confidence. *Run after her? Leave her alone?* Half-formed decisions ping-ponging wildly, he went after her a step shy of a sprint.

"Natalie, wait! Please!"

She stopped suddenly and pivoted. Color had returned to her face—lots of it—and her murderous eyes sliced into him. But moisture rimmed her lower lashes, and her bottom lip wobbled.

It gutted him.

Don't cry, don't cry, don't cry!

He held up his hands in surrender. "Natalie, I—"

She stabbed her finger in his general direction, growling, "Don't you *dare* come closer!" Then she swiped at her cheeks and squared up her shoulders. A monolith of fury. "*Are* you T.J. Shanstrom?"

He dropped his head back and yelled, "Fuck!" at the sky, hoping it would swallow him whole, but the sky didn't give a shit. So he looked into the heat of her flaming eyes and nodded dejectedly. "Yes."

It was hard to believe her eyes could blaze any brighter, but they flashed as though gas had been added to their flame. "What the hell!" she yelped and vaulted at him, open palm striking his chest, rocking him backward. "You used me! You've been playing me this whole fucking time!"

He threw his arms wide, making it easier for her to beat her fists against him, if that's what she wanted. When he spoke, his voice was oddly calm. "I didn't know who you were when I first met you. I swear. And I wanted to tell you. God, so many times. Weeks ago. The other night. Today. That's what I was trying to do bef—"

"Before your girlfriend in there started sucking your face? Why should I listen to *anything* that comes out of your mouth?"

"She's not my girlfriend. I haven't seen her in years. But she's not the point here."

Natalie's chest was rising and falling quickly, her petite nostrils flaring with each breath. Arms cinched over her chest, she gritted out, "The *point* is you're not who you led me to believe you are. You used me, used your *dog*! You're a despicable, lying sack of shit."

She looked at him as though he made her sick to her stomach.

His heavy heart thudded in his chest. "You're right. I'm a lying sack, and I led you to believe I was someone else."

"So you could pump me for information about Kevin. How could you *do* that?" Her voice quaked, and he couldn't tell if it was from anger or hurt.

"I know I have *no right* to ask you to believe me, but I'm begging you to believe I did *not* use you. This was never about getting information. I asked about Kevin because I wanted to know. Because I give a shit."

He raked a hand through his hair and over his jaw. Her eyes bored into him with naked hatred, and he flinched inside.

"I should've told you sooner," he ventured. "No question. I meant to. Wanted to. I never intended for it to go this far. To go *anywhere*. But I got to know you, and you were so ... And I ... Jesus, I felt so bad about what I did. I just wanted to help—"

"Help?" she screeched, lending her a slightly hysterical tone. "You selfish, deceitful, conceited ... This was all a big game to you, wasn't it? You make me sick." She pivoted, and he gripped her upper arm.

"Natalie, please."

She glanced down at his hand, and he released her. Her voice was like cold steel knifing into him. "I want nothing to do with you."

He swallowed hard. "I made a colossal mistake. I should've told you right away."

People ambled past, shooting them curious glances. A bald guy took up station ten feet away, legs spread, arms over his chest, giving him the stink-eye like he was some goddamn bodyguard.

T.J. dropped his voice, though his plea shot through it. "I never intended it to come to this. Ever."

Natalie sidestepped him, hissing, "Just get the hell away from me."

Resigned, he said, "I will. As soon as I get my dog back." Taking Ford to her house before lunch was the *only* stroke of genius he'd had the entire time he'd known her. She'd have to face him one last time to hand Ford over.

A lone, fragile teardrop glistened, then spilled down her cheek. Instinctively, he caught it on his finger. She jerked backward, and the bodyguard took a step forward. T.J. clenched his fist and fired him a warning glare.

"I'm fine," Natalie snapped at Baldie, and he eased, a part-skeptical, part-confused look on his face.

T.J. lifted his chin toward his Hummer. "C'mon. I'll take you home, get Ford, and we'll get out of your life."

She fisted her hands on her hips. "I'll walk."

"Don't be ridiculous," he said, idiot that he was. "You need a ride, and I need to get my dog."

He reached for her arm again, but she wrenched it away. "I'll Uber."

A few new guys now flanked Baldie. *Just what we need to add to this shit-show.* Headlines blasted in his brain: *T.J. Shanstrom tries to tap Kevin May's GF, gets in brawl in restaurant parking lot.*

Fucking awesome PR. Not that he cared about the PR.

"I still have to pick up Ford. No point in you paying for a ride when I'm going to the same place," he urged softly.

She didn't move, her expression frozen in a stubborn frown, her eyes glinting with anger. And she was absolutely gorgeous. His heart squeezed.

"No talking," she bit out.

Sweet relief spread through his limbs like warm shots of whiskey, and he gave her a nod.

He had ten minutes.

Chapter 24

Open Kimono

Natalie stared out the Hummer's window without seeing a damn thing, her emotions snapping from shock to outrage to hurt to humiliation on a loop. She felt like an inflatable nylon tube person, whipping and cracking in the wind. Just like "Tyler" whipped from one identity to another.

Tyler, the devoted dog owner, aka *T.J.*, the heartless hitman.

He'd totally played her. How had she let that happen? *Because con artists are good at fooling people.* He'd even stooped to blatant puppy eyes since the shocking, mortifying spectacle at the restaurant.

He made her sick.

She glared at him as realization continued to bloom. Her temper spiraled upward. "T.J. is short for Tyler Johnson." A statement, not a question.

Behind the steering wheel, Tyler-T.J. nodded his head slowly—about as slowly as he was driving. Why was the man so damn pokey?

"You must be a Gemini." *Crazy-ass Geminis and their split personalities.* Not that she believed in astrology.

He darted her a bewildered look.

"So what do I call you?" She tucked her arms across her chest. "Besides *asshole*," she clarified. "Do you prefer T.J.? Tyler? What?"

A sidelong glance. "I answer to them all, but I prefer T.J. Though I gotta admit, Tyler sounds nice when *you* say it."

"Asshole it is," Natalie grumbled and looked away. "I have questions."

He nodded in her peripheral. "I'm open kimono here."

An image of Tyler-T.J. wearing nothing but that full-wattage, deadly smile playing on his rugged features popped into her brain. To her consternation, tingles raced along her arms, and other parts followed. *Damn it, Hailey!*

She quickly changed her mind's channel. "Start at the beginning. If you weren't playing enemy spy, then why the hell did you insinuate yourself into my life?"

He rubbed the back of his head, then settled his hand back on the steering wheel. "The truth?"

"That would be refreshing."

"When I first saw you in the hospital parking lot, when Meathead escaped ... You were this—you took my breath away." He shifted as though nervous, his gaze focused forward. "Literally," he added in that rumbly voice of his. "It wasn't until that day in the cafeteria that I figured out who you were. I didn't know what to say. And then I saw your car, and I thought you could use some financial shoring up. I wanted to help. I didn't think you'd accept money outright, but if I became your client ... As time went on, it got harder to confess. I dreaded seeing the look you're giving me right now. So I put it off." He paused to expel a sigh, turning his eyes to her. "I had no right, Nat, but I fell for you. Hard. Harder than I've fallen for anyone."

She hadn't anticipated *this* answer, and a surprising, traitorous, zing sizzled through her. His intense moss-green eyes reminded her of tourmalines, and they gleamed as though they'd just been buffed by a jeweler's cloth. *Focus, Nat.* Breaking eye contact when he looked at the road helped Natalie catch her breath.

"So you got Ford just so you could be a dog-sitting client? Then paid months up-front for seven-day-a-week service?" *Who does that?*

"I did."

Stilted silence stretched between them as thoughts ricocheted in her head. She chased them as she fumed, trying to sort them, but it was like trying to catch a trout with her bare hands.

"Unbelievable," she grumbled, looking away, unsure how to process the contradictions bombarding her. He was a cheat. Fraud, phony, fake. Thug. The man had *adopted a dog* to become a client. And she'd been dazzled by that stack of cash. Of course he could afford it because he was a mega-million-dollar-a-year hockey player!

Realization scoured the goo from her brain cells. "Oh my God, your job! It all makes sense now." She erupted in an off-kilter laugh bordering on hysteria. Yep, she was losing it.

Not a porn star or a drug dealer. "You overpaid for dog-sitting to make up for ... I am *not* paying you back."

"I don't want you to."

More silence. Tyler-T.J.'s voice knifed through the quiet. "You know what? It might have started as BS, but I have no regrets because I love that stupid dog ... and then there's you."

"Save it." *Don't you dare say something nice and muddle my mad right now.* "So why *did* you try to kill Kevin?"

His shoulders seemed to shudder. "Ice is fast. If a player overthinks, he screws up. It can be the difference maker in a game. So he goes on instinct. Sometimes his instinct is wrong, and by the time he figures that out, it's too late."

Kevin had told her basically the same thing. *Heat of the battle,* he'd called it.

"And for the record," Tyler-T.J. added, "I wasn't out to *kill* him. Not that it matters now."

Her emotional yo-yo was spinning on a tight axis, up and down, yanked along on a cord she wasn't controlling. She opened her mouth to let loose a string of words she hadn't yet cobbled together. "Hmph." Yep, her intelligent comeback.

She darted her eyes out the window, replaying the awful hit in her head. T.J. punching Kevin. Kevin dropping to the ice. Players piling on. A stark-white jersey with "eight" and "four" turtling over Kevin.

"Natalie?" Tyler's sad eyes were back on her.

Locking them out, she pulled in a breath. "So you felt guilty and decided to play the knight coming to my rescue," she huffed, infusing her tone with as much indignation as possible. "I can take care of myself. Physically *and* financially."

A slow bob of his head. "I know that. I didn't when I met you." He cocked an eyebrow her way. "You're independent, resourceful. You don't need anyone—especially a dumbass like me—helping you."

On the verge of agreeing—primarily with the dumbass part—a mean little poke stopped her. He was quick to put himself down, and she had neither the desire nor the energy to jump aboard his self-pity train.

A moment of silence later, he slowed at a yellow light before it turned red. She felt his eyes lasering into her. "Natalie, right or wrong, I wanted an excuse to be around you. Plain and simple. I couldn't get you out of my mind."

Had anyone ever said anything like that to her before? And meant it? She was temporarily stunned. Disarmed. Word-impaired.

Cody had charmed her with a slick silver tongue, but he'd been smoke and mirrors. A hamburger without the meat. No substance.

She softened for a moment, then stopped herself. Deception couldn't be forgiven. When trust was broken, it was irreparable. Black and white.

Steely resolve narrowed her eyes. "Let me see if I have this straight. You see a woman you're attracted to—who happens to be dating a guy you put in the hospital—and act like you're *rescuing* her while pretending to be someone you're not. Is *that* your MO?" Outrage surged again.

"It's not my *MO*. I don't have an MO," he said so quietly she barely heard him.

Her brain was short-circuiting, flashing *disengage* in glaring neon. She needed space to put order to the jumble inside her. But instead, she ran headlong into the storm.

"Is this why your last girlfriend dumped you? She found out you were a liar?"

He heaved a strangled breath and shot her a pained look that sent a pang of guilt through her. She ignored it.

"No. She wanted serious, and I'm not a picket-fence, family-dinner kinda guy."

His words echoed in her ears: *It was a casual thing.* Genuinely curious, Natalie tossed out, "Why?"

Finger tapping a rhythm on the steering wheel, his eyes fastened on something beyond the windshield. Had he heard her?

"Too cold?" she prodded. "Your kimono's closed now?"

She thought he whispered, "Smartass."

"I tried once and got burned. I don't want to get that close again."

The light turned green, but he didn't move. Rankled by what, she wasn't sure, she motioned toward the windshield. "Can we go already?"

Horns blared behind them. His jaw firmed, a muscle twitching. He rolled into the intersection at a glacial pace. Smothering silence blanketed them as he puttered along busy streets. He had picked the *worst* route. It would take them twice as long to get home, and all she could do was stew in her juices until she could escape him and think straight.

The list of pros and cons floated through her consciousness, and she nearly laughed aloud. She had plenty for the cons column now. Mentally, she crumpled the list and chucked it into the trash.

When he turned onto her street, she spotted Drew's Subaru, and her lungs seized.

Shit! Might as well get it over with in one bloody go.

She sprang from the car before Tyler-T.J. could open her door. He followed her through the front door, muttering about getting Ford and getting out of her life.

Drew looked up from a big-ass sandwich he was wrestling in both hands, full mouth chomping, mayonnaise leaking from one corner of his mouth. His eyes darted over her shoulder and widened.

"Nice of you to help yourself to my food *again*, Bro." She dropped her purse and jabbed a thumb over her shoulder. "Meet Hummer Man, Tyler 'T.J.' Shanstrom. Don't kill him *in* the house, please. I don't want blood everywhere."

Fuck me and my horse, can this get any worse?

When T.J.'s eyes first landed on Drew, the question shooting through his mind had been, "Who the hell's the douchebag looking so comfortable in Natalie's kitchen?" Cue up jealousy. Yep, the old green monster hadn't visited in ages, but he was alive and well and ready to throw his weight around. T.J. was oddly relieved that the guy facing him was Natalie's big brother.

Drew rose deliberately, sizing T.J. up as he chewed his sandwich. Tall, though not as tall as T.J., he had a lean, powerful build and his sister's coloring—except his dark brown eyes, which held none of Natalie's golden-copper light.

Inwardly, T.J. applauded Drew's obvious hostility; her brother *should* want to pound him, especially if he was snapping the puzzle pieces of T.J.'s lie together. Hopefully, T.J. wasn't about to find out how strong Drew was. No question he could take him, but it would give Natalie more reason to hate his ass, and she had plenty of ammo stockpiled as it was.

T.J. gave Drew the "Hey, how's it going, we're all cool here" man-nod. His gaze boring into T.J., Drew swallowed. "Dafuck, Nat?"

Yep, that'd be my reaction too.

Natalie erupted in laughter, yanking their attention her way. Drew shot her a perplexed look.

"Drew, the good news is he's not a porn star or a drug dealer." After a few hitching breaths and a swipe at her cheeks, she burst out laughing all over again.

Borrowing from Drew, *Dafuck?* "Uh, excuse me?"

She flapped a hand at him. "Drew … We thought …" More hysterical laughter.

Drew gave her an eye-roll. "Breathe, Nat. Use your words." At least he wasn't fixated on T.J.—for now.

"Oh my God!" She whooshed out a few breaths. "I'm better now." Her expression told a different story; she looked as though she might dissolve into hysterics again.

Another shuddering breath, and she folded her arms across her chest. "I couldn't figure out what you did for a living. And D-D-Drew …" A pause while her shoulders shook. "Drew thought you were either a porn star or a drug dealer."

T.J.'s thoughts swam. Was this funny? *No clue.* "Why?"

"Oh God, this is hilarious!" Her voice cracked. Seeming to recover, she began counting off on her fingers. "One, your badass Hummer. Two, you're in really good shape."

He checked his grin—he liked that she'd noticed. Maybe this *was* funny.

"Three, you know celebrities like Beckett Miller."

So do you.

"And finally," she said with a note of triumph, "you're in the entertainment industry. Add them up, and presto! A porn star." She started howling again.

"Uh, I've been called a lot of things—"

"Yeah, I'll bet," Drew snorted, joining the party.

"Oh, and Drew," she continued, darting her eyes to the ceiling, "I added MMA fighter, male escort, and stripper to the list."

"What?" T.J. and Drew chorused. The random occupations ping-ponged through T.J.'s brain. He put them aside for later analysis.

Drew didn't seem amused. "Nat, will you tell me what the hell is *actually* going on?"

She pulled in a steadying breath. "As soon as Tyler-T.J. here gets his dog and leaves."

"So you *don't* want me to beat his ass?" Was that a hint of relief in Drew's voice?

Natalie shook her head. "No, unless he tries to weasel his way back into my life again."

Hello, standing right *here*, T.J. wanted to say but motioned toward the sunporch instead, silently signaling he was getting Ford. She trailed him, and his heart lightened with hope—only to crash down when she bagged up and handed him Ford's toys, bowl, and food.

In a final act of ejecting T.J. from her life, she kneeled in front of the dog and ruffled his neck. "I'm sorry, buddy." Ford licked her chin, and T.J. thought she sniffled. "You can't come here anymore. I'm going to miss you." She threw her arms around the dog's neck. Ford seemed to smile smugly, as if to say, "She's hugging on *me*, not you."

Yeah, you don't get it, dumbass. We're both out.

She rose, walked T.J. to the door, and opened it, giving him a look that lacerated him. "Everything you've done or said is bullshit." Her voice was laden with ice, scratching at him like nails on a chalkboard.

Defeated, dejected, he cast her a regretful glance. "Not everything, Natalie."

She closed the door in his face without another word.

Chapter 25

No Excuses

Paige scooped up a clipboard and bag. "We'll go in my truck, Natalie," she sang, "But first I need to drop something off for Beck."

"Sure." Natalie was excited to see the progress on Paige's latest project. She'd visited it a few weeks ago, but now tile was laid and cabinets set. It was field trips like this that made her love working for Paige—and kept her mind off one maddening hockey player she hadn't communicated with since their falling-out a week prior. Oh, he'd been bugging her, the pest. She'd replied with a single—and final—text telling him she was *not* keeping Ford while he attended his charity whatever. *End of story.* Except she missed that damn dog. And a part of her *might* have missed that guy who made her laugh and who fixed everything, especially when her fence blew down during a storm, damn it.

Paige had been chatting away, and Natalie didn't notice where they were until the Blizzard practice arena loomed. Her boss slid into a parking spot behind the building, snatched the bag from the back, and hopped out. "Coming?"

"Wait. Beckett's *here*?"

"Yeah. He's helping some disabled guys while he's home for a few days. Let's go."

"Um, okay." Natalie darted her eyes around the parking lot, hunting for a black H1. To her relief, she only recognized Beckett's white

Mercedes-Maybach S 560, which was parked beside a brand new blue Audi A8.

She hustled to keep up as Paige scurried through the entrance to one of the arena's three rinks. When Paige reached the glass, she waved frantically, her profile glowing with a Beckett beam. It didn't take long before her hulking husband was tapping at the glass separating them, his broad smile mirroring hers.

"How's my baby?" Natalie heard him say through the barrier.

Oh, puh-leeze! He probably meant the baby in Paige's belly, but still! They'd just left each other an hour ago. *Ugh.*

Paige shook the bag. "Brought you something."

When his brows furrowed in question, she continued, "You left your hoodie at home." His puzzled look deepened, and Paige shot Natalie a guilty look over her shoulder.

Paige was obviously up to *something,* and Natalie's spidey-senses went on high alert. Scanning the ice, she took in men strapped to sleds, shortened sticks in their gloved hands. They seemed to be scrimmaging. Riveted by the play, she blindly trailed Paige, who headed toward a rink door. The players were chasing a puck, checking one another, popping back up, whooping, hollering. Having the time of their lives.

Only one person stood upright among them, holding a regulation stick as he smoothly skated into a small fracas. Electricity bolted through her at the sight of his familiar form. Long, thick legs in blue jeans, a T-shirt that hugged chiseled shoulders and chest, backward ball cap keeping a lid on his dark, wayward curls.

Tyler Johnson Shanstrom.

With a face-splitting grin that plucked her reluctant heartstrings, Tyler tapped one of the players. "Mark! Two minutes!"

The guy named Mark struck an astonished look. "For what? That was a clean hit!"

"It was a tackle. This is hockey, not football."

Tyler pointed toward the side of the rink where Natalie now hid in Beckett's shadow. Beckett had opened the door and was hugging on his wife, the two lovebirds oblivious to Natalie's presence. Natalie rocked on her feet, impatient to flee before Tyler spotted her.

Beckett suddenly stepped aside and looked down at Mark, who'd made his way over and had eyes on Paige. "Hey, cutie. Ready to dump Sasquatch for a real man?"

Paige chortled. "What would your wife say?"

"Carla would be the first to agree I'm a real man." His eyes lit on Natalie. "Oh hey! You the stripper Miller hired for after the game?" Mark somehow winked at Paige and Natalie simultaneously. To Beckett, he said, "Good job! This one's really hot! Unlike that skank you—"

Beckett gave him a none-too-gentle shove, toppling him sideways. "I didn't hire a stripper," he said to Paige.

She patted his cheek. "I know. I'd have killed you."

"Watch your mouth," Beckett said to Mark as he jerked his head toward Natalie. "This lady happens to be Shanny's, uh—" He darted help-me-out eyes to Paige, who shook her head. "Dog-sitter," he added.

Mark's eyes lit up. "*You're* Natalie? Oh wow! Shanny said you were gorgeous, but if the guys had known *how* gorgeous, they'd've all listened to him and hired you to dog-sit—whether they had dogs or not."

The convoluted compliment jabbed at the sore spot left by Tyler's deception. Heat crept up Natalie's chest and neck, flaming her cheeks. The urge to run seemed to grow wings. "Thank you, Mark. Um, Paige, I'll just wait …" Natalie jabbed her thumb behind her.

Just then, Tyler yelled at Mark. "Penalty's up! Stop flirting and get your ass—" His mouth swung open as he locked eyes on her. "Natalie?" He pushed off and headed straight for her, and her heart took off like a thoroughbred vying for a Kentucky Derby victory.

She spun, taking long strides powered by a frenzy of emotions playing tug-of-war inside her. Excitement. Shock. Elation. Embarrassment. Contrition.

Grace Guilt was dueling Hailey Hormones.

Natalie came to a stop by a corridor. She leaned against the wall, eyes closed, hand on her stomach, trying to catch her runaway breath. She opened her eyes to a soft whirring noise.

"Hi," came a voice beside her. "You here to watch the No Excuses!?"

Looking down, she peered into silver-gray eyes belonging to a blond man in a motorized wheelchair.

"I'm with Paige ... Miller," she said lamely.

"Nice. I'm Troy, the team manager." His eyes and mouth moved, but little else.

She recovered herself. "I'm Natalie."

A knowing smile. "T.J.'s friend."

Her head bobbed. *God, how many people has he told about me?*

Troy's eyes twinkled. "No doubt you already know what a great guy he is, but I still gotta sing his praises. We're really grateful to him."

Dumbfounded, she continued nodding.

Troy seemed to appraise her. "He didn't tell you, did he?"

Now she shook her head, feeling like a confused bobblehead.

He laughed. "No, of course not. He's not the type to toot his own horn. Well, I'll toot it for him. We were struggling to find court time for our basketball team. He hadn't known us long, but he took it on himself to help us out. We never asked; he just saw a need and jumped in. He'll tell you he doesn't know a thing about setting stuff like this up and that it's all Miller, but the truth is T.J.'s the one who brought Miller along. *And* T.J.'s the one who got the Blizzard organization to back him. Not only did he fix it so we have a regular court slot, but he arranged ice time. On top of that, he got Miller and a few other hockey pros to coach the guys.

"And the best part? It doesn't cost us a dime. I don't know if he's paying for it himself, and he won't say. He just tells me, 'Don't worry about it.'"

Troy blinked rapidly. Was he tearing up? Speechless, Natalie shifted uneasily. With a sniff, Troy continued, "What a difference maker. The guys are loving it."

The tattoo sprang into her brain. "Your team's called the No Excuses!?"

"Yes."

"Did you know your team name is tattooed on his chest?"

"I didn't, but it kinda sums it up, doesn't it?" Troy's gaze traveled over her. "You must hear this all the time, but he's one of the genuine good guys. Like most enforcers, he takes a lot of heat for his role on the ice and doesn't get the credit he deserves. What most people fail to see is how much heart he's got. They only see the on-ice persona."

"But an enforcer is so ... I mean, they play dirty."

Troy cocked an eyebrow. "They play *tough*. Personally, the guy in that position's my favorite on the squad. He's the ultimate team player. Think about it. Night in, night out, he lays it on the line. It might not be a role he wants to fill, but he does it because his team's depending on him. He's about loyalty and heart."

"Natalie?" Paige's voice preceded her. "There you are. Oh hey, Troy."

"Hi, Paige." Troy beamed. "I was telling Natalie how much we appreciate everything T.J.'s done."

Paige darted Natalie a sheepish look. "Beck and I think the world of him. I'm sorry if I put you on the spot."

"No, you're not," Natalie chuffed, masking a chuckle in her throat. "You planned this. Just like you withheld his real identity, which I've forgiven you and Katie for, by the way."

Paige raised her hand. "Guilty. But it was just me this time, and T.J. didn't know. He was pretty disappointed when you took off, by the way."

It occurred to Natalie she was a little disappointed too—he hadn't come after her.

"Shanny, you suck!" Bent over, wheezing the words out loud to himself, T.J. was literally sucking air into his burning lungs. The team had lost the night before, and Coach LeBrun was putting them *all* through a punishing practice.

"Again! Again!" Coach barked like he was the ghost of Herb Fucking Brooks.

The mantra *I suck, I suck, I suck* was one T.J. had repeated to himself since Natalie had shut him out of her life. Texts, calls, emails went unanswered. Seeing her a few days ago—no, watching her run away—had rammed the message home. She wanted nothing to do with him.

A stick tapped the backs of his knees, and he straightened to look into Dave Grimson's toothless, grinning face. The guy reminded T.J. of a pasty jack-o'-lantern.

"Hey, lover boy. Save some of that energy for Kendra tonight." Grims waggled his eyebrows. "You're gonna need it."

Right. The charity dinner T.J. didn't want to go to, with the date he didn't want to take. Grims had been harassing him all week about Kendra, how she couldn't stop chattering about hooking up with T.J. He'd ribbed him with comments like, "About time your right hand got a night off, Shanny," or, "Someone's finally gettin' lucky." Once upon a time, the remarks might've been funny, but now they only pissed T.J. off.

Yeah, he hadn't even met the girl, but the money was on him getting laid if he wanted to. And he *should* want to—it had been months.

Hours later, after cleaning up, wrestling on his tux, and dropping Ford at Katie's, he parked outside Grims's house in his new Audi A8. Before he could get out, a stunning blond with tanned legs opened the passenger door and slid in. An overpowering, spicy scent drifted off her.

"You must be T.J. I'm Kendra." She gave him a lingering once-over followed by a predatory smile. As his eyes traveled over her, he took in a tight silver dress and the smoking hot body filling it. She leaned over, offering him an excellent view, and kissed the corner of his mouth.

"Nice to meet you, Kendra," he near-croaked. Yep, he was getting laid tonight.

Chapter 26

I Brought You Something

Cozied up on her couch, Natalie watched *Destination Wedding*— or tried to. She was having difficulty focusing, even on Keanu. The same had happened with her all-time favorite, *Lake House*. Unheard of.

"What are you saying, Keanu? Stop mumbling and speak up!" she whisper-yelled at the TV. She'd rewound the same scene a half-dozen times. It might have explained why it was past eleven and she was three hours into a movie that ran ninety minutes.

She reversed again, and just as she hit play, someone pounded on her front door, launching her from her seat.

What the hell?

"Natalie Foster? You awake?" came a man's muffled voice.

Not a voice she recognized. Her heart kicked into overdrive, furiously pumping blood through her veins. She plunged her hand under the couch cushions and gripped a foot-long length of metal pipe. Pushing her sweater up on her shoulder, she rose and tiptoed to the door.

Another knock, and the door rattled in its frame.

Oh shit, oh shit, oh shit!

"Natalie? I haven't had the pleasure of meeting you yet, and I apologize for the circumstances, but I'm a friend of T.J. Shanstrom. Our boy's kinda messed up, and I'm here to help him get his dog."

What the—?

Eye to a peephole said T.J. Shanstrom had installed for her safety, she steadied her tremors. A Chad Michael Murray lookalike in a crisp tuxedo stood on her stoop holding a dark, human-shaped heap. She inched the door open, and Chad gave her a tentative smile.

"Hi. Natalie? I'm Gage Nelson." He was holding up a bleary-eyed Tyler, also in a tuxedo, though his resembled an unmade bed. Gage's eyes traveled down to her hand, and the smile slid from his face.

Time froze. Natalie took in the scene before her while Gage took her in, frowning.

"I don't have Ford," she blurted.

"Uh, Shanny said he left his dog here."

"Ford's not here," she repeated.

A few garbled words sounding suspiciously like, "Told you she was beautiful," rumbled from Tyler.

"Yeah, dude, you were right." Tyler's knees began buckling, and Gage appeared to struggle under his weight. "Can you stand up?" He began losing his grip, and he darted his eyes to Natalie. "Can I bring him in for a sec?" Behind him, engine running, was the blue Audi A8 she'd seen in the Blizzard parking lot several days ago. A beautiful blond in shimmering silver sat in the front passenger seat, neck craned toward them.

"Um, okay. Just put him on the couch."

"Thanks." Gage part-marched, part-dragged Tyler to the couch and heaved him onto it. Tyler listed to one side and sank into the cushions with a groan, bowtie undone and askew, jacket hanging at an angle she was sure Armani *never* intended.

"What happened?" she asked.

Panting, Gage's eyes flicked back to her hand, and the half-smile returned. "That thing loaded?"

Adrenaline waved through her body, and she tightened her grip on the pipe. "Yes. You gonna tell me what's going on?"

"Sir Galahad," he tilted his head at Tyler, "got a little drunk tonight. Apparently, he preferred Jameson to his date. She's out in the car now, and I'm trying to get her home."

Retching noises came from the couch, and Natalie's eyes widened. So did Gage's. "Bathroom?" He reached for Tyler.

She pointed. "Back there! On the right! And there's a spare toothbrush and toothpaste in the top right-hand drawer."

While the men were busy in the bathroom, she motioned for Tyler's date to come in, but the woman shook her head forcefully. She didn't look pleased.

Sporting a Tyler cape, Gage emerged a few minutes later. "He's better—at least for a few minutes." Gage shucked his load onto her couch, then draped Tyler's jacket and tie over an armchair. Tyler moaned and nuzzled the cushions.

"I know this is asking a lot, but can I leave him here while I get his date home? I'll come back for him." Gage's face was guileless, earnest, and Natalie felt an unwelcome yank at her heart. The thought of Tyler sick in Gage's car—and Gage cleaning it up—knocked about in her head, and she heard herself say, "Okay," before Lily Logical could slap some sense into her.

Gage gave her a head dip. "Good night, Miss Natalie."

"See you soon, Gage."

Natalie glanced at the large lump on her couch. *Definitely a case of stray dog syndrome.* And speaking of stray dogs, where *was* Ford?

Thumping alerted Natalie something big was staggering around her house.

Crap!

She shot out of bed and switched on the lamp, glimpsing Keanu Reeves and Winona Ryder frozen on the TV screen in the living room, sporting the same half-lidded, open-mouthed poses they'd sported when Gage and Tyler first arrived.

A shirtless, pantless Tyler loomed and filled her hallway, looking around himself as though lost. She tore her eyes from his perfectly cut body because he was about to toss his Jameson cookies again. Which was why his abs, his pecs, his biceps—pretty much every perfect muscle on him—was contracting.

She flipped on the overhead light and pointed at the bathroom door. "That way!"

He looked at her through slitted eyes. The man didn't just *look* lost. He *was* lost. She reached him, grasped his biceps, and yanked. He didn't move. Just looked down at her as if trying to puzzle out a pesky insect buzzing him.

"Nat?" he croaked.

Her hands didn't span his biceps, so she shoved at his shoulders.

"Bathroom's there," she puffed.

He shuffled his feet and lurched sideways into the bathroom barely bigger than a closet. She slammed the door just in time to dull the sound of his heaving. She leaned against it, praying he'd hit the toilet.

"You alive in there?" she ventured when everything had quieted.

A grunt. He still lived, thank God. A sprint to the refrigerator, and she had a blue Gatorade in hand. Back at the bathroom door, she knocked softly and jumped back when he opened it.

"I'm sorry," he rasped. His face was wet where he'd splashed it with water, and his head hung miserably.

She slid past him, careful not to brush against him, and grabbed a hand towel, which she threw at him before wrapping her arm around his waist. Trying to block out the feel of smooth, warm skin stretched over hard, sculpted muscle, she let his heavy body lean against hers. His weighty arm draped over her shoulders.

"Let's put you to bed until Gage gets here." *Where* is *Gage?* "Here's some Gatorade," she added as they stutter-stepped their way to her bedroom.

Partway there, he stopped, looked down at her, and moaned. "God, you must hate me." A hint of mint drifted from him.

She ignored him because no, she *didn't* hate him. What she hated was that she'd missed him and that touching him was sending all sorts of tingles sailing through her betraying body. *Slow your roll, Hailey.* Natalie refused to give her conflicting emotions free rein; she would *not* have this discussion with herself right now.

"C'mon, chief. Let's get you to bed."

"Chief," he snorted. "I like that. *Way* better than asshole."

She snatched up the covers, and he slid beneath them with a loud sigh. She uncapped the Gatorade and handed it to him. Propped on an elbow, he chugged half the bottle and passed it back to her, then flopped his head on the pillow with a moan. He blinked a few times and looked at her as if seeing her for the first time, his eyes a muddy combination of green and brown. Like a Louisiana bayou—something she'd seen in pictures but never in person. *I should go there sometime, maybe take in New Orleans during Mardi—*

"I love you, Natalie Amber Eyes."

What? Her heart slammed against her rib cage. Acrobats flipped and tumbled in her stomach as she stared at the hot mess of a man in her bed. *Is he talking to me?*

Natalie Amber Eyes. Even bet he was talking to her.

Pulse racing furiously, she finally found her voice, and it carried an outrage she wasn't feeling at the moment. Besides stirred up, she wasn't sure *what* she felt. "Seriously, T.J.?"

His face creased, and he dragged a hand across his stubbly jaw, then covered his eyes.

Man, that scruff! Did he do that just for his date tonight? Like, he started growing the damn beard three days ago to impress her? Natalie's heart caved a little as she recalled the slinky little blond— whose sickly perfume wafted from Tyler's clothes and skin.

Ugh.

In a rumbling slur, his voice sliced through the fog of her thoughts like a lighthouse beacon. "Jesus Christ on a fucking cracker, I'm in love with you, and I sure as shit don't want to be." He gulped a breath. "But you won't get off the fucking pedestal."

Her mouth dropped open. Thank God his hand still covered his eyes. *Am I dreaming?* All thoughts of sexy blond date forgotten, she tried to process his dizzying words.

I'm in love with you, and I sure as shit don't want to be. A far cry from a romantic declaration, she told herself. More like a kiss followed by a slap. How did one respond to that? *Um, thank you?* As for the pedestal comment, she had no idea.

"Gatorade's right here, and I'm on the couch if you need me." She pushed an errant curl off his forehead. His hair was thick and soft.

"Mmm, that's nice." He sank into her mattress.

He'd really said he loved her, hadn't he?

Before Hailey Hormones had her curling up next to him, she clicked off the bedside lamp and squeezed the door shut on her way to the couch. Her phone droned on her coffee table like a lethargic, overloaded bumblebee.

Gage: *TJ behaving himself?*

Natalie: *No choice. Sick as a dog.*

Gage: *About that. You still want me to get him tonight?*

Her brain stopped for a tick, like an electrical blip—one that lasted just long enough to make you reset every digital clock in your home.

Natalie: *Maybe best to leave him. Transporting him might kill him.*

Gage: *Ok. Good.*

Natalie: *Thank you. You're a good friend.*

Gage: *So are you.*

She set the phone down and smiled. For a guy she'd judged irredeemable, a lot of nice people liked T.J.

Natalie startled awake, propped against couch cushions, pillow in her lap. It was pitch-black outside, light filtering from Keanu and Winona, who were still frozen but in different poses. So she'd advanced to a new scene. Progress.

Facing her from the depths of an armchair, still clad in only knit boxers, T.J. Shanstrom fixed his eyes on her like a locked-and-loaded laser weapon.

"Omigod!" she yelped. "You scared the shit out of me."

He straightened and put his hands up, which did wonders to expose his bare chest, shoulders, and stomach. "Sorry. Don't shoot."

She gusted out a breath. "*Sorry* seems to be your favorite word lately."

"I have a lot to be sorry for."

She was in his gun sights, though she had little clue what thoughts lurked behind his penetrating gaze. *Is he sober? Less drunk at least?*

"I, uh, was gonna call a ride and get the hell out of your life, but I can't find my phone or my clothes." His deep timbre was a tad muzzy.

She crossed her arms, and her sweater slid down her arm. The movement seemed to break his focus because his eyes immediately darted to her shoulder, then to her chest, where it lingered. As if remembering himself, his gaze shot back up to hers. She yanked the sweater up her arm, but it merely slipped down again. "Where'd you leave Ford?"

"At Katie's."

"She didn't tell me." Something poked at her. A pang of jealousy? "Phone's charging on the kitchen counter, and your clothes are hanging in the bathroom. How are you feeling?"

"I'll live. I'll just get my stuff and go before I embarrass myself further. Thanks for the Gatorade and …" He motioned vaguely toward the bedroom.

She shrugged. "What are friends for?"

His watery eyes seemed to light up a notch on the brightness scale. "We're friends?"

Off guard, sleep-relaxed, yet taut as a fully-extended bungee-jump cord, she gave in to reflex and nodded. "For now. And this friend says you should climb back in bed." She flipped her hand at him as if shooing him away.

He shook his head gingerly. "That's *your* bed. I'll take the couch."

She looked him up and down, then cast a glance at her couch. "You don't fit. *I* barely fit."

He dropped his head in his hands. "Which is why I should go."

Clicking off the TV, she rose from the couch, took one of his hands in hers, and tugged. "I don't think so. C'mon."

"Where are we going?"

"The bed's big enough for both of us. You can sleep there as long as you keep your hands—and other body parts—to yourself." *What in the actual hell am I doing? Letting "I love you, Natalie Amber Eyes" run roughshod over me. Sap.*

He trudged after her, huffing, "My body's barely functioning as it is. I don't think you're in any danger."

She wriggled out of her jeans and yanked the sweater over her head, leaving her in black cami and boy shorts, while he stood motionless on the other side of the bed and watched her.

"What are you waiting for?" she blurted.

"Uh, you." He raised his hand to tug his hair, and the masculine visuals assaulted her. Bunched bicep, dark armpit thatch, flexing chest and stomach muscles, shallow navel, dark hair arrowing below the low-slung waistband of his boxers. Hailey whooped. Natalie dared not let her eyes travel any lower, instead fixing on his breathtaking tattoo, illuminated in the glow of the bedside lamp.

Dashing her eyes away, she piled under the covers and thrashed her way into the semblance of a comfortable position on her back. *Suddenly wide awake here.*

He seemed to take his cue from her, waiting until she'd settled before slipping between the sheets. The mattress dipped drunkenly under his weight, and she inched her butt to her edge to keep from rolling against him—or on him. *Action item: replace saggy mattress.*

Lacing his hands over his bare chest, he cleared his throat. "Should I turn off the light?"

"Yes," she squeaked. "Although, for the record, I'm not one of those women who objects to doing it with the lights on." *Omigod! What is wrong with me?* She suppressed the urge to clamp her hand over her fat mouth.

He slid his eyes her way. "Good to know." Then he rolled on his side and reached for the lamp. She stole a peek at his broad, smooth back and shoulders, biting back an inner moan.

I thought this was a good idea, why?

Chapter 27

Open Kimono Redux

Despite a pounding skull and a stomach that sloshed like a green hurricane sea, T.J.'s body parts were all functioning, and one in particular was having difficulty settling down because, Jesus, he was surrounded by Natalie. Her scent drifted from the bedding, the pillow—hell, it floated from her skin mere feet away. It had him captured and bound in silk and air, and there was no escaping. Did he want to escape? Fuck no. He wanted to pull her against him, climb inside her, and stay there forever.

Instead, he lay on his side, every muscle bunched, struggling to ignore how his dick was drawn to her like a witching rod to water. Didn't help that her last words had branded an indelible image on his brain—one where she straddled him, gloriously naked. With the lights on.

Think of something, anything else.

Kendra.

Oh shit, where had he left her? Vague recollections of Nelson driving his car surfaced, and he eased.

When he'd picked Kendra up, he'd been optimistic he could lose himself with her and break his dry spell. She'd certainly done her part, coming on strong. Really strong. The attention stroked his ego and *should've* broken out a song-and-dance routine in his pants. Unfortunately, he couldn't get the dog-sitter beside him out of his head, and the hopeful celebration south of his belt never got off the ground, instead fizzling like a spent party popper.

So he'd backed away. Right into a bottle of Jameson.

And wound up in Natalie's bed.

I've wanted to be here since the first day I saw her.

Trouble was Natalie hated him. But if she hated him, why was she letting him lie next to her, half-naked? *Especially* after his humiliating display?

The memory of her sweater sliding down, exposing the smooth, tawny skin on her shoulder with only a thin, black strap made him hard. The image of her *after* she'd pulled the jeans and sweater *off*—in a tiny top and short shorts—made him harder still. Unbearably hard.

He drew in a breath and tamped down a few hope bubbles that were effervescing their way into his consciousness. *I'm in Natalie's bed.* He didn't dare let those bubbles grow and pop.

Her arm, silky and warm, snaked over his side, surprising him, delighting him, raising goosebumps on his skin. She flattened her palm against his upper abdomen, splaying her small fingers.

"Is this okay?" she whispered behind him.

Yes. No.

He clamped his hand around her forearm and pulled, snugging her to his back, then covered her hand with his to keep her there. Her heat spread through him, enveloping him, and he relaxed into the mattress and her hold on him. The dog clock ticked. In the distance, a train horn wailed plaintively.

"Are you still open kimono?" she asked.

A chuckle vibrated his chest. "I'd call lying here in just my underwear pretty much open kimono."

"What happened that soured you on relationships?"

The question froze his blood, and he must have tensed because she rubbed her cheek against his back, soothing, murmuring, "Never mind if it's too personal. But I'd like to know."

Jesus, he didn't want to go there. Ever again. But what did he have to lose? It wasn't like he was going to sleep. Not like this.

He closed his eyes and traveled back through the graveyard of his memories. "The night I was drafted, I was on top of the world."

A hard swallow. "My girl was with me. Melissa. She'd been my girl since I was old enough to care about the differences between boys and girls. In high school, I billeted and played all over, so we didn't see much of each other, but we stayed close. She was always there when I came home." He paused, and Natalie squeezed his hand, silently urging him on. "I got the call straight out of high school, so we went to Montreal for the draft. I'd borrowed money from her dad so I could bring her. My entire future was right there, so damn dazzling I needed sunglasses."

Natalie softly sang the chorus to the old Timbuk 3 song, "The Future's So Bright, I Gotta Wear Shades," making him smile despite the nausea waving through him. For an instant, he felt like a kid whose mom crooned a lullaby while she held him close. The moment was vivid but fleeting, like a shooting star.

"The month before, I'd asked her to marry me on the anniversary of our first date, and she'd said yes. I was ecstatic. Finally, my life was on the track I'd always dreamt of. She acted like she was thrilled too."

He checked the urge to lurch upright. Natalie seemed to notice his body language and traced fingertips along his back, calming him. God, that felt good. *She* felt good. He eased back against her. "This girl was it for me—the one I was building my life around. And there we were, on the brink of something incredible. At least that's what I thought."

A beat to catch his breath. Two. His voice dropped low. "The LA Kings picked me thirty-second overall in the draft. I was celebrating my ass off at an after-party. She told me she'd fallen for someone else and was leaving. That night. Turns out the whole trip had been an act."

A sharp intake of air, and Natalie's body stiffened behind him.

He let out a mirthless laugh. "Yeah, that was my reaction too, along with a few choice words and threats to destroy the motherfucker."

"Did you know him?"

His angry words came out in a growl. "Oh yeah. I knew him. My best friend. It had been going on for months."

"*What?* Who does that? And why *that* night, of all nights?" She seemed to be grasping for a way to fathom the unfathomable. *Welcome to my world.*

Breath ripped from his chest, and it was as if his heart was being ripped out all over again. He thought he'd grown a callus over it, safeguarded it for the rest of his life, but the pain was fresh and raw. He stared at the dim edges of her nightstand with unseeing eyes.

"She said she'd been trying to find the right time to tell me, and she decided to tell me that night because nothing could bring me down from my high."

She couldn't have been more wrong.

Natalie lay in silence with him, unmoving, for long minutes, only the clock ticking out its rhythm in the background. Her closeness lulled more memories from the deep recesses where he'd buried them years ago, and he let them come.

He'd been so lost that night. Small and alone in a sea of people partying like Armageddon loomed. But his personal Armageddon had just detonated, turning every piece of his heart into shrapnel so miniscule it would never be reassembled again.

Not much of a drinker in those days, he was staring down his fate utterly sober and losing the battle. One of the girls at the party zeroed in on him, and when she offered him a drink, he threw it back without tasting it. More drinks followed, until he was numb and didn't know who he was anymore.

Soon they were dancing and kissing in the midst of swaying bodies. She brought him to her room. He was desperate to leave himself on the floor with his clothes, but she felt all wrong. Apparently, he was just sober enough that his mind could still direct his dick, telling it this was not *his* girl—the girl he was preprogrammed for.

In hindsight, he shouldn't have been surprised. When he'd been with Melissa, no one else measured up. It had never occurred to him to stray, and not just because he was an inexperienced punk. He'd never wanted to. Which made him a pathetically invested one-woman man. A candy-ass, his dad would have said.

Eventually, he grew icicles over his heart and became cyborg-like, looking real but functioning like a machine. Women were playthings he engaged with his body, never his heart.

Natalie's lilting voice pulled him from his inky misery. "How old were you?"

"Eighteen. A stupid kid playing at being a man. I had *big* plans," he mocked. "We'd live together while I paid my dues in the minors, working my ass off to break into the NHL. Then we'd get married. I'd have been in my early twenties then. We always talked about having kids—I wanted six—and she could've stayed home if she wanted. Hell, we could've afforded one nanny per kid."

Christ, now I'm vomiting information.

Lying in bed, talking, should have been surreal. Being horizontal with women was normally a sporting event involving little talk. But somehow, doing this with Natalie was … freeing. No judgment. No ridicule. Natural. Sheltered from a raging storm.

Ironic that it was with *her*, given their history.

Pushing the thought aside, he relished the feel of her against his back. She was like a superhero cape, making him invincible.

As though she sensed it, she curled her body into him, tucking her knees behind his, and little pieces of him—lifeless pieces that had been flung far and wide for years—began collecting themselves in small, solid shapes. At their center, his heart started beating again.

The connection to her was excruciating … but safe somehow.

"That must have been terrible," she said softly, "realizing one dream while another one was being shattered."

"I assumed," he faltered, "we'd always be together. That it was destiny or some fucking romantic bullshit like that. Instead, she's saying yes to me while she's banging my buddy. Christ, did she ever play me for an idiot." The stab, tender and deep, throbbed in his chest, but not as sharply as it had before. Coincidentally, Natalie's hand was pressed into the very spot, as though safeguarding it.

"The issue was hers, not yours."

"So you're a shrink?" he teased, trying to get back to a lighter place.

"No, but I stayed at a Holiday Inn once."

"Always with the jokes."

"My dad used to say, 'Humor greases the skids of life.' And Mom's motto is 'Smile even if you ain't feelin' it 'cause sunshine'll follow.'" Natalie's voice sounded lazy, sleepy, adorable.

"I wish I'd known your dad. Your mom's ... sweet. Generous."
Loyal. How a mom should be. Without thinking, he laced their fingers together. "Like her daughter."

"What about your family?" she murmured minutes later. "Were they with you on draft night? They must've been so proud of you."

A familiar spike, sharp like a thistle between the toes, sent his defensive shields skyrocketing. His father's voice rattled around in his brain like a steel ball in an old pachinko machine. *You're a stupid, whiny little shit. Why do you think your mother left? She left because of you.*

No matter how comfortable he felt in Natalie's arms, he couldn't go there. "Melissa was the only family I had."

Silence strained the air. He could practically hear her gears grinding. She hugged him closer and stroked his chest. The caress wasn't erotic; it was reassuring. "So your mom wasn't there? Your dad?"

"He wasn't invited."

A calming press of her hand. "Why not?"

He expelled a lungful of air. "He has a temper. I didn't want to take the chance he'd go off. Let's leave it at that." Invisible bands constricted his chest, his throat, cinching down hard.

"I'm sorry. I didn't mean to bring up bad memories," she continued in her dog-whisperer voice. "Do you worry you're like him?"

"Always."

She breathed out a sweet little "oh."

He scrubbed a hand over his scratchy beard and pressed finger and thumb into eyes that felt as though they'd been propped wide open during a blasting sandstorm. "Believe it or not, I wasn't a hothead growing up." He cleared his sticky throat. "But breaking up with Melissa really messed me up. I was gunning for trouble, and the anger showed in my game. I was also filling out, growing stronger, getting bigger every day. I started bringing an aggressive edge to my play that hadn't been there before. It made me feel powerful, like I could actually control something. Coaches began to notice, encouraged it, helped me channel it."

"That explains your intensity."

Luck, desperation, and a colossal amount of hard work had gotten him where he was. Intensity? You bet. Mix in a healthy dose of attitude that rivaled a pissed-off grizzly bear, and he possessed the secret sauce to making it in the bigs. Something he never took for granted.

Thousands of hockey players would step into his skates without thinking about the cost. Spit out all their front chiclets? *Where do I sign?* Tear a groin muscle? *No problem.* Take an eighty-mile-an-hour puck to the face that breaks a jaw or orbital bone? *A shot of cortisol and some stitches, and I'm back on the ice without missing a shift.*

She lay quietly.

"You still with me, or have I killed you with boredom?"

She squeezed his fingers. "Still here. Just processing. Keep going. I want to learn more." With a little sigh, she added, "I love the sound of your voice."

That made his cock stir. He tried to ignore the tightening his thin boxers wouldn't contain. "I made it to The Show earlier than I expected. That's when I met Becks. He was a helluva good hockey player, one I'd always admired. He took me under his wing."

"In the hockey department or the party department?"

"Man, you're nosey."

She snickered. "I prefer *inquisitive.* You were saying ..."

"I'll admit I wanted to match Becks on *and* off the ice, though I didn't touch the drugs. The alcohol I took care of on my own."

"Mr. Jameson?"

His stomach executed a slow roll, like a rotisserie spit speared through a dripping, greasy hunk of meat. "Shit, don't remind me."

"You *did* earn it."

"Smartass. Yeah, I did. Anyway, there I was, this kid with no home, no ties, making tons of money, trying to leave my past behind, so I went a little nuts."

"Understandable," she said softly. "Did it work?"

He tugged her hand up a little higher and wrapped his arms around it. "For a while. I was playing hockey, having lots of fun, meeting my hockey heroes, but it started to catch up. Guess you can't run from your demons forever."

Why was he even going there? Because he could. He could talk about this with her like he'd never opened up to anyone. Maybe it was the alcohol still floating in his system, or maybe it was lying in the dark, but some of the shackles of his past seemed to loosen.

Natalie shook her head, and her hair tickled his bare skin. "Those demons can be pretty tenacious. You've got to show them you're tougher."

He rolled onto his back. She was backlit by the moon outside her window, and he took her in, this fierce warrior woman. The thin black strap of her camisole hugged the curve of her shoulder. Her hair, long and loose, draped onto the pillow. Everything about Natalie glowed: her skin, her dark waves, her eyes. God, she was beautiful.

His heart burst with an *I love you,* taking him by surprise. Jesus, he'd said it earlier, hadn't he? Out loud, when he'd been wasted. He cringed inside with the realization.

Natalie blinked. "Right?"

"What?"

"Give the demons a John Wick ass-kicking."

He chuckled. "Easier said than done." He twiddled a strand of her hair and cupped her cheek. She leaned into his touch. Her face was small and cool in his hand, her skin light compared to his. She was silk, a whipped meringue to his burlap and chaff.

An image of a bloodied, bruised woman's face, her bones shattered, barreled into his consciousness, making him recoil inside, sending his heart crashing against his ribs.

Mom.

Natalie must have sensed the shift inside him because she laid her head on his shoulder and, in a voice as soft as a breeze, said, "Can you tell me about your parents?"

God, he didn't want to dive any deeper than he already had tonight, hunting his demons down. He'd rather open a vein and bleed out slowly. But wasn't that exactly what he'd *been* doing his entire adult life?

"Don't think I can go there right now," he said.

She nodded against him. His racing pulse ratcheted back a few notches as he toyed with her tresses. He closed his eyes, breathing in the scent of her hair, her skin, her serenity, fortifying himself against the familiar, agonizing question that tore at him.

Was he capable of his father's viciousness?

Chapter 28

Still Waters

Gears were locking into place. Everything was beginning to fit now, and Natalie had a better understanding of the enigma that was T.J. Shanstrom. And her heart ached for him. The stoic façade, arm's-length relationships, and hooded eyes served one purpose: to keep a very tender heart well out of harm's way.

He'd been hurt badly. Melissa had trampled him. *Who does that anyway?* Natalie held back her gust of contempt.

Beneath her hand, T.J. lay frozen, every muscle taut, coiled as though he prepared to spring into action. She'd stirred something big and bad inside him, and the kimono was closed, cinched tight.

Deflect. "Tell me about the tattoo?"

His body relaxed a fraction, then a fraction more. "Now?" His deep timbre rolled from his chest in calm waves. "How about I take you to breakfast first? Then we'll get Ford." He peered at her, and though the room was dim, she felt his eyes, like tractor beams, locked on her.

I love you, Natalie Amber Eyes. Had he meant it? Or had it been a drunken mumble?

"Actually, I have a better idea." He was grinning now, white teeth flashing in the gloom. Hailey cartwheeled through her stomach. *Yes!*

"How about I take you to breakfast and tonight I take you out for dinner?"

"Like a date?" she squeaked. God, she sounded laughable, like a teenager dragging her sneaker toe in the dirt, unable to look at the hunky captain of the football team talking to her. Holding her. Without his clothes on. Yeah, okay, so she'd cut herself some slack. She was, after all, only human.

He rumbled a laugh. "Not *like* a date. A *real* date."

"Uh ..."

"Seriously? I've thrown up in your bathroom. We've shared a pillow, and we've been lying in bed half-naked the last few hours. Don't you think it's time we tried dating?"

"What about Kevin?"

Tension buzzed in the quiet, and she cursed herself.

Fortunately, he recovered. "I don't want to date Kevin."

Relieved at his playfulness, she smacked his very hard chest. "I *meant* shouldn't one of us tell him, smartass."

"I thought *you* were the smartass in this relationship." He tweaked her hair. She loved that. "So? Dinner tonight?"

Bubbles began fizzing in her stomach. "Okay."

Thank God the light was muted because her face was on fire.

T.J. opened a towering nine-foot door and held it for her, and she stepped inside his lair. His home. Even at first glance, the space was small, though it felt huge and empty. Stark. Cold. She curbed an urge to hug herself.

"You live here, or do you just stop by for showers and changes of clothes?" she teased, anticipating an echo from bare walls.

His eyes bounced from concrete ceiling to hardwood floor to a wall of glass that faced the mountains. "It works for now." He toed off his shoes and tossed his jacket and bowtie over the back of an office chair tucked under a built-in desk in the hallway. At the kitchen counter, he unloaded his pockets into a pewter bowl. "I've never had any complaints about the decorating. Then again, only my buddies have been here—and Paige apparently, though I wasn't living here then."

His hands went to his belt, and he began unbuckling—and stopped. "Oh shit. Sorry. Forgot. I'll just ..." He pointed vaguely toward an open doorway around a corner.

By the time the shower began running, she'd surveyed everything in the living area. She sidled to the doorway he'd disappeared through and took in a rumpled bed, two vacant nightstands, and a utilitarian lamp. On the wall opposite was a closed barn-style frosted glass door. *Bathroom?*

The room smelled strongly of him—cedarwood, man, and musk—and she stepped farther inside, her nose plucking his scent from the air. Gingerly, she lowered herself onto the foot of his bed and ran her hand over a dark gray comforter. Not much to look at here either—no hockey memorabilia, not even a poster—except one good-sized framed painting swirled with golds and browns that faced the bed.

She rose to examine it. An ethereal image of a woman's face with little but her eyes showing. It looked original and expensive—the gold frame alone must've cost a small fortune. Though it was only the woman's eyes, they radiated liveliness, femininity, and strength. Whoever had painted it had captured a mischievous, seductive spark in her golden irises, and as Natalie leaned in, she realized those irises resembled star clouds filled with dozens and dozens of pinpoints of color. It was stunning. The artist had obviously been under the woman's spell.

Her eyes scanned the bottom and corners for a signature but found nothing until they caught on a wave of brown hair that resembled a scroll. Embedded were three words in ocher, and she began reading to herself. "Natal—"

"Like it?" T.J.'s deep voice nearly shot her out of her shoes.

She'd been so focused she hadn't heard him come into the room. Now she felt like that employee who'd been caught playing solitaire on her computer.

"I just, um, yes. I hope you don't mind. It's beautiful, and I wondered who the artist was."

Scrubbing a towel over his damp curls, he filled the now open doorway, bare-chested, tattooed, and wearing jeans that rode low on his hips. In his other hand, he held a shirt.

Oh mama! She suppressed an urge to bite the heel of her hand.

T.J. flung the towel on the bed and snapped the shirt. Then he trailed a tender gaze from her eyes to her hair and landed on her mouth.

When they'd left her house, he'd had a green-gray cast and looked pathetic. Now all trace of pathetic was gone. In its place, robust. And genuine. Heartfelt. Handsome and genuine. And broad. Hulking, handsome, and heartfelt.

Damn it.

"I am." He yanked an ivory long-sleeved Henley over his head, stretching it down his torso. The shirt would've been boring but for what it molded to and showcased.

"You are what?" *Mouthwateringly chiseled? A perfect sculpture? My fantasy come true?*

"I'm the artist."

"Oh." Confusion dissipated into disappointment. "Oh! *You* painted … Is this Melissa?"

He shook his head, jouncing a few curls, and tilted his head at the painting. "She had blue eyes. I only know one woman with gorgeous eyes like that." His hazel gaze intensified and caught hers.

As realization dawned, breath spiraled from her lungs. She had to remind herself to breathe. "And she would be …"

A grin split his face. "Having breakfast with me. C'mon, Natalie Amber Eyes. My body craves grease."

Natalie Amber Eyes! He freakin' painted my … Omigod! He painted me! That's so … so heart meltingly wonderful. Is this guy for real?

No one, ever, had done anything like that. The picture was beautiful beyond words. And he'd painted *her* eyes through his own. A meek voice reminded her of his duplicity, but she shrugged it away. It vaguely occurred to her that somewhere along the way, he'd become *T.J.*, supplanting Tyler in her mind.

Overwhelmed, giddy, and suddenly shy, she nodded dumbly and followed him out of his condo, her impression of him canted another degree on its axis. He was one delightful surprise atop another, and she struggled to remember why she'd been angry with him.

T.J. stood on the opposite side of the elevator from Natalie, scrolling through his phone, pretending she wasn't a mere five feet away and overloading his senses.

Nelson got Kendra home. I owe him big-time. Maybe a bottle of—fuck no. No booze. Nelson also apologized—with a winky emoji—for not understanding where Ford was last night when he took T.J. to Natalie's, and for not coming back for him. Yeah, T.J. owed him *big-time*.

He stole a glance at Natalie, who seemed transfixed by the only button glowing in the elevator. *Yeah, she's gonna ditch my ass. First I stalk her, then I lie to her, then I show up dead-drunk and throw up all over her bathroom—because really, the other two weren't bad enough—then she sees the painting. Open kimono? Yeah, it's all hanging out there. Just kill me now.*

She turned her gaze to him. "Did you mean what you said last night?"

Deflect, deflect! "I said a lot of things last night, and I was drunk for most of 'em. I wouldn't believe a word if I were you."

Her eyebrows touched, then quickly eased. "Right."

"Why? What did I say?" *Maybe she doesn't remember the "I love you."*

"Does it matter? I mean, if it's not believable."

Alarm bells began clanging in his head, and it hurt like a motherfucker. Events were fuzzy, but he didn't recall blacking out. "Please tell me I didn't say something *really* inappropriate." *Like how I can't stop thinking about you, about how badly I want to taste you and be inside you. Or all the other things I want to do to you. Christ, please tell me I didn't go there.* He groaned inwardly as other possibilities popped into his head.

"Sometimes I say too much," he muttered.

"It was nice."

Confusion must have shown all over his face, because she followed with, "I mean it was kinda weird when you think about it."

What the hell did I do?

"You know, you showing up drunk as a skunk, me ready to throw you out, then we end up cuddling and talking. Intimate without being … intimate. Weird, but nice."

This conversation, and the recollection of last night's, should've made his skin prickle and crawl, but it didn't. It *was* weird but nice. Really nice. He couldn't imagine doing that with anyone else. And she was still talking to him. Hell, she was going to breakfast with him!

"So you don't hate me?" *Wait. Did she say* intimate?

She tilted her head. "No, I don't hate you. Besides, you've got that well covered all by yourself."

"What does that mean?"

"Kinda hard for others to love you when *you* don't love you. Maybe cut yourself some slack?"

He looked around himself. "Dr. Phil, what have you done with Natalie Foster?"

She gave him an eye-roll. "Always with the jokes."

"Some smartass told me humor's good for greasing something."

Electric razor in hand and Ford at his feet, T.J. stared at his reflection in the mirror. He tugged on his jaw. "What do you think, buddy? Clean-shaven or trim what's here? Women like the stubble, right?"

Yesterday, he couldn't have given a rat's ass what his date thought of how he looked. The stubble hadn't been deliberate—just the result of several days' laziness. It wasn't as if he needed to disguise himself anymore. Which, admittedly, felt pretty good.

"Heads, I keep it. Tails, it goes." He glanced at Ford, who wagged his tail. "Tails it is. Good call. Less likelihood of beard burn. Assuming I get that close. And if you tell her I said that, no Pup-Peroni for you."

While he shaved, a sizzle and pop coursed through his system, as if he'd been hooked up to electrical current. Natalie was all he'd thought about all day. He should've been tired, but he was amped up. Should've been hungry, but he couldn't eat. Shouldn't have been primed after jacking off—twice—just thinking about lying next to her last night, but he was ready. And hopeful. And damn nervous.

A half hour later, he stood on her stoop with Ford. When she opened the front door, it occurred to him he'd need to rub out a third one. His breath caught in his throat, and he did a double-take, his brain racing to process what he was seeing. Was this the same woman? His body had *no* problem processing, voicing its approval with a silent salute and general chaos breaking out in his pants.

Fuuuuuck me!

Please.

She was devastatingly dressed in a black, sleeveless number that hugged her slim waist and every curve, sheathing and showcasing her perfect hips. The dress stopped above her knees, exposing mile-long legs and short high-heeled boots. Her glossy chestnut hair spilled in loose curls over her shoulders, down her front, curving under her breasts like a pair of hands lovingly cupping them. Like *his* hands longed to do.

"You're early." She laughed.

"Is that bad?"

"No. It just tells me you're hungry. As usual."

Something about the way she said it calmed his firing nerves. Like she knew him well. Shared his secrets with him. Of course, if she *really* knew him, she'd know how little interest food held for him in that moment. In fact, he wasn't sure when he'd be able to eat tonight for all the somersaulting in his stomach.

She flicked her eyes to his car. "That's *your* Audi?"

"Yeah, I traded the H1 for something more practical. Like it?"

"Love it. I thought it was Gage's."

Ford followed her inside the house, shooting him a look that said, "You coming, dumbass, or you just gonna drool on her doorstep?" T.J. mouthed, *She likes the car,* at him, two-stepped into the living room, and closed the door. "You sure Ford's okay to stay here while we're out?"

"Of course." She looked at T.J.'s side and blinked. "Are all those for me?"

Reminded of the flowers he held, he thrust the bag at her, along with a wrapped present.

Her eyes widened as she cradled the gifts in her arms. "Wow! Did you buy out the entire flower shop?"

His hand shot to his nape and smoothed. "I, uh, didn't know what you liked, so I got an assortment." Having never given a woman flowers before, he'd had little idea what to buy. So he bought it all.

"I'm not sure I have enough vases." Another lilting laugh that enveloped him like melted caramel sauce. She headed for the kitchen, and he trailed behind, entranced. "I'll just put these in water." While he stared blatantly, roving his eyes all over her, she grabbed a bucket from under the sink and filled it. "There must be six bouquets here!"

"Nine."

She began wrestling with the gift, which was more scotch tape than paper—he'd never wrapped a present in his life—and he began to panic when she finally freed it and arched an eyebrow. *"John Wick: Chapter 2?"*

"I know how much you like Keanu ..." Jesus! What had he been thinking? He hadn't—because his blood hadn't been circulating to his brain for most of the day, nor was it about to work its way above his neck anytime soon. What an idiot! He should've brought diamonds or a car. Yeah, a car. She needed one of those. Maybe he should give her the Audi ...

"I love it!" she gushed, and relief flooded him. "That was really thoughtful. Maybe we can curl up on the couch and watch it later."

She was killing him. *Wanna skip dinner?* He swallowed hard. "You look, uh, amazing."

"Thank you. It's fun to get dressed up for a change."

"Yeah. Right." *Fan-fucking-tastic!* He couldn't even string a simple sentence together. "And no dog slobber," he added, then mentally slapped himself.

She gave him an impish grin. "Are you still sick?"

"No. I'm, ah ..." *Just missing my brain.* His eyes flicked over her again. He couldn't stop himself. Christ, she was so fucking gorgeous! "A little tired maybe."

She smirked. "Well, we won't keep you up too late, then."

Oh, please keep me up.

Dinner was a blur of white linen in a dark booth, candles, and conversation. His body finally uncoiled—except one part—but he still felt as though he skated on one blade, trying to hold his balance and remain upright.

He remembered little of their exchange except when she asked about his interest in Roman history.

"I listen to make myself smart," he'd replied.

She'd eyed him over the rim of her wineglass. "You don't think you're smart?"

When he'd shaken his head, she'd added, "Could've fooled me," making bubbles dance in his blood.

On the ride home, his mind whirred through possible scenarios. Watch *John Wick* and go for that cozy-on-the-couch thing? Kiss her as soon as they got inside the door? Yeah, but what if she didn't want to go there? Before his mind could amble farther down its current path, her phone rang.

"Hey, Mom." Natalie side-eyed him. "Just heading home after dinner out with Tyler, um, T.J." A pause. "I'll let you know, okay? Yeah, love you too."

His gut constricted. "You told her?"

Natalie stared straight out the windshield. "Mm-hmm."

He dragged a hand across his jaw, muttering, "She'll never speak to me again." The thought inexplicably saddened him. *Good-bye, Rockwell.*

"Oh, I doubt that. She wants you to join us for Sunday potluck."

His eyebrows leapt to his hairline. "Seriously?" A grin quirked his lips.

"Seriously. You even get a pass on bringing a dish. She thinks what you did ... the Ford thing ... is romantic."

His pulse sped up. "What does her daughter think?"

Natalie twisted in her seat, partially facing him. "*She's* still pondering."

A laugh burst from his chest. "You probably have spreadsheets you're analyzing the hell out of, am I right?"

When he glanced over at her, she faced front again, busily smoothing her dress. He reached out and took one of her hands. She nestled it into his like it belonged there.

"Let me know how I can up my plus-minus rating on your stats sheet." He sent her a wink.

It was dark in the car, but he could've sworn she blushed. He'd take it.

Inside her house, she tossed her purse on a chair, beelined for the sunroom, and let Ford in. The dog hurtled at T.J., slapping his legs with his tail while Natalie opened a cabinet and stretched her hand toward the top shelf, leaning over the bucket of flowers in the sink. The lights were still off. "I need to put these into vases."

One graceful leg extended behind her, turning her into a human fulcrum.

Stepping toward her, he shot his hand up beside hers. "I got it."

Ford chose that moment to knock himself into T.J.'s legs. Arms braced against the counter on either side of Natalie, T.J. barely averted falling against her back. The warmth rising from her body and her vanilla-and-flowers fragrance mingled, invading his senses, intoxicating him as they wrapped around him. His dancing cock burgeoned into a full hard-on. The air was thick with restrained desire. His mind blanked.

There in the kitchen shadows, he dropped his hand to her neck and brushed her hair aside. It felt like silk against his fingers. She made a noise that sounded distinctly like a sigh. Arm braced on one side of her, he ran his fingertips along her neck, to her throat, holding her still while he pressed his lips to the bare skin at the slope of her neck. Another sigh escaped her.

Heart thumping like a bass drum, he trailed languid kisses up her neck, nuzzling the skin behind her ear. Her head tilted to the side, giving him more surface to explore. He flicked his tongue out, and that little taste spurred him to nip and suck softly, the tip of his tongue dancing over her sweet skin. She leaned against him on a whispered moan.

Arms bracketing her body, he continued his onslaught, nibbling and tasting, feeding the raging hard-on pressed against her ass. She lifted her hands and tunneled her fingers in his hair. Exuberant ripples raced from his scalp to every margin of his body. He swept his hands up her sides, then cupped and caressed her breasts through silk and lace. She arched into his touch, fingers twisting in his hair, undulating the length of her back against him in a sensual rhythm. The tingling in his body exploded in microbursts until he was no longer sure where he started or ended. His hands glided down her sides, along her thighs, over her hip bones, back up her stomach to her breasts. She felt wonderful. More moans rose in her throat. Every part of him was on fire. If he died being devoured by the flames, he was okay with that.

She turned slowly and faced him, sliding her hands to his shoulders. Her lips curved in a sultry smile, speaking a language that went straight to his cock straining against his fly. Another sizzle shot through him. While one hand held her to him, anchoring her hips to his, he stroked the length of her silky cheek with the back of his other hand.

"You are the most beautiful thing I've ever seen."

She scanned him from chin to scalp and cradled his face in her slender hands. Helpless to stop her even if he wanted to, he let her pull his mouth to hers, landing on her oh-so-soft lips. The kiss was gentle, two people finding just the right fit. And when that fit was found—that perfect, seamless joining of lips—instinct kicked in, and his arms cinched her close as his mouth took hers. Her hands wrapped around his head. With a hand grasping her waist, he tangled the other into her thick waves. His tongue glided along her lips, eager to explore. She let him in, and he tilted her head to drive the kiss deeper. He plundered her mouth to his heart's content while he tightened his hold on her. Little mewling noises escaped her, making him throb with need.

Her mouth was pliant, lush, matching his, captivating him. She tasted like wine and sweetness and warmth. Unrelenting desire seized him.

God, he wanted her.

As he kissed her, he roamed his hands over her back and snugged her against his steely length. She was right there with him, her hands on his butt, dragging him closer. His fingers crept down her thighs, inching the hem of her dress up, stroking her achingly soft skin as he went. He couldn't get enough of it. When he reached her ass, his engine went into overdrive. Nothing divided his fingers from her skin but the strings of a thong. He barely kept himself in check as he caressed her.

Her pelvis tipped against him, pulling a series of groans from his chest. His breathing kicked into high gear as urgency bloomed.

Breaking the kiss, he looked into eyes as warm as whiskey and brimming with desire. "Jesus, Nat, I want you so bad." His voice was gruff, full of hunger, surprising him.

"Show me," she breathed, plowing her fingers through his scalp.

Oh fuck yes!

Kissing her again, he released the hem of her dress and ran his hands over her, stopping at her zipper. Coaxing it down, he peeled away the dress. It slid down her body and puddled around her boots. As his tongue stroked hers, his hands stroked her back, her side, all that soft skin, then snaked between her breasts, where he unclasped her lacy bra. He brushed her flesh and the hard beads of her nipples, and she let go a whimper in his mouth. Now both his hands were cupping, massaging. Discovering. She was all softness, female, and sex. Heat raced up and down his back, pooling at the base of his spine. His senses were on overload.

He untangled his mouth from hers, his breathing rapid and ragged. The room was dim, but light through the kitchen window glowed golden on her outline. Through half-lidded eyes, she peered at him as he slid the bra straps off her shoulders and arms. Clad in a thong and ankle boots, her body exposed to him, she watched as he took her in, running his fingers over her flawless skin and stunning breasts. He leaned in, wedging his thigh between hers, as his mouth sought hers. Her eyes were fully open now, holding his gaze while he teased her nipples between his fingers and thumbs.

"Harder," she whispered. He complied. A gasp escaped her moist, parted lips, echoing the breath he sucked into his lungs. She kept her eyes riveted to his and began rocking against his thigh as he kneaded her flesh, feeling every inch of her. A slight shift, and he bent to one breast, latching on, exploring with his tongue while his fingers explored her other breast. He suckled first one, then the other, her hands clenched on either side of his head, positioning him where she wanted, her pelvis grinding against him as he intensified his licking, tugging, and nipping. Her rising moans and murmured *yeses* and *oh Gods* urged him on, sending flashes of heat straight to his aching cock.

Everything about her was hot, raw, primal.

Sinking to his knees, he blazed a trail of open-mouthed kisses over her ribs, her flat stomach, and hooked his thumbs on either side of her thong. Slowly, he slid the lace down her long legs, all his attention on the view before him, dimly aware she kicked the underwear off the toe of her boot. He feasted his eyes on this glorious, naked woman looking down at him, her chest and stomach rising and falling with her heavy breaths.

He was stirred to his core like he'd never been. A burning man dying to devour her on the spot.

Splaying his hands on her thighs, he lifted one onto his shoulder, opening her to him, breathing in the scent of her arousal. Nectar and musk. God, she smelled like heaven. She hissed something inaudible when he ran his tongue over her. He didn't stop. He lapped, licked, nibbled softly, sucked hard, teasing, stroking, thrusting, and plunging his tongue and fingers, torturing her, torturing himself, until her legs quivered and her entire body seized. Rising swiftly, he took her mouth hard, capturing the orgasm rolling through her. The sensation staggered him, firing every nerve with scorching heat.

He held her to him, kissing her neck, caressing her shoulders and back, while the storm in her body subsided. The tempest raging in his own body had been building and was simmering within him. He kept it tightly leashed while she hung boneless in his arms, snug against his chest. Finally, she dragged in a shuddering breath and laughed.

He stroked her hair. "What's funny?"

"We're in my kitchen," came her muffled voice. "I'm only wearing my boots, and you're fully dressed. And I'm pretty sure your dog watched the entire time."

He let out a soft chuckle. "He was coaching me."

"Well, he did a damn fine job."

His heart ballooned. "Yeah?"

She propped her chin on his chest. "Oh yeah." Then she ran her hand along his rock-hard shaft and cupped him through his pants. "Interested in a fair trade?"

His eyes rolled back in his head as he tried to lock out the feverish pulsing, the mounting explosion. When he couldn't, he moved her hand away. "If I let you do that much longer, I'll embarrass myself."

The sight of her very bare, very beautiful body was one he could stare at twenty-four-seven and never tire of, though right now he wasn't sure how much he could take. She stood brazenly under his lustful scrutiny, as if challenging him to touch her. It was a challenge he gladly took on, running the backs of his hand along her cheeks, across her shoulders, down her arms, her skin like warm silk. His gaze dropped to her breasts, and he palmed them, caressing her nipples stiff with his thumbs. "How about an *unfair* trade?"

One side of her mouth curled up. "What's that?"

"It means yeah, I want a turn, but I want you to have another turn too. Under me." He wiggled his eyebrows, then pulled her to him. Jesus, he was killing himself here, fighting the urge to take her right there on the kitchen floor. The counter. The table. He didn't care.

Ford yipped beside him.

"I think he needs to go out." Pressed against him, she skimmed her lips over his neck, shooting chills down his back, his arms.

He released her and put distance between them, but his hands lingered a beat on her body, reluctant to let go. Finally, struggling to even his breathing, he walked to the sunporch door and let the dog out. With a backward glance, he glimpsed her gathering her clothes from the floor, and his heart gathered speed again. He wanted that girl naked. So much.

In one swooping motion, he hoisted her over his shoulder in a fireman's hold, his hand firmly planted on her naked ass.

Dangling down his back, she giggled. "Where are we going?"

"Where do you think? I'm far from done with you," he growled as he angled toward the bedroom.

A few strides, and he threw her atop the bed and toed off his shoes, but she popped right back up, still giggling. He was about to push her back down when she gripped his belt and hauled him onto the bed with her. "Someone has on waaaay too many clothes."

"I can fix that." His body buzzed with her touch. The smell of her on and around him launched a burst of impatience. He lunged at her with a kiss and hungrily worked over her throat and ear.

"Right now," she panted.

"Demanding, aren't we?" he mumbled against her skin.

He rose above her, kneeling, and took over unbuckling his belt. His pants were off in a nanosecond while she ditched her boots and tackled his buttons. Boxers and socks hit the floor before she'd reached the third button. He sat up and grasped the back of his shirt, wrestling it over his head. A few buttons popped and bounced on the floor. A second later, his undershirt joined his other clothes, and he paused to catch his breath.

Her eyes roved over him, taking in his scars, all of him, without stuttering. Looking at *her* physically hurt, spiraling him into a whirlpool of need and ache and want. He'd never been here before, and the thought occurred he might drown.

He was a goner.

Chapter 29
You Can Pick Your Friends, but You Can't Pick Your Family

T J. was breathing hard as he sat on her bed, his last shred of clothing on the floor. All that kept Natalie from gasping out loud at the sight of him was that she *couldn't* breathe. The man was magnificent. All corded muscle and smooth skin and male perfection. Looking at him supercharged her every nerve, setting her skin on fire. But she probably hadn't come down off the high she'd climbed in the kitchen.

Oh mama, she'd never experienced an orgasm *that* explosive. Especially while standing up. From someone going down on her. Against a sink. With a dog watching her.

Right now she nearly trembled, anticipating his impressive erection pressed against her, inside her, filling her. And fill her he certainly would.

Tingling sensations sped through her bloodstream. She'd never felt anything so intense. It must've been what a skydiver felt right before a plunge.

T.J. was looking her over like a wolf surveying a bunny rabbit, gauging where to start feasting. The thought sent another zing through her, and moisture surged between her legs. Her nipples nearly stood up and happy-danced.

"Um, I have a condom if you don't," she offered.

His eyebrows arched. "You keep your own supply for … *guests?*" Frowning now, he began looking around the room. Was he looking for "guests"? *Way to kill the mood, Nat.*

She let out a nervous laugh. "No, but when I was in the restroom tonight, they had a machine, and I thought … I'd come prepared. I mean, *be* prepared. Just in case. You know. Like a boy scout." She paused for breath. "And it makes a great missile in a water balloon fight." *Oh my God, you dork! Just shut up!* A flush crept up her chest, her throat, over her cheeks.

He flashed her a wicked grin. "You're gorgeous when you're embarrassed." His voice was doing that low, rumbly thing that pooled delicious warmth low in her tummy.

She sent him a sheepish look.

Snatching her wrist, he hauled her to him, rolled her on her back, and climbed on top of her, covering her with his heavy body. His skin was hot and melted with hers, and she sank into the mattress in a state of utter bliss. His arousal, undiminished, nudged her inner thigh.

He curled long, strong fingers around her neck. "You're gorgeous *all* the time, *especially* naked," he whispered. His lips began blazing a trail along her neck, making her eyes roll backward. "I have my own, by the way," he murmured.

"Of course you do." Her voice sounded throaty, probably because her breath had picked up speed again, what with his open-mouthed kisses heading for her breasts. "It's, ah, been a long time for me." She tunneled her fingers in his luscious curls.

He lifted his head and pierced her with his eyes, all hazel and thick lashes. "Me too."

She smirked. "I'm sure it's been much longer for me than you."

He shrugged.

"So how long has it been?" she teased, inwardly questioning why the hell she was asking. *Please don't say last night … or even last week.*

"So long I'm not sure I remember how. Can you teach me?" His mouth closed over her nipple, pulling an inadvertent moan from her.

"You seem to be remembering just fine. Besides, I hear it's like riding a bike."

Up went his head. "Really?" He scratched his chin dramatically. "So all I have to do is find a bike, straddle it, and start pumping?"

Giggles bubbled from her like a champagne fountain. "Oh my God! Did you just say that?"

"What?" he chuckled. "I was referring to pedaling." He tapped her nose with his finger. "You have a dirty mind." Then he winked. "I like it. Now stop talking and kiss me, smartass."

She did, long and deep, running her fingers over his muscular shoulders, digging into his flexing back. And his hands were everywhere on her, caressing, squeezing, clutching. He was a mind-numbing blend of rough and tender, demanding and giving, seductive and raw. All hot, hard man.

Soon they were a frenzy of arms and legs, thrashing together in something akin to a wrestling match. He manhandled her, flipping her on her back or her stomach like she was a doll. The more she urged him, the more physical he became. And she loved it. He opened doors she didn't know she had.

He came to rest, straddling her, panting. "I won't last much longer."

Before she could tell him she wouldn't either, he parted her legs over his shoulders and pinned her hips down while he stroked her with his tongue and tormented her in the very best way. Again.

"You taste so fucking good, Natalie," he mumbled against her. "I want to eat you up."

His words alone sent her into orbit, and her orgasm crashed over her before it could even build. But he didn't wait for her to come down this time. He reared up in all his glory and snagged a packet from the corner of the bed, sheathing himself in the time it took her to blink. *Condom ninja.*

His hot, wet mouth was back on hers, and she wrapped her legs around his hips. He shifted his weight to one beefy arm and, with the other, positioned her how he wanted. One thrust, and he plunged inside her with a rumbling groan, pulling a gasp from her lungs.

He stopped moving. Uncoupling his mouth from hers, he locked eyes with her, his breathing labored, his fingertips dancing over her face. "Is this okay?"

She nodded, speechless, adjusting to the sensation of him inside her while drowning in his eyes. Everything about him rocked her, set her ablaze. She was suspended between this world and a world she'd never been to before.

Holding her gaze, he withdrew slowly, his tip not quite clearing, then drove into her again with a raspy, "Holy shit!" Dropping his head into the crook of her neck, he flexed his hips, moving inside her with a steady rhythm, picking up speed and intensity. She grabbed his ass like she was hanging onto a bronc. Another orgasm blossomed, gathering steam with his pounding thrusts.

"Jesus Fucking Christ, Natalie," he gritted. "You feel fucking incredible."

That did it.

She came apart, shattered, went over a cliff with a cry, fireworks filling her head. His shouts joined with hers until they were a guttural, exploding, carnal chorus.

When she came to, she was dragging in breath, her chest slick against his, and he was panting against her neck. She turned and opened her eyes. He was staring at her. One side of his mouth curved up.

"My God, woman!"

"Not God. Just Natalie." She let out a laugh. "What *was* that?"

"In-fucking-credible, that's what it was."

Their breathing calmed, and he swept her hair from her face. She basked in the tenderness shining in his eyes. "You are amazing, Natalie Amber Eyes." He laid sweet kisses over her forehead, on her eyelids, her nose, her cheeks.

She smoothed his hair. "You're not so bad yourself."

A quick kiss, and he got up to dispose of the condom. When he returned, he climbed into bed and spooned her, wrapping her up in big, strong arms. She settled against him as though cuddling under a quilt.

"Maybe we can do that again sometime," she hummed.

"How about fifteen minutes from now?" he murmured, snuggling against her back, kissing her shoulder. A simple, sweet, intimate gesture. She drifted off in a sea of warm contentment.

When she next woke, a dog was licking her hand and predawn lit her window. T.J. slept soundly beside her, his hand palming her ass. He never asked to spend the night, and she never invited him. It just happened, like it had always been that way. Easy, natural.

She rolled out of bed, threw on her robe, and padded to the back door to let Ford out. When she returned, T.J. was propped up on his elbows, curl-tousled and sleepy-eyed. His face lit up when he saw her, and her heart cartwheeled.

"I'm sorry I fell asleep on you, sweetheart. I must've been more tired than I realized."

Sweetheart. The endearment warmed her to her toes. She leaned down and kissed him. "It's okay. You can make it up to me."

"How about right now?" He tugged her robe open and slid his warm, rough hand inside.

God, she loved his big hands on her. His eyes on her. *Him* on her. She could get used to this.

Their lovemaking was languid and long as they explored the landscape of one another's bodies. Though they'd explored plenty the night before, this morning's pace was a one-eighty, and Natalie reveled in the slow, deep rhythm thrumming between them. This was new for her, striking this achingly intimate chord with a lover. They could've been two parts of the same instrument vibrating in concert. A perfect fit. He must've felt it too.

Countless orgasms and hours later, they lay with their limbs intertwined, her head lolling on his chest. He separated her strands with his fingers, examining each one as though it were spun from gold.

"Your hair has so many different shades," he said with wonder.

She lifted her head and rested her chin on his tattooed pec. "The artist's perspective?"

"Artist?" he scoffed. "Hardly. Just a guy who's fascinated by all the colors in your hair." He grinned at her. "And eyes." He ran a fingertip over the bridge of her nose. "And freckles."

"I don't have freckles." She raised up and lightly tapped his tattoo. "Am I ever gonna hear what's behind this beautiful design?"

"What do you want to know?" He sat up, reached for a water bottle on the nightstand, and guzzled it.

Mesmerized, she watched his neck muscles ripple as they shipped the liquid down his throat. Her eyes swept his chest and shoulder. "Where does it start?"

He pointed at his bicep and the tip of a wing comprised of red and blue feathers. The wing swept up his shoulder where it seemed to sprout from a bird's green body immersed in flames.

"A phoenix," he explained. "For rebirth. Rising up after annihilation." His finger tracked from his shoulder to his chest, and now she saw the bird's head holding a pocket watch in its beak. The short hand pointed to a Roman numeral twelve, with the long hand positioned about quarter past. "Twelve-seventeen," he said. No other explanation.

Clutched in the bird's talons was a perfect red rose with a thorny vine that wound around the bird's feet and a heart resting atop the scroll. The thorns punctured the heart in several places. "The rose means love and balance, and the thorns are for recklessness, loss, and defense. And the scroll you already know."

"No excuses." She stared at the intricate design, entranced, her fingertips trailing over it. "Bleak and beautiful at the same time."

He answered with a single nod.

"Hopeless and hopeful." She flicked her eyes to his. "What does twelve-seventeen signify? When your girlfriend dumped you?"

"No." He glanced over his shoulder out the window. "Sun's climbing." He looked back at her, a piercing, sorrowful expression on his face.

"You're not going to tell me."

He drew her to him and pulled the coverlet up, draping it over them like a shroud. She sighed against him, relishing his smooth, warm skin against hers. After a beat, his voice rumbled through his chest, vibrating her cheek. "You make me feel things I haven't felt in a long time, Natalie. Things I didn't want to feel again. It's a lot to take in all at once. Give me time." He kissed the top of her head. "I want to get there."

The earnestness in his voice made her ache for him. Did she want him to *get there*? Yes.

Because she loved this man.

The realization didn't hit her like a tumbling brick wall. Rather like the creeping warmth of a heated blanket that seeps into your bones. *I love you* nestled in her heart.

"I'm off today. What do you want to do before dinner at Mom's?" he said with a chuckle.

She peered up at him.

He arched a considerable eyebrow. "Today's Sunday. Potluck night?"

"Right. I got distracted. What do *you* want to do today?"

He shrugged. "I was thinking we could do Naked Day."

A laugh burst from her. "Naked Day?"

"Yeah. We hang out naked. You cook naked, we eat naked, we watch *John Wick* naked. Naked Day." There was that devilish grin again. "We'd be doing our part for the planet. Fewer clothes to wash."

"If I'm fixing you bacon for breakfast, I'll need an apron," she purred in his ear before nipping his earlobe.

His hand traveled to her ass and squeezed. "I'm loving *both* of those ideas. Being fed and you in nothing but an apron."

She tiptoed her fingers over the covers to his groin, toying with the erector set tenting the coverlet. "There's the proof," he added, his voice husky. "Maybe we should work up a bigger appetite?"

Her phone buzzed on the nightstand, and she wantonly dragged herself over him.

"Drewbert."

"Calling about tonight, Nat."

T.J. had rolled on top of her, mumbling about distracting her while his hands caressed her skin and his talented mouth worked over her, leaving icy-hot tingles with every touch.

"Uh, can I call you back?" She bit her bottom lip to hold back a moan.

"Just tell me this. Is Mom pulling my leg, or are you bringing *him* over?"

Every muscle tensed in response; her stomach contracted. T.J. lifted his head, hazel eyes staring at her, brows furrowed, mouthing, "Everything okay?" She nodded vigorously and gathered herself upright. With a deep inhale, she answered Drew. "Yes, I am."

T.J. slid his long legs off the bed, catching up his boxers and pants on his way to the bathroom. She let out the breath she didn't know she'd been holding.

Drew's voice, tight and flinty, shocked her back into breathlessness. "In that case, I won't be there."

"*What?* Why?"

"Because I don't want to be under the same roof as that dick."

"He's *not* a dick," she hissed.

"Have you completely lost your mind? Shanstrom's facing a lawsuit. Maybe criminal charges. Even if he *isn't* using you, he'll pull you down with him."

Natalie's head jerked back as though he'd physically slapped her. "You're wrong!"

"No, little sis, *he's* wrong. Wake the fuck up!"

Hands trembling, she disconnected, tears stinging her eyes. T.J.'s approaching footsteps had her swiping her lashes. Pants on, he stood in the doorway with a questioning look.

"No Naked Day, huh?" Her stab at humor died on the quaver in her voice.

"I'll do whatever you want, sweetheart, but I have a feeling Naked Day is the last thing on your mind right now." His voice was warm, full of empathy.

She shook her head and cursed herself inwardly for the tears still building behind her eyes. "Just an everyday brother-sister fight."

"Because?"

"Because he's an asshole," she spat. "Do you mind if we skip Mom's tonight?"

Concern etched T.J.'s features. "Your call. I got you, whatever you want to do."

"I want to forget it. Let's have fun today. Maybe take Ford for a hike?"

Though he looked unconvinced, he played along. *Bless him.* When he left the room to get Ford, she quickly texted her mom.

Can't come tonight. Love you. xxxooo

Then she texted Drew that Mom was all his tonight. As she hit send, a hiccupping sob squeezed her chest.

T.J. had no idea what passed between Natalie and her brother that morning, but after she brushed off his repeated questions, he let it go. Ignoring his own warning systems, he immersed himself in Natalie World. It was a wonderful place to be—all sugar and spice—and for a week, he floated in its silky warmth like being carried along Willie Wonka's chocolate river.

Wrapping himself up in Natalie and Ford was a balm, calming his mind and soothing his soul, and it resurrected memories he'd thought extinct. Sweet ones, where his mom brushed his hair from his forehead and planted a kiss there, then told him he was a good boy and that she loved him. Loving Natalie had pulled that from him, and as long as his defenses remained decommissioned, he was safe, oblivious, and drunkenly happy. And it wasn't just the mind-blowing, scream-from-the-rooftops sex. That was all bonus.

By the end of the week, though, his fortifications began ramping up, taking on the form of the damn Oompa Loompas singing out that he was a greedy bastard living in a fantasy world. Though he had no way of predicting when the skate would drop, Natalie *would* leave.

The inevitability curdled his stomach.

Sharing a beer with Wheelie Mark and Nelson one evening while Natalie ran long on a project, T.J.'s mind took a familiar detour to the

300

horror show that defined his life. *Air and space are wasted on you. That's why your mother left.*

Mark's voice floated into T.J.'s consciousness and stalled his descent into Misery City. "Man, I was a ball of hate. Didn't help that I grew up pissed off. I had to do *something*."

T.J.'s focus lasered in.

"My therapist said, 'Meditate! Do yoga!' I figured only chicks do yoga, so why not?" he chuckled. "That's how I met Carla. She was the instructor. I came on to her from day one, and she shut me down every time. God, I was a dick! I'm surprised she didn't kick me out of the class. I finally asked what it would take for her to go out with me."

T.J. raised an expectant eyebrow.

Mark took a swig of his brew. "She said when I got my head out of my ass, I could take her out for coffee. Coffee!" he chuffed. "I nearly left it there. But what she said started to sink in. The way I looked at the world started shifting until one day a switch flipped on. I decided I could be a victim, or I could take control." He clacked his bottle against Nelson's. "That day I realized I had something to offer. I wasn't a loser, and I was gonna be okay."

Absentmindedly shredding the label on his bottle, T.J. let unasked questions bob up in his mind. Was *he* choosing victimhood? If he took control, which version of himself would emerge? His brutish father's clone, or the man he saw reflected in Natalie's eyes?

Chapter 30

Done and Dusted

The next morning, T.J., dripping, stepped from Natalie's shower and looked around himself. "Nat? Sweetheart? Is there a clean towel somewhere?"

The door opened, and she poked her head in, swept her eyes over him with an approving smile, then pulled a thick towel from a cupboard and handed it to him.

"If you're gonna stay here every night, you need to figure out where things are."

This was new for him, staying with a girlfriend twenty-four-seven. He'd always kept his distance, but with Natalie, he *couldn't* stay away. Another first for him: they'd stopped using condoms, relying on her birth control. The feel of her that first time had annihilated any qualms.

"Well, you weren't *here,* taking a shower with me, even though I asked nicely," he winked at her, "and I didn't want to rifle your stuff."

"You can rifle my *stuff* anytime, big boy."

With a headshake and a half-smile, he unfolded the towel and wrapped it around his waist, surprised at its size. "Big towel."

She canted her head. "I bought you a bath sheet."

"You bought me my own towel?" The thought warmed him all over.

"You have a lot of real estate to cover."

His smile widened. "Why, thank you, Ms. Foster. That's the nicest compliment I've ever gotten."

An eye-roll. "Cocky jerk. I meant your general," she waved her hand up and down, "tallness. *Nothing's* big enough for that ego of yours."

Her feistiness had his dick twitching appreciatively. She turned, giving him a seductive over-the-shoulder look, and he followed her swaying ass into the bedroom. Like a puppy. With its tongue hanging out. *She* owns *you, Shanny.*

Whip fast, he lunged, reeled her in, and wound his arms around her. He lowered his mouth to her neck and went to work.

"Stop!" she gasped between delightful squeals.

"Not until you apologize for being a smartass," he mumbled against her skin. She smelled sweet and tasted even better.

Unintelligible words pitched from her.

"What's that?"

"N-no ap-apple …"

He intensified his hold, trapping her in his arms. Mouth locked on her neck, tongue lashing her skin, he walked her backward.

"No apples? Not hungry? Too bad because I've got something for you."

Oh, this was fun—and a colossal turn-on.

She inhaled sharply, which made her chest swell against his.

"No apologies," fled from her in one breathless rush.

He'd maneuvered them to the edge of the bed, and when he let her go, he pushed her none too gently on her back. Laughing so hard she was snorting now, she rolled to her side, but he yanked her leg back so she was splayed wide. And then he pounced, pinning her beneath him with his weight, settling between her legs. She wriggled, but he was too heavy, and she couldn't budge him. He grasped her slender wrists and pulled them up over her head, effortlessly holding them in one hand. This left his other hand to roam freely, and he took full advantage, pulling her T-shirt up and unfastening her bra in a few deft moves.

Laughter thundered in his chest, but he quickly reined it in and put on a stern face. His fingers zeroed in on her stiffening nipple and teased it into a tight, round pearl he ached to get his mouth on.

"Do you know what happens to bad girls who don't apologize?"

Her hips writhed with everything they had as she began wiggling out from under him. He threw out a leg and corralled her.

"Love means never having to say you're sorry!" she shrieked.

"Hold up," he panted. "Did you use a cheesy old movie quote to say the L-word?"

She stilled and stared at him with her big doe eyes. God, she was beautiful. Hands still trapped above her head, everything about her softened, and she nodded slowly, a hesitant smile forming on her face. "Is it okay that I say I love you?"

His heart caught fire. He thought it might combust. "Yeah, it's okay," he rasped. *Because I fucking love you too.*

Time took a long pause. He became acutely aware of her chest rising and falling under his, her warm breath on his lips, and her soft flesh beneath his fingertips. Alarms were going off in his head, but his conscious brain checked out, putting up a "Gone Fishing" sign.

Her eyes dropped to his mouth, then languidly slid back up. "Aren't you going to show me what you do to bad girls?"

His cock, which had been paying attention during their playtime, steeled into a ramrod ready to slam its charge home. He was drunk on her, addicted, forever needing the next fix.

She loves me.

Her hands were relaxed in his, her body pliant beneath him. Long and lean, she arched her back like a cat stretching in a patch of sunshine, thrusting her breast fully into his palm. Lifting her chin to his, she purred, "Put your mouth on me, T.J."

Holy fuck!

Breath stuttering in his chest, a beat or three passed before he recovered his few remaining wits, released her hands, and made quick work of his towel and her clothes. Then he climbed back on top of her and dipped his head, laving her nipple before his mouth closed around it. She let out a long, throaty moan and plowed her fingers through his hair, angling his head where she wanted it. He didn't fight her. Couldn't.

She loves me.

She could've dragged his naked ass across an icy rink and he wouldn't have cared.

Instead, he worshipped and served her as though she were a high priestess and he her slave. Whatever she wanted, he gave her with abandon. He delighted in her, sucking, skimming, licking, nipping, kissing, tugging, tasting, and caressing every beautiful inch of her, his mouth and hands instruments to bring her pleasure. All for her. Because he loved her.

In the time and space defined by her bedroom, his only purpose was to drive her to carnal insanity so he could hear the sweet sound of his name falling from her lips again and again and know she loved him.

When her moaning cries crescendoed into an urgent plea, he lay back and pulled her astride him, running his hands along her smooth sides and over her breasts. With feline grace, she lifted herself and sank down, taking him in an inch at a time, driving him to a head-spinning edge where he couldn't breathe, where he was about to lose it. Or die.

He clamped down on her hips to keep her from rocking until his lungs could inflate and his heart could start pumping again. She dropped her head back, giving him a breathtaking view of glowing golden skin, pale throat, sharp collar bones, maple-sugar-tipped breasts trembling with ragged breaths, triangle of dark hair impaled on him, and long tawny legs. She was perfection, and he feasted his eyes until he couldn't hold back.

He started moving inside her. "Tell me again," he demanded.

She leaned over him and cradled his face in her hands. Warm whiskey eyes pierced his as she rode him. "I love you, T.J."

Holding her gaze, he murmured, "Good, because I love you, Natalie Amber Eyes."

She came hard, hot, and fast all over him, and he followed with his own spine-melting climax.

He held her to him while they descended from the clouds together, his mind wandering to how this woman had turned his heart. From the moment he first saw her, he wanted to fuck her forever. But this wasn't fucking. They were making love. And *that* he wanted to do forever too.

Later that afternoon, he sprawled on Natalie's couch, watching NHL Network while she worked in her home office. As his mind lingered on how he'd gotten here, on how he'd let her in and given her the strings to his heart, the image on the screen snapped him out of his reverie.

A sports reporter stood in front of a popular restaurant. Below her, the words "Kevin May Retiring" were superimposed. T.J. sat forward, cranking up the volume on the remote.

"We caught up with Kevin May last night, and here's what he had to say."

The mic and camera swung to May standing close to a woman. A sharp pain crashed through T.J., like a bone-crushing check to the solar plexus. Breath *whooshed* from him.

What. The. Actual. Fuck?

Right before the camera narrowed in on May's face, T.J. glimpsed Natalie at his side. He hit the remote's rewind button, hoping his eyes had reported bad information to his brain. They hadn't. Recognition inverted his stomach and sent his blood into a pressure-cooker boil. He leapt to his feet.

May was talking, but the words were a loud buzz in T.J.'s head. A multitude of emotions whirlpooled inside him—crushing betrayal, anger, hurt—and they funneled into one searing white blast that surged through him. He was a powder keg ready to detonate.

Hands fisting and unfisting at his sides, pulling in a lungful of air, he told himself not to blow. "Nat!"

The tone of his voice must've jarred her because she came flying out of her office, eyes wide. "What is it?" Ford padded over and parked his butt in front of her, eyes on T.J.

T.J. stared at her, stuck in a place where reason was leaking fast from the hole in his soul.

Worry etched her features. She tried stepping forward, but Ford thwarted her. "Are you all right?"

"No, I'm not," he gritted out. "I just saw you on TV. With May."

Guilt flickered through her eyes.

Fury and dread snaked a cold trail up his back. "You had dinner with him last night when you told me you were working. You fucking *lied* to me."

Her brows drew together. "I didn't lie. I never said I was working. As for Kevin, yes, I was with him, but not the way you think. I was going to tell you today, but I hadn't found the right time yet."

"Oh, that's fucking rich! After all the shit you gave me about Ford—"

"That's different."

T.J.'s cheeks flamed. "Really? Why don't you enlighten me? Shit! Forget it." He flapped a dismissive hand at her. "You're just like Melissa. Fucking someone else and leading me on."

Her expression darkened, reminding him of gathering storm clouds. "I admit I called him. I wanted to be honest and let him know about us. He suggested dinner. *Fucking* wasn't part of the conversation. Ever."

T.J.'s pulse was a runaway train, and his chest was rapid-firing with ragged breaths. "So you wanted to be honest with *him* but not me?"

"No! You're putting words in my mouth."

His hands flew to his hair, and he tugged. Hard. "Jesus!" He was about to lose it, and he took a few steps backward. "I'm out."

Amber eyes flashed. "*Out?* What does that mean?"

"It means I've been a complete idiot, playing house," he yelled, waving his hand, "pretending this was all going to work. *Out* means I'm done."

Her mouth swung open. "Over *this?*"

Wordlessly, he strode past her to her bedroom, collecting the possessions that actually registered in his brain. In that moment, very little registered except the need to get the hell out of there.

Behind him, he was vaguely aware of her standing in the door frame, Ford at her side. When she spoke, her voice quavered with— what? Hurt? Outrage? Didn't matter. "I don't believe this! Could I have handled it better? Yes. But one strike, and I'm out with no chance to explain. Just like that," she snapped her fingers, "you walk."

He threw a few things on the bed, then dropped to his knees and checked underneath.

"Telling Kevin felt like the right thing to do," she continued, her voice steadier. "I also thought … I thought if I talked to him, he might consider dropping the lawsuit."

Upright again, he wheeled and faced her. "*What?* Where the fuck do you get off fighting my battles for me?" Yeah, he was in full-on dick mode.

She straightened and folded her arms over her chest. "It's what people who care about each other do. They have their backs."

He ignored her. His eyes scoured the room, but a red fog kept him from seeing.

"Wow. I see." Her voice was feigned indifference, edged with a bite. "You were already looking for your way out. And now you've found your excuse. One more *casual relationship* in your ledger."

Though he couldn't reason why, her last words sliced right through him. He lashed out. "This, whatever it is," he motioned between them, "was par for the course. I thought it was different, but guess what? I was wrong. Again."

Stuffing his clothes into his overnight bag, he prepared to exit before he could see his vicious words reflected in her eyes—or admit to her that *this* had never been par for the course.

Whatever this is?

Stung, Natalie recoiled inside. "Wrong how?"

Anger blazed her cheeks, and she cinched her arms tight across her chest. Before she could gather thoughts into a more coherent stream, T.J. began talking, his voice low and tight.

"You want to know what twelve-seventeen means? It's a date, not a time." His eyes flared. "That's the day Mom left. It's also the day my dad killed my dog. He made my sister and me watch, 'setting an example,' so we'd *understand* what would happen to us if we crossed him."

Horror shook Natalie to her core, setting her mind awhirl. No words came.

His eyes glazed over, and he darted them to the ceiling, where he fixed them, as though the memory was a bad movie streaming behind his eyes. "December seventeenth. I was six years old. Merry Fucking Christmas." He continued in hitches, his voice unsteady. "Duffy— that's my dad—used to beat my mom. I tried to stop it, but I was puny. He put her in the hospital. A lot. The last time, he took Trish and me to visit her. He fawned over her like he had nothing to do with putting her there. Made me sick." A gusting exhale. "I guess she'd had enough. She checked herself out of the hospital and never came back. She left her kids behind … with a monster."

Natalie's heart caved. Checked tears stung her eyes, congealing in her throat. She swallowed around the lump. "Did you ever hear from her?"

He pressed a thumb into one eye, put on a mask of coolness, then shuttered his eyes. "Nope."

"Did you try to find her?"

A too-casual shrug. "Once or twice. I have no idea if she's alive, if she's got a different family, or if she's rotting in a grave."

"What about your sister?"

Eyes back to the ceiling. "Without Mom there, Duffy turned his fury on Trish and me. Trish especially. She was sixteen, working some shit job, and promised me we'd get the hell out of there. 'T,' she'd say, 'don't worry. I'll get us a safe place where Dad can't find us. I promise I'll take care of you. Pinkie swear.' And like the dumb fuck I was, I thought pinkie swear actually meant something."

Natalie sucked in a breath, but he didn't seem to register it. He dropped his bag and began moving like a caged lion, pacing back and forth, all ferocity and restlessness. She sensed he'd retreated to a painful place, somewhere she didn't belong. He was in a world completely his own.

"Trish married some random guy and moved out before she graduated high school. He was her ticket out. I begged her, like a little pussy-ass, to take me. 'I'll come for you, T. Soon as I get things settled.' But she disappeared, just like Mom. So I became my dad's favorite punching bag. Know what it feels like to take a bat to the gut? When you're seven? Not all these scars are from hockey."

Natalie pressed her lips between her teeth, her tears threatening to break her dam of composure. Her heavy heart fractured for the little boy who loved to paint. Who loved a mother, a sister, and a sweetheart who'd cast him off. Mind spiraling to a pitiable place, she wanted to pull him to her, comfort him, but he stood like a forbidding tower, a mixture of loathing and hurt twisting his features. Ford leaned against her legs as though protecting her. She barely recognized the man before her, but she wasn't frightened. Only moved.

"Have you looked for Trish?" she whispered.

His expression and voice were like chilly steel tethering pain and fury. "What's the point? Women leave. All. The. Time. They pull you along, tell you what you want to hear, then wham! Done and dusted. Loyalty isn't in their DNA."

Whoa! "And you think I'm in that category."

"I don't know." He seemed to deflate. "It wouldn't have worked anyway." Defeat laced his words. "I'm broken. I'm my father's son, with a temper to match."

Natalie blinked. "Have you ever hit a woman? Melissa … On draft night?"

Something akin to disgust flashed in his eyes. "Christ, no. Never. That would make me just like *him*." He picked up his stuff again.

"But you've convinced yourself you *are* just like him. He still controls you." Tears spilled down her cheeks. Damn it! She took angry swipes at her face while thoughts streaked through her mind. How could she make him stay and *listen*? How could she make him see himself the way *she* did? The right words were like precious gems in that moment, embedded in rock where she couldn't extract them.

His hard lines softened with a momentary flicker of regret. He stared at her a long beat. "You'll be fine, Natalie Amber Eyes. You're a cat, and they land on all fours."

Natalie's heart about imploded with the finality of his words. "I'm a dog. They flop on their sides, and it hurts like hell." She paused to

310

collect herself. "I'm in love with you, T.J., and I thought you were in love with me."

Something flashed in his hazel eyes. "I can't do this."

"Can't? Or won't?" Her voice climbed to an embarrassingly fierce squawk.

"Does it matter? You'll get over me in a nanosecond. Same as I'll get over you."

Thunk! She'd never been struck with an arrow, but she could've sworn one pierced her heart just then. Pulling in a lung-filling breath, unworldly calm and clarity settled over her, bringing with it an understanding. "I have something for you." Without waiting for a response, she hurried into her office, slid a handwritten paper from a drawer, folded it, and stuffed it in an envelope. Back in the living room, she handed it to him.

Turning it over, he frowned. "What's this?"

"It's something I wrote after our fishing trip. I meant to throw it away when I found out who you really were, but when I reread it, I realized it's all true. Take it. And," she pointed at his chest, "read that scroll over and over until you believe it."

He strode to the front door, Ford falling in behind him. The dog gave her a melancholy glance that made her tears come hard, thick, fast. Man and dog walked out of her house and out of her life, tearing a gash deep inside her.

T.J. was still reeling when he stumbled into his condo, Ford close behind. Sanctuary. Except he couldn't hide from his miserable thoughts.

It was early afternoon, but he reached for the Jameson anyway, trying to halt the loop in his head. A three-finger pour and quick swallow burned but didn't chase Natalie from his thoughts. Her scent clung to him, her taste lingered on his tongue, and her smooth skin ghosted under his fingertips. A physical craving for her throbbed within him.

He sank into his couch and twiddled the unopened envelope. Ford hopped up beside him, resting his chin on T.J.'s thigh. Absentmindedly, he fingered the dog's ear before sliding the paper from the envelope and unfolding it. The top was labeled *Pros* and *Cons*, and words filled two columns in Natalie's neat printing.

As he read, emotions began a vigorous tap dance inside him. "What the—" he said aloud. Concerned, crossed copper eyes fastened on him.

"These must be reasons why she thinks I suck," he muttered. "'Porn star, gigolo, stripper.' Jesus, I'd never do those jobs. Way too hard. And what's so bad about living in California? 'Guarded, evasive.' Yeah, she got those right."

What he found unbelievable, though he read the list twice, were the reasons she thought he *didn't* suck. *Especially* the part about him being smart. "Girl's delusional." *Has to be.*

"They should make T-shirts that say, 'Intimacy isn't for pussies.'" Ford let out a whine, and T.J. ruffled his neck.

Thoughts came at him like colors in a spinning kaleidoscope.

An image of Natalie reared up, filling his mind's eye. Mere hours ago, she'd been naked underneath him, her eyes dancing and sparkling. And sweet Jesus, what came next had blown his everlovin' mind. A connection, deep and powerful, had moved his body, heart, *and* spirit. It had terrified him. Though he'd expected some sense of relief after walking out, his heartache overpowered everything else.

He was hopelessly, helplessly in love with her.

She'd sparked dead emotions to life, and like a limb that had been asleep too long, the wakening was prickly and painful. The intimacy—exquisite, yet excruciating—had aroused a feeling so overwhelming it had shattered his defenses. Feelings he'd *never* experienced before clawed at his throat.

He didn't want to just be with Natalie. He wanted to cradle her, protect her, love her, and never let her go.

But that very desire put him at her mercy, leaving him exposed, gasping for air, like a hooked fish waiting to be gutted.

Except he was already gutted.

When morning came, T.J.'s chest felt as though weights compressed it. Moving didn't alleviate the crushing sensation in his heart.

He rolled over cold sheets and checked his phone, disappointed—though not surprised—to find no message from Natalie. He flopped on his back. God, this hurt like a motherfucker; taking a puck to the face was less painful.

But pushing her away was best for her, right? *Didn't I feed myself that shit once before?*

And what about *his* own good?

"You are so fucked up!" ripped from his chest, and Ford jolted beside him. He scratched his pup's neck. "I'm not talking about you, buddy. You're pretty near perfect." He let out a gust of air. "And so is she."

He reached for his phone again and tapped in a message.

Can we talk?

Chapter 31

When Life Gives You Lemons, Chuck 'em Back

Puffy-eyed and exhausted, Natalie stared at T.J.'s text. Indecision had her in its grip. Anger still flared in the ash heap of hurt in her heart, but love lived there too.

Natalie: *Why?*

T.J.: *I fucked up. Big-time.*

Natalie: *Yeah you did.*

T.J.: *Can I come over and apologize?*

A sad sigh escaped. Seeing him might make her cave, and caving wouldn't do either of them any good.

Natalie: *Not a good idea.*

T.J.: *Why not?*

She hauled in a huge breath and blew it out. Though Lily Logical understood he'd lashed out like a cornered, wounded animal yesterday, Natalie's pain and doubt were too raw to erase with a few contrite words.

Natalie: *You walked away.*

T.J.: *I was scared as fuck. Ur nothing like Melissa.*

Natalie: *What happens next time we hit a speedbump and you get scared?*

T.J.: *I'll learn to deal.*

Unconvinced, she replied: *Think you need to figure out a few things first.*

Moments skated by before he answered: *Like?*

Natalie: *Like what's really important to you, what you're willing to risk.*

The clock's tail ticked back and forth, marking time.

T.J.: *Did u mean what u wrote?*

Natalie: *Every word.*

T.J.: *Having hard time buying it.*

"And that's just it," she murmured through fresh tears.

Natalie: *You are full of excuses but no trust.*

"I can't fix you," she wanted to add. *Can't do this,* she tapped instead.

T.J.: *Can't or won't?*

Tears blurred her vision. With a sob, she thumbed a final *Won't.*

T.J.: *I'm SO sorry, Nat. I love you.* Following his words were three broken heart emojis.

She ran for the bedroom, tossing her phone on the couch. Collapsing on her bed, she wrapped herself around the pillow that smelled of him, and she sobbed.

Two weeks later, Natalie cradled a cup of marshmallow-infused hot chocolate at her mom's kitchen table. Drew munched peanuts while a huge pot of stew simmered on the stove, filling the room with a savory aroma. But Natalie wasn't hungry.

Mom bent, gave her shoulder a squeeze, and kissed her temple. "Tyler's loss."

In the deafening quiet since their breakup, Natalie's anger had evaporated, but the ache in her heart hadn't dulled.

Absently, she scratched at an embroidered cherry on the tablecloth. "It *is* his loss. In so many ways. He's never had a real family, and I think he caught a glimpse of ours and liked it. But it also scared him.

He's like a moth—drawn to the flame but afraid to get burned." Her gaze bounced from her brother to her mother. "I don't say it enough, but you guys are the best. You're what family is all about."

Loyalty. And though he was loyal to the core, T.J. couldn't accept it in return from anyone but his revolving door of teammates. He was his own worst enemy, forever sabotaging himself. The thought saddened her.

Tears welled up. God, she had to stop blubbering! Maybe a Keanu marathon …

Drew brought her back to the present, scoffing in typical big bro fashion. "Don't go getting all soft and mushy on us now."

Natalie blinked away tears while her mother looked on with a pained smile that said, "I want you to be happy." Warmth pooled in Natalie's belly and spread, filling gaps in her splintered heart like mosaic glue. Yeah, she was lucky.

T.J. was a man on the run, and nothing she could do would change that; he couldn't see himself the way she did. The way everybody did. His pain was too enormous, had too many tentacles, like a cancer that sneaks and hides and latches on to healthy tissue and feeds on it and grows in the dark, destroying everything good. Only he could vanquish it. And he had to want to.

T.J.'s teammates were yukking it up around him while they cleaned out their lockers. The season was over, and he wouldn't see some of these faces in this locker room again. He took it all in with a twinge of melancholy.

Beside him, Nelson packed his duffel, whistling like he marched with the seven dwarves. Guy was happy to be heading home to the Bay Area.

Home.

Where was that for T.J.? Coach LeBrun assured him they weren't trading him, so with luck and Paige's help, it would be a sweet house with a yard for Ford.

Images of house hunting with Natalie jabbed him. *Pure fantasy.* God, he missed her. He'd reread her list so many times the damn paper was tearing at the folds.

After autographing shit for the organization and each other, back-slapping, and exchanging bro hugs with teammates, T.J. headed to a different end-of-season gathering. The No Excuses! and their significant others were hosting a picnic in the park. The event was a rare bright spot he'd been looking forward to since breaking up with Natalie two weeks and three days ago. Not that he was counting. Not that he hadn't died inside more each day. Not that he was hollow.

At the park, he popped open a cold brew and joined the guys as they talked excitedly about next season. Troy had been swamped with requests from other disabled athletes wanting to join their program. The No Excuses! roster was expanding because they had the resources now, and T.J. was proud of the part he'd played in that new normal.

Glancing at Miller manning the grill, he caught Paige staring at him, her tiny frame front-heavy with the melon growing in her belly. He ambled toward them.

"You're here alone?" she asked.

Obviously. "Yep."

She perched her hands on her hips and scrunched her eyebrows together.

T.J. darted a *WTF?* look at Miller. Miller gave him a shrug and kept working his spatula on the steaks.

Okaaaay. "What'd I do?"

"You didn't bring Natalie," she barked.

Taken aback, he busted out a nervous laugh. "Why would I?" *More like, why would she give me the time of day?*

Miller gave him an eye-roll that said, "Wrong answer, dumbass."

T.J. had never seen Paige mad, but she seemed to be winding up. *Uh-oh.*

"Because she's beautiful, smart, and she has a huge heart. I mean, she overlooked *all* your shenanigans."

"You do know I tried to talk to her, but she refused, right?"

"That's all you've got? You let her go just like that, you big dummy!" She snapped her fingers. "I thought you were made of grittier stuff."

A little flame of hope flickered inside him. "Did she say something?"

"No."

The little flame sputtered.

A beat later, Miller said, "Feel better, pixie?"

She hmphed. "Much."

T.J. masked the sting. "Am I fired as a client?"

She threw up her hands and spun to leave. Miller's gaze tracked her impassively as he flipped a steak.

Another quick pivot, and she faced T.J. again. Her anger seemed to have drained away. "Clearly you've moved on, so you won't care if I set her up." A statement, not a question. It fired something green and spiky in T.J.'s belly.

Paige glanced at Miller. "You remember Ethan Lind from the Wildlife benefit, right?"

"Buff blond guy with the sweet Maserati GT? Sha! He's single?"

Shit. Who's this blond douchebag?

"*Very* single." A self-satisfied smirk spread over Paige's face. T.J. hadn't seen her devious side before; he wasn't thrilled to be making its acquaintance now. The spiky green thing in his gut began shaking its cage. He needed to calm it the fuck down. Unfortunately, what came next didn't help.

"He's a catch; she's a catch," Paige prattled. "He likes numbers; *she* likes numbers. This could work." She walked off, beaming.

The wrestling match with Spiky Green wasn't going T.J.'s way. He raked his fingers through his hair. "So who's this guy, Millsy? A narcissistic jerk who treats women like shit?"

Miller narrowed his gaze. "You *do* know you're a fucking idiot, right? Seriously, if you're so worried about it, why don't you get your head out of your ass and *do* something?"

T.J. gripped his beer a little tighter, his temper on simmer. "Like what?" As it left his mouth, he was fully aware how stupid the question was.

"Oh, I don't know," Miller said sarcastically. "Maybe start by apologizing for being such a tool?"

T.J.'s anger diffused. "I tried."

"Try again." A beat went by. "A few words of advice?"

"Do I have a choice?" T.J. snorted.

"If you want Natalie, then listen up. Relationship 101: Grovel. In your case, I recommend *extreme* groveling. Think of it as an endurance sport with some sweet bennies at the end."

"Speaking from experience?"

"No way. I *know* how to take care of *my* woman."

"Who's taking care of a woman, and can I watch?" came Wheelie Mark's voice.

Shit. Just what I need.

Miller pointed the spatula at T.J. "This asshat has a thing for a certain hottie, but he's too stupid to do anything about it."

Mark looked T.J. up and down. "If we're talking about Natalie, then you *are* stupid. If I was single, I'd—"

"But you're *not* single," T.J. snarled. A sip of his beer to coat his parched throat, and he pushed a cleansing breath through his lungs. "Anyway, she's smart to steer clear of my wreckage."

"Got that right," Miller huffed. "'Course, she seems to *like* wreckage. She stuck by May. Now *that's* what I call loyalty."

Mark chimed in. "Who of us *isn't* a wreck? Look at me, man. You can be a wreck alone, *or* you can be a wreck that wakes up every morning like I do, pinching myself because there's a beautiful woman beside me."

"Know what I don't get?" Miller said to no one in particular. "How someone as smart as Natalie falls for a guy who mopes around feeling sorry for himself."

T.J.'s pissed-off-o-meter climbed. "Fuck you, Miller, *and* the high horse you rode in on."

Miller smirked and took a pull of his beer.

"Making the leap takes balls," Mark added helpfully. "Asking Carla to marry me scared the everlovin' shit out of me." He shrugged. "But I persevered."

Mark glanced over at Carla and winked. She blew him a kiss. He mimed catching it before turning back to T.J. "Here's what you gotta decide, my man. Do you want to go through life *with* her or *without* her? If it's *with,* you've got your work cut out. And I wouldn't wait too long. *That* girl won't stay on the market."

"Who says she's on the market?" T.J. muttered under his breath. His intel told him she wasn't—yet.

Looking at T.J., Miller jerked his chin toward Mark. "What he said." A beat later, he added, "Friends don't let friends lose their girls to dicks like Ethan Lind. Grovel."

Mark chuckled. "Groveling's good."

Paige and Carla came over, and T.J. mentally disconnected, studying the surrounding trees and the bright blue sky arcing above. So much color.

Comprehension clobbered him like a hundred-mile-an-hour slapshot. Before Natalie, his world had been shaded in grays. Like now. *With* her, it had been vibrant, bursting with the spectrum of a full paint palette. She was the best fucking thing that had ever happened to him.

In that moment, he made up his mind he wanted color. He *deserved* color.

It was time he owned it.

Chapter 32

Truly, Madly, Deeply

Ten days after the regular season ended, Natalie's phone lit up with an unexpected number.

"Kevin? Hey!"

"Hey, Nat."

"How are Kris and Emma?"

His voice cracked. "Kris and I decided to re-tie the knot."

A thrill shot through her. "I'm so happy for you both! When?"

"Early August. But that's not why I called."

Confusion took up space alongside her happy bubbles. "Oh?"

He laughed. "Don't worry."

She let out a mirthless laugh. "Be happy."

"Seriously, I wanted to call and find out if you knew what Shanstrom did."

Her bewilderment blossomed. "What he did?"

"I didn't think so," he chuckled. "He came to visit me last week. To work something out between the two of us without lawyers in the way. That took guts. And we got it done. The attorneys wrote up the agreement, and we signed it today. He's no longer part of the lawsuit."

Her mouth fell slack, her eyes softly focused on the arm of her couch.

When no words came out, he said, "You there?"

"Yes, I'm here."

"He handed over some very compelling evidence that'll help us go after the team. I don't know what all happened between you two, but I thought you should know. Guy's not all bad."

Three days later, Natalie was home working on Paige's books when her phone chimed a text.

T.J.: *Hey. Got any dog-sitting openings?*

She stared at her screen for so long another text chirped.

T.J.: *Hello?*

Natalie: *Um, hello.*

T.J.: *Haven't contacted u b/c couldn't figure out a way to show u how sorry I was.*

Natalie shook her head to be sure she wasn't dreaming before answering: *And you found a way?*

T.J.: *Think so. HOPE so. Can I tell u in person?*

Natalie: *When?*

T.J.: *Now?*

Natalie: *Where?*

T.J.: *Outside ur front door.*

Her eyes flew to the window. A bright blue Audi sat out front. Her heart lurched against her ribs, and her tummy wobbled. *Should I be happy? Indignant?* Unsure which emotion to call on, she stood slowly, finger-combing her hair and smoothing her top.

Rapping sounded. She skittered toward the front door, only to brake, taking deliberate steps. *He can wait.* She broke into another scurry, and her hand was on the knob in a nanosecond. *Oh, what the hell.* She yanked the door open.

T.J. Shanstrom stood on her stoop holding a huge box. He gave her that grin, the one that puddled her insides into pudding. "Can I come in?"

A swarm of butterflies took flight in her stomach all at once. Ecstatic to see him but befuddled and off-kilter, she stood aside. "Uh, sure?"

Sporting shorts and a T-shirt that matched his moss-green eyes, he brushed past her, his cedarwood man-scent filling her nose. Ooh, he smelled good. And the T-shirt showed off every carved muscle on his torso. The butterflies were flapping furiously now.

He stood in her living room, his mouth quirking. The scar on his lip was a broken pale pink line, and the memory of nibbling it bloomed. *Down, Hailey!*

The box seemed to move ... and snuffle?

She eyed it closely. "Um, whatever that is, do you want to set it down? It looks heavy."

"Maybe in your sunroom?"

She led him through the door. Scuffling noises came from the mystery box, and she grew more baffled.

He placed it in the middle of the room and gingerly opened the lid. She peered inside, and her hand flew to her chest on a gasp. A cluster of fat puppies wagged, wiggled, and scrabbled. Brown, black, yellow squirming balls of fur. Natalie barked out her astonishment with a laugh.

"Not a bucket, but hopefully a box of puppies will substitute," he said. "I also noticed your porch light is loose. I can fix that." Before she could restart her heart, he pointed at the box. "May I?"

She nodded dumbly as he grabbed a pair of pups and set them carefully on the floor at her feet where they sprawled. Stumbling and falling, they tried to climb her legs, their little needle teeth gnawing her bare toes.

"Oh my God!" she yelped, giggles gurgling inside her. "Where did you get them?"

"The Dumb Friends League came to my rescue—in exchange for helping out with one of their fundraisers."

More puppies joined the first two, and she knelt beside the box to help free the rest. Soon her neck and face were assaulted by pink puppy tongues, and she couldn't stop laughing. She plopped down and let the roly-polies crawl over her, licking and wagging as they went. "Eight puppies?"

T.J. dropped beside her, and they pounced on him. "Yeah. Aren't they great? They're almost all spoken for."

She held a chubby little guy in her hands, and he lapped at her chin.

T.J. cleared his throat. "This woman I'm in love with—who's sweet and sassy and smart and sexy as hell, by the way—told me it's impossible to refuse a person with a passel of puppies. And I sure as hell hope she's right because I'm asking her to forget what an idiot I've been and forgive me."

She gaped at him. His eyes twinkled, and she found herself submerging in their hopeful hazel depths while the puppies grunted, whimpered, and snorted.

T.J. suddenly looked hesitant. "Lame?"

Joy fizzed deep inside her, bubbling over, and happy tears stung her eyes. "Not lame. It's ridiculously wonderful!"

He gave her a look that shot straight to her heart. "Yeah?"

"Yeah."

He held a brown puppy nose to nose. "I need to have these back in an hour, but I'm considering keeping this one for Ford. What do you think?"

She wiped her moist eyes. "I think it's a great idea."

He snuggled the puppy against his chest. "Only thing is, I need a dog-sitter who's willing to take on a puppy. Among other things." He waggled his eyebrows.

She gawked at the gorgeous man seated in a pile of puppies, holding a squirming, furry meatball in his big man-hand. Who could say no? She was only human.

Ford ran into the sunroom and began a boisterous sniff-a-thon, his tail set to *high* on the wag-o-meter. People filed in behind him. Her chin nearly hit the floor at the sight of Mom, Drew, Paige, and Beckett standing in a semicircle. She felt her cheeks blaze.

Heart thundering inside her chest, she glanced at Drew. "What's going on?"

Drew, grinning like a madman, jerked his chin at T.J. "Ask *him*. It's his party."

T.J. rose and extended his hands to her. Dazed, she grasped them, and he pulled her up. Holding on to her, he looked around at her family and friends. Then he locked on her eyes.

"Natalie, I know what your family means to you, so I, uh, asked them to ..."

If she kept her mouth open any longer, flies were bound to move in, so she snapped it shut.

He sucked in a huge breath. "I'll just come out and say it."

Please do. She nodded encouragement.

"I figured out some things. One, I love you, Natalie. Jesus, so much. I need you like my next breath. Two, I'll do whatever it takes to make you mine because the thought of going through life without you is scarier than having John Wick after me. Three, God knows I'm no prize. I behaved like a—"

"Dude, you're supposed to *sell* yourself," Miller chuckled. Paige shushed him.

T.J. side-eyed him. "Groveling here." Turning back to Natalie, his voice cracked. "I'm a mess without you." His expression shifted, and a sheen glazed his eyes. "Being with you makes me want to be a better man. To be the best version of myself. For you." Tears spilled from his gorgeous hazel eyes.

She melted, unable to fight the ones pooling in hers.

This man was laying himself bare, putting it all on the line. Open kimono. And she knew what that cost him.

He took in another chest-filling inhale. "I've been wrong about so many things, but one thing I'm sure of is that *you* are the best thing that's ever happened to me. If you can find it in your heart to forgive me, if you'll have me, I'll spend the rest of my life making sure you know how much I love you. No excuses. Natalie Amber Eyes, please say you'll marry me."

Her hand flew to her mouth, but it couldn't hold back her stuttering sobs. Joyful tears burned a trail over her cheeks. He extended his hand to Beckett, who handed him a small aqua-colored box. T.J. dropped to a knee, but before he could open the box, the puppies mobbed him, Ford leapt against his chest, and he tipped over. His hand shot upward, still holding the box while fur swarmed over him. Laughing and crying, Natalie joined him on the floor and helped him sit up. He plucked the ring from the box—an emerald-cut solitaire diamond in a simple platinum band—and held it out to her. He cocked his head in question.

She nodded—couldn't stop, as a matter of fact—and held out her hand. He slid the ring on. It fit her perfectly. Just like him.

His eyes lit. "Is that a yes?"

"Yes!"

He pulled her to him and kissed her long and sweet while the small crowd clapped and the canines capered around them.

When T.J. and she finally climbed to their feet, Natalie pointed at the group. "You were all in on this?"

"Oh yeah," Drew said. "We've been hatching all kinds of devious plots behind your back. I was gonna beat his ass for you, Nat, I really was. Besides the fact he *might* have a slight advantage, I didn't want to make his face any uglier." He high-fived T.J.

In man-lingo, her brother had told her T.J. was accepted into the fold, and her already-full heart flooded.

T.J. interlaced his fingers with hers, leaned in, and kissed her softly. "Drew, your sister could beat *both* our asses."

"I love you," she breathed. Those words couldn't do justice to the warmth thrumming inside her, the swelling tenderness in her heart, or the nerves firing from his touch. "I'll show you how much later," she added. His expression switched from surprised to smoldering.

She flashed her ring at her mom. "You helped pick this out, didn't you?"

Mom came to her, wiping her eyes, and hugged her tight. "I did. He asked for my help." She winked at him. "We had fun shopping, didn't we?"

"Yeah, Mary. We did," T.J. laughed.

More tears spilled from Natalie's eyes as she looked at T.J. over her shoulder. "I absolutely love it. You both did good."

Mom squeezed her hands. "So did you, Natbug."

Then Mom turned to T.J., cradled his face and, on tiptoe, kissed his cheek. "You're part of *our* family now."

Mine.

Much later, after family and friends had left and the puppies—save one—were returned to the shelter, T.J. was finally alone with Natalie. His eyes followed her as she cuddled their new addition and stowed him in a crate for the night. Standing in her living room, T.J. floated in a fog of joy, pinching himself. She was his—really his—and he was all hers.

Forever.

He also had her family, and he was okay with that because they were part of *her*. Learning to be the brother, the son he'd never been would be as awkward as skating on a polished wood floor, but he'd get there.

Natalie latched the crate, and the puppy whimpered as she walked away. Ford stuffed his nose against the gridded window.

"I'll share her with you, little guy," T.J. called to the pup, "but let's get one thing straight. You've had her all afternoon, and it's *my* turn now."

"What should we name him?" she asked as she drew near.

Reaching for her wrist, he tugged her to him and encircled her with his arms. "That's up to you. I shouldn't be allowed to name a dog ever again." Her fresh, floral scent invaded his senses. She felt good, her curves all warm, soft woman, and his dick hoisted a flag of appreciation.

"You're right. I'll name him." She slid her hands over his chest and smiled. "Bucket of puppies? You don't mess around."

"Hey, desperate times call for desperate measures. I figured I only had one shot to get it right—if even that—so I pulled out all the stops. No excuses!" He flashed her a grin, the same one that had been frozen on his face since she'd said yes.

"This is my future, huh?"

"Every day for the rest of your life, sweetheart. Get used to it." He scanned her face, then let out a slow, steady breath. "And, if you're game, I think I'm ready to look for my mom and sister." He'd given it a lot of thought. With Natalie in his corner, he had the strength to take whatever discovery brought.

She threw her arms around his shoulders. "Absolutely," she whispered against his neck. "I got you."

God, he loved this woman.

One hand in her hair, he pulled her head back and scanned her eyes. "I promise you will always be well loved by me. And speaking of being well loved, weren't you planning on showing me how much *you* love *me*?" He waggled his eyebrows.

She laughed. "Honestly, what am I going to do with you?"

"Oh, I can think of all kinds of things. For starters ..." He hauled her to the couch and sat, pulling her into his lap. He tightened his hold and breathed her in. God, he could die like this.

A beat later, he said, "Why are you always so damn ... so damn ..." So many words bombarded his brain he couldn't pick one. *Sexy. Beautiful. Bossy. Lovable. Adorable.*

"Why am I always what? So damn cute? Drop-dead gorgeous? Irresistible? Shall I hold this side of the conversation for you? I hope so because I'm going to sound way more awesome than I might otherwise."

He chuckled. "Such a smartass was what I *meant* to say." Then he grew serious and ran his fingertip over her full lips—lips he'd get to kiss for the rest of his life. "I couldn't come up with a single con, but your pros list is jam-packed."

Eyes as warm as whiskey shone with smoky intensity. "You made a list?"

"Oh yeah." He caressed her cheek with his thumb pad. "When I bumped into you that day in the parking lot, I convinced myself you needed me to save you. And that's what I set out to do. But you turned the tables and saved *me*. I still don't know how that happened, but Christ, am I glad it did. I love you more than life, Natalie Amber Eyes."

"And I love you, Tyler Johnson Shanstrom." She brushed a tear from his cheek as she swiped at her own. With a laugh, she said, "Are we done with all this romantic girlie crap? Can we get down to the good stuff? Like Naked Day?"

Smiling, he cupped her face and pulled her mouth to his. Right before he kissed her, he whispered, "Absolutely. Now stop talking and kiss me, smartass."

THE END

Want more of T.J. and Natalie's story?

Go to my website at www.griffin-brady.com to get your free copy of the bonus Epilogue!

GAGE BROKE HIS OWN RULES for a one-night stand, and now he wants forever. But Lily's heart belongs to a rival he can't beat. Here's an excerpt from *Gauging the Player*, Book 3:

Gage scanned the cars, his neon-pink-sign radar on high alert. He checked the icon on the real-time map again. The car seemed to be stuck in the same position it had been stuck in six minutes ago.

How did I end up here again? Wrong place, wrong time. All because Travis the Troll wanted to play BMOC and strut in with a contingent of hockey players. Now that he had what he wanted—namely lots of dancers' attention—Gage could finally escape his intoxicated teammates *and* Travis.

He double-checked the Lyft's position. Ah. Only *five* minutes away now, he thought dryly. What the hell was the hold-up at eleven thirty at night?

"Hey, Admiral!" Quinn hollered behind him.

Gage turned and eyeballed his linemate trotting over to him. "Run out of money for another lap dance?"

Quinn shook his head. "That wasn't me getting the lap dances. I was just making sure Hunter and Wyatt stayed out of trouble."

"And now?"

"And now I don't give a shit. I just wanna go home." Quinn shrugged. "If they get in trouble, it's someone else's problem. I'm tired of babysitting those idiots. I was hoping to catch a ride with you to the arena."

As Gage was opening his mouth to reply, his attention snagged on a woman with long curly blond hair talking to a guy in the adjacent parking lot. He squinted to get a better look. Her arms were crossed, and she seemed to be leaning away from the guy. Nothing threatening, but she looked uncomfortable as hell. He took a few steps in their direction.

"Nelson, where are you going?"

"Just need to check on something. Keep an eye out for a white Altima with a pink Lyft sign. That's our ride."

Gage increased his stride. As his focus sharpened, his breath caught.

"Lily?"

The woman lifted saucer-wide eyes to him, and the dude, a forty-something, swiveled his head, surprise all over his face.

"Uh, hey, Professor," she squeaked. "How's it going?"

Gage pointed at the man. "Is he bothering you?"

A few inches shorter than Gage and obviously not in good shape, the guy took a few steps back. "I-I just wanted to be sure she got in her car safely," he stuttered.

Confused, Gage looked between the two. Lily's expression bordered on alarm—whether it was caused by the dude or her seeing him, he had no idea. He made a snap judgment call and addressed the dude. "I'll make sure she gets where she needs to go. You can take off."

The guy scrambled away and hopped into a car, though Gage hardly registered it for being hyper-focused on Lily. His heart pounded in his chest.

"You are Lily, right?" He didn't need to ask. He'd recognize her anywhere.

She seemed flustered. "Identical twin?"

"Nice try." *Shit, she still wants nothing to do with me. What the hell did I do?* He blew a forceful breath through his nose, his mind careening like one of Disneyland's spinning teacups. *Where's she been? Why did she take off?*

Behind him, Quinn called, "Lyft's here."

Gage spun, which was when he noticed the guy was still sitting in his car, eyeing him warily. Was this guy playing guard dog? "You take it, Quinn," he shouted back.

Quinn saluted and grinned. "Admiral, I expect you to behave yourself and be at practice on time." There was no mistaking Quinn's repeat of one of Gage's worn caveats. In his own defense, however, any guy wearing the *A* needed to act the part with his teammates—even if it meant keeping their asses out of trouble at strip joints.

Gage watched as the Lyft pulled away. To Lily, he said, "Do you want to go somewhere so this weasel leaves you the hell alone?"

"He's not a weasel. He's just …"

He arched his eyebrows. "So you want him following you?"

She shook her head.

"This your car?" He pointed at a gray Toyota Highlander beside her.

"Yes. Could I give you a ride somewhere since yours just took off?" Her eyes darted back to the dude, and she waved at him as if to say, "You can leave now."

"That would be fantastic." He followed her to her driver's side door, opened it for her, then retreated to the passenger side and clambered into the seat, but not before shooting a glare in Weasel's direction. Weasel seemed satisfied—or defeated—and pulled away slowly.

Good. Because right now all of Gage was zeroed in on his goal: to find out where this woman had disappeared to last summer and why.

Get your copy of *Gauging the Player* at Amazon and see if Gage can convince Lily to give up the ghosts of her past and make room for him in her heart.

A Note from the Author

Thank you so much for reading *Third Man In*! I'm a dog lover, and writing about Ford Fido's antics was a lot of fun for me, along with his cast of supporting characters that sprang to life.

If you enjoyed T.J. and Natalie's story, I would love it if you would leave a review on Amazon, BookBub, or Goodreads to help readers like you find the story. And if you do leave a review, I would love to read it! Email me the link at gkbrady@griffin-brady.com.

Stay up to date on upcoming releases, cover reveals, giveaways, and discount deals by joining my newsletter. Simply go to: https://www.griffin-brady.com/contemporary-romance/contact/.

Trouble is brewing. Disaster strikes. Can they conjure a mistletoe miracle? Claim your free copy of *Puck the Halls* (Book 7.5), a Playmakers novella, when you join.

The playlist for *Third Man In* can be found on Spotify.

Ways to connect:
Facebook: www.facebook.com/AuthorG.K.Brady/
Twitter: twitter.com/GKBrady_Writes
BookBub: www.bookbub.com/authors/g-k-brady
GoodReads:
www.goodreads.com/author/show/19488321.G_K_Brady
Amazon Author Page: www.amazon.com/author/gkbrady
Or email me! gkbrady@griffin-brady.com

Acknowledgements

I am indebted to everyone who supported me throughout the birth of this book. I am so blessed and so very grateful to have you all behind me.

As always, a huge shout-out to my wonderful beta readers and critiquers: the Marbles, Janet R., and MJ. Thank you for being generous with your honesty and your knowledge. And to Julia W., a bucket of hugs for a marathon sprint. Your critical eye and words of encouragement helped more than you know.

Jenny Q., my unparalleled developmental and copy editor. How on earth did I get so lucky? Thank you for not holding back and for telling me where things went off the rails. Your candor helps me craft better characters for a better story. I trust you implicitly.

Persnickety, I treasure your meticulous attention to detail and your suggestions for a smoother read. In addition, your kind words were a balm for my ever-lingering doubts about this story.

My husband Tim, I couldn't do this without your love and support. Your unwavering belief in me and your unflagging encouragement to chase my dreams help me push through. I love you beyond measure.

Last but never least, you, the reader. Without you, there would be no reason to create these characters and their stories. I thank you from the bottom of my heart.

The Playmakers Series

Book 0 – *Line Change*
Book 1 - *Taming Beckett*
Book 3 - *Gauging the Player*
Book 4 - *The Winning Score*
Book 5 - *Defending the Reaper*
Book 6 - *No Touch Zone*
Book 7 - *Twisted Wrister*
Book 7.5 - *Puck the Halls*
Book 8 - *Besting the Blueliner*
Book 9 - *Guarding the Crease* (available July 2023)

Historical Fiction

The Heart of a Hussar **(Book 1 of 2)**
A Hussar's Promise **(Book 2 of 2)**
The Hussar's Duty **(Book 3)**

About the Author

Since childhood, all sorts of stories and characters have lived in G.K. Brady's imagination, elbowing one another for attention, so she's thrilled (as are they) to be giving them their voice on the written page.

An award-winning writer of contemporary romance, she loves telling tales of the less-than-perfect hero or heroine who transforms with each turn of a page.

G.K. is a wife and the proud mom of three grown sons. She also writes historical fiction under the pen name Griffin Brady. She currently resides in Colorado with her very patient husband.

Made in United States
North Haven, CT
04 February 2024

48300024R00211